I0699146

TRIALS OF THE NEKOMANCER

Book 2

by

Dungeon Ducky

Trials of the Nekomancer 2

Copyright © 2024 by Dungeon Ducky

All rights reserved.

The characters and events portrayed in this book are fictitious. Any similarities to real persons, living or dead, are coincidental and not intended by the author.

No part of this book may be reproduced, stored in a retrieval system, or transmitted in any form or by any means, electronic, mechanical, photocopying, recording, or otherwise, without express written permission of the publisher.

Any use of this publication to teach, modify, improve, or train generative artificial intelligence (AI) technologies to generate text is expressly prohibited. The author and publisher reserve all rights to license any use of this work for generative AI training and development of machine learning language models.

ISBN (print): 979-8-88993-039-6

Written by Dungeon Ducky
Edited by A. Kiesche

Published 2024 by MoonQuill
www.moonquill.com

Table of Contents

Catpurr 1
Another Season of Catnanigans

It was a day like any other as the pink-haired woman, clad in a tattered brown cloak and half-mask, stepped into the lobby of the rustic Adventurers' Guild.

The noise of the bustling hall died as dozens of curious eyes peered at her and the bloody bundle of goblin heads clutched in her offhand.

She calmly approached the service counter, the room's deathly silence only broken by her quiet humming. The maid at the counter looked up from the stacks of wanted posters, each depicting a young boy named Adam, and smiled at her.

"Oh. Uhm... Hello. How—How can we be of s-service?" the maid asked. The tag on her uniform noted her name as Ruebella.

"Sup, Rueb. Turning in proof of death for the goblin extermination contract," Liza said. The teenaged woman dropped the bundle of decapitated heads on the counter, splattering the lacquered wood with droplets of green blood. From the side approached a blue-haired woman in a maid's uniform.

"You are aware that we only require the ears, right?" a maid named Sinclair asked as a shirtless mountain of a man shuffled by, wearing only a cook's apron with trays of food teetered upon his arms. One of which was a piping-hot plate of fish that caused Liza's stomach to grumble.

"Yeah, but my partner says that this is to make doubly sure that it's properly *counted* with no funny business," Liza drawled, clearly imitating her friend. Then she leaned over the desk, pointedly tapping her silver adventurer's card against it. "After all, a lot of creatures share similar ears."

"O-Okay..." Ruebella stuttered and punched in a series of numbers on a machine as she tallied the heads on the counter. "Thirty-three heads. Five copper a piece. One silver and s-sixty-five coppers."

The young girl clicked her tongue. "Eh, ya get what ya can get, I s'pose. Say, how much for one of those fish trays?"

"Dining in or out?" Sinclair asked. The storage device built into the wooden furniture activated, forming a blue vortex. She swept the heads inside, leaving only the small splatters of green as a sign that they were ever there.

"Out. Oh, and give me extra, please."

"How much extra?" Sinclair asked, fixing her glasses and replacing Ruebella behind the register as the other maid handed over the bounty payment.

"How much for a silver?" Liza asked. A wide smile spread across her half-obscured face.

* * *

"Alright... Surely this will be the week." Adam groaned to himself, pulling out strands of his red hair as he sat in the dirt underneath the forest canopy, staring at his Gacha System.

Deep breaths, Adam. Deep, deep breaths. You're stronger than this. You're more disciplined than this. You didn't piss off a bunch of gods just to fail here!

He pushed the floating translucent button. The slot machine spinning as it calculated his rewards.

[Ding!]
[CONCATULATIONS! You've won 2 Cicero Coins!]

"Uuuuuugggghhhhh."

[Daily attempts left: 01!]

With clear exhaustion, he eyed the eighty-eight gacha coins he had left.

"Okay. One more try for today." The boy closed his eyes, touching the screen and waiting for the familiar ding.

[Ding!]

Adam opened his eyes.

[CONCATULATIONS! You've won 5 Cicero Coins!]

"OH, COME ON!"

[Daily attempts left: 00!]
Gacha Coins: 92

"WHY! WHY! WHYYY?!" The nekomancer raised his tiny fist to the merciless heavens, cursing the cruel and capricious gods.

Adam was on the verge of tears, his gacha coins nigh unusable as each time he rolled the slot machine, he would only receive more coins.

"If you keep making all that racket, you'll attract unwanted attention," Junith spat, the half-naked nekogirl busy doing push-ups to pass the time.

"Why are you so on edge? I told you my skeletons are out patrolling. Nothing around us but trees, trees, and more trees," her reluctant master retorted, pulling up his System menu.

BETA SYSTEM v1.05
TITLE: The Primordial Eli's Chosen
+20% Mana Recovery, +5 Arcana. Undead Favorability
NAME: Adam F. Glow
SPECIES: Nekoboy
LEVEL: 43
EXP BAR: 860/18000
MAIN CLASS: Nekomancer
HP: 360/360
MANA: 315/785
EVOLUTION POINTS: 0
GACHA COINS: 92
FREE POINTS: 0
Bonded Followers: 02
Junith Oatheart: T2 Lvl 19
Eh'liza Oktober: T1 Lvl 37
STR: 15
CON: 36
DEX: 25
ARC: 150+7 (EQ)
SEN: 23
EGO: 33

RESISTANCES: Fire (5%), Inertia (10%)

Buffs: Loved by Undead (Unique), Blessing of Eli (Unique), Eyes of a Predator V1, Corrupted Blessing of Nyx (Unique), Adherent of Death V1. Explosive Renaissance V1, Pain Tolerance V1

Debuffs: Ha! You Sacrificed Your Stats for a Cat?! V1 (Curse) Catsification V1 (Curse) Wet (Catsification)

SKILLS: Animate Bones V2, Irritating Touch V1, Cat Claws V1, Identify V1, Summon Greater Skeleton V3 (+++), Mana Bolt V1 (++), Artificial Linguistics {Rigellian}, Genocidal Aura, Summon Morian Crab, Mana Claws V1 (+), Summon Red-Eyed Death Knight of the Bronx V1 (++), Mana Dash V1 (+), Bone Wall V2 (++), Mana Shell V2

Skill Points: 0

*Twenty points into **Summon Death Knight** and I still can't use it...* Adam lamented. Despite dumping almost all his skill points into optimization to use his new skill, he was barred by a stat check for Ego, something the skill hadn't mentioned beforehand. *Because the gods conspire to screw me once more.*

Junith stood, wiping her brow before cleaning the rest of her sweaty body with a towel left hanging beside a mismatched suit of armor.

"Attitude like that is why you'll lose, necromancer," she said, unsheathing her iron sword from its scabbard to begin the next set of exercises. "A knight must always be vigilant, always ready for threats that may remain unseen until an opport—"

"YOOHOO, I'm back—"

At the sound of Liza's voice Junith spun, striking a box out of the other nekogirl's hands.

The object flew, seemingly spinning in slow motion through the air as Liza reached out for it, screaming "NOOOOOOOOOOO!" Her cry fell upon deaf ears as it landed on the ground and spilled its contents.

"OUR FOOD!" Liza wailed, rushing over to see what was salvageable. "WHY DID YOU DO THAT?! LOOK AT WHAT YOU'VE DONE!"

Junith blinked, dumbfounded for a moment before her expression soured. "It's not my fault! You failed to identify yourself! Who sneaks up on people in the middle of the woods?!"

"I SAID 'YOOHOO?!'" The taller girl pointed at Junith. "What more could you want?!"

Adam pinched the bridge of his nose.

"Can you two argue elsewhere, please? I'm trying to focus," he said, his back still turned. "Did you get the payment?"

"I did, but Judgy here just spilled half of it on the dirt!"

Adam spun, fanged mouth opening to question her further, until his eyes landed upon the soiled pile of cooked fish. "Wait, did you spend half a silver on fish?"

"Yeah, I figured we deserved something after that last bounty."

Adam fumed at her nonchalance. "You meatbag! I gave you one task! One task!"

"Relaaax, it's not like we can't just earn more money."

"That's not the point!" he grumbled, stalking over to Liza as he grabbed her fluffy, pink ears and began violently yanking her head back and forth.

"You overgrown cat! Do you not have a brain in your brain case?! We need all the money we can scrounge for potions and gear!"

"Nyaaaah! Yamete kudasai, Senpai!" Liza moaned out. Her voice high-pitched and made Adam's face twist with disgust, and he immediately let her go.

After their second trial, the nekotrio had been stuck on the road with provisions and equipment being at an all-time low. Due to a certain incident involving slimes, the daughter of a duchess, and millions of golds' worth in damages, Adam was a wanted man... Well, nekoboy.

Vilenciel City was now drowning not in slimes, but posters, all depicting hand-drawn portraits of himself and offering various rewards for his capture and delivery to the daughter of the duchess, whose fascination with him had gone beyond crazy. There were even hand-drawn posters of him in lewd positions, making out with a cartoon character. One particularly memorable poster had him curled up in the lap of the daughter of the duchess herself.

Adam shuddered just recalling it.

"What's the point of nickel and diming if we don't splurge a little now and then?" Liza asked, taking the tricker's persona off her face. The illusion warping her features vanished, revealing her true face.

"What? Because we're poor! Broke! No money! Do I have to spell it out?!" By now the fish were covered in sand, dirt, and ants, Adam observed as he crouched above them. "Junith, come over here and help me collect everything."

"What? Why?" the paladin asked, brow raised as she slowly assembled her leather armor.

"Well, obviously because we're going to eat it."

"You... can't be serious."

"For half a silver, I'm as serious as Voltrain trying to kill us. Now scrape out the refuse, clean the debris, and reheat it over a fire. Perhaps the ants can be extra proteins."

At the mention of extra proteins, Liza winced.

"I'm not a slave! Why do I have to do it?!" Junith spat, the ouroboros crest on her chest glowing. "I thought we had a truce!"

"You spilled it, dum-dum. Of course you should clean after yourself," Liza sang, earning her a glare from her fellow nekogirl.

"WHAT?!"

Adam winced at the imminent explosion. *Ah, crapbaskets, here we go.*

"I'm not dumb! I'm sick and tired of you guys calling me dumb!"

"Well, maybe if you didn't do dumb things, we wouldn't call you dumb, dummy."

"Call me dumb again. I dare you! I double dare you!" Junith spat. The catgirl's button for rampage mode activated.

"Oh, is the little shrimp gonna attack my ankles? Bring it, dumb-dumb."

"ARRRRRGH!" Junith charged, only for her quarry—her much, *much* taller quarry—to stick out an arm, halting with the ex-paladin's assault with a single condescending hand on her furry, cat-eared head.

"SERIOUSLY?!" the girl shrieked, arms flailing madly about in a desperate attempt to reach Liza. "This isn't fair! Why do you get to evolve?! I WANT MY BODY BACK ALREADY!"

"Hahahaha! You're so short, it's adorable!" the taller nekogirl laughed, shoving Junith back. As she burned with unfiltered wrath, so too her hands burned with glowing energy.

"I'LL SHOW YOU ADORABLE!"

"Will both of you shut up and get to work?!" Adam interjected. the two women suddenly glowing from their brands acting up. The crests that bound the two to his will activating as they resisted his order.

He tried to reason with them. "We barely have enough supplies as is. We need everything we can get and we're burning daylight."

Adam reasoned, handing the pair each a stack of despoiled fish before plucking the rolled-up parchment tied to Liza's waistband.

"Please and thank you," he finished, smacking both on the head with the scroll as he turned away.

The two nekogirls glared at one another, both hissing, their hair standing on end before taking off in different directions.

Finally.

When they were out of sight, Adam sighed, unfurling the guild bounty in his hands.

His golden eyes quickly scanned the paper, narrowing as he took in the information it contained. It took no time at all for the nekoboy's expression to sour.

"Seriously? SERIOUSLY?! I SAID NO EXPLORATION MISSIONS!" he screamed, throwing the parchment into the dirt. "WHY DOES NO ONE EVER LISTEN TO ME?!"

Catpurr 2

Hike Through the Forest

One day later.

[Ding!]
[CONCATULATIONS! You've won 2 Cicero Coins!]
[Daily attempts left: 00!]

"Uuuuugh…" Adam groaned, head in his hands as yet another batch of coins was awarded, bringing his grand total to ninety-seven.

"No luck?" Liza asked, hanging upside down by her toes from a nearby tree, observing as her companion slowly lost his mind in a small clearing surrounded by trees.

"Nope." He sighed, pulling up the list of available items in the gacha pool.

~Gacha~

Ring of Holding Upgrade x1 (5/5 available in Tier 1 Machine)
Thunder Stone x1 (1/1 available in Tier 1 Machine)
Fire Stone x1 (1/1 available in Tier 1 Machine)
Shadow Stone x1 (1/1 available in Tier 1 Machine)
Divine Catnip x1 (1/1 available in Tier 1 Machine)
Evolution Point x1 (1/2 available in Tier 1 Machine)

EXP Booster x1

Cicero's Gacha Coin x2

HP Up x1 (2/2 available in Tier 1 Machine)

MP Up (2/2 available in Tier 1 Machine)

Cicero's Gacha Coin x5

Water Stone (1/1 available in Tier 1 Machine)

Flower Stone (1/1 available in Tier 1 Machine)

Cape of Shielding (1/1 available in Tier 1 Machine)

Pebble of Smiting x1 (1/1 available in Tier 1 Machine)

Amulet of Eli x1 (1/1 available in Tier 1 Machine)

She made a sympathetic noise. "Another day, then?"

"Yup."

"Why even bother at this point?"

"Because there's nothing else to do and I want to grab that evolution point," he groaned, his voice muffled by the quiet of the forested night. "Or literally anything that can be useful or I can sell."

"Have you tried leveling up Luck?"

He hesitated for a moment, then blinked and met her gaze. Liza stared back at him, slit-pupiled eyes a familiar shade of gold.

"What?"

"Luck..." At his continued silence, she raised a brow. "Do you not have a Luck stat?"

"NOOO?!" Adam exclaimed, his expression warping. "Is this another hidden stat, like Faith?!"

"Oh... I guess." Liza dropped out of the tree with a shrug, twisting to land on her feet beside Adam. The boy was frozen, wracking his brains at the revelation of the new stat.

"Wait, what's your Luck stat at?" he asked. While he could see Junith and Liza's HP and mana levels from his Followers menu, their specific stats and skills remained a mystery to him. It wasn't just a pain now; it had been endlessly annoying when trying to optimize them, too.

"Mmhm, thirty-five," Liza replied, which seemed awfully high to Adam.

"Did you allocate all your points into Luck?"

"No, I don't have control of my stats."

"Ah, right." He had forgotten. Junith and Liza's stats were determined by their vocations, automatically distributing points with each level-up. Unlike his current System, they couldn't self-allocate.

Great.

"There's gotta be a way to tamper with my Luck, maybe even unlock Faith," he thought aloud. He was just wondering what his Luck stat could be, when through the tree branches the sky was touched by the first signs of dawn. "Bah, I'm never gonna figure it out just staring at my screen like this... We should get going. Where's Judgy at?"

"Oh, you know, somewhere around here, swinging her sword, complaining about skeletons. The usual," Liza replied. She scanned the dense foliage surrounding the clearing, but no screaming nekogirl appeared.

"Get her, please. It's about time we broke camp and headed out." Adam sighed, watching the rising sun. As the light grew brighter, he retrieved his map of the Vilenciel Duchy and nearby area, unfurling it before him.

From his estimation, the trio were just on the outskirts of Canton Forest, a sprawling sea of shrubbery located beside Vilenciel City. A few more miles and they would be close to Rolo Fortress, the first line of defense against wayward threats to Vilenciel City, as well as home to the Duchy's black market.

Adam had seen the fortress while on his way to Sellight Village, traveling with Titania and Sehn on their contract from Clocktower Master Beifong, but they hadn't had an opportunity to visit said locale.

Not that he wished to, now that he was a wanted man.

Adam sighed again. His head hung as he gazed sightlessly at the map until a familiar *clack*ing sound pricked his ears. The smooth, cool texture of bones pressed up against his ankles.

"Hey, buddy." He smiled at one of his many skeletal summons.

Crouching down, Adam petted his skeleton. In return, the skeletal cat dropped the dead rodent held in its bony mandibles, offering it to its master.

Adam smiled, taking the rodent. "Good cat."

Although his Catsification meant they weren't the humanoid skeletons he was used to summoning, these skeletons were just as strong, if not stronger than, their bipedal counterparts. With their lithe frames and the innate weapons of their bone fangs and claws the skelecats were hyper-efficient mini machines of death, especially since he didn't need to equip them with weapons like a regular humanoid skeleton.

"Dumb-dumb! Dumb-duuuuuuuumb!" Liza called out, interrupting Adam's moment with his cat as she searched for their most temperamental companion.

He closed his eyes, pinching the bridge of his nose.

"Why do you insist on antagonizing her?" he finally asked, fixing the teenager with a neutral gaze.

"I dunno... Bored, I guess," Liza replied casually.

Suddenly a nearby bush rustled. An armored and scowling Junith emerged, sweaty and with disheveled hair.

Oh boy, here we go.

"No!" He jabbed at her with a single extended finger, causing her to startle at the sudden outburst.

"Wha—"

"NO!"

"But—"

"No!"

"She—"

"NO! We don't have time for this! We need to move," Adam snapped, his tone final.

Junith grumbled darkly as Liza began to giggle, the shorter nekogirl folding her arms and fixing the other with a death glare.

* * *

Upon scattering leaves and branches to cover their tracks Adam and the pair were on the way, walking through the woods as the nekomancer kept his eyes on the nearby highway, using it as a marker to navigate.

"Ugh. Great, we'll reach the crossroads at noon," he said. Even this early, his feet were sore. It was times like these that he missed his old floating skills.

"Ya know, if you weren't being so paranoid and making us waste so much time covering our tracks, we'd probably have made it before noon," Liza remarked, seeming entirely too relaxed as she hummed and sauntered in the rear.

"Well, when you've spent years on the run from a religious lunatic hellbent on skewering you, you tend to be just a little concerned about trackers," he quipped. Junith turned away from his brief, but quite pointed, look.

A quick reaction, but not one that escaped Liza's eyes.

She smiled.

"So, we've been together for about a week, yet I can't help but realize I don't know anything about you two," the taller girl remarked, eyeing the others with mischief.

"Nothing to know," Junith growled, flashing her a look of warning.

"I concur," Adam said, pausing as a skelecat dropped out of a tree. One of his scouts. "The area ahead is clear, we can pick up the pace."

Liza licked her lips, picking up her pace as Adam took off.

"All I'm saying is that if we're stuck with each other, we might as well get to know one another better," she insisted. "Strengths and weaknesses, likes and dislikes. Like Junith, why do you train with your armor on? Or Adam, why are you still child-sized even though you're at a higher level? And why do you two hate each other?"

"So that's what this is about," he said.

"I mean, I know the why, but just the surface level," Liza said. "She tried to kill you, you said no, she failed—"

Junith growled. "I didn't fail! A higher power intervened..."

"Sounds like you failed."

"No! Failure implies the task can no longer be accomplished. The execution has just been delayed," she retorted, causing Adam to snicker.

"Yeah. Good luck."

"What? You think I can't do it?!" Junith spat. The brand on her chest glowed as she reached for her new shortsword, bought with Adam's money.

"No, I think you'll be in for a rude awakening," the boy in question replied, eyes buried in his map as a skelecat leapt from a nearby tree and hissed at Junith. "Especially when your friends realize that you've been claimed by a foreign god. Unlike me, I doubt they'll be so forgiving."

Junith's sudden silence spoke volumes, while Liza shifted uncomfortably as the silence went on.

"Sooo, tell me about the world you two come from," Liza said, attempting to break the silence that had befallen the trio. "I'm from Earth, a place called Hamburg."

"Hamburg?" Adam's ears twitched. For the first time, the nekoboy raised his head from the map. "Like hamburgers?"

"So you guys have hamburgers!"

"Patties of boar meat molded together and grilled to be served between bread, right?" he asked, only to be met by a confused Liza.

"No, those are pork burgers. A hamburger is meat from a cow."

"Cow?" He tilted his head. "Is that like a different type of boar?"

"No? You guys don't have cows?" she asked. It seemed bizarre that they'd have pigs and boars, but not another ubiquitous farm animal like a *cow*. Black-and-white creature, udders that dispense milk, usually says 'moooo.' Some even have horns." She lifted two fingers to her temples, mooing.

Adam's brows only furrowed deeper.

"So it's not a boar?" he asked. "Why do they call it a hamburger when there's no ham?"

"Ah! I actually know this one." Her ears perked up at the chance to share some trivia from her world. "Because hamburgers were first introduced in Hamburg as the Hamburg steak by a group of nomads, and then when the dish traveled to New York, bread was added, and then it was called a hamburger. Do you guys seriously not have cows? How do ya get milk?"

"Interesting," Adam mused, pausing as the tip of Rolo Fortress came into view from behind the distant horizon. "Spiders."

Liza's smile faded.

"What?"

"You asked how we get milk. Spiders."

"Like... *spider*-spiders? Eight-legged creepy bugs with a bunch of eyes?" A sudden image of a spider with udders appeared in her mind.

"Yup."

"What? Afraid of spiders?" Junith smirked at the look of horror on Liza's face.

"N-No. Don't be ridiculous! Spiders are lovely creatures," the other said, waving Junith off as her expression became jovial.

"Really?"

"Yup! They're some of my favorite animals!"

"Oh, I see," Junith said. A wide smile blossomed across her face. "So that's why you aren't freaking out from the giant spider on your shoulder."

"Huh?" Liza froze. Golden eyes blinked once in bafflement until the girl turned her head slowly to behold the eight-legged creature hitching a ride on her shoulder.

Liza's breathing picked up, her chest heaving up and down, growing faster every second. Behind her, the girl's tail puffed out, body seizing with tremors as eight beady eyes met her own. Chelicerae seemed to wiggle in greeting.

* * *

Elsewhere.

"AAAAAAAAAHH!"

A black-haired adventurer in leather armor pulled the reins on his rented-out donkeys, stopping the wooden cart as the sound of a girlish scream caught his attention.

He narrowed his dark eyes, looking around, scanning the nearby foliage that flanked the Vilenciel highway.

"Did you—"

"Hear that? Yes, Sehn, kind of hard not to," said Titania, poking her head out from the covered wagon with the sun catching the green-colored hair of the Fighter of Freya.

"Sounded like a kid," Sehn said, briefly checking his magic coffin that stored his weapons. Then he turned to the rainbow-haired maid sleeping on the floor of the wagon, curled in the space between transported supplies. "Should we check it out?"

"If you want to. We *are* on a timetable, though. Valentine is gonna be pissed if we don't show up on time for the next quest."

"You're right..." Sehn replied, gritting his teeth.

"Eh, don't worry about it. Probably just some dumb kid. It was just one scream. Probably saw a spider or something," she reasoned, taking a seat beside Sehn and reclining back. "No need to get involved unless she screams again. Remember what happened last time we helped a kid?"

The two shared a laugh, recalling a certain red-haired nekoboy. But the laughter died too quickly, their gazes falling to the cuffs on their wrists.

Catpurr 3
I DEMAND WORKERS' RIGHTS

"THAT WASN'T FUNNY!" Liza shouted, skulking behind a cackling Junith.

"Of course it was. You should have seen your face," Junith said. The girl held up her palm as a mote of black light appeared and grew eight hairy legs. "Here, you want it?"

Liza hissed, baring her fangs.

"Cut it out, you two. We've got a journey ahead of us," Adam cut in. His skelecats dispersed as he began to leave without the nekogirls. "Seriously, no more summoning illusions to mess with Liza."

"Tsk. You've always got to ruin my day, don't you?" Junith growled, dispelling her illusion.

"It's one of the simple pleasures I have left in life."

As part of her skill set as a Priestess of Eli, Junith was capable of summoning motes of black light to attack with and defend herself. It was energy that Adam quickly learned to be voidlight, a volatile substance that was versatile and rare, a seldom found ability among system users. With voidlight she could manipulate the particles to infuse her body or weapons, giving her an edge in close quarters combat, or harness the volatile nature of the energy to decimate foes from afar. A class that was no doubt S-tier judging from Adam's estimation.

The trio walked for a time mostly in silence without any further shenanigans or arguments, until Liza finally spoke up.

"Ugggh. Are we there yet?" she complained, lagging a ways behind the nekopair as the grand citadel in the distance loomed closer and closer with every step.

"Nearly at the crossroads," Adam replied. It was another hour before Liza opened her mouth to complain once more.

"We'll get there when we get there," Adam said, chastising the woman.

Another hour passed.

"You said we'd be there already!" Liza whined, tugging at her leather armor and cloak, both now soaked with sweat.

"No, I said we'd get there when we get there," Adam repeated, his eyes still locked on his map.

Another hour passed.

"Why hasn't anyone invented cars yet?!" Liza groaned. After sitting down in protest and refusing to move, a compromise had been reached—a team of skelecats now carried the nekogirl's limp body.

"You picked this mission," Junith retorted, adjusting the short sword on her hip. "Not sure why you're complaining so much, we've only been walking for six hours."

"YOU ACT AS IF THAT'S NORMAL!" At the outburst, the nekomancer and priestess both looked over before looking away again.

"It is, your realm is just full of lazy people," Junith said.

"NUH-UH! It's called convenience! Something this realm sorely lacks! No bathrooms, no cell phones, no cars, no tampons! I can't even order food anymore from an app and I'm always starving!" Liza lamented. "This world sucks!"

The nekoduo paid the woman no mind, continuing their trek.

"I did tell you to limit the missions to the nearby area," Adam said, eyes down on his map. "Maybe I should send Junith next time to supervise you."

"I'm not a kid! I don't need supervision from a shrimp!"

"Said the dummy who didn't limit the mission radius," Junith shot back.

Hmm, a car would be nice, Adam thought to himself. He had been meaning to look into the production of automobiles since the last trial. Meanwhile, his two companions fell back into arguing

"BUT I DID! I DID, I DID!" Liza cried, lifting her head and protesting to Adam. "On the map it looked so much closer! How was I supposed to know that it was an *eternity* away!"

"Voltrain above, you are so dramatic." Adam snorted in laughter at the priestess' reply. "What? What's so funny?"

"Junith. The irony is so appalling, it's maddening in its scope, and so sad it's wrapped back around to being comical." He looked up from his map. "And the fact you say it so brazenly gives me comfort that truthfully warms my heart."

Despite not understanding the nekomancer's point, Junith growled at him all the same.

"What? Why have we stopped? Are we there yet?" Liza asked. Around her, the skelecats chattered.

"No... actually, I believe we may have taken a misstep."

Silence descended once more at Adam's words.

"You've gotta be kidding me," Liza moaned.

"Are you saying we're lost?!" Junith asked.

"Uhhh... I wouldn't say lost, just... geographically misplaced," Adam replied, looking at the nearby scenery.

"In Voltrain's name..."

"We're going to die out here!" Liza cried, already sobbing.

"Now hold on, we're not lost. We just need to walk to Rolo Fortress and then take the road leading to the crossroads."

"That's like another hour!"

"So it is," Adam replied, tucking the map under his arm and taking off. He had hoped to try and take a shortcut, but the constant bickering and arguments had distracted him, and they inadvertently walked past their destination.

The pair groaned, Junith at least sharing Liza's sentiment.

* * *

Nearing the outskirts of the bastion of humanity, Adam, Junith, and Liza stuck close together as they kept their hoods up and heads down. Within the tents and carts set up around the high walls of the stone fortress, they began to spot human activity.

"Ugh, it's sooo hot," Liza complained as they stepped fully onto the highway. Before they'd had the cover of the forest's dense to shield them from the sun. Now there was nothing to protect them from the merciless rays. "Can we just book an inn?"

"Do you have inn money?"

"N-No," Liza half-cried.

"There's your answer," Adam replied, tugging at his leather armor, clammy and smelly as it peeled off his skin. "There's an inn past the crossroads. If we're swift, we can book a room for the night before pressing on to the Selkuin ruins."

"B-B-B-But—That's hours away!"

"You chose this mission. Let this be a lesson for next time." The boy snapped his fingers, dispelling all twenty of the skelecats that had been roaming around the woods.

"Can... Can we at least get food?" Liza begged.

Adam glanced over to the hunched-over woman who held a look of defeat.

"What do you think?" he replied, causing Liza to bite her quivering lip in frustration.

"THAT'S IT! I QUIT! I'M RUNNING AWAY! If worker unions back home saw how you were working us, they'd be appalled!" Liza boldly declared, drawing no reaction from either of her companions.

"Sure, go ahead. Less mouths for me to feed." The nekoboy shrugged, turning around and walking off with Junith in tow, leaving Liza behind.

"H-Hey! I mean it! I'll really run away!" she screamed.

"Go for it! Good luck!" Adam waved back as Junith flashed a thumbs up.

A moment passed before Liza's feet began to shuffle.

"H-Hey! Wait up! Wait! I was kidding!" she yelled, taking off after the pair.

Junith smacked her lips, sighing to herself before she addressed Adam.

"As much as I'm loath to agree with her, maybe we should stop and rest a bit," she said. "We've been marching for nearly seven hours. I understand time is of the essence, but it could be dangerous if we're too fatigued in case of an ambush."

Adam turned to Junith, staring until her brow went up.

"What?"

"Nothing. Wasn't expecting a sound suggestion with logic behind it from you."

"Rude."

"Being rude to you is one of the few pleasures I've had since you catnapped my Schrödinger."

Junith pursed her lips.

"I'm not going to apologize."

"I don't expect you to," he said.

As he came to the edge of the human encampment he paused, and Liza staggered towards them, body wracked by loud wheezing. The girl fell to her knees dramatically, draping her head upon Adam's shoulder.

"We'll see about visiting a food vendor and stopping for a bit to rest and recover. Then it's onwards from there," he said, wincing as Liza let out a high-pitched "YAY!" Exhaustion forgotten, she immediately perked up, her gaze darting to and fro in search of promising food vendors.

Adam pinched the bridge of his nose before opening his coin purse, noting the single gold in a small nest of silvers and coppers. Between buying a language crystal for Liza, outfitting both girls with armor and weapons, and then procuring daily supplies, their funds were low; something he heavily lamented.

If only I still had my ring of sustenance, he again cried internally. But there was nothing for it. Resigned to parting with yet more coin he trudged into the encampment, until an unexpected voice called out to him, freezing him in place.

"Adam?"

The boy in question blinked, his foot hovering over the blades of glass as he slowly turned to the sound. Not far away were Sehn and Titania, sticks of pork held in their mouths as they stood stone-still, carrying crates in their arms.

Oh... Oh, crapbaskets.

Catpurr 4

Poisoning Yourself Because You Don't Listen

"Adam?" Titania repeated. The wooden box held in her hands fell to the ground.

Immediately Adam pivoted, turning around to run off only for Titania to scream his name.

"Ah, crapbaskets," he muttered, pursing his lips together as Sehn and Titania approached. The sound of their footsteps against the grass caused his ears to twitch underneath his hood.

"Hey, guys!" Asam turned, brandishing an innocent smile as if he hadn't disappeared for a month after causing incalculable costs in damage, kidnapping the daughter of the Duchess, and breaking and entering into said duchess' castle, all before blowing it up.

"Adam..." Titania whispered, slowly approaching as though Adam were a wild animal that could flee at any moment.

The woman stretched out her hands as though she meant to hug him, fingers hovering just inches from touching him—only to place her palms firmly against his temples.

"Huh?" he asked.

"YOU IDIOT! DO YOU KNOW HOW MUCH TROUBLE YOU ARE IN?!" she screamed, lifting the boy up by his head as he instinctively flailed and writhed.

"YOU! YOU!" For a moment Titania struggled to find the words. "BAD CAT!"

Despite the absurdity of the statement, there was a sudden, sharp sting in Adam's chest.

"IT WASN'T MY FAULT THOUGH!" he protested, his feet kicking about. "I TOLD THEM TO LEAVE ME ALONE! BUT DID THEY LISTEN?! NOOOO! BECAUSE NO ONE EVER LISTENS TO ME!"

Finally, he stopped writhing, simply hanging limp as Titania held him in place. He met her green eyes, a pout on his face.

She then hugged him, bringing Adam close to the warmth of her body.

She sighed. "Sorry, I'm just happy you're safe."

"Ah..." he let out, completely at a loss for words as Sehn ruffled his hair.

Great... Now I feel bad again for leading them on...

"Good job passing trial two," Sehn said, gazing at Adam with a wry smile. His eyes swept across Liza and Junith. "Are these your friends? Hey, I'm Sehn—"

He crouched down, immediately attempting to pet the covered Junith on the head. His reward was a feral hiss as she backed away.

"T'nod hcuot em!" Junith spat. "*Peek* ruoy sdnah ot flesruoy, citereh!"

Oh, that's right, Adam thought to himself. Due to funds being low he could only afford one language crystal for Liza, and a cheap one at that. Then again, perhaps the language barrier was a good thing. At least Junith wouldn't be able to run her mouth.

"These are my... sisters," he finally said, causing Liza to raise her brow momentarily before picking up on the boy's hints.

"Hello!" Liza said, suddenly grabbing and shaking Sehn's hand. As she did so, Adam's eyes were drawn to a giant manacle shackled around the man's wrist, inscribed with glowing runes. Adam's eyes darted to Titania, confirming she had one as well. "I'm Liza. Adam's older sister."

The nekoboy took note of how easily Liza melted into the role, her demeanor returning to the upbeat and cheerful one from their first encounter.

Suddenly, Liza hugged Sehn, causing the man to blink as she began purring.

"Oh... You speak our language," Sehn replied. His hands hovered in the air awkwardly, clearly unsure where to put them.

"Yup yup. Nyah!" Liza beamed, pulling away. "Thank you for taking care of my younger brother. If there's anything we can do for you, don't hesitate to ask."

Titania looked at Sehn.

"So you're all... nekofolk?" Titania asked, leaning forward as her voice dropped to a whisper on the last word.

"Yup!" Liza replied. "We aren't from around here, so still getting the lay of the land. If you could show us places to eat or drink, we wouldn't mind treating you."

WHAT?!

Adam broke into a coughing fit, the unsolicited offer causing his heart to briefly stop.

Titania and Sehn seemed to silently debate amongst themselves before they both shrugged. "Sure, why not."

NOOOOOO, Adam inwardly cried.

* * *

At a wooden stall from which emanated mouth-watering scents as chefs gathered around an open fire, Adam was fighting for his life. The nekoboy grappled with the tall stool, struggling to scamper up it while Liza and the others were already seated and awaiting their food.

Damn short legs, he mentally griped, finally finding purchase as Junith scoffed and called him a weakling.

"I'm not weak, they just make these stools too tall," he shot back before finally reading the menu carved into the side of the wooden stall.

Tsk. Seriously? Four hundred coppers for a bowl of noodles?! What is this, a highway robbery? he grumbled, but kept his complaints to himself as he eyed the nearby bulletin board filled with wanted posters, at the top of which had several hand drawn fliers with his face on it.

Why does life conspire against me?

"Dōmo arigatō gozaimasu," Liza said as a bowl of noodles topped with vegetables and meat was placed before her, Adam raising a brow at the unfamiliar language.

"Thanks for the treat," Titania said, taking a bite of her salad.

"Yeah, no problem, it's the least we could do," Liza said, placing a gold coin on the table for the chef.

Adam blinked, immediately checking his coin purse to see that his own money was all accounted for.

How... Wait. He frowned, remembering when Liza had abruptly hugged Sehn. *She must have—*

It took all of Adam's inner strength not to smack the teenager on the back of the head. Judging from the face she made upon noticing Adam's glare, at least she knew she was in trouble.

But for now she paid him no head, instead burying herself into her food as Adam placed an order for Junith.

"Are you not going to eat?" Titania asked as the nekoboy sat with folded arms.

"I'm fine. I had a *nice* meal on the way here. Big enough to punish anyone that comes at me," he replied, glaring at Liza. Eventually curiosity got the better of him when he noticed the manacle on Titania's wrist again. "What's with the shackles?"

"Oh..." Titania replied, a leaf sticking out of her mouth. "Well, after your incident, Madam Valentine revoked our guild licenses—"

"She did what?!" Adam interjected. Just what had happened in his absence?!

"Don't worry about it. The duchess needed a scapegoat after the incident and to set an example. The guild was strong armed because you have ties to us. Officially we're Repentas operating under Madam Valentine, like Ruebella and the other Seven Virtues, but unofficially we're just doing the same thing we've always been doing," she explained.

"Yes, but now with fancy tracking devices," Sehn added, brandishing the cuff on wrist before slurping on some noodles.

"It's honestly not that bad!" Titania repeated, noticing Adam's expression. "We still get paid, still have access to all the guild facilities, and even get paid time off now!"

"Yeah, we just aren't allowed to go anywhere without consent," Sehn grumbled. "Or supervision."

His actions had caused the pair to suffer.

Wait? Supervision? Immediately Adam's eyes darted around, scanning for any signs of threats in the area.

"Relax, if you're looking for our handler, Tilith is asleep in the wagon," Sehn assured. "So, you want to tell us what happened? How in the name of the six gods you managed to blow up half the city?"

Adam let out a sigh, some tension escaping his shoulders. "Look, I just... I just want to start off by saying I'm—"

"ULHK! UGK!"

Liza began to choke, clutching her throat as her eyes boggled. Immediately Adam turned to help but was seized by the nekogirl. She shook him violently, clawed fingers digging into his shoulders as her eyes watered and her face puffed up.

THE HELL?! Adam's eyes widened, unsure of what to do, until something green caught his eye—the remains of a squeezed lime beside her bowl of soup.

"You! ABSOLUTE BUFFOON!" Adam spat. The others leapt out of their chairs to assess the situation as Liza sputtered and hung on to Adam for dear life.

"What's wrong with her?!" Titania asked. Beside her, Sehn flourished a knife at the distraught chef.

"DID YOU POISON US?!"

"N-N-No, mister, I swear!"

As Sehn threatened the chef, Liza collapsed to the floor, dragging her life-sized stress ball down with her.

"JUNITH! Heal her! She's been poisoned from consuming lime!" Adam barked, standing up as the girl's HP plummeted rapidly. Hives broke out across her now-purplish body as Liza trembled in a puddle of sweat.

Junith hopped off her chair, palms glowing with violet light as she crouched beside her companion. The result was almost immediate, as her complexion shifted from ashen purple to something altogether healthier. In the air above them hovered the symbol of a serpent devouring itself—the ouroboros.

Sehn and Titania watched with fascination as a crowd gathered to gawk at the spectacle of a System User using their abilities to heal what appeared to be a dying teenage girl.

As Liza's HP reached its maximum and the girl opened her eyes, Adam sighed, pinching the bridge of his nose. His ears twitched in the cool breeze.

Now that the excitement was over, he loomed about Liza and shook his head.

"Didn't I tell you lime was poisonous to us?"

"Yes..." the girl croaked out, her face flustering from the chastisement.

"But did you listen?"

"No..."

"Do you ever listen?"

"No..."

"Are you even listening to me now?"

"Noooo. I just wanted to eat. I didn't think it'd be that bad!" Liza cried as Adam rubbed his uncovered head, realizing that she—

Adam paused, touching his red hair, no longer hidden by his hood. Suddenly he was all too aware of the crowd's eyes on him—some people in it being decked out in armor and weapons. The nearby adventurers' gazes began to shift from Adam to the nearby wanted sign of his before looking back at him, then back to the sign, then back to him.

Though Adam's rational brain told him he might be hallucinating, he could swear that money signs appeared in their eyes.

"Oooh. Crap. Oh, crap. OH CRAP!" Adam muttered lowly, voice gradually rising in pitch with every word. He grabbed at his daggers as the adventurers began to unsheathe their weapons.

Catpurr 5

Backrooming an Angry Mob

With Liza on Adam's back and Junith keeping pace beside him, the trio sprinted through an open field of lilies, stretching out as far as the eye could see. The day would have been just a normal, average, everyday kind of day. The weather was lovely with a nice breeze, high sun, and terrific blue sky that was perfect for a lunch picnic for any blessedly ordinary person.

But this wasn't any average day, and Adam and his gang weren't ordinary people. Instead of coming here for a scenic walk, the nekotrio were being chased by a contingent of money-hungry adventurers. Nearly a hundred rabid mercenaries were all vying to capture the red-haired neko for the Duchess's reward money.

"YOU ARE IN *SO* MUCH TROUBLE WHEN WE GET OUT OF THIS!" Adam screamed, ducking as an arrow with a boxing glove sailed past his shoulder, and pulverizing the ground nearby.

"I SAID I WAS SOWRY!" Liza cried woefully, alternating between vomiting rainbows and crying as she bounced atop the boy's back.

"Sorry doesn't cut it!" Adam yelled before sensing an abrupt increase in temperature. Jolting to the left, Adam's ear fur was singed as he narrowly avoided a fireball. "SORRYDOESNTCUTIT!"

"STOP YAMMERING AND KEEP RUNNING!" Junith barked, twisting and raising an arm to blast the man who had cast the spell with a bolt of energy. He was sent flying backwards into the stampeding crowd, where he was quickly trampled underfoot.

Running, Adam could see the treeline, the passageway to safety. All the trio had to do was reach it and disappear. Simple in theory, harder in practice; especially when one was burdened by a child's stubby legs and carrying a vomiting Liza.

Adam grimaced, realizing he wouldn't make it at the rate they were going.

GAH! I really didn't want to reveal this!

"GO! ATTACK THEM BUT DON'T KILL!" he barked, calling forth at least two dozen cat-shaped glowing portals, cutting off the over-eager crowd. With his optimization being what it was, he could summon the lowest tier skeleton at the low cost of twenty MP. The only issue being they required verbal commands and orders.

The adventurers momentarily stalled, tripping over themselves as dozens of animated cat skeletons came bounding out of the portals.

"SK–SK–SKELETONS!"

"MONSTERS!"

"GRAB MACES! MACES!"

"SWITCH TO BLUNT WEAPONS!"

"THEY'RE FAST! DON'T CHASE! LET THEM COME TO YOU!"

The adventures began to yell amongst themselves, coordinating like the professional bounty hunters they were and engaging Adam's tide of bones.

Adam clicked his tongue. His skeletons wouldn't last long at the rate the crowd was charging through them. "Junith!"

"WHAT?!" she replied, ducking underneath what appeared to be a boot that someone had taken off and thrown at them.

"Illusions! Can you conjure one in the shape of us to split their attention?!" he barked, expending more of his mana to throw more skeletons at his pursuers.

"I can try if I focus!"

"Don't try! Do it!" he snapped as Liza begged for mercy, vomiting once more.

"Grr... The skill is more complicat—"

"You're always saying you aren't an idiot! Well, now's the time to prove to me that you're a genius, or at least have some competence!" he interjected, wincing as another skeleton was destroyed. A jolt of pain lanced through his psyche.

"GAH!" Junith groaned. Sparking from her hands appeared a half-dozen spheres of crackling light, her brow furrowed in concentration.

"Hurry up!" Adam coaxed.

The woods were not far off, just a few more yards—but their pursuers were still hot on their tails.

"I'M TRYING!" Junith snapped.

"TRY HARDER! OR DO YOU WANT TO END UP BACK IN THAT DUNGEON?!"

At his words, Junith took a deep breath before she froze in place, lagging behind as Adam pelted forwards.

"Screw it!" she yelled with rage, her expression contorting with fury as her legs ached beneath her. Adam spun, about to yell at the nekogirl to hurry up, but the words died in her throat. The tiny pinpricks of light suddenly exploded into massive spheres of voidlight, orbiting her palms.

Oh. Adam's brow went up, realizing what Junith was about to do. Although he had his reservations, at this point he couldn't fault her.

Exhausting all of her mana, Junith pushed the two spheres of voidlight together, merging them, and condensing them into a small ball of volatile energy. Her palms crackled with wild energy.

All attacks converged on the little girl casting some kind of spell. Nets were launched, arrows fired, some even pelted her with more shoes. But all projectiles were blocked when Liza raised her shaky hands, conjuring a bubble of purple energy around the Priestess of Eli. The items were all caught in mid-air as the energy grew wilder, more violent.

"VOID RUPTURE!" Junith yelled, activating her skill. She thrust her palms forward. A wave of black energy swept across the open plains.

Some calls went out for shields and barriers to activate in the moments before the spell reached them. Others just shrieked "OH, SHI—" All were quickly extinguished by the all-devouring roar of Junith's attack. Light and shadow both lost meaning, fading to a blank white void in the unending brightness.

When the sound died down, all that remained was a long crater. Scattered in the barren land were weapons and clothes, things which had formerly belonged to the pursuing adventurers, now nowhere to be seen. Any survivors quickly scattered, screaming hysterical warnings about a demon child.

"J-Junith," Adam muttered, stunned by the overwhelming attack. In a menu beside him, Junith's MP dropped to zero. "Did... Did you just... kill all of them?!"

Junith, visibly haggard, turned to Adam.

"No... I just... displaced them, I think?" She stumbled, falling on all fours with her HP visibly dropping.

Adam narrowed his eyes, gazing out at all the loot that had been left behind. "Where did... Where did you send them?"

"I... don't know," Junith replied before passing out.

* * *

Elsewhere.

In a dank room devoid of sunlight, a skeleton in a pink bathrobe stood in front of a large, black cauldron, stirring it slowly as he read out of a book he'd borrowed, which he certainly had not stolen. The cauldron's obsidian sides were decorated with golden etchings and arcane runes, gleaming with a strange light as a fire kept the cauldron's contents bubbling. Per recommendation from the minor god of war named Islandr and harassment from the god of wildlife, Freya, Eli was strong-armed into trying his hand at a hobby known as *cooking*.

The ladle was a delicate and pristine-white affair, crafted from the bones of a creature known as a Pengwing. These large, flightless birds had gone extinct long ago, native to a realm long ago swallowed up by the void. He lifted a bit of the bubbling orange broth to his skull for a taste.

The soup flowed straight through his skull and spattered his favorite bathrobe. It didn't even taste like anything.

"Oh... Right. I need taste buds and a meat suit," Eli said, pondering for a moment as red dots began to spot his pristine white skull. Soon those red dots began to spread, coating nearly every inch of the bottom half of his skull until it was covered in a red, mushy material that quickly began to inflate. Within seconds, the mushy material turned meaty. Muscles, ligaments, and other parts of a working human jaw formed, culminating in the creation of a mouth, tongue and all.

Eli tasted the soup again, this time displacing the material as it fell through his neck hole and sending it into the void.

"Hmmm. Is this supposed to be what is considered good?" he mused before willing the tiny skeleton perched upon his cookbook to change the page. The glowing blue orbs that served as his eyes settled upon the new pages of text.

"Hmmm... Smell is eighty percent of taste... And we should savor the aroma first before tasting..." Eli read aloud, turning around to place the book down on a nearby shelf just as a portal opened up and spilled dozens of humans all across his kitchen. One particularly loud one screamed as he exited the portal until he fell straight into Eli's cauldron.

The Primordial God paid the newcomers no heed. He was on a timetable, after all. Instead, Eli tapped the crystal on his skull and swiped down, creating a mask of working flesh that connected with his mouth and formed the full features of a face many would consider handsome and regal.

Eli moved his jaw back and forth, squinting a few times with his newly created eyeballs. The golden irises within rolled around, acclimating to the new face he had created. Satisfied that everything seemed to work, Eli turned, dipping his ladle back into the steaming soup as a stark-naked man screamed and thrashed around inside.

The god paused, taking a moment to savor the scent of cooking meat.

"Hmmm," Eli hummed, removing the soup-filled ladle and bringing it to his lips. He smacked his lips repeatedly, savoring the taste as multiple humans began to run away in a panic from the twenty-foot-tall skeleton in his kitchen. "Islandr has odd tastes. Let's just hope they enjoy it."

"MONSTER!"

"DEMON!"

"WHERE ARE WE?!"

"RUN!"

Suddenly, the rickety door of his kitchen opened, revealing the green-haired goddess of hunt and wildlife. Accompanying her as she entered was the short stack, green-skinned Islandr as well as a woman with wings. The trio were talking in the midst of what seemed to be a happy discussion before they all paused, staring at all of the naked humans running around in a blind panic as Eli dipped his ladle into a cauldron occupied by a screaming man.

"Ah, salutations, dinner will be ready shortly," Eli said as calmly as if he were welcoming guests.

Freya facepalmed and Islandr stuck her foot out to trip a man running for the exit. Behind them the last person, the god of light and creation, Voltrain, now in a female host, took a breath and screamed Eli's name at the top of her lungs.

Catpurr 6

A Necromancer, Paladin, and a Thief Walk into an Inn...

"Idiot! Idiot! Idiot! Idiot!"

Under a moonlit sky Adam stood beneath the canopy of large trees, an animated silhouette amidst stoic shadows that yelled over and over again as he smacked Liza on the head repeatedly with his rolled-up map. "Do you not have a brain in your brain case?! Is your head only for show?! I know undead with more intelligence than you! AND MOST OF THEM DON'T HAVE BRAINS!"

"I said I was sowy!" Liza cried as he berated her, clutching her head as the nekoboy kept thwapping her with his map.

"No! Your fake tears won't work on me! How hard is it to listen?! Why does no one listen to me?! Is there something wrong with me?! Are my vocal cords deficient?! ARE YOU HARD OF HEARING?! WHY, DAMN IT?! WHY?!"

Adam paused, taking a deep breath to calm his strung-out nerves. If he were in his past world, this would be the moment where he would relax and pet Schrödinger for comfort. But now all he had were animated cat skeletons which, while soothing, only had cold bones where his companion had soft and fluffy fur.

"Uuuuugh," Adam groaned aloud, holding his head up as he pinched his nose. Within his own skull a headache was forming. "I really wish I had my cat."

Adam glanced around, his natural night vision illuminating the forest floor clearly as if it were day.

He sighed, gazing over to the slumbering Junith propped up on a nearby tree. Between the passed out ex-paladin and the crying nekogirl in a teenager's body, Adam's shoulders could only sag with weight.

Idiots. I'm surrounded by idiots.

"You're such a bully!" Liza cried, falling on all fours before curling up on her side. "You're so mean! Meanie!"

"Gah, stop crying and get up. We've got a trek ahead of us and I want to make it to the inn before daybreak," Adam said, grabbing Junith by her bushy black tail and dragging her along. The nekoboy was by now too tired to be bothered carrying her.

"Tsk," Liza replied, laying out on the ground spread-eagle before finally rising. "Fiiine."

* * *

Staggering in the moonlight that made it past the dense forest branches were two gremlins. At times they would trade off while dragging a third. The whole trio was left dirty and haggard. Occasionally, dark growls would emanate from them, or the third would make frightful sounds as her body struck a rock.

Of course, these three were named Adam, Liza, and Junith. And after several hours of walking, their stomachs were getting loud enough to scare the forest nightlife.

Man... Maybe I should have gotten something to eat, Adam lamented, his feet sluggish as he paused for a moment to get his bearings.

The boy sucked in a deep breath. In the distance he spotted a dim, faint glow, some light source that he assumed belonged to their destination, the inn.

"Nearly there," Adam assured Liza who only grunted in response. Soon the pair reached the edge of the bushes and foliage, where they took a moment to check if any prying eyes watched.

Satisfied that no one was around, the pair stepped onto the paved highway, leading towards a wooden two-story lodge where a nearby sign lit by a lone torch declared that it was the **GALE INN, Open 24/6!**

"Heh..." Liza said.

"What?"

"Open twenty-four six," Liza replied, drawing a confused look from Adam. "Back in my world, usually places that are open all week are open twenty-four seven and... Well, it was just something funny, don't worry about it."

Adam shook his head, peering more closely at the sign. More specifically, the smaller text beneath the inn's name with letters that read **Demi Friendly!**

Adam could not say whether the words were a curse or a long-awaited blessing. However, he *could* say that he was tired, hungry, stinky, and had had enough of touching grass for one day, perhaps even one month. If Liza's complaints were to be believed, the same was doubly true for her.

"Alright. You know the plan, Liza."

The nekogirl sighed as Adam handed her the trickster's persona and summoned several skelecats. If something went wrong, his cats would alert him.

"Noooo problem, little bro," the teenager said, dropping Junith as she fixed her clothes, donned her mask, and cracked her neck. She entered the faint torchlight, following the stone-tile path to the door. Adam followed suit, putting Junith on his back and making sure her tail was tucked into her belt loop before stopping beside Liza. He had double-checked that his hood covered his twitching ears.

Liza knocked on the wooden door, and both tensed as they readied themselves for anything.

Nothing happened.

Adam rounded the corner to peer through a side window spilling light, but quickly realized he was not tall enough to look through, even when standing tiptoe.

Ugh.

Liza knocked again.

A few seconds passed before the nekogirl reached up to knock against the door. But before she could announce her presence again, a loud *bang!* interrupted her, followed by a torrent of swears.

"I TOLD YOU RIGELLIAN DOGS! IT DOESN'T MATTER WHO YOU SEND! I'M NOT PAYING TAXES!" a voice shouted as the door was ripped open, revealing a squat, elderly man with graying hair, standing at Adam's height. Clutched in his weathered hands was what appeared to be a miniature cannon. "Ah, pulling at my heartstrings now, are ya?! Sending CHILDREN TO DO YAH DIRTY WORK?!"

The man shoved past Adam and Liza, raising his fist into the open air. "I'M NOT PAYING TAXES!"

"Uhm, excuse me, s-s-sir," Liza squeaked, still sticking to the script of a weary traveler. "We—"

The man hit a button on his black cylinder, releasing a *boom* that momentarily deafened Adam. Somewhere in the distance, the silhouette of a tree was visibly dissected as one half fell to the forest ground.

Hmmm... Maybe we should just sleep in the woods, Adam thought to himself. Slowly, Adam began to back away but froze in place when the man finally noticed his guests and whirled on them.

"WHAT DO YOU WANT, VILENCIEL DOGS?!" The short man spat, spittle flying as his brown eyes danced with madness.

"Oh—Uhm. We were... hoping to rent a room for the n-night," Liza replied as Adam shrunk into himself. The man blinked at the shaking nekogirl's words, his wrinkled features finally relaxing.

"You want to rent a room here?"

"Uhm. Yes, we aren't from around here and saw your inn on the map." At her words the man scowled as if she'd fed him something wretched. "We've been walking for a while and—"

The man huffed.

"Say nothing else, lassy." The innkeeper looked over at Adam. Propped up on his shoulder was a drooling Junith. "Hundred coppers a night. Sorry, but I have to charge, otherwise I get labeled as a shelter instead. Can you do that?"

Something must be wrong, Adam thought to himself. The price of admission was way too low.

"Adam?" Liza turned and beckoned, hand outstretched for the coins.

"I don't know... I'm scared," he said quietly, the phrase to move on.

"Oh... Okay." She retracted her hand, embracing him instead. "It's okay. If you don't want to stay here, we can just camp in the woods again."

"N-NONSENSE!" the stubby man barked, shouldering his cannon and pointing at his doorway. "Fifty coppers a night, and I'll even throw in some grub and ale! Go on! Get! I ain't gonna let some kids shiver in the cold!"

"FIFTY?" Adam unintentionally blurted. His stomach howled like a beast as greed overwrote his sense of self-preservation. The boy made no attempt to resist as the old shorty shoved them all inside.

"Make yourselves comfortable, I don't get much traffic since the Duchy put my inn on the map," the innkeeper said, walking past the trio of nekofolk to stop behind behind a finely crafted wooden bar. "I'll take payment in the morning."

In fact, the entire interior of the inn was beautifully crafted. Ornate wooden pillars dotted the room decorated with intricate carvings. The walls were brightly painted with images of flowers, and the floor was decorated with hard stone tile, the kind of tile Adam had seen in a place called a 'convenience store' from his last trial.

"Wow... What a beautiful place."

"Thank you. Crafted it all myself, I did."

"Really?!" Liza exclaimed as the innkeeper threw his cannon onto a shelf and began loudly rummaging underneath the counter. "Hard to believe you don't get any traffic."

"Oh, lass, I used to! But then those idiot bureaucrats put me on their little map and outed me out as a demi. Between the tax collectors trying to collect on *land I own*! And those zealots of Voltrain trying to run me out, no one wants to sleep in an inn that's constantly raided by the inquisition and tax collectors," the innkeeper complained.

"You're... a demi-human?" Adam asked, brow raised.

"What? You never seen a stout before?" the man asked, his head just barely peeking over the counter, one brow perked. He produced a ring of keys and unhooked one.

"Uh, no," Adam replied. The man stepped out again from behind the counter.

"Never heard of us?"

"No," he repeated as Liza took the key.

"Are you sure?" the innkeeper asked. "The Vs like to call us squats, or shorties, maybe you've heard of my kind that way?"

"Uh. I can't say I have." Adam replied.

"We participated in the battle of Shroud lands, aided mankind against the beastfolk threat?"

Adam looked off to the side, hazily recalling a passage about humanity's allies during the formation of the Rigellian Empire, but not what its contents were.

"I thought you were a dwarf," Liza commented, causing the man's expression to shift.

"HA! I like you, lassy. Yeah, if I were ten feet tall, dangling from a tree and eating pinecones, I guess I would be a dwarf."

"Haha... Riiight," Liza replied with the innkeeper not realizing she wasn't joking.

"I'm Ritzgerald Barnaby Woodcutter," the Innkeeper said, extending his hand. "But you can call me Barny."

Woodcutter? Odd name, Adam thought but said nothing, his feet aching as he stood in the fancy inn.

"Liza," she replied, shaking the man's hand enthusiastically.

"A—" Adam began but remembered the wanted posters with his name plastered on them. "—bel. And this lump of meat on my back is Judgy."

"Odd names, but it's a pleasure to meet yah. Up the stairs to the left, the room matching the symbol on the key is yours. No hot water yet for a bath at this hour, but if ya need anything, just holla," Barny said. They thanked Barny before taking off, their bones in dire need of a restful night.

Catpurr 7
Insanity, Obsession, and Cats***
Crazy 101

In the bowels of Vilenciel City, in the deepest recesses of the dukedom, a woman clad in a black velvet nightgown lay. Cradled in her lap was a piece of fine black cloth, cushioning strands of bright red hair.

The woman breathed in the fibers, quivering as she lay in the absolute darkness of the dungeon she had crafted for her perverted desires.

"Soon... Soon... Soon," Alencia Vilenciel muttered over and over again. The oldest daughter of the duchess waited in the dark, fantasizing about her idealized reunion with the nekoboy who had managed to elude her thus far.

Suddenly, the sound of a knob turning broke the silence. The heavy oaken door was shoved open with a creak, faint light spilling out to combat the darkness.

"Pardon the intrusion, Lady—"

"OUT! OUT! OOOOUT!" Alencia screamed. The light of the fixture held in the knight's hand illuminated the ornate, king-size bed she lay upon, hand-drawn portraits of Adam covering every inch of the silken sheets. "I SAID I WAS NOT TO BE DISTURBED, NABARA!"

"My sincerest—"

"OUT!"

"—apolo—"

"I SAID OUT!"

"—gies."

"ARE YOU DISOBEYING ME?!"

"—HOWEVER–I–BRING–NEWS–OF–ADAM," the knight blurted. At the very mention of the name, the woman's entire demeanor transformed.

"Really? Really? Tell me. TELL ME!" Alencia was up, leaping from her bed to stand before the knight whose eyes seemed to dim.

"Reports from Rolo Fortress—" Nabara began, removing a stack of reports from a bag—only for Alenia to snatch them away, hungrily tearing through them. "—state the fugitive was spotted in the outskirts of the refugee market area."

Alencia stepped away, reading and rereading the reports and accounts taken from various survivors and eyewitnesses from the incident dubbed *The Catastrophe of the Selkuin Forest.*

Her eyes widened, absorbing the reports from various adventurers who spotted the cat-eared boy, along with a teenaged nekogirl and a little girl assumed to be another demi human.

"There's more of him..." Alencia whispered, her voice sending chills down Nabara's spine. A look of disgust formed across the knight's face. Fortunately, a helmet obscured her expression, the only thing visible being her eyes as they gazed upon her liege's back.

Please return home, Luluca... Nabara said to herself, closing her eyes. A squeal from Alencia caused them to bolt open again.

"There's more of them! MORE! Do you know what that means, Nabara?!" Lady Alencia spun to lock eyes with Nabara. Her own eyes were bloodshot and manic as the knight suppressed a shudder.

"No, I do not, Your Grace," Nabara replied deadpan as the woman approached, grabbing her by the shoulders to shake her.

"*We* can capture one of them and have them take us to their colony!" Alencia screamed in delight. "Can you imagine?! All the nekoboys and girls we could ever want!"

"That sounds lovely, milady."

"Isn't it?! Ahhh, all my years of research, all this time hunting for the fabled nekoboys and he's at the tip of my fingernails!" Alencia screamed, twirling before landing in the bed. A cloud of Adam posters fluttered up into the air.

A moment passed, then another.

"Deploy my personal troops. Lock down the highway and have my carriage ready." Alencia sprung up, her eyes were those of a hawk that had just spotted dinner.

"Locking down the highway... Are you sure that is wise? Your mother—"

"DOESN'T APPRECIATE THE ENORMITY OF THE SITUATION!" Alencia barked, eyes narrowing as she fished out glasses and stood, making her way across the room. "Judging from these casualty reports, these demi-humans are powerful. It's obvious we can't rely on the wayward adventurer and mercenary now that such a massacre has taken place."

The duchess' daughter paused, standing beside a rack filled with nets, darts, bear traps, and various hunting tools. "No... If we want something done, it's best we do it ourselves."

"Lady Alencia, I caution against taking to the field. System Users and Chosen are exceptionally dangerous. May I suggest instead waiting for his next trial as Lady Vilenciel ordered? Once he arrives at the temple—"

"WE ALREADY WAITED! Yet he eluded us! That bitch, Coco!" Alencia shrieked. Her hand clenched into a fist. The noble lady drew it back before punching the rack. "Sheltering the demi-humans! Rubbing it in my face with her damn cat-eared headband! No more! No more! No more! I will not be kept *another second* apart from my beloved!"

Alencia began pulling her hair, fuming before Nabara coughed to remind the woman of her presence.

"Yes. Right. I shouldn't lose focus," Alencia said. "Do as I have ordered, mother will understand. She always understands. This I do not just for myself, but for all humanity. Once we have him, we'll go to work exterminating the rest—save for the few to be kept as pets."

Nabara blinked, happy that the woman couldn't see her expression.

"As you will, milady," Nabara replied, bowing before taking her leave. Once she heard the mighty doors slam shut behind her, she wasted no time quickening her steps.

As the door closed, Alencia turned, waiting for a moment before she approached a massive velvet curtain that jutted out from the wall.

She walked through the wall of velvet, entering a protected sanctuary dedicated to the future she hoped to achieve. On the wall was a massive a drawing of Adam curled at her feet as she sat upon a throne.

"Soon..." she said, half prayer, half promise. The woman fell to her knees, wrinkling the fine velvet dress as she clutched at the shrine with trembling, reverent hands. Contained safely within was a treasure more precious than rubies, garnets, or carmine. More valuable than anything in the Duchy. A crimson vial of Adam's blood.

"Soon..."

Catpurr 8

A Necromancer, Paladin, and a Thief Set an Inn on Fire

Adam stood naked beneath the starry sky, watching as fire consumed the inn sporting a new massive hole in its roof. Beside him, Liza laughed as Junith ran in circles, screaming, most likely due to her fuzzy black tail currently being on fire.

"How... *Why* do stupid things keep happening?" he bemoaned, pinching the bridge of his nose as he recounted the events that had led to this moment.

* * *

Twenty minutes prior.

Entering into the upstairs room, Adam looked around; it was a carpeted space with three beds covered by large purple comforters.

"Hmm." Liza walked to a nearby dresser, running her hand across the surface. "Dusty."

"Well... looks safe," Adam said, eyeing the window nearby. He unceremoniously dropped Junith on the ground with a thud and approached it, pushing the dusty blue curtains aside.

Nothing but trees... His golden eyes darted from side to side, scanning the area below the inn as one of his skelecats came into view.

Suddenly, a bang at the door tore his attention away from the woods. From the other side of the door, the innkeeper shouted.

"Oi, I'm heating some water and doing laundry, if yah want yer clothes cleaned."

"Alright! Give us a minute!" Liza called back before Adam could respond.

"Just leave them at the door, and I'll collect 'em. I can also wash yer armor free of charge but can't do anything 'bout repairs."

"Okay!" Liza said. She turned, only to run into Adam's fist as he bonked her head. Looking at his feet, it became apparent he was standing atop a table to reach her height.

"What are you doing? I don't want to give a stranger my gear!" Adam hissed, glaring at the woman dragging Junith onto a bed.

"Have you smelled yourself?" Liza asked, plopping Junith onto the bed where she began unlacing the straps of the nekogirl's boots. "That's month-long bacteria, mildew, and mold growing on yourself, a recipe for disaster if you don't wash."

Adam paused, looking down at the soiled, scuffed up, and dirt-stained cloak and armor he'd been wearing for a month straight. He hadn't realized how badly he stank. Knowing she had a point, Adam grumbled, unclipping his cloak and removing his sweaty, dirty armor.

It didn't take long before he was standing in his underwear, nearly naked. He watched with arms folded as Liza unsuccessfully struggled to undress Junith.

"Why are there so many latches?" she complained, tugging at the girl's armor. "It's like when I remove one plate, there's latches under latches under latches!"

"Move aside," Adam said, rolling Junith over and undoing the lace that tied a portion of her plate to the other. With deft hands, he quickly removed the armor, tossing it into the pile at the door where all his clothes and gear were before he began working on her clothes.

He tugged at her tunic, pulling it over her shoulders and exposing her skin. Tufts of fur covered her small body as the crest stood out starkly over her breasts. He wasted no time undoing her leather belt and subsequently moving to remove her pants.

"Eh?"

Adam paused. Junith's body suddenly stiffened as her eyes shot open, then widened as she watched a half-naked Adam undress her.

"EH?!"

"Oh, you're awake, good—" was all Adam could say before he was sent flying across the room by Junith's foot planting itself into his face.

"PERVERTED HERETIC! I ALWAYS KNEW YOU WANTED MY BODY!" Junith screamed, leaping up and rolling out of bed with her hands raised, ready to fight. In the corner of the room, Liza giggled at the impromptu show.

Adam got up, blinking blearily as he pinched his bleeding nose. "What the Nyx was that for, meatbag?!"

"How dare you try and take advantage of a defenseless woman!" Liza chimed in, pointing at Adam with an accusatory look. She hugged Junith from behind, her expression one of feigned sadness. "I tried to stop him, but he used his command seal to stop me, and I was powerless! *Powerless* against his dark desires!"

"Command seal?" Adam echoed. Light gathered around Junith's body, and the confusion disappeared as apprehension seized him. "WAITWAITWAIT!"

Energy crackled in the air. Runes blazed to brilliant life all across her body as a churning vortex of electrical energy surrounded the girl. In the Followers menu Junith's health plummeted rapidly, but that did nothing to dissuade her from opening fire, unleashing a blast of void energy to annihilate the perceived pervert.

Adam dodged, hitting the floor just in time to avoid the torrent of purple energy that devoured the roof and opened a hole in the ceiling.

When the blast died down, he spun on his back, warily eyeing the moon and night sky pocketed with stars as it stared back at him.

"You idiot! What if that had hit me?!" he yelled as Liza stood to the side, shaking in a fit of uncontrollable laughter.

"Then the world would be a better place!" Junith screamed as blood leaked out from her eyes. "HOW DARE YOU ATTEMPT TO ASSAULT ME?!"

"I WAS TRYING TO REMOVE YOUR CLOTHES!"

"I'LL KILL YOU!"

Liza only laughed harder, reaching a point where she began choking. The girl staggered drunkenly, bumping into things in the room. As she jostled the wardrobe dust spewed everywhere, flying up her nose and causing her to sneeze up glitter.

As Junith tackled Adam and wrapped her hands around his throat, Liza blinked. Her laughter stopped as the sparkling particles caught her attention. They briefly seemed to hang in the air before she sneezed again, sending more glitter to join them.

"Huh..."

Soon Liza found herself unable to stop sneezing until a cloud of glitter formed, catching Adam's eyes. He watched as his companion fell backwards, sneezing into a lit candle. The boy had just enough time to think *"Oh, crap,"* as the entire glittering cloud was set aflame.

In an instant, fire was everywhere. The bed sheets, the curtains, every inch of the bedroom where Liza had sneezed was now a deadly inferno as the scattered glitter instantly combusted.

Liza let out a scream, running around as her cloak caught flame.

Suddenly the door of their room kicked open.

"WHAT IN POHATU'S NAME IS GOING—" Barnaby froze, the little stoat staring at the trio of chaotic nekofolk as flames consumed throughout the bedroom. "—OUT! EVERYONE OUT!"

He turned and ran. Adam kicked Junith off him and hastily gathered what he could before grabbing Junith by her ear, dragging her along as he ran out of the burning room with Liza.

The trio quickly followed after Barnaby as the innkeeper held the door of the lounge open, beckoning to the scurrying group of nekofolk fleeing from the spreading flames.

Outside, the nekoboy caught his breath before he turned to gaze at the flames engulfing the inn, which only seconds prior had been a lovely establishment for weary and wayward adventurers.

Ah... crapbaskets.

"Your tail! Your tail is on fire!" Liza yelled. Adam's tired gaze fell upon Junith, whose tail had indeed caught fire during their frantic escape. The nekogirl leaped straight up, before running around in a blind panic. "STOP, DROP, AND ROLL! STOP, DROP, AND ROLL!"

I'm surrounded by idiots.

Adam pinched the bridge of his nose and rubbed his face with both hands, a headache forming as he tried to make sense of everything that had transpired within a couple of minutes. Then he looked up, taking in the sight of Barnaby who was standing in front of his flaming shop. Despite his entire livelihood going up in flames, the little innkeeper looked oddly calm.

"We... should probably run," Adam muttered to himself, watching as the stout took a deep breath, before taking out what appeared to be a small wand.

Adam slowly took a step back as the wand extended, revealing a staff. Alarm bells rang inside Adam's head as the staff began to glow, emitting a power that marked the tiny man as a bona fide threat. However, the stout didn't attack the trio responsible for the destruction of his entire life. Instead, he slammed the black metal staff into the ground, and a ripple of power exploded from the point of impact, wrapping around the inn.

Time seemed to rewind. The flames were snuffed out entirely as a soft, green light enveloped the entire building. Arcane runes appeared on the ground as the inn rebuilt itself from the ground up. The roof began to wiggle as what appeared to be tree roots sprouted from the ceiling, closing the hole.

Huh...

Before Adam knew it, he was taking notes, sketching up the scene playing out in front of him of the stout using magic to restore the inn to its former appearance. Within minutes, the innkeeper was done. He flashed a glare at the naked Adam, who could only purse his lips and look away.

"Wow," Liza commented, laying atop a squirming Junith to pin her to the ground.

Adam approached Barnaby.

"Uhm... Sorry?"

"Sorry?!" Barnaby bellowed, his voice ringing out through the darkness of the night. "SORRY?! YOU AND YOUR LOT NEARLY DAMN WELL BURNED DOWN MY HOME!"

Adam took a deep breath, once again warily eying the metal staff in the innkeeper's hand. Metal engravings covered its surface, seeming to dance and shift in the moonlight. "That would be an accurate assessment of current events."

"Accurate? ASSESSMENT?! Why I oughta—" Barnaby raised his fist, but then fell silent, eyes narrowing as his gaze fixed onto something behind the child. When Adam turned to look, he frowned. He didn't need dark vision to see what had concerned the innkeeper.

There were lights in the distance. Tiny orbs, flickering and moving, all at human eye level and moving in such coordination that it could only mean one thing.

People.

"Tsk! Get inside! I'll deal with you lot later!" Barnaby yelled, ordering everyone in with a grunt.

Adam didn't waste a second. He knew trouble was coming judging from the innkeeper's expression, and whatever it was, it seemed worse than a trio of nekofolk nearly burning down his residence.

Liza picked up the still-fuming Junith, one arm wrapped underneath her armpits while the other was clasped on her mouth, preventing the nekogirl from openly swearing. Her screams were muffled as she thrashed around.

Barnaby entered last, walking into the inn. A smell of smoke still lingered in the air, but otherwise the formerly aflame building had been left completely unscathed.

Fascinating, Adam thought to himself. But his admiration of the spell or skill was cut short as Barnaby slammed the door shut and moved a table to bar it. He eyed the three nekofolk.

Then he ran off, heading behind the counter. The stout hit a switch, and a ladder abruptly fell from the ceiling.

An illusionary wall? Adam's eyes went wide. The magics of this inn were far more than met the eye.

"Into the attic! Go! Go now!" Barnaby hurried them.

"What's going on?!" Adam demanded. Outside, the sound of yelling was getting louder.

"Followers of Voltrain! No doubt brought here by the flames!" Barnaby yelled, causing Junith's ears to perk up. "If they spot you they'll drag you off and cuff me! Now up! Go!"

Adam didn't need to be told twice. He scampered up the wooden ladder with feline grace, phasing through the ceiling to reveal a crowded attic space filled with boxes and random knick knacks. His eyes scanned the entire room, pupils wide for any threats, yet all he saw were dust, boxes, and statues.

"Go! Up! What are you waiting for, boy?!" the innkeeper cried, hurrying the boy along.

The others followed suit. Once there were no tails in the way, Barnaby retracted the ladder. The hole closed just as a banging sounded at the door.

Catpurr 9
THEY ARE IN ZE ATTIC!

In the attic, Adam sat still, the creak of the inn door clear as day to his fluffy, red ears pressed against the wood floor. He narrowed his eyes, putting his finger up to hush the squirming Junith in Liza's arms, the former of which was still in her bra and visibly upset.

"MMMh! MMMH!" Junith cried out, muffled by Liza's hand over her throat.

Good thing I didn't give her the berserker class, he considered, then rolled his eyes.

"Shut up!" Adam hissed. At this command, the brand on her chest flashed, just in time to shut her up as a loud, suave voice echoed up from the room below.

"*Good evening.* I am Inspector Lenius Verduin. Are you perhaps Ritzgerald Barnaby Woodcutter? Of the Barnaby clan? Proprietor of the Gale Inn, this fine establishment we currently stand within, glaring at one another?" the man asked.

"What do you think? You know many stouts in the area that can tolerate your stench?" Barnaby spat. Something below went *click*.

"My, of course not! But your kind look alike and breed like rats. Honestly, it's difficult to tell sometimes," the Inspector said with a laugh.

Barnaby was unamused. "You have ten seconds to leave before I blast you with my cannon."

"HA! A stout with a sense of humor!"

"One," the innkeeper began.

"An ultimatum? Oh, I do love your kind's stubbornness."

"Two."

"Please don't be unreasonable, Mr. Woodcutter."

"Three."

"Mr. Woodcutter, I have with me twelve constables from the Ministry of the Federal Alignment Party—"

"Four."

"If you fire upon me, my men—"

"Five."

"—will arrest you and burn this hovel in the middle of nowhere to the ground!" the Inspector at last got out.

The counting stopped. For several long moments there was only silence. None of the nekos in the attic even daring to breathe.

The faux smile in Inspector Verduin's voice was as obvious as it was sickening. "Ah, I see that you're becoming more amicable to my presence, Mr. Woodcutter. Thank you."

After a moment of silence, Barnaby relented. "What do you people want?" Something heavy thudded down upon wood. If Adam had to guess, the stout had just placed his miniature cannon back upon the counter.

"First and foremost, Mr. Woodcutter, how are you?"

"Worse, having to look at you. What do you people want?" Barnaby repeated, his tone a growl.

Inspector Verduin was undeterred. "Why, to see if you are in good health, Mr. Woodcutter! Me and my men were in the area when we saw the blaze from a distance and couldn't help but be worried. Is everything alright? Everything okay? We rushed here so quickly Little

Jogn was complaining about how parched he was, isn't that right, Little Jogn?"

"Absolutely parched," a voice agreed, presumably the man named Little Jogn.

"Garnet River is just up the road, plenty of depth for all of you to go and collectively drown yourselves," Barnaby replied.

As the inn's lobby grew silent again, the three in the attic collectively pressed their ears to the floor, straining for any hint of sound.

From Adam's understanding, every word that Inspector Verduin had said was a lie. The inn was being watched, surveilled by nearby agents of Voltrain. How he and his group had avoided being spotted seemed a miracle.

Or maybe they did spot us but waited until we were comfortable to surround us.

Adam gritted his teeth, closing his eyes to focus on his skelecats. Even now they were prowling around the outskirts of the inn, ready to strike at his foes.

"Mr. Woodcutter. Are you aware of the fugitive named Adam Glow?" Inspector Verduin asked.

"No, I can't say I am."

His response was all mock-surprise. "*Really?* I must say I am surprised; Adam Glow is quite the celebrity. I was told that Inspector Vahki had personally delivered flyers from the Duchess herself, yet *somehow,* I do not spot a single one of the bounties... Quite strange, wouldn't you agree, Mr. Woodcutter?"

"Must have gotten lost. You know how clumsy us stouts are."

"Hm. Quite," remarked the Inspector.

The voices gave way to footsteps pacing against the hardwood floor. They stopped, and Inspector Verduin spoke again, all his affability fell away in favor of a cold ultimatum.

"Mr. Woodcutter. Here is what is going to happen. My men and I will search the premises."

Adam's heart stopped. *Crap.*

Barnaby snapped, "Over my dead body—"

"That can be arranged!" the Inspector bit back. Beneath his voice came the tromping of many feet. "You see, I know you are harboring the demi-human named Adam. My agents have tracked this little minx here."

"I don't know what you're talking about."

"Yes, yes, of course you don't. Pardon our intrusion, Mueller, Ghotz, stay with Mr. Woodcutter while we search the premises. If he moves, you have permission to try and extend his legs."

Both the agents in question chorused their enthusiastic consent. "

Then there was an explosion of movement and sound as the men below began to turn the establishment upside-down.

"Crapbaskets," Adam muttered aloud. In the chaos of trying to evacuate the inn during the blaze, Junith's armor and his gear had been left in their room. He exchanged a rapid look with Liza. The pink-eared nekogirl's hands were already on her daggers; was ready to spring into action.

No, he mouthed instead. With so many inspectors, acting rashly could still make things worse. If there was one thing he was constantly learning, it was that things could always become worse.

"INSPECTOR!"

And just as expected, Junith's armor had been uncovered. The Inspector in question sucked in a breath through his teeth and began to scold the innkeeper.

"Mr. Woodcutter. I am, if anything, a patient man. However, I feel as though we have engaged in enough foreplay for one session, tell me... Where is the fugitive known as Adam Glow?"

Adam shut his eyes, ear pressed tightly to the floor, heart in his throat.

Across from him, Junith frowned as Liza held her close.

"If you are talking about the cat boy, he fled during the blaze."

The nekoboy in question released his breath, surprised by the innkeeper's decision.

"Excellent! Now we are getting somewhere! *Now,* are you sure about your statement, Mr. Woodcutter? Positively sure?"

"Yes. He isn't here," Barnaby repeated. Adam's teeth clenched as his muscles tensed. "He saw your torches and immediately fled with his entourage."

"BAH! See, I told Little Jogn that we shouldn't have used torches. Ghotz, didn't I tell Little Jogn that we shouldn't use torches?"

"You did, Inspector," a man replied.

"But! Not all is lost—no, no! In fact, we seem to have gotten some intel, Ghotz! Mr. Woodcutter, how many companions would you say our fugitive had?"

"Five."

"Five? *Five?!*"

"Yes," Barnaby replied. In the darkness, Adam squinted. Despite everything, the innkeeper was still helping them. "Three tall adults, two children."

"Interesting... Our reports said our target was accompanied by only two companions, Little Jogn."

"Yes, Inspector?" the familiar voice of Little Jogn replied.

"Take note that it has been reported that Adam Glow travels with four additional companions. Two adults, two children. It seems we may be dealing with a family or a den."

"Yes, Inspector!" Little Jogn replied.

"Now!" said Inspector Verduin, all faux cheer once more. "Back to you, Mr. Woodcutter, I... am a forgiving man. An *understanding* man. Unlike my cohorts and colleagues in the Federal Alignment Party, I believe in second chances."

Upon mentioning the Federal Alignment Party, Liza smiled, drawing an odd look from Adam.

In the darkness, the nekogirl's face was growing red. Frantically, he shook his head.

NO! Adam mouthed, brow furrowing. But Liza could not help herself.

Liza slapped her hand down on her mouth, but it was too late—a tiny snort escaped her. Adam froze, every hair on his body standing erect with some mix of utter terror and outrage".

Nyx below, we're going to die.

Adam closed his eyes, waiting for the inevitable. But no reaction came from below.

The trio sat in silence, listening in as Liza's outburst appeared to go completely unnoticed.

"There are few that would openly declare their domiciles safe havens for demi-humans," the Inspector said, his footsteps creaking the floor. "And fewer still who openly bite back at humanity. I respect you, Mr. Woodcutter, and out of respect I give you this opportunity."

"Opportunity?" Barnaby echoed.

"Yes, an opportunity. When Adam Glow returns, and he *will* return, you are to hand him is effects and notify FAP Agents immediately—"

Liza choked with laughter, her face tomato red.

WHAT IS SO FUNNY?! Adam almost shouted. Somehow he held himself back, consumed with need to hear what would be said next.

"—do this for me, Mr. Woodcutter, and perhaps we can see about reduced taxes and fewer visits from Inspectors."

"What makes yah so sure he'll return?" Barnaby replied. "He could be halfway to the Delian Plains by now, or near the Imari Valley."

"Unlikely. I have hunted many fugitives in my time as an Inspector. Like moths to a flame, he cannot help himself. The illusion of safety, the promise of an ally is often too sweet for a man on the run to pass up, especially a family. No... He will return. It is only a matter of time."

"So, I'm bait?"

The inspector clapped his hands together. "Precisely! So, what will it be, Mr. Woodcutter? Will you be part of the solution? Or will you be part of the problem? I can assure you that any information or help leading to Adam's capture will be rewarded *substantially.*"

Barnaby seemed to think the offer over as the Inspector awaited the stout's answer

"If he shows, I'll send a bird," Barnaby finally replied.

"Excellent! Excellent!" the inspector exclaimed, his boot slamming against the floor. "See how much we can accomplish when we just talk? You should be thankful, Mr. Woodcutter, Little Jogn here wanted to slice you open and torture you. Isn't that right, *Little Jogn?*"

"Had my big knife ready and everything, sir," Jogn replied nonchalantly.

"We expect to hear back from you soon, Mr. Woodcutter. Now! I must depart, the fugitives and dissidents won't hunt themselves. Have a nice day."

And with that, the agents filed out of the inn, accompanied by the heavy stomping of many booted feet against hardwood. Slowly the noise died down and the door slammed shut, replaced by Barnaby's grumbling.

Some minutes later the illusionary entrance reappeared, and the wrinkly face of their host and savior poked up into the attack, glaring at the huddled trio of nekofolk.

"Get the Nyx out of my inn."

Catpurr 10
The Selkuin Ruins

"How poetic... A German hiding in an attic and escaping through a tunnel to avoid men from the government hunting them," Liza said. Currently she was crouching while walking through an underground escape tunnel as the trio left the inn. From the front with torch in hand, Adam let out a sound of frustration.

"Tsk, fifty coppers... FIFTY COPPERS! I knew it was too good to be true, this is the last time we ever stop for an inn!" he complained. Presently, the nekoboy only had half his gear on. Namely, his leather armor, his cloak, and boots. Everything else had been left behind, as the Inspectors who had so kindly visited would no doubt notice if his gear suddenly disappeared from Barnaby's inn.

"Somehow! Not only did we fail to find any freebies or discounts, we've doubled the debt in the time since this morning, Junith has mismatched armor and no sword, and I'M MISSING PANTS!" he continued to gripe. "From here on out, it's nothing but camping in trees and caves!"

Liza sulked at the proclamation. "Oh, come on, it's not that bad. Once we finish this mission, we'll be good."

He groaned. "I shoulda just fed you to my skeletons. Why didn't I feed you to my skeletons? My life would be so much easier without you giving me a constant headache."

"Ooooh, stawp it!" Liza said, draping her arm around Adam, who flinched away with a look of disgust. "If you killed me, you wouldn't have anyone to brighten up the mood and run errands for you in town. You and I both know Judgy would just mess it up somehow, and you'd both get caught."

The nekogirl currently bringing up the rear let out a growl at the sound of her name. "Says the airhead who couldn't contain her laughter and almost got us apprehended by those men from FAP."

At the mention of FAP, Liza snorted.

"Alright. What in the Nyx is so funny?" Adam finally asked, turning to face his fellow nekos.

"What? Oh, come on, don't tell me you don't know what FAP stands for," Liza said, a confused smile on her face.

"Federal Alignment Party. Just as the man described," Adam replied deadpan. Liza turned to Junith, who only raised a brow in response. The taller nekogirl's mouth fell open.

"You can't be serious. Ever heard of the phrase 'jerking off'?"

"No, can't say I have. Is that about pulling jerky?" Adam said. At last, it was Liza's turn to shut her eyes and pinch the bridge of her nose.

"Oh, you naive souls," she mused for one wistful moment, before explaining the meaning behind fap and jerking off.

"Disgusting!" Junith snapped, her face red. From the front, Adam released a world-weary sigh, seeming to reverberate up from the very depths of his soul.

He hesitated, eyes shut and hands lingering at his chest level as if debating something.

The moment passed. Rather than saying anything, the nekomancer turned and stalked off. The three continued wordlessly through the winding tunnel until it ended at a hatch. "Looks like this is it."

Liza immediately stepped forwards, only for Junith to bar her path.

"Stop!"

"What?"

"What are you going to do if this is a trap?" Junith demanded.

"Oh, come on, I doubt it's a trap. If the old shortstack wanted us to die, he'd have ratted us out," Liza replied.

"Or maybe he didn't want us burning down his inn. *Again*. Have you thought about that?"

"I'm sorry, how was *I* supposed to know that I sneezed glitter?" Liza shot back. Adam rubbed at his poor, pounding head.

"Please... Shut up. Both of you," he said, feeling as if his IQ was being lowered just by being with the pair. "Junith, open the hatch."

"What? Why do I have to do it?!"

"Because you're the tank with more HP than both of us. If an explosion does occur, you'll at least be useful and block most of the damage." Junith only grumbled at his deadpan reply.

"Truce, my bum!"

There was a brief standoff between the two hissing nekogirls, until Junith pushed past the other and scampered up the ladder. At the top was the hatch. The ex-paladin turned its handle and popped it open, as for what must have been the first time in years, a fresh breeze moved the stale cavern air.

After a moment of peeking out the hatch, she climbed out, calling the others to her.

"Great. Now, time to figure out where we are," Adam said, following her out of the tunnel to get his bearings.

Surrounding them were ruins, effectively a forest of decrepit and rotting stone structures. The ancient ruins were in the process of being swallowed by a more literal forest, slowly being covered by trees, vines, lichen, and cobwebs. The sight was made yet more eerie by the silver moonlight gently beaming down from above.

"Ah..." They must have found their destination, the Selkuin Ruins. Immediately, Adam raised his hand, summoning a pack of skelecats to his side. "Go, hunt down any threat to us."

The cats took off, fleeing the stone building they stood in.

"See? Everything worked out," Liza said, prancing around.

"Alright, spread out and see if we can't find the source of the lights the villagers reported," Adam ordered, walking out of the ruins. Judging from the height of some of these structures, the Selkuin Ruins were the remnants of an ancient city.

"I object," Junith interjected. "We should rest, make camp for the night and observe everything during the morning."

"But then the lights would be gone," Liza said. Despite the long journey, she was apparently still bursting with energy. "The quest states that the lights are only visible at night."

"Then we camp for the night and wait till they show up. A warrior that is fatigued is of no use to anyone. Plus, we don't even have weapons, and are missing half our gear," Junith countered, causing a smile to touch the corners of Liza's lips.

"Ya know, Junith, it's moments like these that make me appreciate you."

"What in Voltrain's name does that mean?"

"It means you're adorable!" Liza said before pouncing at Junith. The little nekogirl's retort was instant, raking her claws across Liza's face.

"As loath as I am to admit it, Junith has a point," Adam said, walking to a sheltered corner of the destroyed building and laying down on a stone slab that had cracks and grass peeking through the architecture. "We'll make camp here in the ruins and pick up tomorrow."

"Ugh, well, at least this place has a roof..." Liza complained before following suit, picking a corner near the adjacent wall as Junith stood at the entrance. The teen tapped the space beside her for Junith to lay but Junith frowned, turning her head.

"I'll take first watch," she declared, folding her arms as she gazed out into the night. Adam didn't need to be told twice. Besides, his skeletons were already on patrol, and he was dead tired. It didn't take long before he was asleep.

* * *

Daylight found Adam stiffly peeling himself off the stony floor of the ruined building.

While stretching, he noticed both nekogirls were absent. His eyes blinked shut as Adam focused on his bonds.

Fortunately, both were close. One remained fixed in one position, while the other was rapidly shifting from close to far, her positioning erratic. From Adam's knowledge of the pair, it was easy to decipher who was who.

Junith was busy with her daily routine while Liza was out hunting or exploring. Judging from how her health was still full, it seemed she had found something interesting to chase.

Being the last to awaken and exit the abandoned structure, Adam withdrew his notebook and pen from his storage ring. The once blank pages were quickly filled with notes and sketches of the surrounding architecture and any remnants of the ancient civilization as the nekomancer roamed the grounds.

It was hours before he crossed paths with either of his companions. Once the sun was high in the sky, a shadow fell across him. Junith stepped over a crumbling wall, dominated by vines, walking to stand beside Adam. By now, the boy was being escorted by several of his skelecats.

"Anything?" he asked, not looking up from his notes.

"Nothing seems amiss. Just lots of rocks," the ex-paladin reported. "I did find these, though."

Junith tossed a pair of ragged, stained pants at Adam, who scooped them up, eyeing the mystery stains. Carefully he put them on, rolling up the pants legs and tying the waist.

"Thanks," he said before returning to his task of documenting. "It'll be dark soon. Have you eaten?"

"I still have some dried jerky, so I'm fine," Junith replied. An awkward silence fell upon the two. Adam seemed unbothered by this as he continued scribbling, Junith standing stoically by his side with folded arms.

"What are you doing?" Liza asked, breaking the silence as she leapt from a nearby roof. The pink-haired teen sauntered over to rest her head on Adam's head, looking down at his sketches. This wasn't the first time she'd seen him sketch, but it was the first she'd asked about it.

"Taking notes," came his response. At no point did his attention drift from his current sketch—a rendering of the wall before them, the layering of the bricks faithfully recreated in ink.

"Of a wall?" Liza raised a brow.

"Of course."

"But... why? This area has probably been surveyed already, you can probably steal a book or ask someone about the ruins."

Adam sighed.

"Yes, but that is second- and sometimes third-hand information. Here it's the real thing, information witnessed by myself that I can trust," he replied, scribbling down on his pad.

"But walls? What's so interesting about a destroyed hovel?"

He let out another sigh.

"This destroyed hovel is the representation of an entire cultural heritage. The remnants of a civilization long since passed that have left behind ruins for us to glimpse into their lives," he explained, beckoning Liza to stand closer to the wall with her torch. "From studying the layering of the brick and stone, we can add another piece of the puzzle that can help form the whole image of the people who lived here."

"Huh... I guess I never thought about it that way," she said as Junith hung just within earshot of the pair. "But why are you so fascinated by it?"

"Because understanding history is how we learn," Adam said. "If I'm ever to build a utopia or help progress humanity, then understanding the pitfalls of previous societies is paramount."

"Huh... So that's your goal..."

"One of many, yes."

The two went on to talk more, but Junith heard no more of it. She moved through the fading evening light as the sun began to set, continuing her patrol. Occasionally she would stop, inspecting the remains of some structure or another, but never for long. She was not technically alone—at times, she spotted Adam's skelecats on the prowl. But they made for poor company, and the ruins were otherwise completely abandoned.

Or so they appeared, until she came across one building protected by a dome of shimmering blue light. Rainbow hues spilled out from the building's doors and windows in a dazzling array.

"Huh," she huffed, almost tempted to approach the magical barrier that had suddenly cropped up. But from her training as a paladin of Voltrain, she knew what a bad idea that could be, instead turning around.

Thanks to her bond with Adam, it was quite easy to return to his side. His presence stood out in her mind like a star against the night sky, growing stronger and brighter the closer she became. When she found them in a different ruined hut, however, the paladin-turned-priestess was treated to a strange sight—the boy was balanced precariously on Liza's shoulder as he tried to study an etching on the ceiling.

"Hold still!" Adam demanded as Liza held onto his ankles.

"What do you think I'm trying to do? You weigh a lot more than you think!"

"Nonsense, just hold still. You have broad shoulders; you can support my weight just fine."

Liza made a face, unsure of what to make of the comment as Junith cleared her throat. The leaning tower of nekos spun to face her.

"I think I found our lights," Junith reported as Adam hopped off Liza's shoulders.

Catpurr 11
The Raving Wizard

"What is it?" Liza asked. The trio, flanked by a squad of skellecats, now stood before Junith's discovery. Filtered through the swirling blue mass of energy, flashing colorful lights were still visible beyond. "I bet there's a rave going on in there."

Adam leaned down, inspecting the barrier. His tiny hand hovered inches away from touching it before quickly retracting. Scattered around the area were various bones and tattered clothes.

"Come," Adam ordered, directing one of his skelecats forwards. It brushed past his legs, rubbing its head on his ankle before moving to touch the barrier with a paw. Immediately the appendage was stuck in the energy.

Adam leaned away from the struggling skeleton as the spinning barrier dragged it inside with an alarmed clattering. The blue gyre spun the skeleton faster and faster before the twisting layers of magic crushed it into pieces. A new rain of white dust and bone fragments fell upon the nekotrio, joining the barrier's previous victims around their feet.

"Sheesh. Good thing you didn't touch it." Liza whistled.

"Hmmm. It's just as I thought," Adam said, pursing his lips. "It's a form of wind barrier."

"Is there any way around it?" she asked.

"Of course. Since it's wind, we just need to dig underneath. Let the wind keep touching the ground."

"Great... More tunnels," Junith muttered.

"Have a problem with being underground?" Liza playfully jabbed Junith in the ribs with her elbow, prompting the priestess to roll her eyes.

"Yes, I'm sick of having to be cramped with you two," The paladin snapped, only for Liza to descend upon her with a tight hug. The nekogirl responded as she always did, violently.

Adam ignored the pair, instead, summoning his cats. Past circumstances had proved digging was a task they excelled in, and today was no exception.

Eventually, a tunnel was made, safely bringing Adam and his gang to the building's entrance.

"Is that... music?" Junith asked. Liza hopped in place, hollering "I knew it!" in a childish manner.

Adam raised a hand, hushing the pair. Even still crouched in the hole, upbeat, rhythmic music was pulsing from within the building. Music which, by his definition, was perfectly obnoxious. Accompanying the thrumming beat was a cloyingly sweet scent.

Great. Well, he wasn't going in first. Adam wasted no time in reminding Junith that that was *her* job.

She grumbled but complied, hopping into the tunnel, two cats trailing behind her, and soon all three reappeared on the other side of the barrier.

"What do you see?" Liza called down the tunnel as Junith peered into the structure dubiously.

"Lots of lights, but you're a buffoon if you think I'm entering without the rest of you," Junith shot back, folding her arms. Adam kicked Liza into the tunnel.

"Hey!" Liza exclaimed.

"The sooner we get this done, the sooner we can afford an inn," he reminded her.

"Really?!" The nekogirl's tail wagged back and forth, almost like a dog's.

"Yes," Adam lied. Without any more complaints, the girl scrambled to join Junith. Adam was slower in following as he hiked up the oversized pants and climbed down, one hand over the other. Finally, he joined the two inside the barrier.

Upon emerging, the overwhelming lights and sounds assaulted his acute feline senses. In stark contrast to his irritated frown and twitching ears, however, Liza seemed to be enjoying herself as she danced in place.

"Let's go, Junith—"

"No! I'm not your meat shield, if you want me to go in, we go in together!" the paladin yelled, stamping her feet.

Adam rolled his eyes.

"Fine," he said before shoving her across the threshold of the building.

"Hey!" she spat. When no great calamity befell her for crossing the threshold, Adam and Liza followed.

Upon beholding the building's interior, Adam's expression twisted, underscoring his disgust. Junith pushed herself up from where she faceplanted on the ground, mouth falling open as the bizarre and otherworldly sight burned itself into her retinas.

Liza was entirely unperturbed, continuing to dance in place.

At the very center of the ruined building was a half-naked hairy man decked out in pink, star-shaped glasses, dancing with a T-shaped hat on his head. Clutched in his hands were two glowing sticks, one red, one green as the man performed a weird, ritualistic dance, twirling them around in conjunction with the awful music's tune.

All around the man was a chorus of purple-colored mushfolk. Clouds of spores floated up from the creatures as they wobbled around the man, all dancing beneath the multicolored light reflecting off a spinning ball's shining surface.

Adam lingered at the doorway, nose twitching, making a face like he was a child asked to eat his greens while Liza entered the building and approached the stranger with a casual air, mimicking his moves.

So much for the element of surprise and safety, Adam sighed inwardly.

The man didn't seem to mind. In fact, he produced a wide, shiny smile, his teeth gleaming so brightly Adam winced.

At last, the stranger turned away. Adam squinted through the strobing lights and drifting spores, looking again. Somehow Liza had produced her own glowing sticks, choreographing dance moves with the strange man.

The nekoboy's first instinct was to facepalm, when his nose twitched involuntarily.

Something was wrong, yet he couldn't quite articulate why.

The man jabbed with his glow sticks towards the pair still lingering in the doorframe. "Hey hey hey! Welcome to Merlin's house of groove," he bellowed, not stopping for a moment as he welcomed Adam and Junith onto the dance floor.

Neither moved, exchanging matching dubious looks as their apparent host continued to beckon them.

"C'mon, chillax, bros. Have a spell and just dance," he said. "Unwiiind."

Adam narrowed his eyes. His head felt strange, but the System showed no abnormalities or status effects.

"Who are you?" he asked. Just outside of view, his skelecats waited for his signal.

"Me? I'm Merlin, baby! Extradimensional wizard, grand caster of King Arthur, high mage of Avalon, party master supreme and groove maestro!" The introduction drew an odd look from Adam.

Wait, extradimensional?

Red ears twitched. Until now, Junith had been his best lead in reuniting with his closest friend, if a useless one that made him wait a full year, but if this wizard, however strange, was telling the truth...

Bad feelings and strange sensations could be put aside, this captured Adam's full attention.

"I see. I'm Adam," he said. It would be better to stay on the wizard's good side for now. "We're adventurers dispatched... dispatched..."

Deep in his chest, his heartbeat was hammering away. Everything was becoming hazy as Adam's concentration slipped, his golden eyes blinking blearily.

"Why don't you just join the party?" Merlin asked as the purple colored mushfolk released another cloud of spores. "Give yourself to the music, laddy? Join the fun."

Adam clutched his head, groaning. Something was wrong. Something was really, *really* wrong. The whole scene tilted and blurred, the strobing making the effect all the worse. A strange urge to giggle rose up in him as Adam's mind flooded with ecstasy.

Am I being drugged?

He turned, trying to leave, but an unexpected sight stopped him and caused his mouth to fall open.

Junith was dancing. Not even in a manner that could be called normal—the nekogirl looked like an eel, wiggling in place with her hands clasped over her head. Her pupils were blown wide, a look of euphoria on her face which made Adam recoil with disgust.

Without realizing it, his foot began to tap involuntarily, his left eye twitching. From ear tip to toe, his body was beginning to become overwhelmed by a warm and floaty sensation.

Crapbaskets!

But when he tried to leave and step away from the dancing man, a firm hand on his shoulder held him in place.

"Where are you going, bud? Music not to your taste?" Merlin smirked as Liza grabbed his other arm.

"Come party with us, Adam. Take a load off and listen to the music," she said. Adam's eyes became saucers.

There was no denying it now—something was obviously wrong. But when Adam tried again to bring up his System, his status screen remained unchanged. And yet, he *knew* his mind was being altered.

"Uhh, I'm okay, I think I left something outside," he said. With some effort he managed to pull away—only to nearly run into Junith.

"We should stay a bit. Enjoy ourselves," she echoed. The nekogirl pressed up against Adam. His face twisted with disgust and outrage as she tried to embrace him.

"BEGONE!" Adam spat, the soft warmth of his euphoria momentarily overwhelmed by wrathful heat. He shoved Junith away, sending her toppling over. With nothing else in his way he sprinted, making it all the way to the exit, when a hand on the hem of his cloak sent him sprawling.

"Where are you going? Don't you want to be happy?!" Junith asked, tugging at his cloak.

"NO! LET ME GO!"

"Come be happy with us!" she screamed as Adam dug his claws into the frame of the door. Despite using every ounce of his strength, the tiny nekogirl seemed his equal. He spun, ripping his cloak with his claws and stumbling away from his drugged-out companion, but now it was Liza's turn to tackle him.

"Where are you going?!" she said, her eyes dilated and filled with mania.

"Get off! GET OFF!" Adam screamed. Between the two of them they dragged him back into the technicolor nightmare kicking and screaming as Merlin danced his way to the trio.

"Let me go! Let go, you imbeciles! You meatsuits without a brain! Let go!" he ordered. On the girls' chests, the ouroboros crests lit up, seeming to promise salvation. But even this backfired—the electrical shocks only caused them both to moan in pleasure as Liza screamed, "More! More! More!"

Dumbfounded by the response, Adam opened his mouth, trying to yell once more. Instead, he sucked in a full dose of purple spores as Merlin towered over him.

The boy hacked and coughed. "SKELETONS! C—ome... to..." He tried to command, but his cry only died out. His tense features relaxed, a gleeful expression slowly spreading across his face. The world swirled, and everywhere Adam looked he was surrounded by skeletons and cats. The creatures called out his name as euphoria took hold in his heart.

Catpurr 12

Spying on Gods

As the sunlight shined through the wind barrier, a catitude of individuals sat in the midst of a building's decrepit ruins, conversing. Every so often, one would say something new, loosing another round of giggles amongst them.

"How do you guys like... know that your memories are real?" Merlin asked, slouched against the stony structure's collapsing wall, beside Adam, Liza, and Junith. All four of them were still inhaling the mushfolk's spores.

"That's such a deep question, dude," Liza said. Beside her, Junith began to grasp at her own face and body as tears leaked from her eyes, wondering if she was truly real.

"I think, therefore I am," Adam said as a sobbing Junith violently shook him.

"Whoa... That's so deep, you should totally write that down," Liza said as Adam blinked. Something was gnawing at the back of his mind, a growing conviction that he needed to get up, needed to move. His eyes flicked down to see purple dust coating his body.

"Weeiiiiiiird," he said, giggling a bit to himself. Suddenly, Merlin reached over, clamping a glowing hand down on the boy's shoulder. Liza and Junith were instantly enraptured, both reaching up to bat at the shiny light. When an invisible barrier kept them from touching the wizard, they whined.

"Shinnnny," Adam said, his eyes widening as the man touched his shoulder. In the next moment, something seemed to happen, a shift, but it was difficult to say what until a notification appeared.

[Blessing of the King Maker Obtained! UR]
[Mana Circuit Efficiency increased! +20% All skills require less mana to use.]
[+10 STR]
[+10 Con]
[+10 EGO]
[+20 Luck!]
[+5 Faith]

Adam's mind cleared momentarily as he read the notifications, a burst of energy pulsing through his body.

"What the Nyx?" Adam yelled. He leaped to his feet and looked to his left at the man called Merlin. The wizard's expression twisted with shock, eyes widening and brows raising, but before anything could happen, both relaxed as another cloud of spores enveloped them both. Adam broke out in a coughing fit.

"What? What was I—" he muttered before his body began to feel funny once more, a smile plastered on his face.

* * *

Night bled into day which faded back into night, and the wizard and nekofolk idled the days away with laughter, while at night they danced among the purple mushfolk.

But each night in the hours just before daybreak, when the feeling of euphoria was at its lowest, Merlin would reach over and touch Adam with his glowing hands.

"Who, like... decided that the alphabet was in order?" Liza asked. The nekogirl was stretched out across Junith as the paladin sprawled across the stony floor, gazing dreamily at the moon.

"I don't know... but I'm like... seeing God right now," Junith said, staring into the open air.

"Which god?"

"All of them." She gazed at apparent nothingness, eyes wide with alarm as on the other side of what should have been a completely unseen tear in the fabric of reality, several beings gazed back.

* * *

"Hey, Bastet. Is this one of yours?" Islandr asked. The short and green-skinned War Goddess called out to the giant, cat-eared Goddess of Fertility and Life, presently somewhat occupied with a naked human flailing about within her giant hand.

"BEFORE YOU KILL ME! PUT ME BETWEEN YOUR BOOBS! YOUR BOOBS! GIVE A MAN HIS DYING WISH! PLACE ME BETWEEN YOUR BOOBS IN MY LIFE IS YOURS!" the man screamed excitedly. Bastet and Freya shared a look of disgust before wiping his memory and hurling him into a portal. Bastet discreetly wiped her hands.

"Alright, that should be the last of them for now, before we can send the rest," the cat goddess said, pinching her nose. "We really need to have a talk with Eli about disrupting the boundaries of the morties. This is beginning to get absurd."

"You helped him design the species. Why didn't you put limits on them?"

"I DID! It's not my fault they're fueled by the power of an Original! Their presence alone is causing warp disruption wherever they walk!" Bastet yelled, slamming her hand into the nearby kitchen table. "Besides, you're the one on Eli duty, why aren't you stopping him from disrupting everything?"

"The same reason you don't. You know he does whatever he wants and not even Voltrain can stop him," Freya retorted. "Besides, I thought you wanted a change of pace."

"I do! But not like this! This is just annoying! Humans are disgusting!"

"Ain't that the truth," a soft voice said in an annoyed tone. From the doorway appeared a comparatively tiny, blue-haired girl. Her aquamarine armor, which should have been worth a fortune, was visibly dented and battle-damaged.

"Unidine?! What in the nine lives happened to you?!" Bastet yelled.

"That idiot Voltrain threw a moon at me!" Unidine grumbled. Her host's brown skin was littered with cracks, from which seeped a light blue energy. "We agreed to no extraterrestrial attacks! But he was like *noooooooo*, the moon was originally part of the planet, so it counts! Bunch of horsecock! Who even throws moons at people?!"

The blue-haired woman looked over to the basket of nude humans. The swarming figures within shrunk back from her towering godly presence.

"What's with the spare parts?" Unidine asked, pointing at the humans.

"Basteeeet," Islandr called out again. The gathered gods turned away from the basket of screaming humans to find a hazy mist in the air.

"Oh. OH! Well that's certainly new," Freya said. She was the first to approach the two-way dimensional scrying screen. Within was a frightened nekogirl, gazing out at the gods with eyes like saucers.

Bastet joined the two staring, waving her hand at the nekogirl, who mimicked her with a look of fascination.

"BOO!" Bastet yelled, causing Junith to leap up into the air and run away screaming as the cat goddess chuckled.

"Isn't that one of Eli's Chosen?" Islandr asked, causing Unidine to scowl.

"One of his Chosen's followers. We really need to have a discussion with Eli about his pawns constantly breaking through to our realm," Freya sighed, stepping closer to inspect the hazy mist. "Wait, are those Voiliticus spores?"

"You know of this phenomenon?" Bastet asked as Islandr pretended to eat one of the squirming, terrified humans. She then stopped, frowning.

"Eww, he's all erect," Islandr said before dropping the man back in the bundle of naked humans.

"Yeah, they're native to the realm of the Tree of Genesis, along with most Mushfolk. This variant shouldn't be in this world, though," Freya said. Her sharp eyes narrowed as she made a series of gestures, grabbing the mist and manipulating it. The image on the screen changed, fixing on Junith again as she shook Adam while screaming incoherently. From somewhere offscreen a man came into view, placing a hand upon the boy's shoulder.

"MYRDDIN?!" Freya shrieked, caught off guard by the image of a wizard she knew too well.

"Wait, is that Myrddin? Let me see! Let me see!" Islandr yelled. The view of the screen was completely blocked by the other gods gathered, who all seemed to tower over her. The war goddess gave a little hop, trying to gain height. "Guys! GUUUYS!"

"And here I thought he died," Unidine mumbled, pushing Islandr back one-handed. "Bastard still owes me a sword."

"He shouldn't be in that realm; I thought he was taken by the warp," Bastet commented as Freya tried to zoom in.

"Let me see! Let me see! Guuuuuuuys! C'mon!" Islandr yelled to no avail. The trio ignored her, trying to figure out just what the man was doing.

"Apparently not," Freya said. "Voltrain might—"

"I SAID LET ME SEE!" Islandr finally exploded. The kitchen flooded with red-hot energy, burning away the spores hanging in the air as the tiny goblin practically exploded with power and nearly consumed the screaming humanoids, who were saved only by the barrier that sprung into existence around the basket, blocking the attack.

The trio of goddesses spun, glaring at the fuming Islandr.

* * *

"ADAM! I'M FREAKING OUT! I'M FREAKING OUT! THE GODS HAVE FORSAKEN US AND ARE ANGRY!" Junith screamed. Adam only winced with annoyance. From his other side the man reached up to touch his arm, shaking him from the spore-induced stupor.

"What in the Nyx do you want?!" Adam snapped, shoving Junith off him. The hand on his shoulder became tighter as Merlin suddenly seized him.

"Listen close! We don't have much time! I need you to summon a skeleton capable of dragging us out of here!"

"What? How do you know I can—"

Merlin practically snarled. "Don't play coy with me! I'm tired of dancing! Do it! Do it now before—"

Something tickled at the edges of Adam's brain, feathery and light. The same infection seemed to affect Merlin as well, and the mage fell silent, both exchanging identical, gleeful grins.

It wasn't until after another cycle of euphoria-induced dancing that Merlin managed to pull himself together. He stalked over to Adam, smacking him in the face until the neko puffed up with anger.

"SUMMON. A SKELETON. TO. GET. US. OUT!" Merlin barked.

With a nosebleed anchoring him to reality, Adam managed to stay lucid long enough to obey, passing the order on to the skeletons guarding the tunnel outside. But even that was not enough. Already the spores were dragging him under again, and he quickly found himself rescinding the order. Whatever it was could wait—surely they could stay and relax just a little longer.

So, the cycle continued. Day by day, Adam and Merlin managed to surface from their spore-induced delirium, but the moments of lucidity were growing increasingly shorter until it became clear that for once, skeletons may not be the answer. Upon that day, Adam tried a different approach. The skelecats were dismissed for the moment, as for the first time he tried a different spell, one picked up in his second trial.

And the Death Knight heeded the call.

Catpurr 13
The Redfield Knight

During his brief moments of lucidity, Adam browsed his System, eyes lingering on his new buff, bestowed upon him by the magician. It was a good one, quite good—but Adam didn't have time to dwell on it. Instead, he raised a single hand.

"COME, DEATH KNIGHT!" he proclaimed. Hanging from his neck like a particularly wet scarf was a crying Junith, whom he ignored, instead pushing all of his mana into the inactive skill.

The ground broke apart, answering his will. From the cracks leaked purple smoke and a hellish red light. One black-clawed gauntlet appeared at the edge of the otherworldly crack, then another. The grim scent of death wafted up from the pit, accompanied by a horrid screech, sending shivers down even Merlin's spine.

The nightmare in onyx armor freed itself from the pit, ebon shadows billowing behind it like a tattered cape. Gleaming eyes wreathed by flames pierced the haze, beneath two tall prongs reminiscent of a cat's ears rose from its helmet.

Regrettably, not even this killed the impeccable vibe of the wretched rave.

"Rescue!" Adam clenched his teeth. Even as he felt the familiar presence of a bond with a summon, the tickle of the spores was breaching his conscious mind again. "Res-cue! Me—hahahahahaha."

He began laughing. Once again, euphoria washed everything else away with thoughts of endless song and dance.

* * *

Sometime later, Adam opened his eyes. The nekoboy was lying in an open field of grass, underneath the canopy of a tree. Immediately he looked left, then right, keeping his body as motionless as possible as he took in his surroundings.

Finally, he was out of that decrepit building, choked with spores and shrooms. In fact, he was nowhere within the ruins at all. The tree was surrounded by a proper forest, and as far as the eye could see stretched trees, sometimes interspersed with stones or wildlife. On a nearby boulder sat a knight in black armor, staring calmly at him. Adam stared back.

It was a bona fide Death Knight—one of the strongest kinds of undead, boasting high defense, offense, and nigh-unlimited stamina. Some called summoning one the crowning achievement of any necromancer, proof of their mastery over death itself, but this one was a little different from other Death Knights, Adam noted as he looked closely.

Unlike the average Death Knight's typical black armor, this one had a few extra embellishments. Its helm was cast in the shape of a cat's head, tall ears stuck up from the top while sharp spikes fanned out from the sides, almost like whiskers. Adorning its left shoulder was a spiked pauldron, and the tips of its gauntleted fingers were sharpened into wicked talons, capable of gutting the average human. But what truly drew its master's attention was the bone-pale tail lazily draped behind it, composed of vertebrae gradually decreasing in size until they became whip-thin. The construct sat at attention, awaiting commands from the small boy who had summoned it.

"Great," Adam sighed. While he was happy that he was able to summon his death knight, he still had some concerns.

Death Knights were intelligent, while also being slavishly loyal. Each Death Knight's very being was twisted and warped to adhere to an oath of absolute loyalty, making them the perfect servants. But the whole thing gave Adam the heebie-jeebies. For that reason, he had always refrained from using any high tier undead that possessed its own soul. Unlike what the church spouted about necromancers, he still had morals, dammit.

Then the Death Knight spoke, dispelling his shame and replacing it with confusion.

"Sup, kid, about time you called me," the knight said in a distinct dialect that made Adam do a double take.

"No way."

"What? You didn't think you could get rid of me that easily, couldja?" the knight said, lifting its slanted visor to reveal the face of Officer Redfield. Pale of course, marked by telltale signs of undeath. His eyes had changed to a glowing red, emanating a menacing aura.

"Shit," Adam said. The death knight raised a brow.

"Well, not the response I was expecting, but I guess it'll do," Redfield said as he stood from the rock. He crossed the field until he stood before Adam, where he kneeled. "I, Leon C. Redfield, swear fealty to my liege. I am yours to command."

Abruptly, Adam remembered the shame from before, but it wasn't like he could reject the man either. He had received Redfield's soul as some sort of reward, after...

Adam clenched his jaw.

"Get up, you don't have to kneel before me," he said. The man who gave his life for him was now his servant. He wasn't sure he liked the feeling.

"It's part of the formality of it all." Redfield shrugged. "I am your sword and shield, a servant bound to you in undeath to slaughter at your grim command."

Adam blinked. "Bit dramatic."

Redfield laughed, his voice vibrating through the air with each octave.

"Come on, let me have this. The other knights drilled me to recite the oath, and it was really cool."

"Other... knights?" Adam repeated. It occurred to him to look for Junith and Liza, but a quick scan of the surrounding area revealed they were nowhere to be seen.

Redfield began to regale Adam about his trip to the realm of Hel. First, he had awoken in a damp room packed with skeletons, calling themselves the Bone Bros. There had been an entire orientation on knightly behavior from there, culminating in swearing an oath along with all the other souls chosen to be Death Knights.

Adam had to admit, hearing about how Death Knights were chosen really was interesti—

NO! Gotta stay focused, gotta figure out where Liza and Junith are. He slapped his cheeks lightly, resolving to ask more about the process later, instead, he asked where the others were.

"Oh? Them? I left them giggling inside the wind barrier."

"What? Why didn't you get them too?"

Redfield seemed to shrug. "Because you were kicking and screaming, biting and clawing at me, along with everyone else trapped inside. I had to knock you out and fist fight a wizard, who nearly killed me twice over."

Adam had an inkling the man called Merlin was strong, but strong enough to go toe to toe with a Death Knight? Strong enough to *fist fight* a Death Knight, when he was a caster class?

"Great... Maybe I should just leave them there," Adam said, debating his options. Redfield folded his arms with a judgmental air.

"Fine, we'll go save them..." Adam grumbled. "Lead the way."

"As you wish, my Lord," Redfield said. Adam paused as a tingling sensation crawled up his spine.

"What? What's wrong?" Red asked Adam, whose face was slack with shock.

"Oh, nothing... Just not used to people following my orders without me yelling at them," Adam said, his voice cracking with emotion as tears seemed to glisten at the corners of his eyes. A tiny, clawed hand rose to cover his mouth.

"Whoa, hey, don't cry! Jeez, kid," Red said, reaching over and patting Adam on the back. The boy pounced at him with a sudden hug.

Catpurr 14

Where Are You Hiding the Nekoboy?!

Adam followed behind Red as the Death Knight led the way back into the ruins until they stood just shy of the wind barrier, gazing at the sky above.

"Plan, sir?" Red asked, waiting on Adam's command.

"One sec," he replied, pulling up his gacha system. On the screen, **Kingmaker's Blessing** and the twenty points it added to his luck stat seemed to be calling his name.

"Seriously?"

"What?"

"You're gambling? At a time like this?"

Adam blinked. "Wait, you can see my System?"

"We're bonded together. Of course I can. Why are you gambling?"

"Relax. I just want to test something out, and I haven't done my dailies yet," Adam said, shooing the knight away.

[Ding!]
[**CONCATULATIONS! You've won 2 Cicero Coins!**]
[**Daily attempts left: 02!**]
Gacha Coins: 98

Of course.

Adam's eyelids fluttered in annoyance. Despite the substantial luck boost, his bad rolls seemed inescapable.

[Ding!]
[CONCATULATIONS! You've won 5 Cicero Coins!]
[Daily attempts left: 01!]
Gacha Coins: 103

Adam sighed.

"Last one for the day, then we can pull them out," he groaned before tapping on his screen for the final time.

[Ding!]
[CONCATULATIONS! You've won 1 Evolution Point! 0 Remaining within Tier 1 Machine!]

"Alright, we can—!" The words died a sudden and memorable death in his throat as it registered that for once, he had pulled something that *wasn't* more coins. For a moment, he was stuck staring in shock at the screen. Then he immediately paged to the interface for the Evolution Tree, scrolling through options to upgrade his body.

FINALLY!

[Cat Tail Module]
[Enhanced Muscular Ligature]
[Reflex Sensitivity Tuning V2]
[Ocular Sharpening]
[Lightweight Body Optimization]
[Bone Density Upgrade]
[Healing Factor Boost]
[Sound Perception Tuning]
[Smell Refinement]
[Sealed until 4/5 Improvements are selected!]

What-to-pick-what-to-pick. Adam narrowed his eyes, mulling over the list with the hyper-focused intensity of a child in a candy store told they could only pick one sweet.

"Ehem," Red coughed.

"Hm?"

"Your companions, sir?"

"What about them?" Briefly Adam's hand hovered over Cat Tail Module, before he forced it to move down.

"We're supposed to rescue them?"

"Oh, right. Yes... Of course." With extreme reluctance, Adam tore his eyes away from the interface to peer through the wind barrier. Inside, Liza spun on her head while Junith did her best imitation of an earthworm.

Adam pulled up his evolution interface again.

"Adam!" Redfield said. His tone had all the sharpness of a parent's lecture.

"UGH! FINE! I guess we'll rescue them," Adam grumbled, closing his System and ordering Redfield in. After all, considering the last time he used an evolution point he passed out, perhaps this wasn't the time for him to do so.

"Go. Rescue Junith," Adam said, giving the verbal command. While Red was capable of independent thought and action, the knights were programmed not to willingly place themselves in fatal situations unless given an explicit order, or in defense of their master.

Considering the unknown depths of Merlin's strength, this certainly counted as a fatal scenario.

Obeying Adam's will, the ex-cop-turned-Death Knight promptly entered through the tunnel. Once on the other side he swiftly snatched Liza by the ankles as she joined Junith on the ground, performing what Adam had since dubbed *the worm.*

Immediately the nekogirl spun, eyeing the undead hand latched onto her ankle. A terrified shriek ripped from her lungs, alerting Junith and Merlin as Red lifted the flailing girl up by her ankle.

"Avada kedavra! Avada kedavra!" Liza screamed. The weird incantation did nothing to the knight holding her.

With one of their spore-ridden companions captured, Merlin and Junith came to Liza's aid, but not before Red punched the terrified, flailing nekogirl in the face.

"Bleh!" Liza went limp. The girl was swiftly tossed into the hole as planned. Suddenly A brilliant white light enveloped Redfield, disintegrating the knight on the spot from the raw might of Merlin's magical attack.

**[Red-Eyed Death Knight of the Bronx Dispelled!
23:59:57 until summon can be used!]**

Oh... Oh crapbaskets.

As Adam blinked dark spots out of his vision, Merlin and Junith reached into the hole, hauling Liza back into the spore-ridden house to resume their dancing.

Great, Adam thought. Seeing how the infected were unwilling to leave the house, he had hoped they wouldn't pursue Liza once she was in the hole. It seemed his hopes were wrong. "Guess it's on to Plan B."

Adam hadn't wanted to use Plan B, but seeing Merlin evaporate his Redfield like a hot sun against ice, he didn't have a choice. He needed to stay safe.

Then again, I'm a faithless heathen and the skill scales with Faith...

Unfortunately, Plan B would have to wait, as it required both Redfield and a *lot* of firepower; firepower that only a Death Knight could bring.

In the meantime, it was time to mull over his potential evolution.

* * *

Standing outside of the wooden inn that sat along the road, Alencia smiled gently as the Inspector kneeled before her.

"Lady Vilenciel, I greet and offer my services to you," the Inspector said, his voice almost reverent as he addressed the legendary demi-hunter before him, accompanied by her black armored Knight.

"Rise, First Class Inspector Lenius Verduin, there is work to be done," Alencia said, her voice regal as she addressed not only the Inspector, but the various knights and hunters gathered around the inn, their faces cast red in the torchlight. She was the model image of a true noble—back stiff as a rod, head held high, and gaze unflinching. A shame that the lovely young lady they all saw was merely a mask for her true self. "I received your report about the fugitive Adam and his whereabouts."

"Y-Yes, your Grace," Verduin said, quickly producing various papers from a burlap satchel on his waist. "Once I heard you were on your way, I produced multiple copies. Here is everything we have gathered thus far on the wanted demi-human."

"Nekoboy."

"P-Pardon, your Grace?"

"When hunting prey, it is best to specify that which we are hunting, so as to not lose sight of our target," Alencia said as she took the papers from Verduin's hands and glanced over the reports. "It is easy to just lump all demi-humans together as part of the same tribe and group, but this is done in error, for by lumping them together we give way to preconceived notions of what they may or may not do and form patterns based on irrelevant information."

"I... see, your Grace. I shall take this lesson to the grave," Verduin said as Alencia's brow furrowed slightly from reading the reports.

Useless. Useless! USELESS! I know all of this already!

Alencia wanted to scream but was patient enough to hold her tongue, instead lowering the papers and smiling at the inspector.

"Thank you for your effort. Now, what is happening here?" Alencia gestured to the row of soldiers standing in formation with their warbows raised.

"The associate of the fugitive refuses to leave the premises or allow anyone within, and any attempt to breach the premises has led to... complications," Verduin reported. Momentarily, his eyes flickered to a group of soldiers being restrained by their comrades. Not long ago they had tried to breach the inn; now they were covered in welts and poison ivy, intermittently screaming "It itches!"

Inspector Verduin returned his attention to Alencia as he said, "Worry not, your Grace. We will remove the vile squatter soon enough."

"Mr. Woodcutter is a citizen of the Empire and a tree magus. We should do this properly," Nabara advised, her voice echoing out of her blacksteel helmet.

"Mr. Woodcutter! This is Alencia Vilenciel! Daughter of Duchess Vilenciel, the owner of these lands upon which you tread!" Alencia barked. "Heed the call of your nation and surrender yourself to be detained!"

A moment passed, then another. Not a soul moved as the Lady of the Lands declared her presence before the man in question.

"This!" a gruff, angry, and annoyed voice barked back from within the inn, "is my own private domicile! And I will not be harassed!"

At the man's unexpected words, many of the soldiers gathered drew their swords, ready to drag the stout out screaming. The lone raised hand of Alencia Vilenciel was the only thing that halted them.

"You are mistaken, Mr. Woodcutter!" Alencia yelled back. "This structure is labeled and registered as a business! A business that has been operating on Vilenciel lands without a single payment of the Queen's tax."

Silence permeated the woods. The old stout apparently had no response for her, other than a loud, cocking sound

Alencia inhaled. Deep within her throat, the desire to scream was building. But now she was in public, and there would be witnesses if she were to truly let loose. No, there would be ample time to vent her stress—later, when she had her beloved in hand. "Bring it to me. Nabara."

"As you wish, your Grace," the knight replied before summoning her one-handed silver morning star, etched with runes which shimmered a striking violet.

Nabara walked forwards. The soldiers easily parted to clear a path for the warrior in onyx, who walked implacably forwards until she stood before the inn's wooden door.

"Alive!" Alencia called out, clarifying. After all, she still needed the stout alive if she were going to interrogate him for information leading to Adam.

"As you command, your Grace," Nabara replied, reaching out and ripping the door off its hinges. Waiting for her on the other side was a massive black cylinder.

"Eh?" Nabara let out, shortly before a sound rang out. Citizens as far as a hundred miles away would be talking about that noise for weeks to come.

Catpurr 15

Bargaining with the Mage of Flowers

BOOM!

Adam jolted up off the stone floor of an abandoned building, the sound of a massive detonation waking him from his slumber.

"The Nyx was that?" he muttered, cautiously peeking out the cracked windowsill to inspect the horizon. Questions burned in his mind, but the sight of his skeletons milling about seemed to indicate that there was no danger.

Adam shrugged, going back to sleep.

* * *

Standing in front of the wind barrier, Adam summoned Redfield. The Death Knight breached the earth, clawing his way out of the dirt to answer Adam's call from the plane of death.

Redfield knelt. "I answer the call."

"Yeah, yeah... Plan B," Adam rushed, watching as the trio of infected beings sat along the wall of the destroyed building, giggling as they pointed at him. "Bunch of idiots."

Redfield nodded. "It will be done."

The Death Knight began radiating black flames as it activated its skill, **Deathly Flame.** Supposedly all Death Knights possessed this skill, something Redfield himself previously confirmed.

Plan B was simple. Redfield would just use his skill to set the sphere on fire. The spores would be cooked, and the building would be robbed of oxygen, knocking out everyone inside. With that done, Redfield would enter and drag the unconscious trio to safety.

Adam wasn't an herbologist, or a druid for that matter, but he was well aware that most spores couldn't survive in hot temperatures.

Redfield approached the wind sphere. A blue heat briefly enveloped him before it coalesced into his weapon of choice—a flaming pistol.

Is that a gun?!

Adam's jaw fell agape as Redfield squeezed the trigger of his burning revolver, unleashing a torrent of fire that quickly engulfed the wind sphere in glorious conflagration.

And now we wait.

Adam took a seat in the grass watching, counting down the seconds. By his estimation, the smoke inhalation and heat would make them pass out in less than five minutes.

Of course, there would probably be long-term effects. But that sounded like a *them* problem, and not an *Adam* problem.

As screams of fear and panic sounded out from within the sphere, Adam began thinking about the future. He was living on the run now, and he needed to plan the necessary steps to survive long enough to return home to his friend.

Looking through his evolution list, he began pondering, wondering what to take. Gradually he laid out the pros and cons on his notepad.

[Enhanced Muscular Ligature]

Pros: More strength to punch Junith easily. Can handle more weight.
Can punch Junith harder.

[Ocular Sharpening]

Pros: Better vision? Easier to spot things at a distance.
Cons: Seeing Junith more clearly? Waste of point?

[Lightweight Body Optimization]
Pros: Faster movement, lighter body.
Cons: Less mass. Susceptible to being blown away and manhandled by Junith.

[Bone Density Upgrade]
Pros: Internals strengthening.
Cons: More mass.

[Healing Factor Boost]
Pros: Healing, increased combat effectiveness.
Cons: None.

[Sound Perception Tuning]
Pros: Increased awareness.
Cons: Sound susceptibility. Hearing Liza's rambling more clearly.

[Smell Refinement]
Pros: Better sense of smell.
Cons: Better sense of smell. Use?

Adam touched his chin, thinking of the sealed function of the Evolution Tree and how it required four points to unlock the hidden portion.

*Hmm. Maybe **Healing Boost,** then everything else?* he thought to himself.

But first, I'd need a safe place to evolve. By now, Red was dragging an unconscious Junith and Merlin out of the tunnel. He unceremoniously deposited the two in the dirt before climbing back in.

Maybe I should make a lair? A dungeon for the time being. Adam furrowed his brow. *Hmmm, but then I'd have to staff it and make protections for when I'm away...*

Unlike other necromancers and magic users, he was aware of who had towers and dungeons, Adam adhered to his master's teachings.

Stay alive, stay mobile. Never stay in one place for more than a day. However, seeing as he needed Coco's temple teleporter for the trials, had multiple companions with... needs, and was always being chased by fanatics, the thought of having a hidey-hole was growing more and more appealing.

"Grrrraaaahhh."

He turned to see Redfieled had appeared again, holding a certain pink-haired nekogirl upside-down by the tail. He inspected her face briefly, before turning to Adam with a baffled look.

"This... isn't who I think it is... is it?" Redfield asked, dangling at arm's length.

"Ah... yes," Adam replied. This was promising to be an awkward conversation. Nevertheless, he did his best to explain the situation and what Liza was doing here with them. "Don't kill her, though. I kinda need her."

Redfield frowned. His revolver twirled in his hand, before pointing at the girl's face. Then with a sigh, he reluctantly put it away.

"As you command," Red said, clearly unhappy as he dropped Liza in a heap. He loomed above, glaring at the woman who had taken his life.

A moment passed, then another, before Adam opened his mouth.

"If you want to dispose of her, I'd understand and would respect your wishes. Despite being bound to me, I don't wish to control you," Adam said. He removed the map from his storage ring, trying to determine the best spot for his would-be lair. "But know that for the time being, she has her uses."

"Like?"

"Pack mule, meat shield, food procurer. And I need her to act as a front to fund my work and survival." With a *thwap,* Adam shut the map and approached the fallen nekogirl.

He crouched down, removing the tricker's persona tucked in her waistband.

"If you wish her to be alive. So be it," Red said. His red eyes flared with blue heat before settling down.

"Yeah... I just need her for now..." Adam said, patting Redfield on his armored shoulder. "I'm sorry."

* * *

It was some time before the first of the unconscious people awakened. Unsurprisingly, the first happened to be Junith who, surprisingly, completely ignored the Death Knight in their midst. Instead, the ex-paladin raved about seeing the gods or something—until Adam smacked her head to bring her back to reality.

Liza was the next to wake. With performative slowness she groaned, slowly stretching out her arms and fluttering her eyes open, whereupon she saw Redfield.

She blinked.

Her eyes slammed shut once again.

"Wait, seriously? Are you seriously going to ignore me?" Redfield asked, his pale face twisted with disbelief. "You know I saw your face, right?"

"You're either a hallucination or a demonic being here to take my soul," Liza replied without missing a beat, her eyes still closed. "Either way, if I ignore you, you'll just go away."

"That's... That's not how that works. That's not at all how any of this works."

"Nuh-uh. You don't know! One moment you were arresting me for shoplifting and the next, goblins started attacking us. Yudunknow—NYAH!" Liza exclaimed as two black hands wrapped around her head and picked her up. "Stawp! Stawp! Red! Yamete! My brain! You're squeezing my brain! My braaaain!"

Adam facepalmed.

"So, you have a Death Knight now?" Junith said, frowning as she sat beside Adam, watching the spectacle. "What happened to not summoning Death Knights and binding undead to your will? Of using souls?"

"I'm just as unhappy as you are," he replied as he watched the still-flaming ball of wind. "The situation required it, for the sake of our continued survival. Redfield consented, although how much of that is his own will and not the geas I do not know. However, I have an inkling he was assigned to me by my... patron."

"Patron? You think your god gave it to you?" Junith asked, her eyes shifting from Adam to Redfield, who was presently holding Liza upside down by her ankles, much to her discontent.

"My patron," Adam corrected.

"Patron, right." Junith rolled her eyes.

"Redfield was awarded to me during the last trial. I didn't know he was the man who helped us until I summoned him," he said. His eyes flicked away from the entrancing flames and back to the skill, still open in his System. The boy's brow furrowed. "I still don't know what the point of these trials are, but it's clear the gods are watching and tracking us. And possess an odd sense of irony."

Junith pursed her lips. As the half-naked Merlin arose, coughing and groaning, her expression soured.

"Ah. I'm free," Merlin groaned, his blue eyes darting towards Adam and Junith as they stood above him. "Salutations, I'm Merlin. I'm eternally indebted to you for rescuing me from the damnable trap."

The half-naked mage sat up, patting his body before standing up and snapping his fingers. A set of blue robes appeared, already draped across his body.

"Ah, much better. And I see you've set fire to those mushfolk, excellent. I tried to contain them myself to limit their spread once I was enraptured by my quarry's trap," Merlin said, his voice much more scholarly and restrained as he rubbed his hands across the smooth, silky robes adorned with images of pink flowers.

Adam raised a brow. "Trap?"

"Oh, yes. I was on the hunt for a woman who stole a certain keepsake from my possessions," Merlin said. He thrust out a palm, and glimmering lights displayed the image of a green-haired woman. Adorning her cheek was a distinctive beauty mark. "She goes by the name Vivian, or Viv, Vivi, Villain, Troglodyte, just to name a few of her aliases. Have you perchance seen her? If so, be forewarned that she is incredibly dangerous and a master manipulator of poisons and politics."

"Uh. No, can't say I have," Adam replied, squinting at the image. The green hair almost reminded him of Titania.

"How about this?" Merlin asked before the picture of a woman named Vivian shifted to an image of a sword Adam instantly recognized.

"If I say yes, do I get a reward?" he asked, causing the mage to lift his brow.

"Depends. I've already given you my blessing, don't you think that's a reward enough?" Merlin said, his eyes shifting to the Death Knight nearby that seemed poised to strike.

"That was conferred out of necessity, not out of gratitude," Adam replied. Merlin seemed overwhelmingly powerful, and gods-be-damned if he wasn't going to milk the mage out of as much as possible.

"So, you're saying I should rescind my blessing?"

"No, I'm saying this is a give and take situation. I could have left you in there and run off, yet I saved you," Adam replied, not backing down despite the threat. "And now I have information you want regarding the Holy Sword Excalibur."

At the mention of the weapon's name, Merlin's eyes widened, his smile vanishing. Runes of power lit up across his body and his jaw visibly clenched. The Mage of Flowers glared at the young boy.

"You are aware that I could disintegrate you with ease, are you not? That I could dismantle each and every one of your companions until you tell me what I want to know?"

"Go for it. You'd be doing me a favor. I hate everyone here," Adam shrugged, despite being subjected to power that made every hair on his body stand on end.

"I OBJECT! He doesn't speak for all of us!" Liza cried. The nekogirl peeked out from beside Junith, claws drawn. Opposite her, Redfield stood behind Merlin, the Death Knight's ghostly gun fixed upon the mage's head.

"You also won't get anything from me," Adam added.

The standoff lasted for several long moments as Merlin fixed the boy in his aquamarine eyes. At last, the mage's shoulders visibly sagged as he sighed.

"Fine... What is it you desire?"

Adam inwardly smiled. With a mage as powerful as Merlin, certainly there was a smorgasbord of powerful items at his fingertips, if only he were to ask. But at this moment, his thoughts were fixed on one thing, and one thing only.

"You said you were a transdimensional mage. Can you teleport me to a different dimension?"

Merlin blinked. "Ah... Did I say that?"

"You did."

"Unfortunately, I can't."

Adam's thoughts came to a screeching halt

"Why not?"

"Dimension hopping is a tricky thing that gets more complicated the more people are involved. Besides the untold horrors beyond your imagination lingering in the boundaries between realms, traveling through realms is extremely dangerous, not only to your body but your soul, and it is quite easy to get lost," Merlin explained, clapping his hands together before pulling them apart. Contained within was what appeared to be a map of the stars. "Nothing short of a divine grade artifact is required for multiple people to make the trip together—"

"What if it were just me?" Adam interjected, causing Junith to frown.

"Still no." Merlin shook his head. "I can barely do it for myself, and even then... Well, you've seen the end result."

Merlin nodded to the sphere of fire.

Great, just great, Adam thought. *And here I was hoping to cut this vacation short.*

"Anything else you might want?"

The boy sighed. "What do you got?"

Catpurr 16
Moving into My New Dungeon

Several days later.

"Perhaps I should have been more clear," Adam said, standing beside Merlin. Before them stood a bright pink building. Salmon-hued shingles lined its roof, matching the peach-colored windowsills. Carved into the white door situated at the building's front was the image of a paw print, below the single word, *Welcome!* "When I asked for a dungeon, this wasn't what I meant."

"Well... It certainly *is* unique," Junith added. The nekogirl brushed past the duo and stopped at a nearby window, standing on tiptoe to peer within.

Merlin scratched his head, plucking from his hair a leaf that had fallen from one of the overgrown trees above.

"Are you sure? I went off the schematic and made the entrance exactly as it was described to me," Merlin said, adjusting the wireframe glasses sitting on the bridge of his nose.

Without shifting his expression Adam looked up and stared blankly at the mage. "What schematic?"

"The one your furry, pink-haired friend gave me?" The mage produced a thin roll of parchment from his floral-patterned robes. "I followed the design to the last detail."

"That—"

"IT'S PERFECT!" came a loud, joyful shriek. Liza darted out from the treeline, making a beeline straight for the bright pink building.

Adam stuck his foot out, tripping the excited teen. Then, at his master's behest, Redfield arose from the earth a moment later.

"Restrain her while I undo this... mess," he said to the Death Knight, pinching the bridge of his nose.

"Wha? NO! My Barbie home!"

"Now, please."

The Death Knight was only too happy to comply. Adam pointedly ignored Liza's tantrum, her desperate *Nooooo!* gradually becoming quieter as Redfield dragged her, kicking and screaming, back into the woods. Instead, the nekoboy turned back to Merlin and asked. "Can you fix it?"

"Once you tell me where Excalibur is, of course." Merlin smiled.

"But if I tell you, you won't finish the work," Adam countered coyly, flashing his own smile in return.

"What do you take me for? A charlatan?"

"Yes," Adam replied, sensing a kindred spirit in the mage. His eyes remained forward, staring at Junith as she entered the structure.

"'Tis fair," the mage replied. "But a little give does go a long way. Anyway, this is just the outer frame, the intestines of the dungeon remain yours to mold once you dominate the core. *If* you can dominate it."

Right. There's still that... Adam said to himself, recalling their recent negotiations. Once he touched the core, he'd have to pass a series of tests in order to take control of the underground structure. Tests designed by the mage before him.

Deep in thought, the boy scratched at his chin in before finally reaching a decision. A torn paper quickly appeared from the depths of his storage, held before the mage. "Here."

Merlin smiled.

"My best estimate."

Merlin frowned.

"Your—"

"Best estimate. Yes. According to rumors—"

"Rumors..." Merlin muttered, a sense of disbelief washing over him before he let out a small laugh. "Rumors. And *I'm* the charlatan."

"Yes," Adam affirmed. Merlin's left eye twitched as he grinned madly. "It is in this realm, though. I tried wielding it but it rejected me."

Merlin unfurled the paper, memorizing the information within.

"You realize that if this is false, I'll drop a city on top of you, right?"

"I believe you are capable of carrying out such a feat, yes," Adam replied.

"As long as we're on the same page." With a smile and a shrug, the Mage of Flowers abruptly disintegrated into a light rain of fluttering flower petals.

Adam's eyes went wide.

"What? Hey! Wait! WAIT!" he yelled, all his suspicions confirmed. "How is this house a dungeon entrance?!"

"*You're smart! You'll make do!*" echoed Merlin's final message before disappearing with the wind.

Adam could only groan. *Gah! How am I supposed to hide if the entrance to my dungeon is a giant, bright-pink house?!*

But the boy's fuming was cut short as a droplet of rain fell upon his head.

Oh, great. Just great. His face twisted.

"Red! Get inside!" he yelled, following Junith into the building as a torrential downpour of rain rolled out across the trees.

* * *

"Anything useful?" Adam asked. Just beyond the doors was a foyer lined with bright pink glow stones, ending at a pink flight of stairs leading into a pitch-black abyss which did *not* match the rest of the decor.

"Liza has horrible taste," Junith said, brushing her hand against the pink wall.

"Rude!" Liza screamed. The nekogirl was drenched, dripping rainwater everywhere as Redfield held her like a shopping bag. "And why am I losing forty percent of my stats?!"

"You don't listen to anything I say, do you?" Adam said, only sparing the girl a glance before descending the stairs. "No one disturb me. There is work to be done, and I require complete concentration."

"You got it, Boss!" Liza called out. Faintly, there was the sound of Junith calling her a kiss-up.

Adam pulled up his quest list, eyeing the timer. As each small foot hit a new step on the staircase, a bright and cheering chime rang out.

[Time Until Next Trial: 147:22:02]

Seven days. Adam smacked his lips. Seven days until his next trial. Only one week and he was missing half his gear, broke, and stuck with two idiots who seemed to be going out of their way to make his life difficult... But at least he had a dungeon now, and his own personal Death Knight.

"Now, where the Nyx did Merlin place the heart?" he muttered as he entered the first floor of his dungeon.

His question was soon to be answered. Tucked into the far end of the room was a large, pink pedestal, a mushy, white sphere hovering just inches above it.

The core.

Time to claim my dungeon. An odd tingle of excitement danced across his spine as he approached. Despite the neon-pink sign above his head, it was still situated in the middle of nowhere, within the dark depths of the Selkuin Forests, guarded by vicious wild monsters. What were the odds someone would stumble across it in the first place?

He approached the sphere, circling the pedestal and eyeing the lumpy shape. Organic veins dominated its surface, pulsing in time like a heartbeat.

S grade, maybe SS? Even from here the power it radiated was palpable; raw mana wrought into solid form.

Adam smiled, realizing he'd gotten more than he was expecting.

He reached out, wrapping his palm around the orb and squeezing the warm heart.

[Unclaimed dungeon detected!]

The notification popped up before him, blotting a good chunk of his vision.

[Would you like to claim?]
[Y / N]

His free hand pressed down upon the Y.

[Prerequisites unmet to claim!]
[Condition to claim: Pass a test from the Prophet of Flowers!]

[Would you like to participate in the test?]
[Y / N]

As he tapped the Y one more time, a wave of dizziness suddenly passed over the boy as darkness encroached on the edges of his vision, quickly claiming him.

* * *

Adam's eyes shot open. His small form seemed to float, surrounded by infinite blackness. Not artificial darkness from a spell, but natural black born from the perfect absence of any light.

He wiggled his body. The breaths filling his lungs were shallow—*too* shallow—as he took stock of his surroundings. Little air, no ability to move comfortably... He was being confined. But by what, and how? Had it been a trap of some kind, a cage? But upon feeling up the edges of his dark prison, Adam realized that this form of confinement was familiar to him. Currently he was lying in a sarcophagus—one he'd laid in before.

Wait.

Immediately, Adam began clawing, punching at the weakened wood that hung centimeters away from his body. A crack sounded out and particles of dirt trickled through the hole he had created. He wasted no time ripping at it, making it bigger, even as his fingers bruised and bled from clawing at the wood.

More dirt fell into his coffin. Quickly he swept it downwards, off his chest and towards his feet. As he pawed at the earthen ceiling, he noticed his battered hands lacked claws. Air was strictly limited down here—he needed to keep his breaths light, and not overexert himself.

The dirt gave way, allowing him to move upwards. The freshly churned earth parted easily for him as he climbed. Adam's underdeveloped muscles burned, and for a moment he worried he'd never reach the surface—but then the earth broke around him, and his hand was enveloped by the cool caress of air.

Suddenly something soft touched his grasping fingers. Whiskers brushed against his skin as he felt dirt rapidly shifting from around his hands.

"Meow!" Schrödinger cried out, the cat frantically digging to free his master from the earth.

"Very good," a soft voice purred as Adam pulled himself out of the dirt. Schrödinger immediately hopped on Adam's shoulder, wrapping itself around its master as a deep purr rumbled in his ears. "I might have to start burying you deeper."

"Master..." Adam whispered.

He stopped examining his teenaged body, turning his blue eyes instead to those of Razalia Des'heart. The archnecromancer stared back at him with pursed black lips and her one good eye, the one not covered by her mechanical golden eyepatch. Slowly he examined every inch of her appearance, matching it up against those warm and distant memories—the wide-brimmed witch hat perched upon her raven-colored hair, the scanty purple silk draped across her figure, the black stockings that only reached her lower thighs; set around her neck was a golden choker. She perfectly matched the Razalia Des'heart of his memories, down to the last hair.

"Huh? What's this about?" Razalia asked, caught off guard as Adam suddenly hugged her. "If you've got so much energy, maybe I should bury you again."

He ignored her words, only hugging the woman tighter as he sank into the warmth of her embrace. Tears pricked at the corners of her eyes. She was warm, she was *here*. Whether this was a dream or simply a very vivid memory, the touch of her skin felt real—*too* real.

Razalia's hand hesitantly rose, resting on Adam's red hair as she allowed her disciple to hug her. No cat ears, Adam noted.

"Master..."

Razalia peeled Adam off of her, kneeling down to lock eyes with the kid who stared at her with a look of stupor.

"What's wrong, Adam? Are you okay? Did something happen down there?" she questioned. Her disciple wasn't usually prone to such obvious affection.

"You're... You're alive."

"Should I be something else?" the necromancer asked.

"I..."

"Please don't tell me you've chosen a class without telling me and developed prophetic powers that have allowed you to witness my demise," Razalia complained. Adam fumbled to pull up his System, but no screens appeared.

"No. No, I haven't," he replied, his brow furrowing as he recomposed himself.

This... This is just a test... This isn't real, He told himself. But the softness of Schrödinger on his shoulder, the warmth of Razalia's hand upon his face... *None of this... is real.*

"And yet you're frowning," Razalia said, standing up. "You've never had a problem with the coffin test, and you've definitely never hugged me before. Did something happen?"

"No," Adam replied, staring up at his former teacher, the woman who had helped shape him, mold him, and instill in him the values of what it meant to be a necromancer and their role in their world burdened by constant wars and suffering.

She seemed so real... so... lifelike. Adam looked at his hands. No longer were his fingertips no longer pointed and angular from his catsification. Again he rubbed his own head, confirming it was free of cat ears. Surrounding them were the familiar ruins filled with skeletons walking around. It was almost as if he'd been transported to the past, sent back just before he had gotten his system and earned his class.

"Well, if you don't want to talk about it, we don't—" The woman turned away, only for Adam's tiny hand to catch at the hem of her robe. "Hm?"

"Can we... Can I just..." he began, his lips trembling just a bit. Despite this being a dream or a figment of some spell, he found himself more than ever wanting to hug the woman who was no longer in his life. "Can I just hug you some more?"

Razalia blinked, her brow going up at Adam's unexpected request. This was the first time he'd ever asked for a hug.

She smiled.

"Sure," Razalia said, removing the wide brim hat on her head and placing it on a nearby skeleton knight. She crouched down and opened her arms wide for the sad, red-haired child.

* * *

Standing above the red-haired nekoboy passed out on the floor beside the dungeon heart, Merlin stroked his chin, observing the events transpiring on one of the many screens in front of him. His forehead creased with wrinkles as he watched.

"Interesting," Merlin said. Displayed on the floating screens were visions of Adam, at various stages throughout his life. Each and every one of the nekoboy's precious memories were laid before the Prophet of Flowers—the man once known as the Kingmaker.

"Very interesting," Merlin said, his aquamarine eyes reflecting the images of Adam's life. "I hope you enjoy your dream."

Catpurr 17
The Gift from the Mage of Flowers

Adam woke, his face wet, eyes red and puffy as he sat up off the dirt floor of the dungeon with a storm of notifications assaulting him.

[Time Until Next Trial: 142:20:22]

From his timer, Adam could calculate about five hours had passed. He took a moment, settling his heart. Once again, his body had returned to its catsified form, claws protruding from his fingertips and triangular ears from the top of his head. Still, those idyllic moments lingered in his memory. That dream... it was bittersweet. But no matter how much he would have loved for that dream to last just a little longer, there was work to be done.

[Dungeon interface unlocked!]
[Please claim dungeon by naming.]

"Hmm." With the back of his wrist, Adam quickly wiped away the remnants of his tears. He took a breath, calming his beating heart before he checked his System.

BETA SYSTEM v1.05
TITLE: The Primordial Eli's Chosen
+20% Mana Recovery, +5 Arcana, Undead Favorability

NAME: Adam F. Glow

SPECIES: Nekoboy

LEVEL: 43

EXP BAR: 878/18000

MAIN CLASS: Nekomancer

HP: 360/360

MANA: 55/785

EVOLUTION POINT: 1

Gacha Coins: 103

Free Points: 0

Bonded Followers: 02

> **Junith Oatheart:** T2 Lvl 19
>
> **Eh'liza Oktober:** T1 Lvl 37

[Dungeon Interface:] >

STATS:

STR: 25

CON: 46

DEX: 25

ARC: 150+12 (EQ)

SEN: 23

EGO: 43

RESISTANCES: Fire (5%) Inertia 10%

BUFFS: Loved by Undead (Unique), Blessing of Eli (Unique), Eyes of a Predator V1, Corrupted Blessing of Nyx (Unique), Adherent of Death V1, Explosive Renaissance V1, Pain Tolerance V1, Blessing of the King Maker (UR)

DEBUFFS: Ha! You Sacrificed Your Stats for a Cat?! V1 (Curse) Catsification V1 (Curse) Wet (Catsification)

SKILLS: Animate Bones V2, Irritating Touch V1, Cat Claws V1, Identify V1, Summon Greater Skeleton V3 (+++), Mana Bolt V1 (++), Artificial Linguistics {Rigellian}, Genocidal Aura, Summon Morian Crab, Mana Claws V1 (+), Summon Red-Eyed Death Knight of the Bronx V1 (++), Mana Dash V1 (+)

Skill Points: 0

Adam sighed, opening the Dungeon menu.

[UR Dungeon Seed (Unnamed)]
[Name Dungeon to claim.]
[Level 01]
[Status: Coalescing mana...]

U-U-UR?! Adam nearly died from shock. This was truly far beyond all his wildest dreams.

He pondered for a moment, staring at the chosen dungeon name before confirming.

[Dungeon named!]

There was an abrupt shift. All around him the walls seemed to tremble, the dirt pressing in before exploding as a connection blazed to life. The room ballooned in size, white bones erupting over the walls.

Far above him came the sounds of Liza's screams as Junith commanded the teen to *Stop! Stop! Stop screaming!*

But before he could wonder what the girls were doing, a sudden blaze of silver stole Adam's attention. The dungeon core pulsed and shined like a star gone nuclear, an echoing heartbeat filling the room, growing louder every second.

[Welcome to Dungeon Dungeon.]
[UR Dungeon: Dungeon]
[Level: 01]
[Status: Coalescing mana]
[Mana Reserves: 789/5000]
[Assistant available!]

Huh... Assistant? This was the first he'd seen or heard of a dungeon having assistants... Maybe this was the dungeon boss.

Blinking before him now was a square icon, below the name Adam had selected for his new dungeon.

As if drawn to the beating core, Adam approached it, until his hand came to rest upon the icon.

[Please envision your assistant.]

Schrödinger's image was the first to appear in Adam's mind as he shut his eyes, but the memory of Razalia quickly appeared beside it. He clenched his jaw, dispelling the image of his former master as he struggled to focus on Schrödinger and Schrödinger alone.

Tendrils of mana shot out of the core, touching Adam, linking his mana with its own and creating a bubble of silver light hovering in the air.

[Designing...]

The cold light grew warmer, caressing the boy's skin as the ground beneath his feet still trembled.

[Dungeon assistant created.]

Adam opened his eyes, blinking rapidly before his pupils expanded. He backed away, staring at the humanoid form taking shape in front of him within the still-growing silver orb.

The light died, revealing a figure that towered over Adam—a woman, donning a wide-brimmed hat and clad in silken robes, a large white tail lazily swished back and forth behind her.

Adam's jaw fell. In front of him was Razalia, or a warped and mutated copy of his master.

The same witch hat framed her face, but instead of the familiar purple robes now they were white, secured to her body by straps of black leather. Her silver eyes blinked as she gazed down at him, the same color as the tattoos marring her body, tufts of white fur barely visible beneath her robes.

"Welcome to your dungeon, how may I be of service, Master Adam?" The woman placed her hand over her heart and bowed, her white tail swishing.

"No no! Nonono! Stop! Don't bow to me!" Adam said quickly, mortified that the image of his former master was bowing to him.

The assistant stood upright, awaiting Adam's command.

"Ah crapbaskets... CRAPBASKETS!" He pinched his nose. "How-to-fix-how-to-fix-how-to-fix?"

"Is there something wrong, Master?"

"Don't!" A trembling finger pointed at the cat-tailed woman as Adam forced his tone back under his control. "Don't call me master."

"As you command," the image of Razalia said.

"WHOA! AWOOGA! WHO'S THE BABE?!"

Why? Adam closed his eyes, drawing a breath of exasperation as Liza came running down the stairs, only to be caught by a black armored claw.

"HULK! Chok—ing! Choking! I'm tapping! I'm tapping out!" Liza spazzed out, twitching and frothing in Redfield's iron grasp.

"Sorry, she distracted me," Redfield said, before dragging the passed-out teenager back upstairs.

Adam turned his attention back to the nekowoman Razalia. The dungeon assistant calmly returned his gaze.

"Do you have a task for me?"

"What... are you?" he asked, struggling to keep a handle on his complicated emotions. "What is your role as my dungeon assistant?"

The being tensed up.

"I am the representation of the Dungeon Interface System. I regulate mana input and output and am the main node that controls all dungeon functions."

"Functions, such as?"

"Room expansions, defense distribution, construction of facilities, and manipulation of the entire dungeon. I also possess an auto function to handle presets and directives chosen by you, the owner of the dungeon *Dungeon*."

Adam scratched his chin as an unexpected wave of guilt for tricking Merlin rose within him.

I'll have to thank him next time I see him, he considered, resolving to aid the mage in some way. Nothing major of course, maybe a potion or something when he got facilities up and running. After all, Adam needed everything he could get to ensure his survival.

"Do you have a name?" he asked. "Can you change your appearance?"

"I am Dungeon, as named by you. As for my appearance, this is what was molded and cannot be undone freely until the core is upgraded," the Razalia in White said, much to Adam's dismay. "Would you like to set a directive from the preset list?"

"Directive? What are my options?" He fidgeted with plain discomfort.

[Invasion Directive]
[Defense in Depth]
[Production Mode]
[Hatchery]
[Expansion Priority]
[Mana Preservation Mode]

A list of options appeared, each a different function of the dungeon.

"Can you explain to me the Defense in Depth function?" Adam asked. Dungeon turned her head to the left, holding her palm out.

A translucent image of an underground blueprint appeared cupped within.

"The Defense in Depth function prioritizes defense of the dungeon at all costs. All resources will be allocated in creating a citadel to beat back intruders," Dungeon explained.

"Resources?" Adam's pupils dilated as he glanced towards the brightly shining core.

"The dungeon gathers mana to power scripts and runes to achieve certain desires," Dungeon said. She waved a hand through the blueprint, banishing it as the image of a skeleton appeared in its stead. "For instance, using scripts we can summon skeletons and other monsters recorded in the dungeon database, or create our own to defend the dungeon from intruders."

"Interesting," Adam muttered.

"You can also specify your needs, of which I shall do my best to accommodate them," Dungeon said, placing her white-gloved hands over her chest.

There was a lot to do here, much to uncover. He furrowed his brow *Hmmm, I wonder if I could produce gunpowder and potions.* The nekoboy's eyes became pleased crescents. With the presence of Red, a person knowledgeable about firearms, and his notes from the previous trial, it should be a simple task to create the necessary materials. *Ah, but then I'd need a smith or such for rifling... Hmmm.*

"Defense in Depth seems the way to go. Prioritize burying the core as far away as possible and setting up defenses to protect the dungeon," Adam ordered. Immediately the silver core pulsed in acknowledgement. "I would also like some accommodations set up, for me and my companions."

"Those in the waiting room?" Dungeon asked. The little details about her mannerisms, like the blinking of her eyes and the visible breaths she seemed to take, made her appear awfully lifelike.

"Yes." The ground shifted again beneath Adam's feet as the pedestal bearing the core sank into the earth.

"Please standby," Dungeon said. "Is there a theme you would like?"

"Practical, homey, I guess?" Adam said uncertainly. He'd never really had a home before or given the idea of one much thought.

"It will be done," Dungeon said as three entrances appeared in the wall nearby, each inscribed with a name.

Junith, Liza, Redfield. Adam raised a brow, wondering where his accommodation was.

He turned his head. The stairway leading deeper into the depths had grown wider, a white boney door covering the entrance. Flanking either side was a humanoid skeleton of average height.

Huh. That was fast. Upon opening the dungeon interface, Adam learned something interesting—the dungeon wasn't bound by his curse. *Hrng, but that means I need to arm the minions…*

[**Welcome to Dungeon Dungeon.**]
[**UR Dungeon: Dungeon**]
[**Level: 01**]
[**Status: Constructing…**]
[**Mana Reserves: 189/5000**]

It doesn't seem very efficient with the mana. Maybe when it levels up its efficiency will increase?

Adam turned to the copy of his former master, staring at him with a smile.

"How do I level up the dungeon?" he asked. "Are there ways for me to outfit the minions with weapons?"

"Once the dungeon has filled the mana reserves, it will be capable of upgrading, improving all functions and my ability to serve you. As for weaponry, that will be left to your purview, unless constructs come with their own."

"I see," he replied, groaning inwardly. "Is it possible to change your voice?"

Dungeon's silver eyes looked left then right before settling on Adam and blinking.

"*Is this perhaps to your liking?*" the dungeon assistant asked in a warped and staticky shriek, twisting its face to accommodate Adam's request.

"N-No. Not really," Adam said, deflating a bit.

"Processing," Dungeon said. "Standby... At this level I am incapable of doing so. My sincerest apologies."

"No. Don't apologize," Adam sighed, pinching his nose as the world seemed to tremble. "Let's see about designing more of this dungeon."

Catpurr 18
Planning for the Trial
[036:21:09]

Adam sighed as another skeleton bumped into him. Thirty-six hours before his next trial and he still needed potions, gear, and weapons. He was less prepared than he had been before his last two trials, with no money to his name but a single gold coin.

On the upside, he now had a dungeon teaming with minions! The downside, however, is that he had a dungeon teaming with minions... so packed in fact, that he could barely make it from one side of the labyrinth to the other. Made all the trickier by how every single undead was possessed of the need to touch his cat ears.

Nyx below I hate this.

"I LOVE THIS!" Liza screamed, wagging her tail back and forth as she rode the undead monstrosity she had reassembled from *his* lackeys. It resembled some sort of carriage of moving bones. They're like legos!"

Adam buried his face into his hands, Liza's obnoxious laughing grating his nerves.

"Should I fix this?" Redfield offered. The Death Knight had yet to pass up on any opportunity to manhandle the nekogirl, who still struggled to remain blissfully ignorant of his existence.

"Please," Adam said. The swish of the nearby air indicated that his orders were being carried out.

"Oh, sup, dead guy! What? Hey! Don't touch that! THIS IS A VERY DELICATE MACHINE! STAWP! STAWP! YAMETE! I worked hard on assembling this!" Liza yelled, followed by cat noises and the clang of claws on metal as she fought with the undead knight.

Adam finally opened his eyes, gazing around the underground dirt hovel before pulling up the dungeon interface. Leveling his new domicile up had only expanded it further.

[UR Dungeon: Dungeon]
[Level: 02]
[Status: Constructing...]
[Floors: Four]
[Minions: 201]

[Resources:
Wood x1
Stone x421
Bones x131
Iron Ore x21
Mana Reserves: 2,389/6,000]

The dungeon had done a great job expanding. In fact, it had done *too* great of a job expanding, forcing Adam to rearrange the directives and ask Dungeon to slow down, otherwise they would attract unwanted attention.

Unfortunately, the dungeon couldn't, so to alleviate the rapid coalescing of mana, Dungeon turned to creating minions and floors.

Which turned out to be a mistake.

Now Adam had an army of the undead, nearly two hundred skeletons all jammed into the rooms the labyrinth created. It wouldn't have been a problem if the cost of each room didn't increase exponentially, but it did and it was a hassle. Now the only thing he could do to de-crowd the halls of animated bones was to wait for more rooms to be crafted.

This is getting out of hand, Adam sighed, shoving past multiple low tier minions to enter a room lit by glowing pink stones. The sounds of grunts and swishes filled the air.

"Junith," he called out, halting the sweating nekogirl's duel with a skeleton, each wielding a femur in lieu of a proper sword.

"Enjoying your lair, my evil overlord?" Junith asked sarcastically, spinning and smacking the head off a skeleton, where it was sent flying into a wall.

"Funny," Adam replied, his eyes shifting to the pile of skeletons missing their legs, crawling around on the ground. "How's the troops?"

"I could take a thousand of them, easily. If these are supposed to be our defenders, then we're sorely lacking."

Adam sighed. He knew it as well. Given time the minions would grow stronger, however time was currently in short supply.

Junith kicked the dirt before planting her femur weapon into the ground and leaning on it. "What do you want?"

"We need to make a trip." He stood beside Junith and unfurled his map, showing the nearby village of Selkuin and the area of Vilenciel.

"Is it that time?" Junith asked, twirling the femur in her palm.

"Yes." He laid the map out onto the dirt and took out his pen. "Red has scouted the route to the village. He'll lead the way, and we'll pick up as much material as possible once in town and see if our way into Vilenciel is still available."

"Why not head directly to the city?" She asked, folding her arms. "Save us time and effort."

"You haven't seen the defenses. Vilenciel is heavily fortified. Leaving isn't too much of a problem, but getting *in* is. Liza has her guild pass and the trickster's persona, but us," he rubbed his cat ears, "well..."

"Right." Junith sighed. "So, how reliable is this resource?"

"For the coin, pretty reliable."

"Aren't we poor?" Junith raised a brow. "How are we going to compensate him?"

The nekoboy stood up, beckoning several of his skeletons to surround him as Redfield answered his master's call.

"You know what to do," he said, nodding to his soul bonded summon as he entered the room.

"As you command," Redfield said, his glowing red orbs shifting before suddenly accosting Junith.

"Huh? What's going on? What is this?" the girl cried. Suddenly Adam stood at the other end of the room, surrounded by his minions.

"Ehem. To answer your question, we are indeed poor, but fortunately I've prepared a countermeasure to our lack of coin," he finally replied, rubbing the storage ring on his finger.

"Oh? And what's that?"

A mischievous grin appeared on his face.

"We still have your armor to bargain with," he said as Junith's eyes made a valiant attempt at escaping her skull.

"YOU ARE NOT SELLING MY ARMOR!" she screamed, kicking and hollering, flailing all around as Red held her.

Adam took a breath, inhaling. "Right. Well. Would you like to play a game?"

"I'LL CLAW OUT YOUR EYES!"

"I've started calling it nap time," he said.

"I'LL KILL YOU!"

"Red, a demonstration."

"VOLTRAIN ABO—Ehk! Ark! RIP! Tear! I'll—"

At Adam's command the Death Knight began choking Junith, wrapping its armored gauntlet around her carotid, causing her to pass out within seconds.

Adam closed his eyes.

"Ah... Can you hear that?" he asked.

"Hear what, sir?" Red asked, draping the nekogirl over his shoulder.

"Peace and quiet," Adam said, rubbing his forehead. "It's so beautiful. I think we should use nap time more regularly."

* * *

Gathering what little supplies the group had, Adam and his gang were soon on the move, heading through the forest with the sun high. Their destination was the black market, situated within a nearby village. If there was one easy way to get them all into Vilenciel, it was the black market. Not that he trusted them not to rat him out, per se, but their competence and professionalism were top notch, two things he sorely needed right now.

"Why do I have to carry Judgy?" Liza complained, even as she hiked Junith up on her back.

"Would you prefer being knocked out and dragged by Red?"

"Maaaybe," Liza whined. "My feet are killing me! I swear all we do is walk, walk, walk!"

"Well, if you find out how to build a car, let me know," Adam replied sardonically before moving past some shrubbery. Beyond, the outskirts of the village came into view.

Huh... We're a lot closer to the village than I would like. He internally groaned, hoping that no one would stumble across the pink house in the woods. *But it looks like they've repaired everything since my last visit.*

"How are we gonna find this guy, anyway?" Liza asked. "You haven't even told me what he looks like or anything."

"He's not very hard to miss," Adam replied.

"Right, that's super helpfu—"

Suddenly, in the distance there was an explosion, followed by a large torrent of fire from a rocky hillside.

Well. That was easy, Adam said to himself, taking off in the direction of the fireworks.

Catpurr 19
Accredited Accounts

Adam sighed.

"Wait here. If anything happens—"

"I'll do what needs to be done to protect you," Red said. The red orbs that served as his eyes flared with energy as they settled on Liza.

"Huh? What'd I do?" As the knight fixed her with a death glare from behind his visor, the nekogirl only raised a brow in confusion.

"Riiight. I don't doubt that. Just be ready in case anything happens... Can you attack at range?" Adam asked.

"I can, sir."

"Good. Then stay at a distance and don't show yourself unless absolutely necessary," he ordered, picking up Junith and tossing the unconscious woman onto his shoulders.

"As you command."

Adam smiled before he took off, creeping along the woods on the outskirts of the town he so desperately wanted to enter for supplies, yet he couldn't. Not without exposing himself and potentially putting others in danger.

After a few minutes of walking, his smile turned into a frown.

This sucks, he said to himself, hiking Junith up further on his shoulders as Liza yapped and went on a tangent about something called BTS and Korean.

"And then they just up and left to join the military!" Liza yelled, throwing her hands up in exasperation as the duo passed by a pair of smoldering trees. "It's not fair! J-Hope came back and then we all thought the band was getting back together, but then noooo, and then to make matters worse that hussie Jennie—"

"Liza."

"Hm?"

"Shut up."

The pair walked in silence after that, their only accompaniment the nearing sounds of explosions and fire.

"Are you sure this guy can be trusted?" Liza asked. The nekopair now stood on the outskirts of a smoldering field. Dancing in the center was a man, donning a cap adorned with two spiraling goat horns and bearing a totem in one hand, the words *Taste the Sun* running up its side. Red hot flames sprayed out from its tip, adding to the conflagration above them. "This seems very sketchy."

"Yes... very," Adam affirmed, fishing out a black card from his waistband.

He sighed, twirling the calling card of the organization before stepping out and revealing himself to the mad magician.

"ADAM GLOOOOOOW! AND YOU'VE BROUGHT FRIENDS!" Tim the Enchanter yelled, his hands lighting up with flames and lightning. "How may I be of assistance, my valued and favorite customer?!"

Adam paused, sensing something wrong. The man was happy—*too* happy. The kind of happiness that triggered red flags and alarms in the boy's mind.

"Favorite?" he asked skeptically.

"Yes! YES!" Tim yelled, sending a burst of flames out of his outstretched palms. "Thanks to you, we've made millions! Millions! Ahahaha!"

"Millions?"

"Yes! Yes! Destruction is good for profit! AHAHAHAHA!"

Destruction? He must be talking about the Vilenciel slime incident...

Suddenly the mage teleported, appearing in front of Adam with a wide smile. "How can I be of service today?!"

"Smuggling," he blurted. The mage smirked, before teleporting elsewhere. "I need to get into Vilenciel, along with these two."

The fire mage glanced over Adam's companions. From beside the unconscious Junith, Liza waved.

"Hmmm, yes, for your trial? It would be about that time," Tim said from atop his cart. "You're just in luck! Rolo is scheduled to be there tonight. It will be difficult, but the Black Hand can get you and your entourage into Vilenciel."

"Great. That's great. How much will it cost?" Adam said, his hand hovering over his storage ring.

"Cost?" Tim raised his brow, a fireball shooting out of his staff and into the air. "Nothing! Your antics have generated significant revenue for our organization. I'll have Rolo pick you up tonight and deliver you as far as the edge of the Temple of the Gods!"

"Really?! That close?"

"Yes! We *could* even deliver you to the priestess herself, but with Vilenciel soldiers surrounding the temple and Paladins of the Order on high alert, it would ruffle a few feathers if we tried."

Adam opened his mouth to say something but stopped, his eyes narrowing. "Wait, how do you know I needed to get to the Temple of the Gods?"

"It's my job to know!" Tim exclaimed. "What kind of merchant would I be if I didn't keep track of everything and do my best to fulfill my customer's needs?"

Adam turned to Liza, looking her up and down. By the time he turned back to the mage, the man was flat on his cart with his legs kicked up.

"Speaking of needs..." Adam said, fishing out his last gold coin. "I need supplies, what can I get for a gold?"

"Put away your money. If it's supplies you need, we've opened up a credit line on your behalf."

"Credit?" Adam asked, his face scrunching, unfamiliar with the terminology.

"Yes! Thanks to your contributions, the powers that be have ordained it necessary to credit you a substantial sum for your aid in generating revenue and profit for our organization," Tim said, disappearing. The red curtain of his wagon shoved aside, revealing that he had teleported within, now brandishing various potions and wares.

"Ooooooh shiiiiiny." Liza was already at the cart, eyeballing several jewels and accessories. As her eyes fell upon a silver tiara studded with green jewels, she let out an eardrum-shattering squeal, tail swishing behind her.

"Wait, how much am I being accredited?" Adam asked, poking at his ringing ear as his eyes swept across the enchanted wares.

"Twenty platinum coins."

Adam coughed. "Sorry, say again?"

"Twenty platinum coins!" Tim announced, his wagon firing off a burst of fireworks.

Adam did the math in his head. By his calculations, a singular platinum coin was worth a hundred gold coins, meaning he had to his name... two *thousand* gold coins!

"Is that a lot?" Liza asked. The nekogirl raised her hand, attempting to paw the silver tiara, only to get smacked on the head by Tim's staff. "Hulhk!"

"Why? How?" Adam asked, his brow furrowing with suspicion. "What?"

"Ah, thanks to your destruction of Vilenciel and elimination of many of our competitors as well as the ravaging of so much of the noble and market sectors, new distributors had to be found," Tim explained, placing a leather bag on the table. "And WHO BETTER THAN THE BLACK HAND?! We've gained full dominance of the upper and under markets, allowing the esteemed organization I serve to secure our claim to Vilenciel and expand our networks."

"I see," Adam said, his eyes greedily glossing over the prepared items laid out in front of him. To the side Liza repeatedly tapped at the tiara, trying to knock it over.

"Is that a lot?" Liza asked again. As she jabbed the tiara once again, it abruptly vanished. "Hey! Aawww."

"Yes. Yes, it is." Adam locked eyes with the merchant, who smiled with teeth that appeared inhuman.

"What would you like to buy today, sir?"

"What do you have?" Adam said, mirroring the merchant's wicked smile.

Catpurr 20
Drip Check Before the Next Trial

[Ding!]
[CONCATULATIONS! You've won 5 Cicero Coins!]
[Daily attempts left: 00!]
Gacha Coins: 115

Adam sighed. He stood in a clearing after finalizing his production order with Tim to have dozens of smiths collaborate on the creation of a weapon hitherto unseen on this world, he'd had nothing better to do while waiting for his contact with the Black Hand to take them into Vilenciel.

Well... of course I couldn't expect everything to even out. But at least I have gear now, He reassured himself, tugging at his green leather armor he now wore. Mentally he took inventory of everything else he had purchased.

Beside new clothes and various bits of armor for Liza, Junith, and himself, Adam had spent a whopping six platinum coins, the equivalent of six hundred gold pieces, leaving him with one thousand, four hundred gold pieces remaining in balance. Of course, this was before he bought other incidentals like food, rope, and traveling supplies, but the vast majority had been spent on magic items.

[Armor of the Pacifist Dryad+1]

[**Item Description:** *Armor crafted by a dryad during the War of the Four Elements to protect her home. As such, this armor possesses heightened resistances to the powers commonly wielded by those who would bring ruin to nature.* **+8% Heat Resistance, +8% Cold Resistance, +15% Blunt Resistance, +8% Wind Resistance to all stats if not the aggressor. If aggressive, stats conferred are halved.**]

[Cloak of Immobile Invisibility]

[**Item Description:** *A prototype for a magical cloak made to replicate the cloak belonging to the "Boy That Lived." This cloak was discarded due to a mishap when binding an activation phrase. As such, the cloak will only activate if the user recites the words* **"What do you mean they're out of pizza?!"** *and remains absolutely still.*]

[Gauntlet of the Magic Hand]

[**Item Description:** *A mechanical silver gauntlet crafted by a dimension hopper known as C-137, in a valiant effort to grab his TV remote when it was out of reach. When activated, a magical copy of the user's hand extends forth from the gauntlet. The hand is capable of grabbing and reaching items as far away as twenty meters. However, the further away the hand is from the gauntlet, the weaker its gripping strength becomes.*]

[Polite Belt of Potions]

[**Item Description:** *A brown Belt of Holding made exclusively for storing potions and other tinctures. Can only be used if the wearer says 'please' and 'thank you' when retrieving or storing potions. If the wearer* *fails to politely request potions enough times, the belt will expel all stored items and call the wearer rude.* **Capacity 18/20**]

[Boots Made for Walking]
[Item Description: *Black Corinthian leather boots, light as a feather and once worn by a ginger colored cat. This enchanted pair of boots eases the fatigue on the wearer's legs, reducing stamina consumption for movement-based actions involving the use of the legs.* **+15% Fall impact negation, +3% Movement Speed, +10% Stamina consumption for moving.**]

Finally, there was the last item Adam bought himself, the twisted shiny silver staff he now held in his hands, a faintly glowing blue gemstone set into its head.

[[SEALED] Depowered Regal Scepter of the Full Moon Queen]
[Item Description: *Supposedly this item can only be wielded by the most intelligent of beings. Its former owner was once the Queen of the Full Moon, consort to a god. After her defeat at the hands of a naked, maidenless warrior using a club, her staff was used to beat various demigods into submission before unconventional usage caused its former splendor and skills to fade. This weapon longs for the day it will return to its former glory.*

Skill: Regal Smash: *Channel mana into the depowered spellstone atop this scepter and deliver a potent concussive magical blast which detonates upon impact with a target.*

Skill: Waning Moon Shield: *Channel mana into the depowered spellstone atop this scepter to activate what remains of its defensive properties and conjure a barrier of moonlight.*
Skill: SEALED
Skill: SEALED
Skill: SEALED
+3% potency to Tier 1 skills, +12% potency to Moonlight skills and abilities, +25% potency to blunt damage when wielding this scepter, +10% natural mana regeneration, +5 ARC]

It was perhaps the most expensive item Adam had purchased, costing an entire two platinum coins on its own. It had been one of the few items in Tim's store to not only possess passives but also skills, increasing Adam's own arsenal. Not to mention the 3 percent increase to his tier one skills—that is, almost *all* his skills.

"THIS SUCKS!" Liza whined, drawing Adam's attention from his gear toward the nekogirl as she toted on her back the massive hiking bag, carrying all their supplies. "Why do you all get to get all the cool things while I get made to carry all our luggage?! It's not fair!"

Liza pointed at Junith. The other nekogirl was still awake, albeit scowling as she sat immobile in the dirt. The new steel armor she now wore had adjusted its size, binding itself to its new master.

[Half-Cursed Immobile Fortress of Smo]
[Item Description: *Curse Armor crafted to entomb a warrior who abandoned his oaths and earned the ire of his liege. When worn, the armor contours around the wearer and confers immense health*

regeneration and near unparalleled defense, with a flat bonus to all physical resistances powered by the user's mana. However, the defensive capabilities of this now partially purified set of armor come at the cost of mobility and weight as well as magical resistances.

A partially successful purging of the curse that affects this suit of armor has alleviated most of the negative effects, but not all.

+400% HP Regeneration, +20 CON, +50 to all Physical Resistances, -80% Movement Speed, -50% Magical Resistance.]

"At least you can move..." Junith grumbled. The paladin now struggled to raise even a finger, but not even that stopped her from slowly flipping off Adam.

"It's not fair!" Liza screamed again, stomping her feet like a little child throwing a tantrum. "I want enchanted gear! Why can't I have stuff like her?! What am I supposed to do if someone runs a spear through me?!"

"Die, I guess."

"Wha?"

"Junith is important, and I need her alive, that's why she has the armor. You, on the other hand, are expendable," Adam replied deadpan. Rather than sparing Liza a glance, his full attention stuck with testing out his new gauntlet. Upon activating, a phantasmal, blue hand appeared. It quickly elongated, snatching an acorn out of a nearby tree.

"WHA?!" Liza repeated, her eyes widening with shock. "THAT'S SO MEAN! How could you say that?!"

Adam shrugged. The nekogirl continued to berate him, tears streaming from her eyes.

"After all we've been through! Does our friendship mean nothing?! Does our bond soaked in blood and forged in hardship have no weight?! Hold no value?!" Liza yelled. Big blobby tears splattered upon the ground as she melodramatically flung herself upon the earth. "Buy me something, *pllleeeease!*"

"Did you forget you tried to kill me?" Adam asked, flicking the acorn away. It bounced off Liza's forehead, leaving a red mark as she gazed at him with heartbroken eyes.

"That wasn't personal! I had orders! Orders, I tell you! Come on! Please, buy me something!"

"No."

"Pleeeease."

"No."

"Pwetty pweeease!"

"Absolutely not."

"Please, with cherry on top?"

"What do cherries have to do with anything?" Adam questioned.

"I don't know, it's just a saying."

"No," he repeated, turning away.

"Pwapwaplaaaz," Liza wailed, slumping onto the ground until she was groveling at Adam's ankles and sobbing onto his boot. "I'm reformed! I'm a changed girl! Please, professor! I'll do anything for an A!"

"What?"

"Buy me something!" she cried, this time looking up at Adam with kitty cat eyes.

This went on for about ten minutes before he finally grunted, her tantrum and his headache overwhelming the remnants of his patience.

"FINE!"

"YAAAAY!" Liza shouted, excitedly taking off towards Tim's cart. Already, the man had a row of items set up and waiting for her.

"You know, if you cave in to her demands, you're only enabling this kind of behavior," Redfield said, hoisting the immobile Junith up by her armpits to set her beside Adam.

Adam pinched the bridge of his nose.

"I know. I know. Gah, so damn annoying. I just want her voice to stop."

"That could be arranged. Just give the word," Red said, his ghostly red eyes flaring. "One and done, back of the head. I'll make it painless."

Adam's eyes swished to the Death Knight. "I didn't realize you were so bloodthirsty."

"Well. When you've been killed, your perspective on the sanctity of life changes a bit."

"Isn't that the truth..." the nekomancer replied with a sigh, drawing a puzzled look from the knight. He remained unaware of Adam's sequential demises at the hands of a certain feathered fowl.

"The tiara! The tiara! GIB ME THE TIARA!" Liza demanded, her head resting sideways on Tim's shop window. Wide golden eyes remained locked on the silver tiara she'd been batting about previously, now safely out of the nekogirl's reach.

"The tiara," Adam grumbled. The black market merchant smiled and handed the tiara off to Liza, who placed it on her head and squealed with glee.

[Gem Studded Tiara]

[Item Description: *A betrothal gift made for a princess of a foreign nation. Besides housing several commonly sought after gems valued* *differently by different cultures, this tiara possesses no special qualities or features of note.*]

"That will be two hundred gold pieces. Shall I deduct it from your balance, or would you like to pay over time?" Tim said, brandishing a wolfish smile.

"T-Two—" Adam blinked, choking slightly. "Two hundred?! That's absurd! The trickster's persona was only fifty without the discount!"

The merchant shrugged. "Different items hold different values to different folks."

"Put it back," Adam said. Liza clutched the tiara tightly like a child with a teddy bear and shrieked a resounding "NO!"

"Put it back!" Adam demanded again, this time grabbing at the tiara as Liza tried to squirm away.

"NOOOO!" she screamed as runes lit up across her body, zapping her.

"RED!"

"As you command," the Death Knight said. Redfield loomed above her with his weapon of choice as quickly as if he had teleported, a smoking revolver already drawn. "Shall I remove the hands or the head first, sir?"

"What? No! Just pry—BY NYX HOW DO YOU POSSESS SO MUCH STRENGTH?!" Adam barked, yanking at the tiara still clutched in the nekogirl's grasping claws.

"N-N-NOOOO—OOOOOO!" Liza screamed. Her voice stuttered as the electricity shocked her again and again.

"DO YOU WANT NAP TIME?! BECAUSE THIS IS HOW YOU GET NAP TIMED!" Adam barked as Liza began to writhe, struggling to escape Redfield's iron grip.

"IT'S SO SHINY! PWAAALS!" Liza begged. "I DON'T ASK FOR MUCH!"

"Are you addle-brained? YOU ASK FOR EVERYTHING! NON-STOP!" Adam yelled, his frustration at a maximum. Two hundred gold pieces were enough to wipe clean his original debt with the adventurer's guild, although the increased sum from his destruction of Vlienciel meant that was beside the point.

"Nap time, sir?" Red asked, holding the shrieking nekogirl aloft.

"I DON'T WANNA GO TO SLWEEp!"

"Do it."

"NooUHK! Choking! Why! I j-just! Wan! Be princess..." With a quick squeeze of Red's gauntlet to her carotid, the girl was out, hands drooping low. The tiara fell from her head and into Adam's clutches.

"Ah, it looks like your way into Vilenciel is here," Tim said, grinning ear to ear as Rolo appeared, wearing his usual black leotard. However, he wasn't alone, this time he showed up with several others in similar black garb. Three others, in fact, the men and women all carrying barrels in their arms.

"Alright. Dump the girls into barrels and let's go," Adam ordered Red. The knight bowed lightly before walking off with Liza on his shoulder.

"Good luck and safe travels, Mr. Glow. I'll make sure all of your requests are processed when you return," Tim said as Adam set the tiara back onto his wagon and turned to walk away. Yet he paused, pinching the bridge of his nose with a groan before he turned back to the enchanter with a deeply annoyed look upon his face.

Catpurr 21
The Second Disaster at Vilenciel

Crouching atop the roof of a tall, high-rise building overlooking the city of Vilenciel was a nekoboy. Casually, he kicked the unconscious body of an adventurer out of the way as he observed the nearby cathedral. Plainly put, it was an obstacle, or the patrols of soldiers, paladins, and Vilenciel guards who stopped and identified all who drew near certainly were.

"So, what's the plan here?" Junith asked. After a compelling argument from Red, Adam had reluctantly agreed to clad Junith in regular, child-sized plate mail while the Death Knight regenerated his mana, only so she could move under her own power as they traveled to their destination.

A precautionary move, one Adam was happy to indulge.

"Unsure," he replied, his eyes set upon his timer. "I'm thinking."

[03:01:11]

Three hours until the trial began.

The Black Hand had proved themselves to be invaluable once again, quickly moving and smuggling the nekos across the Duchy and into the city with practiced ease, fitting into his estimate of how long he'd have to prep to enter the church, crawling with soldiers.

From his vantage point, Adam could make out numerous adventurers, mercenaries mixed in with the heroes. Leaping from building to building were additional patrols of men and women, no doubt taking more initiative in hunting him down. Fortunately, the Black Hand had cleaned up this roof for him, quietly dispatching the four mercenaries atop this belltower and providing their charge with an observation area.

There were several ways he could tackle this.

Brute force was an obvious first choice. Many people would get hurt, but it would also expose his necromantic powers and give the enemy intel on his capacities.

Stealth, meanwhile, was an old friend. He could try sneaking in, or even drawing the Vilenciel guards away with a distraction some kind so that he—

Wait. Why am I overthinking this? Yes, the soldiers were patrolling around the cathedral in droves—but only *around* the cathedral. The marble stairwell leading inside was completely empty of them.

All Adam had to do was reach the stairwell. Once there, he'd be on temple property, meaning the Vilenciel soldiers weren't allowed to interfere, as he was a qualified trial participant with an abyssal ticket.

At least, that's what he understood.

He turned to Junith. The paladin was perched atop a meowing barrel. Liza was presently stuffed inside, refusing to leave as part of her childish display of defiance

Hmm, maybe I can just throw her at the stairwell.

"Get ready," he ordered as Junith hopped off the barrel.

"What about her?" she asked. "We could just throw her at the temple."

"The thought did cross my mind," Adam said, prying the top open. Within, the pink-haired nekogirl was curled into the fetal position, crying. "C'mon. Let's go. Time is ticking."

"I don't wanna."

Adam sighed. Unfortunately, he couldn't carry Liza *and* make his way into the temple. But summoning Redfield would make stealth impossible, and expose his strongest card

"And why not?"

"You're mean," Liza replied.

Adam smacked his lips, gazing skywards in exasperation.

Refreshing air flooded his lungs. With impressive calm, he reached into his cloak and retrieved something, which fell with a *clang* into Liza's barrel. The light struck it, revealing a shiny metal band.

"Whaa?" Liza muttered. There was a brief silence before the barrel exploded as the nekogirl rocketed into the air. She held up the tiara to the sun, grinning with sparkling tears in her eyes. "Y-Y-You—You! YOU! YOU!"

"Oh great. You broke her," Junith said, fidgeting with the pommel of her new sword.

"OH, THANK YOU! THANK YOU! THANK YOU!" Liza screamed, leaping up and embracing Adam. He only sighed, exhaustion laced into his very bones.

"Please shut up."

"I can't believe you got me the tiara!"

Liza began to prance around, placing the silver crown on her head and acting out some strange play.

"So, are you going to tell her it's a knock off or am I?" Junith leaned over and whispered, a slight smirk on her face.

"Do it and I'll throw you off this roof." Well, that was technically the plan anyway.

"Fine. I'll just save this for later."

Adam clapped his hands, drawing the two's attention back to him.

"May I please have my potions," he said, activating his potion belt and retrieving three vials from the enchanted belt. "Thank you."

"Hehehe!" Liza giggled.

"Alright, so here's the plan," he continued, then turned and pointed towards the temple. "We just need to get onto temple grounds. The Black Hand has— Hold on a second—"

One of the men on the ground was groaning, slowly rousing from unconsciousness. A quick kick to the face from Adam sorted that out nicely

"—has delivered us this far. All we need now is to get onto the grounds and we'll be safe," Adam finished.

"How do you suppose we do that?" Junith asked, taking a vial as it was handed to her.

"Simple." Adam uncorked the vial in his hand and downed the clear, viscous liquid within. "We're going to jump."

[Buff: Temp Skill Acquired!]
[**Parachute:** *Once activated, greatly slows the rate of descent, allowing the caster to land safely. This skill disappears upon use.*]

Junith blinked. "Come again?"

"We're going to get a running start, then jump," Adam replied, pointing at the church as Liza uncorked the vial and sniffed it, before taking a sip and recoiling.

"I'm sorry. Can you repeat that? I believe you just said we're going to jump?" Junith repeated. "From a hundred-foot-tall building."

"Yes. That's correct."

"Suicide is against my religion."

Adam pinched the bridge of his nose.

"That's what the potion of parachute is for. We're going to run, jump, activate the skill, and land safely on temple grounds."

"What if we gain too much air and splat into the side of the building?" Junith asked. "There's got to be a better—"

"Then don't splat into the building," Adam said with finality, standing in the middle of the roof. "Now, by my calculations, if we start at this point and take off at full—"

"YEET!" Liza screamed, running past Adam at full sprint and leaping off the bell tower with a scream as she plummeted a hundred stories below.

"Crapbaskets. ALRIGHT! We're doing this!" Adam yelled before taking off, chasing after Liza. But as he did so, he noticed Junith was still stuck in the center of the roof, plainly hesitating.

Great. Adam shifted his direction, aiming his trajectory towards Junith, whose eyes widened.

"WAITWAITWAIT!" she hollered. The nekomancer collided with the paladin and both fell from the bell tower. "WHY?! WHYWHYWHYWHY?!"

Adam's eyes narrowed. As they tumbled through the air he tried to hold tight to the writhing nekogirl, but her screams were drawing attention from everyone below.

"STOP SQUIRMING!" he barked, struggling to orient their bodies correctly as the marble stairwell grew closer and closer. "Ow. Ow. OW! WHY ARE YOU BITING ME?!"

"THAT'S THE FUGITIVE! OPEN FIRE!" a man yelled. A dozen spells, arrows, and various objects soared through the air at Adam as he activated **parachute** and began slowing his descent.

Just then a barrier erupted. The weapons clanged against the oval shield that surrounded the temple grounds, protecting Adam from the threat of the Vilenciel soldiers' weapons.

Unfortunately, the boy had vastly misjudged the description of his potion. Instead of just slowing his descent to a manageable fall, the potion made him appear to hover in place, descending at a snail's pace as Junith hung on for dear life with her arms crushing his chest. Sharp claws and teeth pierced his skin as she clung on.

"Well... Good thing we're on temple grounds," he muttered, eyeing the now hundreds of arrows, skills, weapons, and what appeared to be a lone gabbage as they *clanged* harmlessly off the temple's barrier.

"Seize them! One platinum coin to whoever brings me his head!" a soldier yelled. Dozens of mercs and soldiers attempted to barge their way onto temple grounds, but their advance was repelled as three dozen knights in silver emerged and formed a shield wall, led by the paladin known as Howard.

A few people tried to rush over the wall of silver armored knights, but magic hands formed of water shot out from the streams and ponds surrounding the church, smacking the invaders away.

"Gabbages! Get your gabbages! Guaranteed to do damage!" a merchant screamed, a familiar man walking by with his cart of gabbages. A number of people quickly bought the green vegetables, arming themselves with unconventional ammunition in the struggle to capture Adam.

This went on for roughly an hour. As Adam and his gang gradually drifted closer to the ground, the soldiers of Vilenciel just as slowly abandoned their crusade, going off to do more productive things—like watching paint dry.

Everyone present stared at Adam as he withered under the attention. He just wished the potion would fall faster already.

Liza on the other hand appeared to enjoy the attention, taunting and yelling at the soldiers below, flicking them off as she did poses in the air.

"Ha! Look at you, dum dums! Idiots! Better luck next time!" she declared, sticking out her tongue and giving the army below them the middle finger.

"How about not taunting them?" Adam said. "You'll just piss them off even more."

"Who cares! It's not like they can come at us anyway, with the paladins holding them off," she fired back, before going back to making faces at the army below. A man threw a boot aimed at her, but the barrier promptly deflected it, and the nekogirl only laughed.

Suddenly, the humans began moving, shifting. The mercs and soldiers unexpectedly formed ranks as hundreds of Vilenciel soldiers descended upon the foot of the temple, led by a man in knight armor riding atop his chestnut-colored horse, brandishing a red and gold scroll.

"All hands! All hands! Now hear ye this! By decree of Lady Alencia Kel Vilenciel, daughter to the Duchess of Vilenciel, Huntress of Beasts. The Temple of the Six Gods are hereby ordered to surrender the fugitive Adam Glow to the custody of the Vilenciel Royal Knights, or face consequences in accordance with military law!" the knight bellowed, using a skill to amplify his voice as hundreds of heavily armored soldiers began stomping their way to line up against the woefully outnumbered paladins of the temple. "What say the Church?!"

Howard, whom Adam recognized as the paladin Sehn owed money to, stood before his line of paladins, hands gripping his halberd.

"The temple answers only to the gods! Lady Vilenciel's jurisdiction ends at the edges of our sanctified grounds. This is our answer. Any attempt to breach our sanctum will be met with force!" Howard yelled, earning some of Adam's respect. Previously he'd considered the man a lowly scammer, but now he'd have to revise his initial impression.

"So be it!" The scroll was rolled up with a sharp *snap* as the knight gave a signal.

Ah... crapbaskets. Adam frowned as a familiar figure approached, whose very presence sent chills down his spine.

Even at a distance, he could feel the maddened gaze of Alencia Vilenciel. Adam should not have been capable of reading her lips from so far away, but he swore he knew precisely what she was whispering: *You're mine.*

"ATTACK!" a soldier yelled. Upon command, hundreds of soldiers charged onto temple grounds, meeting the paladins in a mighty clash.

The skirmish resumed as the presence of their lord reinvigorated the attackers. With the assistance of the Royal Guards, they were visibly pushing the paladins back.

Ah crap. Crapcrap. Crap! Adam turned to Liza. "You just had to open your mouth!"

"What did I do?"

"YOU JINXED US!" Adam yelled. The ground was tantalizingly close now, mere feet away, but they still would not reach it quickly enough. "Now we're going to get captured and experimented on!"

"Experimented?"

"Yeah! I hope you liked having a tail!" Adam barked. Several soldiers broke past the shield wall, marching up the stairs and closing in on the floating nekofolk. His heart seized.

Great. Just great!

"Wait, what do you mean my tail?! I love this thing!" Liza screamed, clutching her pink furry tail before a faint, familiar echo began sounding in Adam's head.

"King! King!"

Wait a minute. Adam's eyes went wide, recognizing the sound of his summoned Morian crab. He'd forgotten all about it after it seemingly abandoned him, but something sounded different about its mental voice now. Adam narrowed his eyes, focusing on the voice—no, the voice*s*. Not a single voice, but dozens—no, hundreds! Thousands!

"GLORY TO THE KING!"

"KING! KING KING!" came the telepathic battlecry.

Suddenly thousands of voices were chanting in unison. The ground beneath the gathered human army shifted and quaked, trembling as the chanting grew louder in Adam's head.

What the Nyx is going on?!

"WE RIDE TO THE KING!"

"KING! KING KING!"

"WE ANSWER THE CALL!"

"KING! KING! KING!"

Without warning the ground erupted, spewing thousands of black dots, which Adam quickly recognized as thousands upon thousands of crabs, assailing the Vilenciel army with all the ferocity of rabid wolves.

KRABBY?! Adam's jaw dropped, his eyes widening as he spotted his little cat-eared summon riding atop a massive red Morian crab as it climbed its way out of the ground and began blasting the humans with bolts of mana.

"GLORY!"

"DEATH!"

"GLORY!"

"DEAAATH!" the crabs chanted in unison. Every second, the crabs multiplied in an unending crimson tide until the human army was drowning in them, knights and guards alike shrieking as bolts of mana ricocheted everywhere, tiny claws snipping at those lucky enough to evade the bolts.

"MY TOES! IT HAS MY TOES! HAAALP!" a man screamed, running around madly before a familiar voice hollered in agony.

"PEE ON IT! THEY DON'T LIKE PEE!" an adventurer hollered out, shortly before a snipping sound was heard and a blood curdling screech echoed out.

"NOT MY GABBAGES! STOP! LEAVE MY PRODUCE ALONE!" the gabbage merchant yelled.

"FOR THE KING!"

"KING! KING! KING!"

"It's... beautiful," Liza said. At last, the trio had touched down upon the marble stairway, but now they found themselves arrested by the spectacle sprawling out before them.

Catpurr 22
Runaway Princess Liza!

"Adam!" Coco called out happily from where the blue-haired temple Priestess lay in a pool of water. She beckoned the nekoboy closer as he scampered across the ornate tile floor.

"Portal, please!" Adam yelled frantically, eyeing the scores of shiny suits of silver armor lining the walls as he neared the priestess.

He paid the guardians no mind, instead rushing up to the pool of water where Coco was already opening the portal, the teleporter rising out of the ground as energy hummed through the temple.

"Thanks! Sorry for the trouble! Portal!" he repeated. Dragging Liza and Junith with him he sprinted to close the distance and reach the obelisk, but a minor explosion and rabid snarl arrested him in his tracks.

Adam's eyes widened. In slow motion his head turned to face the monster clawing her way into the temple from the outside courtyard.

"ADAAAAAAM!" Alencia screamed. The woman looked like a scene from a nightmare. Her fine black dress was ripped to shreds and drenched in blood. Pinching crabs clung to every exposed inch of flesh and hair, and yet she still sported a wicked smile.

"PORTALPORTPORTALPORTALPORTAL RIGHTNOW!" Adam screamed, shaking Coco as Vilenciel soldiers flooded into the temple.

"Whoa! Hey! Stop that, or you'll break my headband!" Coco yelled to no avail—visions of being strung up and tortured danced about in the boy's head. "Relax. I'm clairvoyant, remember? Do you think I'd be this calm if anything bad was going to happen to me?"

"It's not you I'm worried about!" He waved the abyssal ticket in front of the obelisk as Alencia's heels clicked closer and closer.

"ADAM!"

Coco sighed, lifting her hand and pointing. Alencia slammed headfirst into a barrier, accompanied by the clanking of metal as the silver suits of armor joined the fray.

"COCO!" Alencia screamed, backing away. "How dare you defy the Empire's will! This is an act of treason!"

"Sue me." Coco stuck her tongue out, her blue eyes flashing brightly. A notification blotted out Adam's field of vision as the obelisk finally activated.

[Do you wish to enter the Abyssal Trials?]
[Time Remaining Until Trial: 01:02:11]
[Yes < No]

YES!

Suddenly the familiar portal of bones appeared, skeletal hands reaching out, beckoning Adam into its embrace.

"Your trial." Coco bowed.

"Oooh, spoopy— WHYA!" Liza said, poking the door, only to be grabbed and yanked in.

Junith backed away, but Adam's foot in her backside put a stop to that.

"Wha—?" She quickly fell into the portal, screaming.

"ADAM!"

The nekoboy in question turned. His teeth ground together, and sweat trickled down the back of his neck as every hair seemed to stand on end.

Alencia Vilenciel stared at her quarry, face squished against the translucent barrier. In her hands were two snapping crabs which she wielded like daggers, repeatedly stabbing the crustaceans into the barrier.

Nope!

"I won't forget this!" Adam spat, leaping into the bone portal as Alencia screamed his name once more.

"Oh, I know you won't," Coco said, watching the portal melt away before turning to the army barging into her temple.

* * *

The night of Vilenciel was immediately swallowed by overwhelming, blinding light as Adam was deposited in an open field. He blinked the spots away from his vision as a notification pinged in front of him.

[CONCATULATIONS! QUEST COMPLETE!]

The Nyx? His pupils dilated as he looked around, taking in the burning, brown grass fields. This place seemed just as chaotic as the temple they'd left behind, but at least none of the screams ringing out were coming from that awful woman.

"Out of the frying pan and into the lava," Liza said as a fireball tore through the night sky.

[SYSTEM LINGUAL TRANSLATOR TURNED ON VIA ADMINISTRATOR COMMAND.]

"Retreat! Retreat! Fall back to the forest!"

Catlike ears pricked. The chaotic noises around them suddenly become comprehensible as a fleeing humanoid screamed orders at the green armored soldiers.

Adam paused, taking a good look at the running beings. Although they resembled humans, there were two glaring traits indicating they weren't: their elongated, pointed ears and their taller builds.

Inspect.

[**Drowthraki:** *A dark-skinned race of humanoids hailing from a land whose sun never sets. The Drowthraki are a subterranean species of evolved humans. As such, members of this race tend to have poor eyesight but excellent hearing and a keen sense of smell.*]
[**Strengths:** *Magic affinity, ???, ???, ???, ???*]
[**Weaknesses:** *Weak frames, ???, ???, ???*]

"Elves!" Liza yelled, pointing at the humanoids. While Adam did agree they had some similarities to elves, they weren't the same. These Drowthraki, as the System identified them, were taller, lankier, with dark purplish skin rather than the pale features he was used to.

"Children? What are children doing here?!" One of the humanoids froze, narrow eyes widening upon seeing children of his race in the middle of an open battlefield.

"HI! HELLO!" Liza called out, waving her hands enthusiastically.

"A princess?! What is a princess doing on the field?!" another elf cried, gaze falling on the tiara atop Liza's head.

Oh no. Adam's breath caught. The nekoboy knew trouble was brewing as the entire crowd of elves stopped, turning to focus on Liza as she waved at them all.

"Run! Flee, Princess! Flee!"

Liza blinked. "Me?"

"To arms! We must save the princess from the dragon!" The army of charred and burnt elves shifted, their retreat changing to a resolute charge. From somewhere behind Adam came a massive boom, the vibrations nearly knocking him off his feet.

His body spun, pupils dilating to drink in the sight before him as his cat claws reflexively sprang out. Here was a beast he had hoped to leave behind him. Approaching them now was a massive, pale creature, glistening with carmine-red scales. It lifted its yellow, toothy bill high into the air as it uttered a wretched battle cry.

"QUACK!"

Oh, you've got to be kidding me! Panic thrummed in his chest once. Here, standing before him again, was the creature that had killed him repeatedly back when this nightmare began. Now it was back in the flesh, barreling towards the small nekoboy.

NONONONO!

The army of dark elves charged the oversized duck, rushing it with their crude weapons, yet despite their heroism they were unable to halt the monster's advance. White-hot flames spewed from its bill as its giant flippers batted away soldiers left and right, crushing them as though they were but ants.

"WHOA! IS THAT A FIRE BREATHING DUCK?!" Liza screamed. "I WANT IT!"

"Stop gawking, you idiot, and run!" Adam yelled, yanking Liza by the collar of her armor as Junith took out her sword. She ran alongside the pair, pushing through the crowd of armored Drowthraki. The warriors parted easily, clearing a path as the nekos raced for the woods.

"FOR THE PRINCESS!"

"FOR THE PRINCESS!" the dark-skinned elves cried in unison. It wasn't long before all that remained on the battlefield were charred ashes and empty husks of half-melted armor. The sole survivor of the one-sided fight, a massive duck bellowing flames into the cloudless sky above.

"This way, your highness!" a drow called out, beckoning Adam's party over to a ragtag collection of survivors. Each was armed with a crossbow as they stood around a black wooden carriage. "This way!"

Liza giggled, entering into the carriage. "I'm a princess!"

Adam tried to enter as well, but the nearby guard shoved him back, barring him from entering, but allowing Junith to hop on.

What the Nyx?!

"You. Walk," a nearby drow said, before closing the door and hopping onto the now moving cart.

Adam blinked, an incredulous look on his face at the unexpected turn of events.

[Welcome to Floor Three! The Dragon Raid!] [0:20:17]

Catpurr 23
Welcome to Trial Three

The night-black carriage creaked along on metal wheels, pulled by several elves. Walking in step with the nearby dark elves escorting their apparent charges, Adam quietly opened his quest tab. But alas, he was met with no quest objective—only the message welcoming him to the trial.

He frowned, eyeing the timer on the side before his eyes shifted to the worn and defeated elven soldiers.

Judging from the title, seems the Duckysaur is the target. Hopefully these guys have more soldiers, Adam thought to himself, imagining the giant duck roasted on a massive pike. *Ah... wouldn't that be nice.*

Thankfully, the Duckysaur didn't seem too keen on pursuing Adam, as he and his entourage were allowed to flee through the dense wood and shrubbery.

It provided him with plenty of time to get to know his new dark-skinned and pointy-eared allies, many of whom appeared injured.

"Uh... Hello?" the nekoboy tried, only to be met with indifference.

He tried again, however the survivors didn't even bat an eye towards Adam.

"Once more, Adam, you are shunned by everyone," Adam grumbled. He followed along behind the carriage until it came to a yawning chasm set inside a mountain wall. The maw was just big enough to fit the carriage in, leading it down deeper into the earth.

Alarm bells rang in Adam's mind. Every one of his instincts shrieked at him not to go in—but he had no choice. In the flight to escape the oversized duck, Junith and Liza had become unwitting hostages, locked within the Drowthraki's iron carriage.

Nothing ventured... He clenched his jaw, walking with the procession of soldiers. *Nothing gained.*

The interior of the cave was smooth, too smooth. Unnaturally so, as if something had molded the walls into a cylinder shape.

There were no torches, only faintly glowing stones of blue that gave off low light. It was still hard to see, but Adam's eyes adjusted quickly, his dark vision taking over.

Well... This is concerning, he considered. Jutting out from the walls were spikes of stone, chains dangling from the ceiling.

Not exactly decor that screams friendly. But quickly, the elves distracted him from the scenery.

"Just a bit further. We must report our failure to our Lady of Silk," an elf said.

"She will not be pleased," another elf added. "Our unit was nearly annihilated. A hundred dead. A princess outside her coven."

"We cannot control our fates. "

"Hush!" interjected another elf. This one carried a staff, half his body covered with burns. "We are near the gate."

Adam narrowed his eyes. Growing in the distance was an imposing iron wall at the end of the unnatural smooth tunnel, a gate set into it their only way of progressing along the path.

"Open the gate!" an elf cried. Then a silence settled over the underground road.

A moment passed, then another. Several of the dark-skinned humanoids exchanged glances with mixed expressions.

Some of them seemed distinctly fearful.

Suddenly something creaked, followed by the sound of machinery grinding.

The gate opened. Elven soldiers rushed out, armed with what appeared to be crossbows. The soldiers took up position, forming ranks as a woman stepped out from the gate. She was clad in golden armor and wielding a great axe, long white hair contrasting her dark Drowthraki skin.

"Lady Cha'tul," the burned elf said. Each of the survivors fell to a knee as the lithe, tall woman swept her purple gaze across them, the very act brimming with power.

Seeing the spectacle, Adam did the same, lowering his body as the elves began to talk.

"Report, Un'el," the woman said. Her voice was slightly snobbish, but her tone brooked no argument as she glared at the survivors. Clearly she was a figure of utmost authority.

"We failed, mi'lady," the burned elf said. Suddenly he toppled to the floor as he was struck.

"You were ordered to fight to the last! To die destroying that abominable beast!" Cha'tul yelled, her eyes glaring as she looked down at the crippled elf laying on the cold hard ground.

Adam clenched his fist, keeping his head low.

"Speak your excuse!" the woman demanded.

"My apologies, mi'lady... But a princess... a princess was on the field..." The elf's trembling fingers rose in the air, pointing towards the carriage.

Oh... Crapbaskets.

Adam didn't like where this was going. He could sense trouble. In fact, it practically radiated off the woman now rapidly closing in on the carriage.

The nekoboy's **mana claws** came out, prepared to strike if need be.

As she passed before him, however, the woman paused, turning her violet eyes to stare at him. A long moment passed as she scrutinized the boy carefully—almost as though she had realized something was wrong.

Adam couldn't say how strong the illusions allowing him to blend into the trial's world were. He couldn't say how it made him appear, or even what his clothes looked like. He could only hope it made him unassuming to all around him.

Thankfully, the woman in armor spun, ripping off the wooden door.

"Oh. Hello!" Liza waved. Immediately the ashen-faced woman went pale, dropping flat on the ground in a bow.

"Your excellence! Your Grace! Daughter of our Lady of Silk!" the woman shrieked, bowing to Liza. "F-Forgive my transgressions!"

Liza went wide eyed, while Junith held her palm on the hilt of her sword. A moment passed, then another. Within the carriage, Adam caught Liza's eye and saw the nekogirl smile to herself.

Oh no. Don't yo—

"That is I! Yes!" Liza exclaimed, going along with the woman's assumptions. "Daughter of the Silk! Princess!"

Great. We're going to be executed, Adam sighed as dozens of soldiers came rushing out of the gate towards them.

Catpurr 24
The Space Dog Administrator

Somewhere else amidst the infinite vastness of space, surrounded by the twinkle of distant stars and nebula, floated a white and brown canine wearing a white spacesuit. Before her was a translucent grey screen which she looked upon with slow, dawning horror.

"No! No! NO!" Laika began to bark in a panic. The Administrator of floor DR-04 let out a low whine as her worst fears were realized.

Eli's Chosen had arrived.

Why me?!

The screen shut down as she paddled her legs, doing a somersault in the airless void. Her body twisted as she reoriented herself, now facing the hulking grey monstrosity she called home.

Laika let out a bark. A light on her collar winked on and off, and the space capsule drifted towards her. Immediately she entered, collapsing on a cushion within.

"Oh no. Ooooh no. Oh no." She buried her head within the gray cushions, gloved paws pressing down on her snoot. Through her nose she sucked in a deep, calming breath, before reopening her admin screen. But despite her self-assurance that everything would be fine, the situation revealed itself to be anything but.

Everything was on fire.

Somehow. Twenty minutes prior to the trial officially starting, Eli's Chosen and his supporters had managed to burn an entire city of Drowthraki.

Everywhere Laika looked, giant, adolescent duckysaurs ran about, the draconic fowls spitting gray fire and acid at anything in their way.

People ran to and fro, buildings crumbled, livestock fled. The underground city said to be impregnable to the surface world was now under siege by fluffy feathered fowls.

You were supposed to have the Drowthraki as allies! What do I do now?!

Laika eyed the timer on the right. Three minutes before the trial was destined to start. Then she focused again on Eli's Chosen and his companions.

Adam Glow.

He stood on a gray obelisk, smacking a teenage duckysaur on the head with his staff as one of his companions hugged its neck. A third, who appeared to be a teenage girl, ran around in a panic chased by a squad of gray baby duckysaurs, barely old enough to have their scales.

Please just die. Pretty please, please, Laika groaned. But alas, even as she eyed the timer praying for a miracle, no such blessing manifested.

The trio proved too tenacious, again and again. They had managed to survive for entirely too long, and now she was forced to teleport them.

"Oooh shucks," she groaned. "Now I gotta work."

The doggo pressed her screen with her snoot, her eyes tearing up a bit before a gray beam of energy encapsulated her and her surroundings were replaced.

* * *

"HUH! HWHA? HAH?!" Adam yelled, swinging his staff into the open air frantically before he blinked. Somehow, the environment had shifted. No longer was he in that burning hellscape, now he'd been transported to a lush and open prairie. "Huh?"

One moment he was smashing his staff against the bill of a duckysaur and the next he was enveloped by a blue beam of energy.

"HHHHAAAAAAAW!" With a cry, Junith fell on top of him.

"Gah! Get off! Meatbag!" Adam yelled before shoving the paladin off him. His stomach churned, but through sheer rage he managed to keep down the bile. "Seriously?! Out of all the places you can land, why on me?!"

"It's not my fault, you necrofilth! I was teleported on top of you!" Junith spat, smacking him.

"We're alive!" Liza cried, interrupting the pair.

"YOU!" Adam spat, his eyes widening with fury as the nekogirl ran to them. "YOU IMBECILE! WHY DID YOU LET THEM OUT OF THEIR CAGE?!"

"How was I supposed to know they were dangerous?"

"I DON'T KNOW?! MAYBE READ THE SIGNS! OR HOW ABOUT THE DROW SAYING NOT TO OPEN THE CAGE!"

"But, Fluffy! If not friend, why friend shaped?!"

"AAAAAAAGH!" Adam yelled before tackling Liza, pinning the girl down and slapping her repeatedly in the face.

"Ow! Ow! Ow! Owowowow! Stawp! Stawp!" she screamed.

"You! Stupid! Stupid! *Stupid!* Meatbag!" Adam yelled, punctuating each word with a slap to her face.

"Stop bullying meh!"

"You're lucky I don't kill you!" he barked, his hands wrapping around the girl's neck.

"But you love me!"

"I HATE YOU!" Adam screamed. "You're so useless! Why do you do the things you do?! Are you trying to make me mad?!"

Liza's eyes widened in shock, her mouth falling agape. Then tears began to line her eyes, her lower lip wobbling as she sniffled.

"You're so mean!"

"BECAUSE OF YOU ALL THE SUPPLIES I BOUGHT ARE GONE!"

"Ehem!" Suddenly a crackly voice coughed, drawing Adam's attention to a floating canine in a white suit. The dog gazed at a blue screen while lying on top a white machine, draped with several colors.

Considering its strange look, it was clear this was the admin for the floor.

"Hello!" the Administrator said. Or rather, the dog barked like a normal dog would, as a voice from its collar translated the words into something the nekos could understand. Slowly Adam got off the sobbing nekogirl, taking the tiara with him. Liza gasped, wailing as it was taken from her, but Adam was focused entirely on the being before him

A talking dog?

"What's the task?" Adam asked, spinning to face the dog as several blue portals opened, dropping off various individuals in gear.

"In a moment," the dog barked, floating high up to address the crowd in the midst of getting their bearings.

"Welcome, contestants, to trial three!" it barked, drawing the attention of the gathered humanoids.

Adam scanned the crowd, instantly recognizing three of the eight additional contestants.

Abdullah, Sethis, and the canine-faced man from Trial Two stood out amidst the crowd of other humanoids.

Of the crowd of newcomers, three seemed to be new contestants, while the final two were followers like Junith and Liza. Seeing as both were wolfmen and growling viciously at Abdullah, it seemed safe to bet they all knew each other and were the more familiar wolfman's followers.

"Surely good tides shall come to those, the pious who temper their wrath!"

Outnumbered, Abdullah recited a prayer. Since Adam had last seen the man, his body had been covered by more scars, but he had not grown any more cowardly. He charged, brandishing his spear as he attacked the serpentine woman and snakefolk. The demi-humans moved to counter.

"No! No fighting!" the Administrator barked, a loud pocket of air erupting between the two parties and blasting them away from each other.

Suddenly multiple ghostly copies of the admin appeared. The dogs barked, herding and controlling the group as the space dog descended from on high. A screen lit up in front of Adam.

[Welcome to Trial Three! The Dragon Raid!]

[Mandatory quest given!]

[Work with your team to hunt and kill Sir Bullert Top Hat, the Almighty Duckysaur!] [0/1]

[The world of Telletos is plagued by rampaging fowls that threaten to exterminate all sentient life in their quest of conquest and destruction.]

[Subquest 1: Retrieve Bullert's Top Hat.] [0/1]

[Subquest 2: Exterminate Duckysaurs!] [0]

[Hidden Scenario x2!]

Catpurr 25

Well, That Was Easy...

As Adam looked over the description and details of the latest trial, his heart sank.

Team? I have to work with a team? He resisted pinching his nose and sighing. Already, he had Junith and Liza to deal with, the last thing he wanted was more people.

Then again...

With more bodies to throw at the problem, his chances of meeting an ill-timed demise would be lessened.

But that begged the question, who would be on his team?

He looked around, glancing at the participants. Aside from Sethis, the canine man and his posse, and Abdullah, there were the three others who Adam knew nothing about. For all he knew, they could be followers of Voltrain.

Of course if they were, Adam had a little surprise for them.

"Here are the details of your trial," the dog said quickly, leaping off its white mechanical home. In Adam's periphery he saw something ping into existence as he looked up and saw an 'X' hovering above him. And he wasn't the only one. Above all the contestants gathered, an 'X' or an 'O' appeared over their heads. Abdullah, Liza, Junith, and a gruff man with blond highlights on his black head of hair, donning floral robes as he wielded twin blades, all joined Adam in the 'X' category.

The rest had 'O's over their heads, indicating each group's assigned team.

"There is no time limit to this trial," the Administrator said as Liza gazed at the dog with something like awe. "The symbols above your heads correspond with your team. 'X's and 'O's. You will work with your team to complete and fulfill your trial goals."

Liza began to fidget, bouncing up and down in the corner of Adam's eye.

"The team that has most most points will—"

"LAIKA!"

The dog in the white suit stopped and turned to Liza.

"Yes?" the Administrator said, its tail wagging.

'You're alive!" Liza yelled before suddenly pouncing on the Administrator. "That's so cool! You're an Administrator now?!"

Confused, Adam could only blink at the brazen display of the woman cuddling the dog. The administrator allowed Liza to scratch its neck and hug it.

"Who's a good girl! Who's a good girl!" Liza exclaimed. As the nekogirl petted it, the dog's leg kicked.

"I am! I am!" the Administrator yipped, much to the dismay of everyone nearby. "Oh, that's nice! That is very nice!"

What is even going on?

This went on for a while, each contestant staring at the debacle before the Administrator finally seemed to gain lucidity and rebuffed Liza, barking and releasing a blast of sound that sent her flying uncontrollably into the distance.

Ah.... Well she's dead, Adam thought, as his companion became another twinkling star in the sky.

"No touchy! Let that be a warning!" Laika barked. The collar on the dog's neck summoned its bed, whereupon it quickly re-ascended into the air. "Ehem! As I was saying before I was rudely interrupted, the team that scores the most points will earn the most rewards. However, the team that scores the fewer—"

[Failure: Trial Reversion]

A message blinked below the trial quest details, prompting Adam to frown.

Reversion?

"w—ill have a trial completion deducted from their tally."

A human newcomer with pale skin and leather armor raised her hand. Upon her back was a bow.

"What does that mean?" she asked for clarification.

Laika pivoted, floppy ears flapping. "That means you'll have to undergo another trial before you can pass on to trial four."

Adam was about to raise his hand to ask a question but slowly lowered his hand as a realization struck him.

The Administrator had said more rewards for the winning team, meaning that the losers would still get rewarded. Which meant...

If I scuff this trial, I can do another one and get more rewards!

With gleaming eyes, the nekoboy evaluated his Followers menu.

[Follower in Critical State!]
[Eh'Liza Oktober!]
[HP BELOW 20%!]

Ah, she survived... Unfortunate, he considered, before closing the interface and sizing up the other contestants.

Beside the two canine-faced adventurers garbed in mismatched gear, the opposing team consisted of Sethis the snake woman, the archer, and a green-skinned man with royal blue armor and bulging red eyes.

On Adam's side, was the grinning, scarred bronze warrior Abdullah as he stared down a hissing Sethis, Junith, and the man wearing floral robes. Not counting Liza, who was off dying somewhere, the fight would be five against six. Not exactly balanced, but Adam had a suspicion this was on purpose, considering the summons at his beck and call.

No, the real challenge would be sniffing out the follower of Voltrain in the trial.

"If there are no further questions, I shall bid thee ado!" the Administrator said, shortly before disappearing. Flames burst from the dog's mechanical bed as thrusters sprung out. The white construct shot up into the sky, leaving behind the contestants.

Well... Simple enough trial. Now all I need to do is find the Voltrain follower. Adam was turning back to the trial description to reread it when an arrow sprouted from his chest.

Or, it would have, had Junith not stepped into the projectile's path, deflecting it with her raised shield.

"HERETIC!" the archer yelled, already preparing another arrow.

"Ah... Well, that was easy," Adam muttered, just as another arrow was fired at him.

Catpurr 26

Right for the Neck

"Die, heretical scum!" the archer yelled, releasing a flaming arrow at Adam. It exploded against Junith's shield, sending the nekogirl flying as Adam dove out of the way, vanishing in the long grass.

I knew I shoulda kept you stuffed in that armor!

Immediately chaos ensued. Abdullah licked his lips before pouncing as Sethis and the three wolf-folk sprang into action.

The green-skinned man and Adam's teammate backed off as Abdullah conjured sand. Twin tendrils of dust extended from his arms, which he whipped towards his prey as Sethis and the canines scattered.

With Abdullah distracting the majority, Adam wasted no time. He charged the archer. She leaped backwards in an attempt to gain distance, but Adam had foreseen her move.

Her fate was already sealed.

"RED!" Adam called out. A jagged black gauntlet snatched the woman's anklet as the Death Knight rose up from the earth.

"Huh?" The woman gasped as she was yanked against the ground, the gauntlet locked in an iron vise.

"Unhand me! By Voltrain's name, thou shalt be smited!" she screamed, fully bound by Red as he hid in the dirt.

Adam wasted no time. The nekoboy darted forwards and slid beside the blonde woman. She snarled as tiny hands grabbed her temples.

Why are you all like this?

"Unhand me, oaf! Thou shalt not tolerate the xeno! Thou art an affront to our golden god's glory!"

"Stop squirming!" Adam yelled, fixing the blonde woman's head until her neck lay exposed.

"What are you doing?" Junith asked. The nekogirl approached Adam from behind as he exposed the woman's jugular.

"Payback," he said sinking his fangs into the woman's flesh.

"WHAT ARE YOU DOING?!" Junith screamed.

"Havin ah snak? Wha dosh ish ook ike I'mh doing?" he said sarcastically, rolling his eyes. Below him the woman shrieked uncontrollably as the nekoboy's fangs dug deeper, drops of blood spotting the pale flesh of her neck.

Immediately the symbol of the ouroboros manifested, the symbol of Eli searing itself onto her flesh, burning her as she screamed for gold, the apparent cure to his curse.

Sometime after returning to Rigellia, Adam had questioned Liza and learned that in the early stage of being infected the process could be reversed if treated with gold.

The archer shouted, screamed, jibbered. Some gaseous light escaped her body as she rocked back and forth. Then her muscles seized as she began to shrink.

"XENOS SCUM!" Adam's victim screamed.

Kathrine Dominica: T1 Lvl 1 (Fearful)

HP: 83/85

MP: 3/25

The familiar status screen popped into view, but as quickly as it came, Adam willed it away. Behind him raged the sounds of battle, but thankfully either no one cared what Adam was doing, or they were all too distracted to deal with him.

At his side, Junith clutched her chest as she gazed at the shrunken body of the newest nekogirl. The blond neko's eyes stared blankly, body unmoving as drool trickled from her now-fanged mouth. *So that's what that looks like,* Junith thought with a suppressed shudder.

Adam yanked at the blonde neko's hair, bringing him up to look him in the eye, gold to newly turned gold. Then he opened his mouth to lay the geas.

"You will not attack me or my allies. You will not bite or infect another. If asked for help, you will render aid to the best of your ability. If I give you an order you *will* follow it."

Behind them, Abdullah had encased himself in sand, taking the form of a sand golem. Alone, he guarded against his four adversaries.

"Oh, and you aren't allowed to be annoying," Adam finished before releasing the woman. But as he stood, he noticed Junith.

"What are you doing?!" he asked the dazed the nekogirl, staring down at the blonde.

Junith spun to face Adam. "Are you just going to leave her?"

"Yeah! Now let's go! She's no longer our problem!" he barked, before taking off.

Junith hesitated for a moment but clenched her jaw. The familiar tingling of Eli's crest kept her in place, preventing her from disobeying. But despite knowing she shouldn't, she pressed against the order. The ex-paladin scurried after the nekomancer, following him into the nearby woods.

* * *

High above a forest choked with viridescent forests and emerald oceans floated a crystalline cathedral. The pristine building, casting opalescent rainbows from its stained-glass windows, would have caused any architect to blind themselves from shame. Standing atop the marble-white roof was a naked woman. With her golden blond hair and matching eyes, she looked like a sculptor's magnum opus come to life, but now, her perfect features were marred by a stormy expression.

"You've got to be kidding me," Voltrain muttered. His host's feminine features contorted further as he watched his Chosen be forcibly transformed, a new mark appearing upon her body.

"Wow... He really went right for the neck on that one," Brynhilda said. Voltrain briefly glanced at the six-winged valkyrie before conjuring up a portal. His hand reached out to the spinning vortex, a bolt of lightning crackling to life.

"No," Brynhilda chastised, grabbing the God of Light's slender wrist. "He is protected against godly wrath by Eli. Amusing as it would be to watch your attack rebound, I'd hate for you to run through another host already."

Voltrain gritted his teeth, knowing the woman was right.

"This isn't fair."

"The universe seldom is," Brynhilda said. "But it is our job to balance things on the grand scale. Why are you so hung up on losing one or two followers when there are hundreds of trials ongoing?"

Voltrain sighed, eyeing his brunette advisor.

"My concern lies more in what Eli is planning and his lack of respect," the god replied. "Interfering with the trials and shoehorning himself in without letting us know is one thing, but corrupting and poaching our Chosen is another."

"Well, you can't say it isn't deserved," the valkyrie said. "After all, you marked him for death."

"For being an anomaly!" Voltrain scowled, his hands arcing with power. "I should just strike him down. It would be a simple matter to atomize him."

"Then you would be in violation of the laws."

"Laws that Eli ignores!" Voltrain spat.

"Well..." Brynhilda paused. "You and I both know that the laws weren't intended for Primordials. Just be thankful Eli hasn't begun picking out more Chosen."

"Gah! This is such a headache."

"May I suggest," Brynhilda began, taking a deep breath, "that you rescind the death mark? Offer a truce with Eli's Chosen?"

"And kowtow to a mortal?!" Voltrain spat. "No. Never. If he wants to fight, I'll just send stronger followers. Ones that can't be corrupted!"

Voltrain took off. The god disappeared in a flash of brilliant light, leaving the valkyrie behind. Bryhilda could only sigh.

If this keeps up, I'll have to train another God of Light...

She frowned, pulling up a new screen. Depicted upon it was an image of Adam.

Catpurr 27
The Coin

"Great. More woods," Junith grumbled, following Adam through the thick shrubbery.

"What? Tired of the great outdoors?" he asked, scanning the tree line as he downed a mana recovery potion strapped to his chest.

Junith only rolled her eyes. "What's the plan?"

"Well, the first step of any adventure is to find out information."

"What about Liza?"

"What about her?" His golden eyes remained on the surrounding trees.

"Are we going to pursue our quest objective without her? Or without our allies?" Junith asked. She kept close, warily observing the dark depths of the surrounding trees

Adam sighed, a headache forming.

"It really doesn't matter to me if she lives or dies at this point. All my extra potions, food, and clothing are gone! Gone!" he yelled, throwing his hands into the air with exasperation.

"Still, if we are to survive there is power to be gained in numbers."

"Said the paladin to the necromancer," Adam muttered. Then he hesitated, one foot held in midair. "Hey."

"What?"

In his head, the memory of Junith protecting him with her shield played and played again. But he said nothing, only shaking his head to dispel the image

"Nothing. We need to press forward."

"An apt plan. Is there any rhyme or reason to our aimless push?"

"Well, once we find a road, we should be able to find a village or a town. Then we can gather information and proceed from there," Adam said, pausing beside a small stream of water.

"You're assuming there are towns or villages nearby. Or even roads."

"There's water. And where there's water, there'll be people. All we have to do now is follow the river upstream until we hit a village or spot a road."

"Bit optimistic. We could be walking for hours. Or even days," Junith groused.

Adam shot her an irritated look. "Then what do you suggest? I don't hear you having any solid plans."

The nekogirl looked away.

"That's what I thought," he said with a huff, then looked up. High above the nekos hung a pair of twin suns. Ever since they'd all been teleported away from the underground caverns of the Drowthraki, the suns hadn't budged an inch. "Thinking isn't your strong suit, just leave it to the professionals."

At his words Junith scowled, picking up speed and attempting to smack Adam. She stumbled instead, and on her way down grabbed at his waistband, yanking his pants down. The redhead's buttcheeks were exposed to the world as she faceplanted in a puddle of mud.

"Hey! What the Nyx was that for?!" Adam screamed, pulling his pants up.

"I wasn't trying to pants you! I was trying to hit you!" the paladin spat, retching mud out of her mouth. Mud caked her face; it would take a thorough washing to make clean again.

"What for?!"

"For calling me an idiot!" She flung some mud at Adam, who ducked.

"Hey! These are new robes!" Adam spat, kicking Junith in the face.

* * *

After following the stream for two hours, the forest was finally interrupted by a paved road. By now, both of the nekos were tired, cranky, and caked in dried mud.

"See? I told you we'd find civilization," Adam said. Two skelecats appeared from cat-shaped portals as he climbed atop them to read a wooden road sign. It was chipped and weathered with age, covered in soot.

Junith moaned, "We haven't found anything. All we've managed to do after two hours is come across a sign."

"A sign of civilization." Adam rubbed off the debris until a line of characters beneath were revealed.

"Which is currently rotted and in disrepair."

Ignoring Junith's pessimism, Adam climbed down and took out his notepad, recording the characters.

Hmm. Avarion left, Corydrun Right.

As in previous trials, the Administrator's translator allowed Adam to read and understand the characters, but it was still worth noting and deciphering the alphabet.

"So, where to now?" Junith asked. As she did so, a familiar presence touched Adam's mind—Liza. He froze up.

What the hell is she up to?

Junith noticed as her companion squinted into the distance

"What? What's wrong?"

"Something..." the nekomancer muttered. "But I don't know what. Liza is happy. And I'm unsure if that's a good thing or a bad thing."

Junith folded her arms, wondering what that half-wit was up to.

"Avarion or Corydrun?" he asked, snapping his fingers to get Junith's attention. There was nothing to do about it, so for now it was better to ignore the feelings coming from Liza. He could only hope it wouldn't bite him in the non-existent tail later.

"What's the difference?"

"How would I know? I'm not from this world," Adam said, matter-of-factly.

"Well, which one is a city?"

"Again. I don't know," he said flatly.

Junith looked left and right, pursing her lips.

"Flip a coin?"

"Eh, why not." He tossed up a silver coin in the air. It glinted in the light as it spun. "Heads Corydrun, tails Avarion?"

Junith and Adam watched the coin arc through the air until it landed in the dirt.

"Huh..." Adam blinked. Against all odds, the coin stood up on its side, perfectly balanced.

"Try... again?" Junith said.

Adam picked up the piece of metal, flipping it again but for a second time, it landed on its side.

"Is this a trick coin?" Adam muttered, wondering if Tim had scammed him.

"Let me try." As Junith flipped the coin, something entirely mundane happened, that now seemed almost unexpected—the coin landed on heads.

Adam plucked the coin out of the dirt, trying again. Once more, it landed standing up.

"What the Nyx?!" Adam spat, his face scrunching as he began flipping the metal piece over and over, the coin landing its edge each time.

He crouched down, putting his head to the dirt, narrowing his eyes as he lifted the coin a few inches off the ground. There would be no bets for guessing how it landed again.

"What even is this? Why?! WHAT?!" Adam asked, completely befuddled as Junith picked the coin up and tossed it. Again it landed on heads.

"Well. It seems Corydrun won," she said, snatching the coin away from a desperate Adam's clutches.

Catpurr 28
Are... Are You Robbing Me?

Hmm, I wonder if it has something to do with my Luck stat? Adam thought, eyeing the coin as it stood straight up in his hand. *But then if it does, how do I unlock it?*

He frowned as he and Junith proceeded down the road at a brisk pace for about three hours. Occasionally the nekomancer would stop to gather samples of alien foliage and flowers, collecting them in his vials.

After another hour, Adam looked up. The suns were still in the same place in the sky.

Maybe this world has a different day and night cycle, he considered. Then he took a moment to sketch the positions of the twin spheres of fire on a diagram in his notebook.

After a moment passed of nothing but the sounds of pen on paper, Adam flipped the book shut, angling his face up towards the suns. He seemed to bask in the light, a sigh of relief escaping his lungs as a lone tear fell along his cheek.

"What? What's wrong?" Junith asked, turning to him.

He shook his head, an almost fond smile on his face. "I never get tired of that sound."

"What? What sound?" Junith asked. Her hand moved to her sword's hilt as golden eyes scanned the treeline for threats, alert ears twitching up.

Adam slowly turned to her, wiping the tear from his eye.

"Silence."

Junith's face went slack, her hand dropping from her sword.

"You are almost just as insufferable as her," she said, rolling her eyes as she pushed Adam out the way. The paladin began marching along the path once more, back straight.

"Are you implying you find me as annoying as that halfwit?"

"Not annoying, *insufferable*. That oaf is twenty times more annoying than you, but at least she doesn't make me hate her."

"Said the woman who saved my life earlier," Adam quipped. He began to follow behind her, but in that instant, she paused, a solitary brow arched.

"What are you even talking about?"

"That archer. She fired an arrow at me that you defended me against," he said, recalling the event. "You could have let it strike me."

Junith scoffed.

"I was compelled to by your brand, this curse placed upon me," Junith spat suddenly.

"I never gave you the command."

"You didn't need to, your geas made me defend you."

Adam raised a brow.

"That's not true. I never set your geas to protect me," he replied, tapping his chin. Junith spun, placing a cold blade's edge against his throat.

"Fine! If you are so keen, you are my quarry! Mine!" Junith spat, her blade against Adam's carotid. "I will be the one to slay the kingslayer! If you are to die, it will be at my hands! Not some oaf who happened to get lucky while you were distracted!"

Adam's face scrunched.

"Said the woman who literally *attacked* me with a catapult and an army of Pegasus riders shooting arrows and magic at me!" Adam countered. "You even tried to decapitate me with an enchanted sword of Aku-Lame or something!"

"Akalym," Junith corrected, removing her blade. "And it's not as though I wanted to. The army was ordered to assemble and move by Duchess Volbrook's command. We all serve masters. If it were up to me the glory of your death would have been mine and mine alone."

Adan shook his head in disbelief.

"Who the Nyx is Volbrook?" he asked, confused.

"The noble whose father you polymorphed into a frog."

"I don't—" Adam froze, the memory of a pompous Duke insulting Schrödinger playing in his mind. "Oh... Oh!" Then he paused and gave a half-shrug. "Well, he deserved it."

"And this is why you're insufferable! Everywhere you go, chaos and death follow," she scoffed.

"That's not true."

Golden eyes narrowed, burning with a hunter's focused intensity. The short nekogirl advanced upon Adam. "Goldenrod City, Saffron City, Mauville, Jubilife, Castelia City. Every one of these places was either burned to the ground, overrun with monsters, or frozen solid! There are still yetis running around everywhere in Castelia!"

"To be fair, how was I supposed to know an ancient Cryo-Phoenix was slumbering beneath the mountain? Who even builds cities in mountains, anyway?"

"AND THEN! NOT TO MENTION! You killed our King, turned a Duke into a frog, destroyed a cultural monument—!"

"Whoa, whoa, whoa! Hold up. The last thing I would *ever* do is try and destroy historical landmarks," Adam said, offended. "I don't even know what you're talking—"

"The labyrinth."

"Oh..."

"WHICH YOU COLLAPSED AND BURIED ME IN! IT TOOK ME FIVE DAYS OF DIGGING WITH MY HELMET TO CLIMB MY WAY OUT!" Junith screamed, her tail lashing. She stepped forwards again, now standing inches from Adam. He winced as spittle spattered his face.

"You survived, didn't you? And that was your fault. I was looking for traces of my master and you wouldn't stop chasing me!"

"BECAUSE YOU'RE A MENACE TO SOCIETY!"

"Said the genocidal paladin to the pioneer! My intentions for society have been nothing but pure!" Adam countered.

Junith thrust out an arm to either side as she shouted, "News flash, heretic! Not everyone agrees with your vision of society!"

"Well, maybe they're wrong! At least my vision doesn't include the wholesale slaughter of innocents!"

"No! Just unchecked destruction wherever you go! Millions, Adam! Millions dead from your last trial alone!"

"And I told you that wasn't my fault! How was I—" he began, but the rustle of leaves interrupted their argument.

Both spun, eyeing the treeline, eyes narrowing and pupils wide as they picked up humanoid silhouettes and movement.

"If you're trying to ambush us, we can see you!" Junith barked, pointing her sword at a silhouette. "Come out!"

The rustling stopped.

"Ha!" a voice cackled, causing both nekos to tense up.

"Well, well, well. What do we have 'ere?" a voice asked. Stepping out from a nearby bush was a bald ruffian with pointed ears, clad in hide armor. "Several would-be heroes, aye?"

Suddenly several more figures emerged, each brandishing crude weapons and mismatched gear.

"Seriously?" Adam said aloud, eyeing the twelve bandits surrounding him and Junith. "You're robbing kids."

"Oh, you ain't just kids, I can sees it, ya know! Your shinies! Ain't no Drowthraki walking the surface that ain't either a richie or a soldier!" the bald man said, wearing a wicked grin. "We'll take ya shinies, then we'll pocket you out for coin!"

Adam closed his eyes for a moment, taking a breath before opening his eyes.

"Let me get this straight," Adam said, holding up a finger. "You're robbing us."

"Dat's right! Hand me your pretty staff and I'll letcha keep your life," the man said. In his hand he held out a knife, waving it as he gestured.

"Riiight," Adam said, his expression shifting.

Despite their differences, if there was one thing Adam and Junith both despised, it was the bandits, highwaymen, and vagabonds that preyed on the weak. Enough so that it distracted the pair from their hatred for each other.

Adam gave his ultimatum as Junith looked on with eyes narrowed. "I'm only going to give you this one warning. Leave. Now."

"Or what?" The man laughed, drawing a chorus of chuckles from the other bandits.

The nekoboy's shoulders slumped.

"Junith... Fold this man into a pretzel," he ordered. A vicious grin, all pointy fangs, broke out across the paladin's face. "And break the others' legs so they can't run. I have questions."

"With pleasure," Junith said, cracking her knuckles.

Catpurr 29

Answering My Questions

"Ya know, Junith…" the nekomancer said, appreciating the human pyramid of interlinked, broken limbs and cries of pain. "I was beginning to think you had no artistic talent, but this is some fine craftsmanship. One could almost declare it art."

"Pllleease. We said we were s-s-sorry," one of the bandits in the pile tearfully moaned.

"Well, I've had a lot of practice," Junith said, dragging two tree branches beside the bandits.

"What are you doing?" Adam asked, looking down at the kindling.

"Preparing the cleansing ceremony."

"Cleansing?" He raised his brow. "Wait, are you trying to set them on fire?!"

"Obviously," she replied. At her words, a low chorus of fearful cries went up from the highwaymen as two of them began to beg. "Hush, scoundrels!"

"Down! Bad paladin! Bad!" Adam reprimanded, bonking Junith on the head with his staff. She growled.

"Oh, thank you, thank you!" the leader sobbed, his forked tongue flicking out.

"Oh, I'm not done with you lot," Adam said, patting the bald man on his cheek.

"Wha—What are you going to do to us? A-Are you going to eat us?"

One of Adam's brows shot up. "Uh. No. I just need directions," he said.

"Directions? Yes! Directions! I can give directions!"

"We can give directions, please don't eat us!" one of the bandit lackeys chimed in while another groaned, "My leeeeegs."

"Good. Good." Adam smiled, tapping the man. "Junith."

"What?" asked the nekogirl as she kicked at the dirt.

"Heal these men."

The paladin blinked. "What? Absolutely not."

"P-P-Please," a bandit twisted into a pretzel moaned.

"Shut up," she spat, punching the offender before her body started to glow. "Why should I waste precious mana on lowlife scum?"

"Because they have something I need," Adam said, picking up one of the crude weapons off the ground. "Plus, there might be reward money if we turn them in."

The nekoboy then paused, turning to the leader of the bandits.

"You guys do have bounties on your heads, right?" Adam asked, rubbing his fingers together.

"B-Bounties? Yes! We're famous! Grig! Tell him! Tell him we're famous!" a bandit cried. The leader, apparently named Grig, agreed, "Y-Yes! We're the Gangpunchers."

"Gangpunchers?" Junith raised a brow. "Crap name."

"It's all of our names combined, starting with me, Grig, then Antho—"

"Excellent!" Adam clapped his hands, interrupting the man. "Junith. Heal them."

The reluctant priestess of Eli frowned, but ultimately went to work disassembling her creation. Those who had yet to pass out from shock wept and cried out from the pain.

Eventually the twelve bandits were left on the side of the road, still groaning in agony, but now with significantly more personal space.

"Now that I've done something for you, you'll have to do something for me," Adam said, staring at the Grig. The bandit leader wasted no time in groveling.

"Oh! Anything! Anything at all!" Grig yelled, kissing Adam's boot.

"Stop it! Get off!" That same boot then kicked the pointy-eared man in the face.

"Sorry! Sorry! Sorry!" Grig whimpered, shoving his head in the dirtThe rest of his followers copied him. "We'll do anything you say, Boss! Anything! Please don't eat us!"

"Really?" Adam said, eyeing the shiny bits of metal decorating the man's fingers and ears. "Strip."

"Wha?"

"Get naked. Right now."

Grig clutched his chest, shying away, his face a little red. "P-P-Please... Please be gentle."

"What?" Adam said. The other men were beginning to weep again, some gazing tearfully at each other. "Just give me all your stuff."

"Oh." Grig chuckled slightly, which soon became a torrent of laughs from the whole group.

"What's so funny?" Junith spat, punching her fist into her palm with a glare.

"N-N-Nothing! Mistress!"

"Then get undressed!" she spat. The bandits quickly shed their clothes, jewelry, and other knick knacks. Soon all twelve men were huddled together in their underwear.

Junith narrowed her eyes.

"Your underwear, too."

"P-Please, please no! Leave us some dignity!"

Grig turned to Adam with large, tearful eyes. The redhead only shrugged.

"Underwear can be sold," he said. Grig hiccupped, and reluctantly moved a hand to his stained underwear.

* * *

"It's... so cold," Grig whined. Plodding alongside the nekopair was the naked collection of vagrants and miscreants, carrying what until recently had been their own belongings.

"Would you like me to heat you up?" Purple flames wreathed Junith's hands.

"N-N-No, mistress."

"Then shut up and don't speak unless spoken to."

Grig whimpered.

"You said we were thirty minutes out from town," Adam said. They had been walking for forty minutes now, with nothing in sight but trees, hills, and rocks. "Where's the town?"

"Uh, that way, Boss." Grig pointed at a nearby hilltop.

Adam turned to the elf. "There's nothing there."

Suddenly the man's legs buckled, his knees kicked from behind by Junith who spun the man around and grabbed him by his ears.

"Ow! OW!" Grig whined as Junith pulled.

"You better not have made us walk for an hour just to lead us to the middle of nowhere!" she yelled.

"I swear! It's there! I swear! Ripping! You're ripping my ears! The city is underground! Please! My ears! They aren't tasty! They're really gamey!"

That was the final straw for one of the bandits who stumbled back, whining, before trying to make a break for it—but Junith wasn't having it. In one fluid motion she dropped Grig and spun, nailing the man in the back of her head with her thrown shield. The bandit collapsed to the ground, and the paladin took her time approaching the downed man. As he lay curled in the dirt, she made quick work breaking both his legs.

A gut-wrenching scream was dragged from his lungs.

"Anyone else want to run?" Junith barked. The other survivors' pale faces and wide eyes gazed back. "No? Good. You." Junith pointed at a tall bandit as the runaway screamed and cried.

"M-Me?"

"Yes, you. Pick up your friend."

"Yes, mistress! Right away, mistress!" the elf yelled, obeying.

Why do they call her mistress? Adam thought to himself, but didn't pursue that train of thought. Instead, he turned to the hill, narrowing his eyes. "Alright. Lead the way."

The bandits looked at one another.

"What?" Adam asked.

"A-Are you—Are you sure you won't eat us?" Grig asked.

"Is there something I'm missing? Why do you keep asking that?"

Grig looked at his fellow elves. They all exchanged baffled looks. Finally Grig turned back to the nekoboy and said, "Because the crime for banditry is being eaten."

Adam blinked as Junith's eyes became wide as moons.

"Wait, are you saying the penalty for banditry is... cannibalism?" Adam asked as Grigs and the other light skinned elves looked at one another.

"Yes," Grit said as if it were the most obvious thing in the world.

Catpurr 30

Learning About the World

"I don't like this," Junith said. She stood amidst several red-leafed trees, interwoven boughs so thick they could have been called a tunnel which supposedly led down to the city they were seeking, somewhere on the other side of the tree-made corridor. "This could be a trap."

"Well, nothing ventured, nothing gained," Adam replied, sifting through the pile of clothes, jewelry, and knick knacks taken from the bandits.

"So then, what are you going to do with them?" A small, clawed finger pointed towards their naked captives shivering in the wind.

"Ask them a few more questions, then probably let them go." Junith looked at Adam oddly. He ignored her, in favor of opening a bag that seemed stuffed with colorful wigs and make-up.

"Wait. What?"

"You heard me," he said, pocketing several coins and stuffing them into the pouches of his leather armor. He grabbed a shirt from the pile of the bandits' possessions, inspecting it with a critical golden eye.

"They're scum! Bandits, who deserve no pity or remorse!" Junith yelled. The group shrunk back in fear as she brandished her sword towards them.

"While I am in agreement with you for once, they are of much more use to me alive than dead," Adam said. He was distracted from one of the shirt's mystery stains by the discovery of a small crest, a crown above a downward-pointing sword. A quick examination revealed that each shirt was marked with the same crest.

"How so?"

"Well, it just occurred to me that we know so little about this world," he said. Carefully he removed one of the silver coins, running a thumb across the same emblem, embossed across it. "What can you tell me about these two items?"

To her credit, Junith did not scoff at the request and gave both items a cursory glance. As she looked closer, her eyes narrowed before she answered, "The emblems are the same."

"Which tells us?"

"They could be deserters of an army." She frowned. "Or they stole the uniforms. Either way, they are scum."

"We won't know unless we ask." Adam snapped his fingers, the crisp sound ringing out. The elf named Grig jolted, before approaching the nekopair.

"Y-Yes, Boss?"

"What are these emblems?" Adam asked.

"Ah..." The man grimaced. "The emblem of Armayas, Boss."

"And Armayas is?"

"A kingdom, B-Boss."

"Were you a soldier?"

"Y-Yes. A kith, Boss," the naked elf said before gesturing to his group. "These are my men."

"Kith?" Adam echoed.

"Our word for Knight," Grig replied. Junith's glare suddenly intensified and Grig withered under the force of it. Adam only raised a brow.

"You? A knight?" The paladin laughed. "Please."

"It's true! I swear it, mistress!" Grig replied. "Sworn to uphold the laws of Armayas and to fight for its people!"

"By robbing passersby?" she spat angrily. But to Adam, it was already a familiar story. Many times during his travels to uncover lichdom, he had come across people like Grig. Soldiers, mercenaries, and peasants, down-on-their-luck people forced to resort to banditry, often after their leaders were defeated.

"Well, Armayas don't exist no more and we all gotta make a living, so—" The man cut his sentence short, bowing his head to avoid Junith's death glare.

"Alright. Down, Junith. Go watch over the others. And no killing," Adam ordered. The nekogirl hissed but did as told. High above, the twin suns beat down upon the earth. The nekomancer gazed at them for a moment, before turning to address the fallen Kith. "Tell me more about Armayas."

* * *

Adam sighed, pondering the information he just received from the bandit leader and his men. Apparently, the continent was known as Cardia, the largest of three landmasses in the world, dominated by the surface nation of Armayas.

Or that had been the case until several months ago. One fateful day, the last bastion of civilization and government, Cadia, fell to Bullert's wrath. The Cardian continent was consumed by chaos, carved up amongst warlords bleakly fighting for their own survival, trying to secure trade routes while fending off the subterranean Drowthraki. Sheltered in massive caverns below the earth, only they had been spared from the fowl apocalypse. Well, until recently, Adam supposed.

"Tell me more about the Webway," he asked. On his lap, his sketchpad was turned to a fresh page, already scrawled over with his notes on this world, and a rudimentary map of the regions Grig had laid out for him.

"It's ruled by the matriarch they call the Lady of Silk and her princesses," Grig explained. "Winding tunnels, the Webway is a buncha cities underground that are filled by Drowthraki. Not to question ya, Boss, but you don't know this?"

"I'm from a different continent," Adam replied bluntly in-between taking notes. "We don't live underground."

"Then ya were spared the feathered fowl?!"

"Uh... Sure," he said, lying through his teeth. "Let's go with that. Tell me more about this continent's Drowthraki."

"They're sick! Cannibals that enslave any man they come across! It's thanks to them we lost the feckin' war!" Grig suddenly yelled. "Them and their backstabbin' crown-wearin' princesses!"

That caused Adam to pause, frowning as several dots in his mind threatened to connect. Not far off, there was a commotion as another of the captured bandits tried to flee. He was quickly caught, pummeled, and thrown back amongst his comrades by Junith as the nekogirl viciously taunted the other cowering bandits, daring them to run.

Explains the crap treatment. And why they thought Liza was a princess... Adam thought, recalling how the woman kept gazing at him with contempt while indulging the nekogirl's whims. *And here I was beginning to think all women just hated me.*

"Enslave men..." he voiced aloud, trailing off as his gaze landed upon the bag of wigs. "I take it this bag has something to do with that."

"Yes!" Grig said proudly. "In order to infiltrate the cities, I! Grig Bilwad of the Gangpunchers, came up with this brilliant plan!"

"By... pretending to be women?" Adam slowly looked up, eyeing the group of bandits who weren't the most... feminine of individuals.

"Brilliant, ain't it?!" Grig said, his chest puffed up. "The ol' darkies can't pick us apart on account of us being light skinned. We all look alike to them!"

"Riiiight." A rhythmic, staccato sound caused Adam's ears to prick up, distracting him from the conversation.

Marching.

"Somethin' wrong, bos—"

"Ssssh." Adam turned his head, eyeing the three dozen or so armored Drowthraki exiting the tunnel entrance in the side of the hill. Protected by them were several Drowthraki men dragging a series of carts, decorated with flying purple banners emblazoned with spider emblems. Reclining atop one of these carts was a Drowthraki woman, heavily veiled in laces and silks.

A warband or an escort, Adam guessed as he watched the procession, but judging by the crown atop the woman's head, if he had to bet money he would have guessed the latter. Once the procession had left the area, the nekoboy turned to the naked elf.

"Is there someone in your band with artistic talent?"

"S-S-Sir?"

"Artistic talent."

"Uh... Thud does," Grig said, pointing out his large, lumbering companion.

Wait, how does that fit into the anagram 'Gangpunchers'?

Adam narrowed his eyes, looking between the bag of wigs and the man, debating his choices and options.

"Grig. How would you like to earn some honest currency?"

"M-M-Me?"

"Oh, not just you, but your entire crew," Adam said. A smile crept across his face, one that caused Grig to shudder.

Catpurr 31
Makeover Edition

"Meow."

—Schrödinger

"Seriously?" Junith asked, her face twisted with disgust as she gazed down at Adam. Crowding him were several bandits working in serious concentration.

"Hush! Don't distract an artist as they work!" a muscular bandit by the name of Thud hissed.

Unexpectedly, Junith backed off, surprised by the bandit's abrupt command, leaving them to their delicate operation.

Thud paused to wipe his brow, the man's scarred face scrunching as he narrowed his green eyes and focused, adding the final touches to his masterpiece.

"There... I've done all I can," he said, backing away as the now half-naked crowd gaped in awe.

"Well... How do I look?" Adam's voice asked. As Thud stepped back, he revealed a pale-skinned girl, hair like moonlight cascading down her shoulders and back. Thick lashes curtained her eyes, and her cheeks were the same color as the rosy dawn. But this wasn't a girl— this was Adam's disguise, courtesy of the wig and make-up.

"Stunnin', Boss," Grig said, stroking his chin as the rest of the bandits nodded in agreement.

"Are you serious? Are we seriously going with the plan suggested by a highwayman?" Junith asked. "You realize how stupid this is, right?"

"Oui!" Grig ordered. But upon drawing the nekogirl's ire once more, he quickly looked away.

"Like it or not, this is our ticket into the city," Adam replied, accepting a mirror Thud handed to him and taking in his new appearance.

"So, am I supposed to call you Adama or something?" Junith snickered. "What happens when someone asks you a question? Are you going to fake a girl's voice?"

"Uh... Sure? I guess?" he said, raising his pitch and tone to practice his voice. "Like this? Like this? Hello? Hello?"

Junith facepalmed as Grig and Thud gave a thumbs up.

"Hmmm, can we make this shorter? I don't want it getting snagged on anything and pulled off," Adam said, playing with his locks.

"Sure thing, Boss," Thud said, producing a pair of scissors. He snipped away at the silver wig until it only reached Adam's shoulders.

"Stunnin', beautiful, a modern work of art. You'd make a fine looker, Boss," Grig complimented as several bandits voiced their assent.

"Really?" Adam said, a glint appearing in his eyes. *Perhaps I could use this to my advantage.*

"Alright. As promised. Payment," he said. At the word the gathered bandits perked up, gradually inching closer.

The nekoboy stood unmoving, staring at the waiting robbers. As time passed, they began to grow antsy, some glancing towards their leader.

"Uh... Not to rusha or anything, Boss..." Grig said, scratching the back of his head. "But errr, where's da payment?"

"You're alive, aren't you?" Adam said, raising a brow. "And I even gave you all back your underwear."

"Uh... I suppose that's true." Grig grimaced, he and his men visibility deflating. "But you did say we'd be earning money."

"Currr—ency," Adam corrected with a smile. "And what more precious commodity than life and blood."

At the nekomancer's words a few of the bandit's faces soured. A look from the armored nekogirl standing behind him, however, was quick to reveal to them the wisdom in the advice.

"Uh... Sure, Boss," Grig said. "D-Does that mean we can go?"

Adam turned to Junith. "What do you think?"

"I say we kill them all," she replied deadpan.

"You're free to go." The bandits quickly scattered at the boy's words as Junith's voice contorted.

"Seriously?! Why even ask for my opinion if you were just going to let them run free?!" she demanded.

"Simple, I'm conducting an experiment where you suggest something, then I do the opposite of that—" The girl grabbed him, pulling back a hand to slap him "—HEY! Watch the make-up, numbskull! Don't ruin my disguise!"

"I'm not a numbskull!" she yelled before electricity zapped her and forced the paladin to let Adam go. "Gah, this is going to get us killed."

"Tsk, I thought you wanted me dead," he retorted, turning towards the entrance to the Drowthraki city of Cordryun.

"By *my* hand. Not by some backwater, underground, dark-skinned, abhuman scum who aren't even blessed by the light of the righteous lord," Junith said, following behind him.

"Riiiight. Righteous." Adam rolled his eyes, stepping out of the bush to walk towards the cave. "Are we still on this?"

Junith clicked her teeth. "This isn't going to work. Won't they find it odd that two children are walking around alone? What if they require ID, or permits or something? Or search us for being suspicious?"

"Well, according to Grig, they don't do any of that as long as you're a woman. And they didn't last time."

"Again, you're trusting the word of a bandit!" Junith yelled, throwing her hands in the air as Adam deposited his staff into his storage ring. "A bandit!"

"And that's why you've got a sword and shield," he said. Carefully he scanned the smooth cavern walls with his dark vision, until he noticed a faint source of light coming from around an upcoming bend. "Besides, with all of our supplies gone, we need sustenance, information, and a safe place to hole up in so I can evolve."

"Evolve?"

"Ah. Don't worry about it." Perhaps his evolution points were better kept to himself, actually.

Junith grimaced but followed the nekomancer's lead. Their march was halted, however, as they came up against an iron gate, torches flickering around it.

"This is a dumb idea," Junith growled again. The iron gate slowly winched open as Drowthraki in purplish-black armor emerged.

"Hush," Adam whispered, observing the soldiers.

The men looked down, observing the nekopair as they stepped to the side in equally perfect formation and silence.

Interesting... In silence, Adam watched the soldiers back. In unison the soldiers bowed, allowing the nekopair through.

"See, I told you everything would be fine," Adam whispered. Beyond the gate was an expansive tunnel, serving as a buffer.

"If this fails, don't say I didn't tell you so," Junith replied.

"Oh ye of little faith. Worst comes to worst, we'll just set fire to everything and raise an army of the dead." Junith's expression became one of horror, and Adam sighed. "I'm kidding."

At last, the two exited the tunnel, stepping into the main system of caverns which housed their destination—the city of Cordryun. Both nekos came to a halt, frozen by the unforgettable sight laid out before them.

"Ah... interesting," Adam said. Hundreds of Drowthraki across the cavern were a little too distracted to greet the two newcomers, far more occupied by their acts of excessive revelry and debauchery.

Catpurr 32

School Arc? Bargaining with Schrödinger

"I want to get out of here," Junith whispered. The woman was visibly uncomfortable as they continued down the path, paved with dark stone. She whispered beneath moans of pleasure and loud music, blaring from the clay and black-stone buildings.

"We will, when I get some supplies," Adam said. He stopped as a bright green banner atop one building caught his eye, emblazoned with the symbol of the Goddess Freya. Several chained men were being led through its ornate double doors.

Slave house... Interesting, he thought to himself. While the idea of owning people was absurd to him, it was still a location worth checking out. For reasons of science and documentation, of course. *I wonder if I could buy a servant for Schrödinger....*

"Why can't we just hunt for food? Like we did before?" Junith reasoned, interrupting Adam's thoughts. Some Drowthraki passersby looked at them oddly.

Hmm... It's a city, yet I haven't seen any children. He took a moment to look up at the ceiling, layered with pipes, before replying to Junith.

"Because there's only so much information to be gleaned from hunting, and I require a place to rest comfortably without the chance of a fire breathing fowl eating me," he said.

He took out the coins pilfered from Grig, his gaze locking onto a nearby inn.

Roodaka's Hovel, Adam read on the sign. The letters were written in gold, suspended by what appeared to be web above the entrance.

Oh, wait. Adam sighed, realizing he'd forgotten to ask the bandit the conversion and worth of the coins.

Great. Nothing ventured...

The boy turned and opened the door. Groups of female Drowthraki patrons stopped to stare at the nekopair as they approached the counter, tended by a tall and slender drow as she busily served drinks.

"Um. Excuse me," Adam squeaked, imitating a girl's voice as Junith facepalmed. "Are there any available rooms to rent out?"

The woman spun, her purple eyes widening upon spotting the pair.

"Room?" the barmaid asked, blinking. "Shouldn't you two be in school?"

Oh, crapbaskets.

"It's... a holiday?" Adam said, the first excuse he could think of bursting from his mouth.

"I know, which is why you girls should be in school, not galavanting around during the Festival of Lshkerdink," the woman said, looking Adam up and down, her eyes narrowing as if something were wrong. "Why do you stink of men?"

"Uh..." he replied, before he cleared his throat. "I was down by the slave market?"

"Take a seat at that table. Bernadotte, watch these two while I scry for the academy truancy officer," the barmaid said as a bald woman in armor with sharp eyes appeared from the ceiling, dropping down beside Adam and Junith.

"Go," the bald woman demanded, folding her arms.

"Is this all part of your plan?" Junith whispered, as the two took a seat at a wooden table in the corner.

"No, but this works greatly in our favor," Adam whispered back, a massive smile on his face.

"How so?!"

"Well, if it's an academy, they'll have all the information I'd need." His heart fluttered in his chest as he imagined such a bastion of academia and knowledge. "Plus! I've never been to an academy! Imagine all the books, the knowledge, and research! All at the cusp of our fingertips!"

"Can you calm down? Your voice is starting to break!" Junith hissed. She was too aware of each time the bald Drowthraki glanced at them from the bar.

"Of course, a knuckle dragger like you wouldn't understand. Your kind burnt down or destroyed most learning institutions."

Junith leaned back, a look of shock on her face. "My kind? What does that even mean?"

"Fan—na—tics," Adam sounded out, pointing at Junith, who scoffed.

"Of course we burnt them down," the paladin said as if it were an obvious choice. "Why would we condone the spreading of knowledge that would slander our lord of light?"

"Ah! So you admit to purposely destroying knowledge to make everyone as dumb as you!" Adam yelled as he pointed at Junith. She quite rationally responded by climbing over the counter and hitting him, repeatedly screaming, "I'm not dumb!"

"Yes, these two right here, Officer Thesla," the barkeeper said, shortly before two hands grabbed and separated the nekopair as they spat and hissed.

"Thanks for reporting this, Roodaka," said the woman in a purple uniform, adorned with various insignia and emblems. She held the two writhing nekos apart from each other, glowering at them. "Alright, you Hvisklicas, let's get you back to the academy."

"Yes!" Adam squeaked. The officer gave him a surprised look but remained otherwise silent. She ushered the children back out the door as she rubbed her hands where she'd be scratched.

* * *

Elsewhere, in a faraway realm...
POV: Schrödinger

"Meow. Meow, meow, meow. Meow meow."

Deep within the sacred depths Holy Sanctum of Voltrain, the prodigious Dominic von Chesty le Blanc, Greatest of All Swordsman of the Church of Voltrain, man blessed in the holy waters of Viliskapor, Slayer of Wingelum the Tyrant Penguin, man of a thousand women, sat cross-legged in a ruined building across from a white fluffy creature, vibrating as it lay curled up atop what had until quite recently been *his* flaming holy sword.

The paladin hesitantly reached out to the weapon's hilt, but no sooner had he barely brushed it did the cat hiss. Von Chesty's fingers flinched back.

"May I please have my sword?" von Chesty asked, fidgeting with his fingers.

"Meow." The cat yawned before it snuggled the blade, ignoring the man.

Von Chesty reached into his pocket, revealing several cat treats.

"Please? I'll trade you. Don't you want a treat?" von Chesty bargained as a pair of scribes struggled to drag a large bed beside the paladin. "We even got you a new bed! It has heating enchantments and back vibration supports! Crafted by Lord Geppeto himself!"

"Meeeeeeeow," the cat dismissed in a disinterested, drawn-out meow. All around the two, a number of clergy and knights looked on as their greatest champion engaged in a heated battle of wits with the necromancer's abominable feline. Several seemed to be questioning if *this* was truly the best use of the Church's time and resources.

"Is everything okay, mi'lord?" a clergyman asked.

"*Of course!*" von Chesty bellowed, rising to his feet instantly with a proud and righteous look. From a hole in the roof a ray of sunlight beamed down, haloing him in a golden glow. "I, Dominic von Chesty le Blanc! Break dance master, champion of the grand prix, slayer of the Kanasaur! Have everything under control! Do you dare question your betters?!"

"O-O-Oh! Of course, mi'lord!" the clergyman squealed before shrinking back. "It was not my intention to question your magnificence, mi'lord!"

Von Chesty let out a laugh, waving the crowd off before leaning down and whispering to Schrödinger, "C'mon, I'm asking nicely! Please! You're embarrassing me in front of all my friends!"

"Meow," Schrödinger replied, opening its mouth and setting the new bed on fire, much to the horror of von Chesty and the scribes gathered.

"WHAT ARE YOU DOING?! THAT WAS A GENUINE GEPPETTO!" von Chesty screamed. But alas, the once luxurious bed, supported by finely carved pillars and made with silken sheets was now hardly better than matchwood.

Von Chesty spun, drawing his sword and slamming it down upon the white cat.

[Attack nullified!]

"GAH!" the holy paladin of Voltrain screamed in frustration as men and women in black and blue striped uniforms descended from above, quickly dousing the flames with water and various cold abilities that snuffed the heat from the air. After a month of constant fireballs, blasts of flames, and breaths of fire, a fire force had been created to quickly deal with any potential outbreak of flames.

Von Chesty sighed, pinching the bridge of his nose.

"What do I have to give you in order for you to be happy?!" he screamed, the paladin on the verge of a breakdown.

Suddenly, Schrödinger stood. The cat strutted off the holy blade, approaching von Chesty with single-minded focus. His eyes widened with surprise and worry, mouth falling open as he staggered backwards.

Then he lunged forwards. Now was his chance to collect his church's sacred weapon! Now, while the foul beast was distracted! His heart thudded in his chest, his palms slick with sweat. But the star of the church of Voltrain was too slow.

HEAVY!

"UHK!" Von Chesty let out a great gasp, staggering under the full weight of the feline fiend as it bore down upon his body, crushing it against the cratered marble floor. Like an upturned insect, his arms flailed futilely.

"MI'LORD!"

"VON CHESTY IS DOWN!"

"THE BEAST IS KILLING THE ONE!"

"SEND FOR THE POPE!"

The scribes all screamed in concert, racing around the room to try and free their champion, left utterly powerless against the feline.

"I can see him! He's alive!" a scribe yelled, peeling at the rubble to spot von Chesty, whose face was red and struggling to breath. "Are you okay, mi'lord?!"

Von Chesty let out in short gasps. "I, Sir Dominic... Von Chesty... bearer of Voltrain's symbol, require... medical assistance!"

Catpurr 33

Ellie the Troublemaker

As the professors droned on—something about chemistry, this time—Ellie couldn't help but heave a sigh. The violet-eyed Drowthraki schoolgirl found it impossible to focus on her lessons, and instead stared out the classroom's window into the dark shadows of the expansive underground.

Ugh. What's the point of this? After a few days we'll all be duck food, she groaned as she set her head down. Her cheek found the pre-existing imprint of her face in the cool, brown wood of the desk.

"Psst! Hey! Keep your head up! Don't sleep," whispered a voice to the side as Ellie felt something nudge her.

"Lemme sleep," Ellie nudged, batting away her friend Karlie as the other Drowthraki girl kept trying to wake her.

Suddenly something bounced off Ellie's head, an eraser thrown at her by Professor Scholl. The long-haired Drowthraki scowled at the student as Ellie raised her weary head.

"I'm sorry, am I boring you, Ms. Hall?"

"Nooo," Ellie said, as all eyes in the classroom turned to her.

"Then why is your head down?"

The girl didn't respond, her gaze drawn back to the window as though by gravity.

"See me after class," the professor said before going back to her work.

* * *

"Your grades are slipping, you're constantly sleeping, and you've been giving all the teachers an attitude for the past week," Professor Scholl said, adjusting her wide brim glasses. "The constables even came up to me looking for you the other day, what's going on?"

Ellie scowled, folding her arms. "You know what's going on."

At Ellie's reply, the teacher could only sigh.

"Those are just rumors. Nothing more, nothing less," the teacher assured, tapping one finger on her wooden desk.

"Yeah, well, that's a lie," Ellie said as she rolled her eyes. "Word travels, ya know? Even if ya keep us imprisoned here, we hear what's happening on the surface world."

"Imprisoned? This isn't a prison, Ellera."

At the use of her full name, Ellie's scowl deepened. "Well, it sure feels like one," she countered. "What's the point of class and continuing the day to day when we're all going to be duck—"

The professor slammed her palm on the desk, stopping Ellie.

"We don't know that for sure!" Professor Scholl snapped before she inhaled, composing herself. "I would be most appreciative if you didn't spread unsubstantiated rumors."

"Tsk." Ellie turned her head.

"I'll have to give you a red mark for sleeping in class. This is the fourth one you've earned, so I'll have to give you detention."

There was the scratch of quill on paper as the processor wrote something down.

"Whatever," Ellie said, taking the slip of paper before marching out of the classroom. Waiting for her in the hall was Karlie.

"Detention?"

"Yup," Ellie sighed.

"You know this goes on your permanent record, right? You shouldn't be sleeping in class and blowing off your studies," Karlie berated, walking arm in arm with Ellie.

"What's the point?" the other girl groaned, her shoulders sagging.

"Oh, by our Lady in Silk, are you still on this? You're so pessimistic! This is why you don't have any friends."

"It's true though, isn't it? What's the point of studying when the duckysaurs are marching their way across the continent? The Bangaas and light skins have already been defeated and last I heard, Cadia fell at Bullert's hand," Ellie countered. The two entered the school cafeteria, taking a seat at one of the many square tables. "It's only a matter of time before they dig their way to us!"

At Ellie's outburst, several students turned to her with matching disapproving looks.

"Sssh. Shut up!" Karlie hissed, stabbing at the buttons on the table that would call their food.

Ellie folded her arms, trembling in her seat until she suddenly exploded, standing up. "I'm tired of this mundane day to day, waiting around until we get killed. I've never seen the ocean, I've never seen the surface, I haven't even had my first kiss!" She punctuated the last words with a sharp, two-palm *smack!* against the table.

Around the pair, whispers were breaking out. Two adults approached the girls, their uniforms marking them as officers.

"Ms. Hall, please check your tone or you will be subject to a red mark," the woman in a blue uniform said, gesturing for her to sit back down.

"Hm." Ellie complied, clutching her face in her hands. Then she suddenly sat back up, hands falling away to reveal an uncharacteristic smile.

"What? Why do you look like that? Why are you smiling?" Karlie asked, narrowing her purple eyes at her friend. Ellie said nothing, instead rising from her seat. "Where are you going? The food is here."

"Outside."

"To the courtyard?" Karlie said. The meal of cooked fish had just arrived, placed on their table by a black-suited man holding what looked like a ball gag in his mouth.

"No. Outside," Ellie said as she narrowed her eyes and planned her escape.

"B-But you have detention! It'll go on your record!" Karlie exclaimed, standing to follow Ellie as the girl left the cafeteria.

Catpurr 34

Calm Before the Catbreak

"Wait here," the truancy officer instructed, leaving Adam and Junith at the iron gate of an enormous structure.

Adam's jaw had long been left on the floor. With eyes as large as saucers he marveled at the structure before him. It resembled an obsidian spire, darker than the dark surrounding it in a way that easily drew the eye, connected to the ceiling by lacey black webs. The mighty pillar seemed to bear not just knowledge, but the very city of Cordyun itself. Patterns in glass dappled its sides offering tantalizing glimpses within, and crystalline balconies traced its side in symmetrical designs. The whole structure seemed like a great world tree, tempting Adam with delicious fruits, which wouldn't be left forbidden for long.

"It's... beautiful," he mused. Junith was gawking, too—not at the building itself, but at how her companion whipped out his sketchbook to draw the structure.

Perhaps I could order Dungeon to adopt a similar design, he considered.

"Alright, you Hvisklicas, let's go," the officer said as she returned.

Hvisklicas? What's that mean? That the world wasn't automatically translated stuck out to him and piqued his curiosity. *Seems like the System isn't infallible.*

Upon passing through the iron gates, Adam followed the tall woman along a gravel path, flanked by lush, luminescent blue flora.

The light cast by the plants gave the entire area a mystical ambience, making it feel as though they had stepped into another realm entirely.

At the center of the garden was an odd statue cast in marble, its pale stone almost glowing against the surrounding dark architecture. Eight spindly legs delicately arced over the ground, coming together to form a spider's abdomen. Sprouting up from the arachnid lower-half was an elegant, humanoid woman's upper torso, wielding an intricately carved staff.

Man, Liza would not appreciate it here, Adam thought, eyeing the hundreds of cobwebs that covered the garden, each crawling with colorful spiders. *Note to self, perhaps this garden holds some religious value. Best not to mess with the spiders.*

At the other end of the garden a wooden door towered above them, iron and gold etched into the polished surface.

Impressive. Though they were foreign to him, Adam could tell that powerful, magical sigils had been embossed upon the door.

"Here they are," the truancy officer said. At last, the small group came to a stop at a reception desk, manned by another purple-uniformed drow. The receptionist sat with a dull expression, not bothering to look up from the see-through figures projected from a crystal.

The receptionist waved apathetically, saying, "The ones who snuck into a slave house? Yeah, I don't recognize them. Just throw them with the two runaways. We'll get it sorted out after the Ghstliki." The officer waved nonchalantly, her focus completely on one see-through character tackling another.

Interesting. Adam's eyes locked on the moving pictures, his feet dragging until the truancy officer shoved him forwards.

"Keep going, no sports for you," Officer Thesla said, as the three walked through a hallway crammed with books.

Adam smiled. Hundreds of tomes, a hallway of knowledge free to be picked up and read. He could hardly wait, in fact, he was beginning to get excited. *Ah, perhaps these trials aren't so bad after all.*

However, his excitement was tempered as Officer Thesla opened a door to a blank room with no signs of furniture, save for an iron slab in the center of the room currently occupied by a pair of teenage drow.

Adam frowned.

"Smooth plan getting us incarcerated," Junith snickered, causing Adam to elbow the paladin.

"Keep your hands to yourselves, Hvisklicas! Go," Officer Thesla said, shoving the pair into the room. Two sets of eyeballs immediately turned to them.

"Ah, fresh meat!" a teenage drow with golden hair greeted, approaching the pair as the door slammed shut. "Looks like they gotchu too, huh?"

Flitting behind her was a white-haired Drowthraki. She tried to say something, but the blonde shoved her.

"Nice trick ditching the uniforms," the girl said, snapping her fingers. "We shoulda done that!"

"Uh... yeah..." Adam agreed non-committedly. He moved to a corner of the room and sat, tucking his legs into his chest.

"I'm Elerra Hall, but you can call me Ellie. What's your name?" the drow asked, beaming with so much positivity Adam felt a pang in his chest as if he'd taken physical damage.

"Uhhh..." He hummed in thought, the sheer force of happiness strong enough to make his face twitch. "Adama?"

There was an audible smack as Junith's hand struck her own face.

"Adama? That's a unique name! Is that Eukaryo? Syanthria? Opisthum?" the girl rattled off, learning in closer and closer to the nekoboy. Then she froze, nose wrinkled. "Huh... You smell weird."

Do I really smell that bad? These elves must have a higher sense of smell! Panicking, Adam turned to Junith, hoping she'd catch a hint and step in, but luckily the blonde drow was grabbed and dragged away by what Adam surmised was her friend.

"Sorry for Elerra, she isn't house trained," the other drow said, holding the blonde drow as she squirmed and writhed. "Especially since she doesn't know how to respect the rules and ended up getting us both sent to holding! Now we're both getting detention!"

"I said I was sorry!" Ellie cried. "You're the one that chose to follow me!"

"Yeah! To stop you from getting in trouble!"

"And whose fault was it I got caught?!" Ellie spat back. Adam only sighed. This was his first time meeting these girls, and yet the argument sounded quite familiar....

"Ah..." Adam said, before remembering to use his girl voice. "Don't worry, I have a couple of untrained cats that are a handful."

"What's that supposed to mean?" Junith growled. "Adam-*ah*."

"It means I'm sick of you," he replied. "Every waking moment is spent with you."

"*Oooh,* trouble in paradise?" Ellie said, smiling at Adam and Junith. "I always love a lover's quarrel!"

""WE'RE NOT LOVERS!"" the nekos yelled simultaneously before blinking and turning to one another.

"SHUT UP!" they yelled in sync again. "NO, YOU SHUT UP!"

"STOP COPYING ME!" As the two glared each other in the eye, arms crossed in a perfect mirror, Ellie chuckled at the show.

"Aww, they're so cute! And so young!" Ellie exclaimed before sighing. "Too bad we're all gonna die soon."

What?

Adam immediately spun, his neck making an audible snap as he faced the young drow. "Ehem, come again?"

"Oh? You haven't heard? The duckysaurs are making their way here. The whole city is going to be destroyed, which is why they're hosting the festivals," she said nonchalantly. Adam's jaw dropped, even as the other drow girl smacked Ellie on the back of her head, chastising her.

"B-B-B-But I just got here!" he cried, as screams began to penetrate from outside the room.

Catpurr 35
Oops

"But I just got here!" Adam cried, his face twisted in a mixture of anguish and disbelief. This sanctuary of knowledge, this vessel of books and arcana was soon to be trampled underfoot by ducks most fowl.

Suddenly there was a *bang!* from the other side of the door, as someone on the other side snarled. Ellie shrieked, leaping back at the unexpected noise, only to gaze intently at the door's small, barred window. Something like recognition ignited in the girl's eyes. "What? WHA?! Miss Teria?"

Adam turned, following Ellie's gaze until his own golden irises went wide with shock—and irritation. Smashing her head against the barred window and snarling was a cat-eared Drowthraki woman.

"Of course," he sighed, pinching the bridge of his nose. "I'm not even going to question how this happened."

"M-Miss Teria?!" the white-haired dark elf gasped. Cautiously she approached the door, only to recoil as the cat-eared woman snarled.

"By Voltrain's light, not again!" Junith smacked Adam on the back of the head. "See! This is what I mean! You're a menace! A *menace!*"

"What did *I* do?! This is probably your fault!"

"*My* fault?! How is it my fault when it's obviously yours!" she yelled back, pointing at the catsified woman trying to stick her hand through the iron bars. Elongated claws had burst from her nail beds.

"What's wrong with her?" Ellie asked. She approached the door as if in a trance, only to be stopped when Adam stuck out an arm.

"I would caution against such curiosity," he said, drawing a look of curiosity from the girl.

"You... You two know something. Did you do something to the teacher?" the blonde drow asked, backing away from the nekopair.

"No, of course not," they said simultaneously. Their defensive attitudes did nothing to soothe the Drowthraki girls' suspicions.

To get a handle on his nerves, Adam took a calming breath, and reflected on how this infection could have happened. The only people he'd had contact with recently were the archer he'd manhandled, and the truancy officer that had—

"Huh," he said aloud.

Junith hadn't bitten anyone, and he was certain his newly converted Voltrain minion wouldn't have disobeyed orders so soon— not to mention, he doubted she was even in his vicinity. That left Liza, but judging by his companion sense, she wasn't anywhere close by either.

So how did someone get infected?

Could it be that biting wasn't the only way to infect another? Were there other vectors for infection? Was it... airborne?!

Adam didn't know, but the thought of an aerial catsification terrified him.

"Adam."

But the two beside him were clearly not infected. Nor were Titania, Sehn, Coco, and anyone else he interacted with outside the trials.

"Adam!"

So that meant it had to be physical.

"Adam!"

Adam wracked his brain, thinking back, it must have happened on the way here, somehow the officer had gotten infected. Did he scratch her? Did Junith's rabid screaming scatter droplets of saliva that infected her? Either way this required testing.

Maybe I should invest in some gloves, he thought to himself, better to be—

"ADAM!" Junith screamed. She forcibly shook the nekoboy, then spun him to face the door. Already multiple infected dark elves were gathered, squeezing their arms through the window in a desperate bid to convert new victims.

"Oh... That may be a problem," he said. Already the hinges of the door were beginning to peel off the wall. He turned to face the Drowthraki girls, who were now holding each other, staring with fear at the door as it bent under the zombies' combined weight.

I wonder if the infected will attack me? Adam silently asked. *They aren't dead, after all.*

Junith drew her short sword from underneath her cloak. Surprisingly, the truancy officer had let her keep her weapons, proving useful in a situation like this one. However, as she placed herself in front of the door, Adam raised a hand, stopping her

"What are you doing?! Move aside!" she demanded.

"Hold on, don't attack. Can't you see they aren't dead? What if we can cure them?" As they grabbed and snapped at potential prey, they weren't ignoring Adam. That told him that the infected were not dead.

They weren't dead, simply rabid. And if the catsification of his bites could be cured with gold, perhaps that was a hint as to what could cure these, too. Of course, this was assuming the feral state wasn't a permanent affliction. But it was still worth a try in Adam's mind. If nothing else, it would be a good distraction as he waited for the trial to time out and end.

"Are... you serious?"

"Of course!" he said. The black brick floor crumbled and split apart as Redfield clawed his way aboveground, heeding his master's will. Against a backdrop of infected catwomen and a black-armored Death Knight, Adam turned back to the frightened pair of girls. "Does this facility have an alchemical laboratory?"

"Y-Y-You're a necromancer," Ellie whispered, her voice almost reverent.

Adam raised a brow, his mouth unwillingly forming into a frown before he declared boldly, "Yes, I am! Now, does this academy have a laboratory? With gold and potion pots?"

"D-D-Do you mean the chem lab?" Ellie asked.

The other girl stepped forwards, shielding her friend from the pair of obvious good-for-nothings. "Hush! Don't answer her! They could be cultists! Part of a terrorist plot! You heard the Dean about the cultists and bandits sneaking in!" she said aloud, narrowing her eyes at Adam. "They could be terrorists! Or worse! *Men.*"

"Fine. Suit yourself, I guess we'll all get infected then." Adam shrugged, ordering Redfield from the door as it began to splinter and buckle. Idly he wondered if he'd also be affected by the rabies.

"Adam! What are you doing?!" Junith demanded.

"Accepting my fate. Since they don't want to tell me information to save our lives, I guess we'll all just die. It was a good run," he said, laying down on the ground with his hands crossed against his chest. "Do you think this is a good death posture? I do hope they don't gnaw the flesh off my face."

"Adam!" Junith yelled. The light of her geas crackled around her as Adam compelled her not to attack. She turned her head, snarling. "This is *not* the time for games!"

"Who says I'm playing around?" he said, closing his eyes as the sound of wood breaking grew louder. "Truth be told, we've had a good run, Judgy, and I'm ready to die. At least we have friends coming along with us."

The door broke apart, more and more. From the other side came dozens of screams as some of the catsified drow raced off in pursuit of easier prey. Adam began to whistle.

"WE DO! WE HAVE AN ALCHEMY LAB!" Ellie finally burst out as the door finally came off its hinges.

Catpurr 36

Gold Experiment

At Ellie's words, Adam snapped his fingers.

"Red."

The Death Knight turned, unleashing a wall of black shadows that pushed back the six infected drow currently barging into the room.

Ellie and her friend's jaw dropped. The pair could only stare at the Death Knight bound to the stranger who seemed their age.

"See what happens when you tell me what I want to know?" Adam said. He stood without fear before the crowd of infected Drowthraki, as they writhed against the inky black shadows binding them. "Everything works out."

Junith rolled her eyes.

"Don't listen to hi—*er*, she causes trouble wherever she goes," she said, drawing an odd look from the two drow.

"Don't listen to the meatbag, she's incapable of cognitive thinking," Adam fired back. The pair was about to get into another argument when suddenly the gaggle of pinned infected drow opened their mouths and collectively let out a shrill scream.

[Skill resisted! Resisted Skill, Cry of the Pack. As Origin of this Pack, this skill does not affect you.]

Adam covered his ears, the grating sound of their wail making the hairs on his arm stand on end. Yet despite his annoyance, below it was a gnawing sense of urgency, a primal instinct to abandon everything and take off in the direction of the sound.

Fortunately, Junith recovered quickly. The paladin simply punched each of the screaming infected until they stopped their incessant screeching.

"Gah! So annoying! What even was that?!" she spat, flicking the bluish blood off her hands.

Adam didn't know. He had never observed people infected with his curse displaying such a skill. But then again, that had been with humans. There was no telling what influence his curse had on other species.

"Interesting," he said, crouching down to observe the unconscious nekofolk. The researcher in him emerged as he recorded the different features of the catsified drow that catsified humans didn't possess. For starters, their tails were furless, more akin to a rat's tail than a cat. Similarly their cat ears were hairless as well.

Adam reached down, lifting one of the infecteds' wrists to more closely observe the bumps along the skin before his eyes wandered towards the woman's swollen lymph nodes. These were features each of the infected possessed, meaning it was a norm, not an exception or mutation.

Oh, how I wish I could experiment more on this... he thought to himself, suppressing the dark urge.

"What... What happened to them?" Ellie asked, getting closer despite the insistent efforts of her friend to hold her back.

"Unfortunate victims of that one's idiocy," Adam said, pointing at Junith, who scowled. "They've been infected with a curse."

"Can you cure it?" Ellie asked, rubbing her nose as she squinted at Adam. Something about the strange drow piqued her curiosity.

Screams echoed from down the hall as drow fled down one corridor.

"We should go!" Ellie's friend exclaimed, tugging at Ellie.

"Maybe," Adam replied to Ellie, stroking his chin as he took out a gold coin from his chest guard.

Eh, worth a shot. Adam moved to test his theory, but before he could, a cacophony of screams and broken objects rang from the hallway.

The nekoboy moved past the cluster of squirming infected and peeked his head around the doorway. Then he ducked back to hide as he glimpsed a stampede of infected drow, charging closer and closer.

Ah... That's a problem.

"We should leave," he said calmly, turning back to the girls.

"What? Why? What's out there?" Ellie's friend asked, as both girls shrunk back.

"Things we should be running from!" Adam said, summoning a sabercat skeleton. A portal appeared, and one skeletal paw emerged, claws clicking on the floor. "Go, delay their advance! But don't kill anyone!"

Immediately the giant bone cat took off, barrelling towards the infected stampede where it slammed its body into the crowd, knocking down rows of drow.

Ellie and her friend both gawked, both peeking outside at the spectacle of the undead cat rolling around and flattening drow.

"Take me to your alchemy lab," Adam said, pulling the two away as he directed Redfield to bring along one of the infected.

* * *

Jogging down the empty halls, the group was unimpeded as they made their way to their destination. Adam was left wondering where everyone was. Outside of the horde of infected adults screeching and catching up behind them, there hadn't been a single soul. Aside from the pair accompanying them, there had not even been other students.

"Here we are," Ellie said, standing outside of a door, the words *Chem Lab* stenciled on a frosted window. Looking at her, she seemed almost reluctant to enter the room, but as another ear-piercing scream echoed from behind them, the choice was taken from her hands. The drow girl opened the door.

Adam let out a low whistle, his eyes darting to and fro taking in the rows of alchemical plants, pots, and various equipment neatly laid throughout the interior.

"Awesome," he muttered. On his face was an uncharacteristically wide smile as he began pocketing vials and other lab equipment. Redfield meanwhile laid out their infected test subject—a teacher— on a table, pinning her down.

"What are you doing?" Ellie asked, as Adam beckoned Redfield over. The nekoboy promptly began dumping any lab equipment that caught his eye into the Death Knight's hands. "Hey! What are you doing?!"

"Uuuuh." Adam paused, looking over to the girl.

"Wait, are you stealing from us?!" Ellie's friend yapped, pointing at the boy. "I knew they were no good!"

"I'm not stealing! I'm..." he turned to Junith. The woman stared at the pair with a deadpan expression and folded arms. "Help me out here, what does the church call it when they steal?"

"Steal? We don't steal!" Junith hissed.

"Oh, yes, tithing! Wait no, appropriating!" Adam said, snapping his fingers. "I'm appropriating a tithe for my services."

"But you two caused this mess!" Ellie's friend yelled.

Adam opened his mouth to respond but paused. "Ah, yes... Well... That... would be correct."

"You really shouldn't take stuff you don't need, sir," Redfield said, chastising his master. "Plus, shouldn't we be focusing on curing this outbreak?"

"Ah, fine, fine, tsk," Adam huffed. He again took out his gold coin and approached the unconscious woman, only to be interrupted again by Ellie's squeal.

"IT CAN TALK?!" the girl screamed, skipping to Redfield with excitement in her eyes.

"The name's Redfield," the Death Knight said. His glowing eyes gazed down at the drow girl from behind his helmet as he stretched out a hand.

"Are you asking for my soul?" Ellie asked. What Redfield did not realize was that the girl had no way of understanding him—Adam's System only translated Redfield's words for him and his followers. From Ellie's perspective, his introduction was little more than gibberish.

"Excuse me!" a feminine voice abruptly hollered, drawing the attention of everyone inside the lab. "What are you doing in my lab? Why aren't you all at the gymnasium ceremony?"

"Oh dung!" Ellie gasped as everyone collectively turned and looked at the adult Drowthraki. She was dressed quite elegantly in glasses and a long, flowing dress, with big white gloves that were spattered with a number of drying substances. Her black hair was tied into a neat bun, and glinting black gemstones adorned her ears. Not even the dark scowl on her face could sour her appearance.

"Do you have a pass? Who is that on my counter? Whose Death Knight is that?!" the teacher asked in rapid succession. Her heels clicked as she approached the table. "What is going on?!"

"Miss Scholl, we can explain!" Ellie said, backing up as the teacher quickly approached the unconscious woman.

"Miss Kometos?" the teacher said with shock and surprise on her face. She fumbled for the woman's wrist, checking for a pulse. "What happened here?! Why are you binding her?! Whose Death Knight is this?!"

Adam backed away, grabbing a heavy stool. His eyes remained locked on the infected woman, noticing as a finger twitched at the shrill noise.

"Miss Kometos! It's Miss Scholl, can you—" Before she could finish her sentence, the nekowoman woke up, immediately snarling and attempting to bite the woman. Fortunately, Miss Scholl was quick and ripped her hand away just barely.

A cry went up from the woman who had once been Miss Kometos. From the hallway came a number of answering cries.

"I don't know what's going on here, but I'm calling the guard!" Miss Scholl declared, heading to the doorway despite Ellie and her friends' attempts to stop her.

But before she could open the door, a stool was smashed over her head, knocking the woman out instantly.

"WHA—? WHY?!" Ellie cried. Both girls raced to the downed teacher.

"What? It was either this or let her open the door and get infected." Adam shrugged as Junith began punching the rabid Miss Komatos until she lost consciousness.

"Nap time!"

Adam ignored the pair, instead crouching beside the incapacitated infectee. Junith rose to her feet, rubbing at her knuckles as she joined him.

"So... What's the plan?" she asked.

"This." The nekoboy pressed the gold coin against the cat-eared woman's head.

A moment passed, then another, with no signs of any curative properties.

"Seriously?" Junith raised her brow. "Here I was hop—"

Suddenly, and without warning, steam rose from where the coin touched skin. It warped and shifted, forming a bubble around the subject's body.

Interesting.

Immediately, the nekowoman's eyes snapped back open. The creature struggled to bolt upright and bit Adam. But even when occupied with holding the door, Redfield's tendrils of darkness held her down and gagged her.

"Huh..." Adam hummed, still holding the coin to the rabid woman's head.

"What?" Junith asked, observing.

"It's just... her eyes aren't gold. Usually when I've turned someone, their eyes turn gold. Hers are blue."

"Okay. But how does that help us find a cure for our condition?" Junith asked, raising a brow.

"Oh, it's not relevant. Just interesting that the curse affects other species differently," he said as Junith rolled her eyes. "Ah, if only I was a bit more immoral."

"What's happening to her?" Ellie asked. The inquisitive girl kept a healthy distance from the pair who were obviously capable of a lot of violence.

"It seems her body is reacting to the coin," Adam said.

"Is that a good thing or a bad thing?" Ellie asked.

"Unsure."

"Unsure? *Unsure?!* I thought you said you could cure them!" the other drow girl yelled.

"The academic's method can't be rushed!" Adam hissed. His eye flickered back to his patient, just as she began to sweat profusely.

Hmmm. He began to wonder if there was any way to speed up the decatsification process.

From the way her tail seemed to be shriveling up and the fur around her wrist was falling off, just prolonged contact with gold seemed capable of curing the infection. Or that's what Adam guessed, as he watched her claws retract back into the nail beds.

Fascinating... I wonder if gold to blood contact would expedite the process. Golden eyes flickered across the flasks and burners lining the classroom walls.

"Plan?" Junith asked.

"Hm?"

"You have a plan," Junith said.

"Yes, I do, but how do you know that?"

"Because you make a stupid face when you're thinking."

"Takes stupid to know stupid," he retorted before stroking his chin. "I have a plan, but... Hey, you!"

"Who? Me?" Ellie's friend asked.

"Yes, you, how high do these burners go?" he asked, gazing once more upon the knobs and magical sigils.

"Uh." The nameless girl shrugged.

"About three thousand Celsius," Ellie answered

"Huh, enough to melt gold... three times as much," he muttered. Then he lifted a flask, his eyes narrowing as he took out several gold coins and weighed his options.

Catpurr 37

What's the Big Idea?

Ellie and Karlie sat far from Adam and Junith, on the other side of the room. As they tended to their unconscious chemistry teacher, each girl shot occasional looks at the mysterious newcomers, especially the white-haired 'girl' who'd been frowning, almost weeping. It left them both anxious about what was to happen next.

"What are they doing over there? You think they were serious about a cure?"" Karlie whispered, frowning at the pair of troublemakers.

"I don't know. But I know they're up to no good." Ellie grimaced, smacking her fist against a palm.

"So, what do we do?" Karlie asked. The door was silent, for now, but the Death Knight still stood braced against it.

All Drowthraki were familiar with Death Knights. They were the pinnacle of a necromancer's arsenal, the symbol of their prestige and might that required years of training and discipline to acquire. To even attempt to summon one was forbidden, without first receiving the blessing of the temple.

Yet the white-haired child had one under their command—and they seemed even younger than Ellie and Karlie.

"I don't know... If they can summon Death Knights, we aren't strong enough to deal with them," Ellie whispered, narrowing her eyes.

It was nigh unheard of for a male to command a Death Knight. They simply lacked the magical might and potency necessary to call forth a warrior of the abyss.

But despite how much he looked like a girl, he couldn't hide his voice. There was also how suspicious it was his friend kept referring to 'Adama' as he and him, while constantly facepalming and cringing at Adama's name and voice. Then again, Junith's girl voice was much more convincing than the other's.

Ellie frowned, wracking her mind as she tried to understand what they wanted. The one called Adama was crying, appearing genuinely distressed. Her chest had tensed up, breaths short and shallow, but despite her grim expression, their attempted cure seemed to be working, as Miss Kometos' body gradually returned to normal. Her fingernails had dulled and shrunk, and her skin was returning to its normal complexion.

Still, whatever they were caught up in, it must be big... A male Drowthraki that was gifted enough to summon a Death Knight—without chanting, at that! And one that seemed to be sapient, even if she couldn't understand its speech? It must be a first in Drowthraki history!

Despite the fear tickling her greshtalki, her heart was elated. Finally, her school days would no longer be quite so dull.

* * *

Adam rubbed his nose as he sniffled, but that didn't stop him from doing what had to be done. Another gold coin was melted and lost over the burner.

I didn't realize how much this would hurt. The sacrifices we make for science... Even as silent tears leaked from his eyes, he whipped out his notebook and turned back to the unconscious drow woman.

The good news was his sacrifice was not in vain. Gold did seem a viable cure for his catsification curse, as Adam jotted down notes on the effects and how long it took to reverse the infection. Of course, any good experiment needed multiple subjects to prove the hypothesis correct.

Adam rubbed his chin.

"So it works," Junith said, standing over the woman.

"So it does," he affirmed. "Now the question is, can this cure us as well?"

Adam reached over, opening the woman's eyelids. The drow's irises had changed color from blue to purple.

"Hey, you, the one named Ellie. Come here," Adam beckoned. The girl was initially hesitant but complied despite her friend's attempts to stop her.

"Yes? What's up?"

"Are these the woman's original eye colors?" He gestured at the woman's eyes, gazing blankly ahead.

"Uh... I think so," Ellie said, shrugging as Adam went back to his notebook.

Subject's irises have returned to what is assumed to be normal color. Possible correlation with curse and eye color. The description was added into his notebook, beside a diagram of a Drowthraki body.

"Excellent. Thank you for being useful," he said as Ellie peered over his shoulder, eyeing the diagrams he was sketching.

"What are you doing?"

"Science." He returned to the body before dropping his pen in shock. It bounced across the floor.

"What? What's wrong?" Junith asked. The paladin's hand was already on her sword.

"I just realized I don't have a control variable."

"Meaning?"

"Meaning my data is incomplete!" he said, before storing his notebook and lifting himself up on top of the table, where he crouched down over the unconscious woman. "Bah, I should have done this when she was still infected. Now I'll have to catch another and undress them."

Confused at Adam's words, Ellie and Junith could only gawk as Adam began unbuttoning the sleeping woman's blouse. When he tried to tug off her shirt, however, their confusion was quickly replaced with rage.

"WHAT ARE YOU DOING, YOU PERVERT?!" Junith barked, knocking Adam from the table with a flying kick. The researcher was thrown into a row of shelves, which collapsed upon him.

"Ow?! What the Nyx, you meatbag?!" he yelled, pulling himself out of a cabinet.

"Why are you trying to take her clothes off?!" Junith demanded.

"For science, of course! How am I supposed to find a cure if I don't have precise, accurate data on our test subject's meatsuit!" he retorted. What was the big deal, anyways? What had gotten the three girls all so worked up?

"You can't! You—!" Junith facepalmed. "You *can't* just undress people!"

"Why not? It's for the academic method! I thought you wanted to be cured!" Ellie and her friend gave Adam an odd look at his words.

"I do, but not by violating others' privacy!" The paladin marched up to her companion, getting in his face as she shouted.

"What? It's just flesh," Adam said, reaching up and squeezing Junith's boob. "See? I don't see what the big—"

* * *

A low groan escaped him as Adam gradually rose, blinking. He pinched the bridge of his nose as he dragged himself into sitting up.

"Ow." A very obvious gift from Junith had been left for him—a black eye dominating the left side of his face, swelling that eye shut. "Rude."

As he got his bearings, however, he frowned. No longer was he in the chem lab, instead, Adam had been left inside a messy, disorganized room. Chairs and books were strewn across the floor, claw marks gouging each of the walls.

"Well... That's concerning," he said. The scent of sulfur and heat hung heavy in the air, and there was a puddle of blood nearby. Even stranger, the doors had been barricaded, but he had been left alone in this room. Adam tipped his head up, following the light source until he saw an open, blue-tinted window.

So they abandoned him. Great.

With a sigh, Adam stood up, approaching the window. He looked out and beheld a city on fire.

"Well... This certainly got out of hand..." he said. Standing in the rubble of what once had been a home, a duckysaur wobbled back and forth. But there was something special about this duckysaur—it didn't take Adam very long to notice its cat ears and massive, bushy tail. Even the duckysaur had been catsified.

Seems it can also infect non-humanoids... The nekoboy frowned, eyeing the packs of infected Drowthraki running around the city, hunting screaming elves. This was bad. *Real* bad. Adam didn't know how long he'd been out, but it was clear the infection had spread outside the academy, with Junith and his knight oddly nowhere to be found.

BETA SYSTEM v1.05

TITLE: The Primordial Eli's Chosen

+20% Mana Recovery, +5 Arcana, Undead Favorability

NAME: Adam F. Glow

SPECIES: Nekoboy

LEVEL: 43

EXP BAR: 860/18000

MAIN CLASS: Nekomancer

HP: 350/360

MANA: 315/810

EVOLUTION POINT: 1

Gacha Coins: 103 [Daily Summoning Available!]

Free Points: 0

Bonded Followers: 03

Junith Oatheart: T2 Lvl 19 (Feralized)

Eh'liza Oktober: T1 Lvl 37

Kathrine Dominica: T1 Lvl 8

[Dungeon Interface:] >

STATS:

STR: 25

CON: 46

DEX: 25

ARC: 150+12(EQ)

SEN: 23

EGO: 43

RESISTANCES: Fire (5%), Inertia 10%, Heat Resistance 8%, Cold Resistance 8%, Blunt Resistance 15%, Wind Resistance 8% (EQ)

Buffs: Loved by Undead (Unique), Blessing of Eli (Unique), Eyes of a Predator V1, Corrupted Blessing of Nyx (Unique), Adherent of Death V1, Explosive Renaissance V1, Pain Tolerance V1, Blessing of the King Maker (UR), Boots Made for Walking (EQ), Regal Scepter of the Full Moon (EQ)

Debuffs: Ha! You Sacrificed Your Stats for a Cat?! V1 (Curse) Catsification V1 (Curse)

SKILLS: Animate Bones V2, Irritating Touch V1, Cat Claws V1, Identify V1, Summon Greater Skeleton V3 (+++), Mana Bolt V1 (++), Artificial Linguistics {Rigellian}, Genocidal Aura, Summon Morian Crab, Mana Claws V1 (+), Summon Red-Eyed Death Knight of the Bronx V1 (3Hrs) (++), Mana Dash V1 (+), Regal Smash (EQ), Waning Moon Shield (EQ)

Skill Points: 0

Judging from his System, it seemed safe to guess Junith had succumbed to the horde, and that Adam would have to find her, strap her down, and cure her. Fortunately, he could tell she was somewhere nearby—he wouldn't have to look very far.

"Uuugh." Adam rubbed his face, a headache forming.

"Seriously, I don't get what the big deal is. All I did was touch her breast and she freaks out. Stupid meatbag." Adam sighed, turning around to eye the barricaded door. It was time to go find his missing link back home, but first...

The nekomancer paused, opening his gacha screen menu. It was time to roll dailies.

Catpurr 38
Oh... Hi There.

[Ding!]
[CONCATULATIONS! You've won 5 Cicero Coins!]
[Daily attempts left: 00!]

"Of course. Even with a blessing granting me a bunch of Luck, it remains ever the same." Adam sighed as he closed his System. "I really need to find a way to edit my Luck..."

The nekoboy turned back to the barricaded doors, eyes lingering on them. Someone had gone to great lengths to protect him, but seeing as that someone was no longer here, they had fled out the window in the end.

He traced their path, moving to the window and looking out upon the destruction of Corydrun. What had once been a bustling metropolis brimming with brick buildings and crystalline spires was now ablaze. Infected duckysaurs and nekodrow roamed the smoldering ruins.

Great. Juuust great. How the Nyx do I fix this? Adam sighed, then resigned to do the only thing he could do—take notes.

Was doing anything more at this stage even possible? Would it be wiser to just cut his losses and run? Adam smacked his lips, seriously considering his options. If Junith was now in a feral state, there was a strong possibility the same could happen to him. A shudder wracked his body at the thought.

There was some hope, however. Early experiments with gold as a possible cure for the infection were looking optimistic, but therein lay the crux of the issue. How the Nyx was he to expose hundreds of people to gold, let alone keep them there long enough for the cure to take effect? Hurling vials of molten gold had been his first plan, but it was one he quickly discarded, the risk of accidental injuries was too high. With Junith at his disposal that might have been an acceptable risk, but that brought him back to his issues.

He had no Junith, and he had no gold, in their stead he had only several hundred infected, and several rampaging catsified fowl.

"What a mess. Well, time to get to work. No use just standing around." The first step was to remove the barricade. If there was a way to create some system that could deliver the cure for thousands, he would bet good money its ingredients were housed within the academy. It would take some time, certainly, but as he had no intention of participating in this trial, time was something he had in great abundance.

With Redfield on cooldown, his replacement came in the form of several summoned skelecats as he slowly opened the unbarricaded door. Next they bounded out the door, scouting the hallways for any potential threats.

After some time had passed, the nekoboy stepped out into the once pristine hallways, now streaked with gore. Claw marks marred the walls, paintings were ripped to shreds, and various objects had been overturned and shattered, leaving the hallway cluttered.

There was a distant scream—another nekodrow alerting its pack that prey had been scented.

"Well, that's not ominous," Adam mumbled, creeping through the hallway. What he really needed was a directory or a sign pole, something that would tell him where to go, but sadly, every sign, every portrait, every scrap of paper had been ripped to shreds.

"Maybe I should create one massive cat scratch post," he said. As he opened another door to check the room within, several pairs of eyes turned to face him, barely lit in the dark. Another pack of nekodrow.

A moment passed, the two parties staring at one another.

"Ah... right. My apologies," Adam said before closing the door just as a nekodrow threw itself at him. He quickly barricaded the door with a nearby statue. It wobbled under the force of the infected's blows. "Just gonna keep that locked."

Adam and his skelecats moved on, searching the halls. As he stealthily advanced through the halls, a sense of guilt gnawed at his insides, growing with every glimpse of destruction.

"How do I fix this?" Adam grimaced, deep in thought, walking aimlessly through a hallway intersection as his mind wandered through possible solutions and fixes to this catastrophe.

But unbeknownst to the young nekomancer, he was gathering a crowd. Within the shadows stalked several feral nekodrows, eyeing him with hungry eyes as he passed them at a brisk pace.

Made curious by the white-haired drow girl's unhurried movements and apparent nonchalance, there was soon a small procession of nekodrow trailing behind Adam, even as he muttered to himself. At his feet clattered his skelecats. Some even leapt up onto his shoulders, headbutting him in a bid for attention.

Adam's trance was only broken as he passed by a window.

Water.

It was raining.

This would be a normal occurrence in any other city, but Corydrun was underground. Ignoring the oddly overly affectionate cats, Adam approached the window.

"Weird," he said. High above the city, he found the source of the water—the pipes that criss-crossed the ceiling had burst.

"Interesting." Gradually the little droplets of water fell in a mimicry of rain, extinguishing the fires.

A fire suppression system or an irrigation unit? Seemed to have been the former. Clever. The nekoboy thoughtfully rubbed his chin. *Would make sense that an underground city would have something to fight the fires. I wonde—*

He blinked, an icy shiver jolting up his spine as he at last realized he was not alone. In his reflection in the glass, a crowd of nekodrow gazed back at him.

"Crapbaskets," Adam muttered. Slowly he turned around, holding out his hands in a placating gesture.

"Heeey, ladies," he said, scanning the crowd of roughly twenty nekodrow, staring at him from where they crouched on all fours. "How's it, uh... How's it going?"

At Adam's words, the crowd of feral nekodrow began to inch closer, their hairless tails swishing back and forth. The tell-tale sign of a cat about to pounce.

"Can we talk about this? We're all cat folk here, right?" Adam said, slowly inching back. In response, several nekodrow in the front row hissed, snarling at him. He looked down, eyeing his skelecats.

"Why didn't you warn me?" he hissed in turn.

In response the skeleton looked up, clacking its mandibles almost in frustration before headbutting Adam's ankle repeatedly.

Okay. Time for a distraction.

"Riiiight. HEY, WHAT'S THAT OVER THERE?!" Adam yelled, pointing to the distance in an exaggerated manner. The cats didn't take the bait, instead they stared at the nekoboy, with some cocking their heads in confusion.

Why did I even think that would work? Alright, plan B.

"May I please have a potion? Thank you," he said, summoning from his pouch a small, clear flask filled with black liquid. Slowly he began moving it back and forth. The pupils of the nekodrow immediately dilated, darting back and forth, following the vial.

"That's right, shiiiny. Track the shiny thing," he muttered. If he hadn't realized it before, this confirmed it for him—the infected were *exactly* like cats.

With no other recourse, Adam threw the potion into the air and took off. In an instant the nekos were climbing atop each other, scrambling to reach the thrown object. Those who fought most viciously and emerged triumphant were rewarded with a faceful of smoke as a dark cloud arose, covering the nekomancer's hasty retreat.

But the distraction would not last him long. It did nothing to cover the sound of running footsteps, which seemed to trigger a predatory instinct in the nekodrow and the swarm quickly became a frenzy, which Adam could only flee in panic.

Ducking, diving, and weaving, he managed to dodge around the infected. Some fell from the smoke cloud, shattering the glass windows as they plummeted.

"AH CRAP!" the boy cried repeatedly, his heart racing as adrenaline filled his veins. Once, before he lost Schrödinger and was saddled with this ridiculous catsification curse, he'd been a prodigious escape artist. Now he used all his energy, all his cunning. Somehow his enchanted boots paired with his reflexes allowed him to dodge the infected, coming at him from everywhere. They were fast, but Adam was faster—barely.

"NAAAAYH!" A nekodrow hissed, leaping at Adam from the above.

His staff appeared on instinct, and the legendary item bashed down into the nekodrow's forehead. Its wielder quickly springboarded off the prone feline form, propelling himself forwards.

He spun in the air, summoning his skeleton sabercat as a shield that mowed down the rows of infected before him, buying time.

Hitting the ground in a roll, Adam immediately pivoted into a corridor where he skidded to a halt.

"Oh, come on!" he yelled in exasperation as dozens of nekodrow turned their heads at the source of uninfected flesh. He turned to flee, to find another path, but retreat was a pipe dream as dozens of infected drow slammed into each other behind him, clogging up the hallway.

"Ah... crapbaskets."

With two forces of nekodrow surrounding him, Adam spun his scepter and slammed it into the ground, activating its skill, **Waning Moonlight Shield**.

"YOU SHALL NOT PASS!"

Immediately a light, bluish energy erupted from the white crystal atop his staff, emitting a bubble of translucent mana that surrounded the nekomancer as dozens of infected charged him from both sides.

"Ha. Hahaha. Ha!" he chuckled at the nekofolk futilely clawing, hissing, and tearing at the bubble in a mad attempt to infect him. But he could waste no time laughing at them, instead he summoned forth Junith's armor of Smo. According to the description, the fullplate armor was nigh-invulnerable to physical attacks.

Taking off his magic cape, Adam wrapped it around the armor before climbing his way inside from the hatch on its back. Once in, the burden of the cursed armor fell heavy upon his shoulders, the weight of the enchanted suits ceasing all movement as it resized itself to perfectly fit its wearer.

Fully encased in armor, Adam gazed through the slits of the helmet, watching as his **Waning Moonlight Shield** began to dim, flickering against the tide of nekodrow clawing at the barrier. He had seconds, maybe not even that before the skill dispelled. Fortunately, that was all he needed. Just as the barrier began to fall as the horde staggered towards him, the nekoboy cried out in a thin voice, "What do you mean they're out of pizza?!"

Catpurr 39
The Librarium Sanctum

An hour of dead silence had passed in the darkened hallway. The carpet of shards of glass and debris had not been disturbed in some time. And so, it sounded particularly loud when a soft *clink, clink* sounded, and a mound of metal appeared from nowhere.

"Huh! I can't believe that worked!" Adam gasped, panting heavily as moving from the fetal position at last broke his invisibility skill.

After about ten minutes' struggle, he finally clambered out of the fortress of Smo. First, he glanced around the vicinity, checking that the coast was certainly clear before placing the armor back into his storage ring and wrapping his cloak around his shoulders.

Moving swiftly but quietly, the nekoboy skulked through the desolate hallways, moving with the grace of a thief in the night searching for his prize.

A more cautious cattitude would benefit him here. Only after his skeiecats gave the all-clear would Adam advance. Each time a nekodrow blocked his advance, he wouldn't risk his own safety. Instead, he'd command his cat summons to lure the infected away and wait them out.

But fortunately, he never had to wait long. The nekodrow were very easily distracted, as it turned out, especially by fast-moving objects. Even other infected could draw their attention. Adam found it a simple matter to access anywhere he wanted.

Finally, after what felt like an eternity, the nekoboy found himself standing in front of a double-door entrance, a plaque hanging above it, reading *Librarium Sanctilli*. The onyx plaque bore scratch marks, but it was still legible.

"Well, what better place to garner knowledge than a library," he said, reaching out and pulling at the bronze handlebar to open the door.

"Huh?" The door refused to budge. As Adam occupied himself with struggling to open it, he failed to notice as a nekodrow rounded the corner and spotted him. Again and again, the boy tugged at the door, rattling it. Only when his skelecat clacked for attention did he notice and spot the infected.

Great. This again.

One more time, he tugged at the door. No such luck.

"Crapbaskets," he muttered and immediately bolted as the nekodrow took off, racing through the hallway after Adam.

He ran back down the way he came, leaping over piles of debris before turning the corner and yelling the activation phrase for his cape.

Immediately the boy turned translucent as his back hit the wall of a corridor, his body now invisible and blending into the tapestry as the nekodrow sailed by.

Good thing their sense of smell is bad! he thought with some relief, closing his eyes and inwardly sighing, thankful that their senses weren't as acute as an actual cat's.

A moment passed, then another before Adam moved, breaking his spell and heading back to the library's doors.

He rubbed his chin, eyeing the entrance way. It would be a small matter to just blow the door down using his staff or a skill, but doing so would wreck the architecture and attract infected, both things he didn't want to do.

"There's gotta be another way into the library," he mused aloud. Golden eyes idly wandered until they fell upon a grate on the ceiling.

"Huh."

A ventilation shaft. Which made sense, given the vastness of the academy.

Blueish energy gathered to create a magic hand as Adam activated his gauntlet. The tendril of energy emanated from his white glove as it extended towards the ceiling. With only some mild prodding, hand waving, and complaining, the grate was soon unscrewed and set to the side, the vent shaft left open. And with that, the magic hand construct was dismissed.

He eyed the opening. Judging from what he could see, it was just big enough for his tiny body to fit. Taking a breath, the nekoboy wiggled and crouched low, steadying himself before throwing his body into the opening. With **mana claws** he tightly latched on and heaved his body up.

"Hup, hup!" he gasped, now fully on all fours and surrounded on nearly every side by metal walls. Fortunately, the way forwards led straight towards the librarium. He crawled until he came across another grate, through which he glimpsed something that made his heart leap with elation.

Books.

Hundreds of books, *thousands* of books. Adam swooned, and found he had to place a hand over his mouth to keep from sobbing for sheer joy. And that was only the books he could see—how many more awaited him, just out of sight, simply begging for a worthy academic to re—

"No! Don't lose focus now, Adam! Concentrate, there will be time... *So* much time to read," he consoled himself. Then he punched the grate. The crumpled metal covering tumbled through air, clattering against the library floor.

The nekoboy froze, waiting with bated breath for any infected within the library to reveal themselves.

A moment passed then another, his eyes wide as sweat condensed on his forehead. After a few minutes, Adam poked his head into the librarium where his jaw immediately dropped.

Books.

Hundreds, thousands, nay! *Millions* of tomes arranged neatly on rows upon rows of beautiful bookshelves that lined every inch of the room. At a distance, the nekomancer could see they were cataloged, each book bearing a spine label that had numbers and letters.

This... This is what he'd dreamed of. A world where such a sanctum of knowledge could exist freely and be accessible to everyone.

When the shock of what he was staring at wore off, Adam sniffed and clutched his heart, a tear rolling from his eyes.

"It's... more beautiful than I could have ever possibly imagined," he whispered fondly, reaching up to brush away a single tear.

Then a massive, infected duckysaur burst through a wall, wrecking it all. It kicked and bucked, its fluffy tail bowling over hundreds of shelves in a wild frenzy.

Then it spit flames, lighting up the librarium. Quickly the facility's fire suppression system activated, as little knobs in the ceiling doused the fire with gallons of water.

Adam could only stare at the spectacle, dumbfounded. The duckysaur slammed through another wall and vanished. The only sign of its existence were its fading quacks and the half-charred, half-sodden mess of wood pulp it left in its wake. Wood pulp that had once been the most beautiful and precious thing in all creation.

"Y-Y-You! NO! NO! NOOOOOO!" Adam screamed as fury built up in his heart. "I'LL KILL YOU!"

Catpurr 40

Catnapping My Archnemesis

Amidst the soggy ruin of the once beautiful librarium, Adam wept on all fours, his eyes welded shut as he cursed the divinities that forced him to witness such a tragedy.

The books. So many books. Trampled. Destroyed. Ruined! Laid to waste by evil most fowl.

Why? Why?! he cried inwardly, stifling his tears. A sanctuary of knowledge laid to ruin by those stupid birds! He clenched his jaw, anger rising as his fists balled.

Before now, he had been content with letting the duckysaurs do as they pleased, to fail the trial and let others clear it while he explored. Now though, Adam wanted nothing more than to hold Schrödinger close and exterminate the feathered monstrosities. Both things competed for his top desire.

Burning him to death with flames that turned his skin into melted cheese? Sure.

Eating him and slowly dissolving him in stomach acid? Okay.

Flattening him against the earth and turning him into a red paste? Alright.

But destroying books?

They'd gone too far. An act like this could not—*would* not—stand!

Golden eyes snapped open, blazing with wrath.

"You've made a grave error," Adam whispered, as he enshrined a silent vow within his tiny heart, a vow that he would not rest, would not sleep, until all the fowl beasts had been exterminated.

But he still had a job to do, before then. Quickly he devised a plan of action.

Step one, cure the infection.

Step two, find Junith.

Step three, *exterminate the duckysaurs.*

His gaze swept across the still-smoking remains of the library as the artificial rain trickled to a halt. They settled on each of the collapsed walls formed by the duckysaur's abrupt entrance and exit.

Debris had filled those holes, and as a result the librarium was still relatively secure. It had come with the heart-wrenching loss of so many books, but at least Adam could still read in some measure of peace. Well... Read what remained.

"Well, Adam... It's time to get to work," he whispered to himself as he stood and began his quest for answers.

* * *

Two weeks later.

Food. Hungry. Scratch. Itchy.

The thoughts chased each other around, again and again, as she haunted her territory on all fours. Scruffy, worn, and wandering aimlessly—this was what had become of the former paladin of Voltrain, Junith Oatheart.

Ever since she'd been bitten while carrying Adam to safety, her feral mind had prioritized one thing—spreading the catsification infection as far as possible. All of her time had been spent hunting, attacking, and infecting what survivors remained.

But after two weeks, she was reaching her limit. Her body was left dehydrated and starved. The need for food was the first lucid thought to break past the infection's madness. The hunger gnawed at her, howled at her. Food had become a scarcity now, a rare commodity lusted after by every feral nekofolk. By now most had grouped up into packs and colonies, for their own protection—and to hunt.

Junith, however, was alone, ostracized despite being infected with the same curse that plagued the minds of so many Drowthraki, leaving her battered and frayed as she hunted on her own.

But now something tempted her, drew her onwards. An aroma nearly forgotten tickled at her nostrils and seemed to animate her limbs. *Food.* As the scent grew stronger, so too strength returned to her body as she barreled down the corridor, towards the source of sustenance.

But as she rounded a corner she paused. There was already a horde of nekodrow here, ripping apart a platter of food laid out on the ground. Upon noticing the newcomer, three of the dark-skinned nekodrow spun and hissed at her, baring their fangs at the nekofolk so similar to them, yet not at all.

Junith prepared herself for battle. Unlike the other infected, she wore armor, something that gave her an advantage against the nekodrow that always aimed to pick fights with her.

She hissed back, her black tail puffing up as her eyes dilated and her claws dug into the tile of the floor.

"Meeeow!" the lead nekodrow caterwauled, a woman wearing a school truancy officer uniform that was torn and ripped to shreds. The outfit did next to nothing to cover her exposed, purple-skinned body, clearly suffering from starvation.

Junith hissed again, her body now releasing energy that sent the nekodrow running away.

Wasting no time, the fallen paladin crawled over, sniffing the platter of cooked meat. Although large chunks of the food had been eaten and torn off by the nekodrow, there were still good bits left.

She reached her head down, nibbling on the bits, completely unaware of the red-haired nekoboy staring at her from the vents above. Or the fact that she was standing over a net of expertly interwoven clothes laid beneath the plate and connected to a pulley system controlled by the same red-haired nekoboy.

Adam smiled, looking down at the paladin who had been relegated to eating contaminated food off the floor. Food he had spiked with herbs and other sleepytime ingredients procured from the chemistry lab and the infirmary.

It had taken him a week to chart the school through the vents, and another week to finalize his base of operations. During that time, he had stumbled across Junith. The nekogirl had fortunately remained within the academy's hallways, rather than fleeing into the roads of the city.

Since then, he'd been tracking her, making note of her hunting grounds, habits, and sleeping pattern, and at last he had determined himself ready, and prepared his trap.

Now he waited, observing as Junith partook of his dish of cooked... whatever it was he found in a trashcan. Gradually her feral, jerky movements slowed and stilled until the nekogirl keeled over, unconscious.

"Oh, how the tables have turned," Adam said to himself. The irony of hunting his archfoe who had spent nearly a lifetime hunting him was not lost on him.

Pulling on the mechanism, the net laid out below him slowly closed around Junith, lifting her up into the vents, from where he could drag her back to his lair.

Catpurr 41
Test Subjects

"Hmmmm."

Dangling before Adam was an unconscious Junith, now strung up in chains looted from the academy's in-house forge and hanging off the librarium's floor. The nekoboy gazed at his fallen foe, stroking his chin.

"Ya know, sir," Redfield said, as the former cop-turned-Death Knight stood beside his master as the nekoboy poked the nude Junith, sketching her body, "this looks really bad."

"So you keep repeating." Tiny hands opened the nekogirl's mouth, prodding at her canines. "But I assure you that my intentions are utterly pure."

"In my world, this would be considered an invasion of privacy. I feel like I'm breaking several laws just standing here," Redfield protested. Another round of meowing caused his head to turn to the side, where several rows of angry nekodrow were strapped to boards. He eyed them cautiously. "Like... a gross invasion."

Adam continued to sketch. "Seeing as you're back, did you get what I sent you for?"

"Uh..." The Death Knight glanced down at the box of gold bars in his armored gauntlets. "Yeah. I asked you five minutes ago where'd you want this."

Oh... Right. It appeared he'd been rather lost in thought.

"Just put it with the others." He waved his summon off, engrossed in his work. Satisfied with her front half, now he circled the girl, making a sketch of her tail and how it connected to her spine. Next, he clipped off a bit of her nails with a pair of pliers.

"Right," Redfield said, turning his ghostly helmet back to the stacks of gold bars and golden jewelry that littered the library, carried in by Redfield and the skelecats. By now, the librarium almost looked more like a dragon's hoard. Adam's summons had taken everything gold and glittery that wasn't literally nailed down and brought it here. "What are we doing with all this gold?"

"Saving the world," came the sardonic reply as Junith's extremities began to twitch. "Well, this one and any future ones we go to."

The nekomancer backed away.

"This is extremely dangerous, you know," Redfield said. "What if she awakens and begins using magic?"

"Are you referring to her skills?" Adam said. "It's doubtful she will. From my prolonged observations she hasn't been doing so. Even when fighting off multiple assailants."

"Then why are you standing behind me?" Redfield asked, as the nekoboy hunkered down.

"It's hot and I wanted some shade."

"We're indoors," Redfield retorted. Junith began thrashing about mid-air, tugging at her chains. The Death Knight cast a wary eye towards her. "Are you sure those can hold her?"

"By my calculations," Adam paused, tensing up at the sound of the chains clinking, "yes."

"Why doesn't that fill me with confidence?"

"You're dead. What do you have to worry about?"

"It still hurts to die, you know," Redfield countered. "When that mage vaporized me, I felt... *Everything.*"

The nekomancer was silent for a moment, digesting that information.

"Right. I hadn't considered that angle. My apologies," he said, stepping out from behind Redfield. Having watched his infected companion for a few moments, he was now certain her chains would hold.

"Don't worry 'bout it."

"See, flawless mathematics." The boy gestured towards the hissing and snapping Junith.

"Okay. So... How do you plan on curing her?" Redfield asked, nudging all the clutter and knick knacks he'd been forced to bring in with a black armored boot. "And the rest of them?"

"Simple!" Adam declared, walking off towards a table cluttered with various items ranging from chemistry beakers to weapons and armor. "Through trial and error."

Golden eyes tracked the items there, taking inventory one final time.

A gold dagger, a bar of gold, shaved bits of gold flakes, and a flask filled with yellow liquid.

The nekoboy gathered in his hands some of the gold flakes, which he'd painstakingly shaved from a solid block of gold.

Then he walked over to a bound nekodrow, sprinkling the gold flakes on the thrashing woman.

Immediately her purple skin began to sizzle, her tail flicking rapidly as she strained against her restraints. From behind the rope gagging her mouth came a throaty growl.

Adam summoned his notebook and recorded the effects and time, watching as the drow's complexion lightened, her tail shriveled up, and her cat ears began to morph back to their default placement.

"One tablespoon of gold flakes, applied to solar plexus area. Effect: Instantaneous. Time..." he muttered, waiting as the cat features on the Drowthraki melted away. "Eleven minutes."

With each of the bound nekodrow, Adam repeated the process and recorded the events. Upon completion of the infection's reversion, each of the dark elf women passed out, allowing him to carry on without a fuss.

Ten to twelve minutes for flakes, he noted. Then, using one of Junith's nail clippings, he reinfected his bound subjects.

"Time for re-catsification, twenty seconds to a minute... Possible acceleration caused by prior catsification," he reported.

"Jesus, you're a walking biological WMD," Redfield commented. Throughout the whole process he had stood beside Adam, staring in some mixture of awe and horror as the test subjects reawakened, squirming as their ears, tails, and fangs regrew.

"WMD?" Adam asked.

"Weapon of mass destruction. Just one of these infected can destroy a world."

"So, you understand what I'm doing here. The importance of it?"

"I do," the Death Knight affirmed, making Adam sigh with relief.

"It's wonderful that we're on the same page," the boy said, walking off to grab an ornamental, gold-plated dagger.

He hesitated only for a moment, sighing to himself. Then he quickly sliced the forearm of one of the nekofolk and waited.

Catpurr 42
Aqua Regia

"Adam—Sir," Redfield said, holding out an armored gauntlet towards Adam. "Perhaps we should put clothes on her *before* waking her up?"

The nekoboy paused, moments from administering the cure to Junith. Or, well, he hoped it would cure her of her rabid state. After such rigorous testing he was fairly certain it would.

"Ah... Good point," Adam said, rubbing the side of his face with a gloved hand as he lowered the flask of golden liquid. "She does get pissy about that sort of thing, doesn't she?"

"Most people tend to not enjoy being... exposed in front of others," Redfield said, flatly.

"I'll make a note of that, I 'spose. Mind knocking her out, or shall I?" He placed the golden flask down on the table, instead picking up a torn shirt and a different flask, containing a colorless liquid, one he had spent hours creating and perfecting.

"Are you sure that's safe, sir?" Redfield asked, as Adam let droplets fall from the vial onto the cloth. "Chloroform is very dangerous. Especially... No offense, but this isn't exactly a quality science lab."

They were still in the messy librarium, now growing cramped with bars of gold, lab equipment, and the squirming catsified test subjects.

"According to the Drowthraki literature, this is their go-to weapon to seduce partners and calm them down."

"You mean subdue."

"Not according to this book," Adam said, holding up a tome whose cover proudly bore the title, *How to Train Your Slave; BDSM Guide to Obedience.* Beneath the words was the image of a skinny Drowthraki woman in leather, smothering a scantily clad, flailing elf. "Very interesting read. Haven't gotten to the point where it tells me what B-D-S-M stands for, but I understand the gist of it."

Redfield was left at a loss for words.

"Okay. Well, putting aside how innocent you truly are, let me do it," Redfield said, plucking the rag and flask out of his master's hand and approaching Junith, quickly covering the rabid girl's fanged mouth with his gauntlet.

"Ow." Valiantly the nekogirl squirmed, trying to escape the Death Knight's grasp, but he held the rag over her nose until finally she fell limp.

"Huh... Five minutes." Adam said, jotting down the time. "Here I thought it would be much faster."

Redfield backed away, gently placing the items on a nearby table. "Chloroform doesn't work like it does in Hollywood. It usually takes about five to ten minutes to knock someone out."

"Hollywood?"

"Uhhh. It's a movie studio," Redfield said, realizing he'd made a mistake.

"Movies?" Adam asked, his ears unconsciously twitching as his interest pricked.

"Focus, sir."

"Right." Quickly he lifted a small pile of fabric and tossed it haphazardly over Junith. Using a needle and thread from his pockets he quickly went to work, expertly sewing a dark blue dress around the nekogirl.

"Huh, you can sew?" Redfield said, clear surprise in his tone.

"When you're on the road for most of your life, you get pretty good at being self-sufficient," the nekomancer said, standing back and admiring his handiwork. "Especially when every new robe you wear gets torn up by a holier-than-thou-maniac."

"You'll have to tell me more about this maniac you're always complaining about," Redfield said as Adam reached over, grabbing the flask he'd set down before again.

"One day. If you tell me more about this Hollywood."

"Sure."

"Alright then," he replied before he took the flask and aimed it at Junith's face. He clenched his jaw, steeling himself before he squeezed the trigger, spraying the rabid nekogirl in the face with the golden mixture.

And then he waited. Golden liquid trickled down her sizzling, boiling skin. Pus pockets formed and just as quickly burst.

But despite the ugly process, catsification was working in her favor. Her innate regeneration, something shared by all those catsified, was quick to heal the damage.

"That looks extremely painful, sir," the Death Knight remarked, wincing as he observed the mixture of hydrochloric acid, nitric acid, and several bars of dissolved gold doing its work, melting the dark hair off the nekogirl's skull, smoke curling from the wounds.

"Oh, yes. Quite."

Redfield's eyes widened. "Uuuh, sir."

"Hm?" In this time, Adam had yet to look up from documenting the chemical's reactions to living flesh.

"In the future, you may want to aim more for her chest area. Sir."

"And why is that?"

"Because you've burned most of her hair off." He pointed to the bald patches atop Junith's head. "She's not going to be happy."

"When is she ever?" Adam shrugged. "Plus, her being bald is funny."

"That's fair, but I do believe this will piss her off. Take it from me, sir, women love their hair."

"Eh, I'll just tell her she fell down some stairs or something." Again, he shrugged as Junith began to wake.

"I don't— I..." Redfield trailed off. The Death Knight quickly gave up arguing his point, instead choosing to facepalm.

"Wha—" Junith began, her eyes fluttering open. Then she let out an ear-piercing wail.

"BASTARD! BASTARD! WHAT ARE YOU DOING TO ME?!" she demanded, hydrochloric acid still dripping off her face as she struggled against her chains.

"Hey, it worked!" Adam exclaimed, smiling to himself.

"WHAT! IS! THIS?! IT BURNS!"

"Oh! Crapbaskets!" he yelled, snapping out of his excitement at a job well done as he grabbed a bucket filled with sodium bicarbonate, a compound that could neutralize the acid.

He doused Junith, covering her in white dust before a skelecat ran up to him, carrying a pail of water.

With Redfield's help, the two went to work cleaning Junith off, making sure she was no longer burning.

"YOU!" she snarled, bearing her fangs at Adam. "DO YOU HAVE ANY IDEA HOW MUCH THAT HURTS?!"

"Hey, you're alive, aren't you?" he said, returning to recording the curative effects of his tincture.

"YOU THREW ACID ON ME!"

"Sprayed."

"What?"

"*Sprayed* acid on you," he corrected. The paladin's eye twitched as a vein on her forehead throbbed. From the side, Redfield watched as the girl's face grew redder and redder.

"I'LL KILL YOU!"

"See, Red, she's always angry," Adam said. "A thank you would be nice. A week ago, you were eating rotting fish off the floor and peeing on carpets."

At Adam's words the nekogirl became flustered, the hairs on her body standing on end. She shrank into herself, and only then did she realize she was no longer wearing her armor.

"G-Get! Get me out of these chains!" she hissed.

Redfield looked at Adam, awaiting his master's command.

"Shall I, sir?"

"Sure, as long as she doesn't bite or infect anyone." At a nonchalant wave, Redfield dutifully uncuffed their prisoner, starting with her ankles.

"Where are we?" Junith asked, as she fell to the floor in a crouch. Her hand bunched the fabric of her dress into a fist. "And what am I wearing?!"

"The Librarium Sanctum, home of most of the academy's literature and knowledge," Adam said, holding up the *How to Train Your Slave* book. Redfield was quick to pluck it away. "As for what you're wearing, I sti—"

"Ehem," Redfield said, standing in front of Adam. "It's a dress we found you in."

Junith looked down, smoothing out the fabric with her hands. "It's nice. Feral me has good taste."

Adam's ears twitched.

"Do you remember your experience as a feral?" he asked, his notebook already in hand.

"No. All I remember was—" Junith's eyes widened with panic. "Ellie!"

"What?"

"Not what, who! She was the teen girl that was with us!" she yelled. "After I got scratched, I handed you off to her so I could buy time and slow down the infected."

"How noble of you."

"Shut up! Have you seen them? Where are they?!" she demanded, shaking Adam.

"No, I haven't. I woke up in a barricaded room all alone."

Junith deflated, her cat ears folding.

Adam was unsure of what to do in this situation as he stared at the depressed nekogirl.

"You should comfort her, sir," Redfield whispered, leaning down to reach the boy's ear.

"What? Why?" he whispered back, his brow raised.

"Because she got infected saving you."

"Yeah, right after she knocked me out."

Redfield was unyielding. "Still, sir. Think of it as team building and strengthening cohesion."

Adam sighed, before stiffly reaching out to the sulking Junith.

"There, there. I'm sure they're okay," he said, tapping on her shoulder.

"Don't touch me!" she hissed. She stormed off, only to abruptly lose steam and collapse upon a stack of nearby books.

"See what happens when I'm nice?" Adam said to Redfield.

"It's the thought that counts," The Death Knight replied. They both moved to stand above Junith, as the girl mumbled directly into the pages of a dusty tome.

"Fewaweb."

"What?" Adam asked, brow raised.

"Fweeeb." One arm reached out, jerkily, as though puppeted on an unseen thread.

"What? I can't understand—"

"FOOD!"

Catpurr 43

Operation: Golden Shower

With a burner liberated from the academy chem lab, Junith and Adam cooked and then silently ate a meal. Well, Junith did; Adam was too busy watching her scarf chunks of meat and vegetables before they'd even cooled down, simply too famished to care if she burned her fingers or tongue in the pursuit of sustenance.

"Oh, lord above! This is so good!" The paladin was almost moved to tears. Adam chewed more quietly, his attention mostly fixed on his book. "You know. Adam, as much as it pains me to admit, you may be a smelly heretical pain that deserves to be flogged, but you can *cook*."

Adam said nothing, his brow furrowed as his gaze intently swept over the contents of his book.

"Hey."

No response.

"Hey!" Junith yelled, punching him on the shoulder and pulling him from his stupor. "I gave you a compliment."

His look of bafflement quickly became a scowl. "Thanks?" With the interaction finished, he went back to his book.

"Say... Where did you get fresh meat from, by the way?" As the nekogirl looked around, she realized she had not seen any kitchens or larders.

"*Don't*. Don't ask," Redfield warned, appearing with a stack of books.

"What? Why?" Junith hissed, her expression narrowing as her face twisted. "Where did you get this food?!"

"Hm? Oh, from a dead Drowthraki body," Adam replied. He bit into another piece of meat, eyes scanning lines of text even as Junith's expression morphed into one of horror.

Her head slowly moved to the meat in her hands, mouth ajar as her eyes twitched and gazed at the—

"Y-Y-Y-You! BLEEEGH." She turned her head and rainbow spew spattered over Adam and his books. He finally looked up, with a face of mild disappointment. "YOU MADE ME INTO A CANNIBAL?!"

"Hm? No," he said casually, wiping the vomit off his face with a sigh. "You are a human turned nekogirl. These are Drowthraki. Dif—"

"DON'T YOU GIVE ME THAT SPIEL! YOU MADE ME! YY-Y-YOU MADE ME EAT A SENTIENT BEING!" she screamed. Claws came out as she tried to pounce on Adam, but Redfield grabbed her by the scruff.

"Having your body consumed to sustain life is one of the highest honors that can be undertaken in Drowthraki culture. A sacred rite performed for the deceased. It would be disrespectful not to honor their customs," Adam replied, continuing to chew. "I know you're worried, but we aren't cannibals, the Drowthraki are."

"Y-Y-Y—" Junith kept stuttering, unable to process what she'd unwittingly been a part of. Her rage seemed to leave her as she deflated, eyes glazing over.

"See. I told you not to ask," Redfield whispered, holding the limp woman until he was sure the fight in her system had flickered out. Gently, he set her on the floor.

"C-C-Cannibal... I'm a cannibal... And it was so tasty..." Junith began to sob, actual tears flowing from the woman's eyes as she stared at the ceiling.

"Oh... Wow. Okay," Redfield said, backing away to stand beside Adam. "I think you broke her, sir."

"She'll be fine," he replied, his focus still on the schematic of the city laid out before him.

"Have you formulated a plan yet?"

"I have," Adam replied, rubbing his chin. "I call it, Operation: Golden Shower."

There was a long and drawn-out creak as Redfield's helmet swiveled, his gaze locking on the small nekoboy.

"Are you serious?"

"Yes," Adam said straight-faced. "Do you see this conduit here?"

He tapped a small image on the map.

"Yes, sir."

"This is the main control gate for the fire suppression system that hangs over the city," Adam explained. The Death Knight's jaw chattered as he caught on to his master's plan. His blazing eyes flickered to the nearby metal barrels, each filled with the liquid solution known as aqua regia.

"I see."

"The plan is simple, really." Adam took a breath. "We break into the water holding tank and refill the tanks with aqua regia. Then we activate the fire suppression system, flooding the city with the cure."

"What about the infected that are indoors? Or the... burning effects?" Redfield asked.

"Right, well... There's nothing I can do about the acid. There's not enough sodium bicarbonate, or a way to distribute it. The regeneration effect will persist for a bit after, but there's no telling if they'll all survive." The boy grimaced. What came next would not be pleasant by any means, but it would be for the greater good. He had seen before what happened when the infection was left to spread unchecked. "For those indoors, we'll have to go one by one to spray them down."

"So that's why you made so many flasks," Redfield said. Arranged in rows on a nearby table were dozens and dozens of spray flasks, along with the small bags of white powder. "The name of the game is containment."

Adam blinked, frowning.

"Yes. We can't risk this getting out." He sighed, eyeing his captives. "Hopefully when I cure and wake these Drowthraki, they'll understand the severity of the situation and aid us."

"Cannibal... Cannibal..." Junith continued to cry.

Adam ignored her.

"We'll need to double check and triple check that there aren't any ways for the survivors to get out. Or the duckysaurs, either," he said. His meal long finished, he stood, moving to the section of the librarium where he stored the lab equipment. Another batch of sodium bicarbonate was being finished, even as he spoke. "If even one catsified person gets out, this world could be doomed."

Redfield's ghostly eyes flickered.

"I understand what's at stake," the Death Knight said. He had been there for the second trial as well, after all, he too knew exactly what sort of destruction catsification was capable of—but that world had been dealing with an undead epidemic.

This was worse.

Catsification gave the living enhanced speed, regeneration, and heightened senses. They were like fictional werewolves, if the werewolves were cats. The only difference was that the nekofolk weren't bound to the whims of the full moon.

Or did that only apply to the characters of Dragon Sphere?

Redfield discarded his thoughts, instead focusing on the task at hand. He followed his master as he prepared to cure and wake up the remaining Drowthraki.

Catpurr 44

Ellie's Last Stand

Fast-paced footsteps echoed in the halls of the inn as Ellie spun, racing into an empty room. The girl could not even pause to breathe. Instead, she threw herself bodily into an open closet, shutting it as gently as she dared behind her.

Held up in a wooden box, she clutched her bar of gold close to her chest. Not inches away, the floorboards creaked.

She held her breath, her eyes quivering. With her left eye, she peered through the crack in the closet door. Beyond that, she barely glimpsed the catsified Drowthraki prowling the room.

Karlie.

Her own best friend was hunting her.

Ellie didn't move. Didn't breathe. Didn't blink. Every fiber of her being was committed to blending in with the dresses in the closet as much as possible.

Ever since she'd run into the two Drowthraki boys pretending to be girls, everything had gone downhill.

First the entire academy had been overrun, then the city. She had found a group of survivors, and had at first teamed up with them, hoping to escape. But the infected had picked them off, one by one by one.

Out of a group of seven, all that was left was Ellie.

It left her starving, tired, and dirty. She hadn't eaten a good meal in days. What she could find were just scraps and trash, the little bits of edible garbage that even the catsified Drowthraki didn't want.

Still, she had a mission. To escape the chaos and bring with her the cure to this magical curse. She and Karlie had barricaded the door and left Adama behind after they'd both been scratched, taking with them the gold bar he had clutched in his hands. The thing he had seemed certain could cure this madness. Getting to the roof had been a treacherous task, and they had risked their lives. Only barely had they avoided turning into feral creatures themselves.

Someone had to warn the others, to tell them of what transpired. Now it looked like Ellie would have to go it alone.

But she was too tired, too haggard to pin and wrestle her friend who was now both physically stronger *and* faster than her.

All she could do was pray to the Earth Mother of Silk that she would survive this tribulation.

Just outside, Karlie sniffed the air. The nekodrow paced the decrepit room on all fours, the room they had sheltered in together not long ago.

Ellie's limbs were trembling. Her full body felt hollow, the results of her long stint without food. She felt a familiar sensation as her innards churned and realized what was about to happen.

No! The girl's eyes went wide, fear overtaking her body, skin tingling as Karlie's golden eyes snapped in her direction.

Please! Please no!

Ellie clutched the golden bar as if it was a lifeline, praying to the Goddess with more fervor than any zealot.

Karlie hissed. From the other side of the closet's door, there was a thump.

"AH!" Ellie yelped. The double doors slammed shut. The sound of claws ripping into hardwood filled her pointed ears.

Pleasepleaseplease! Earth Mother!

The door burst open. Ellie's sight was filled with Karlie's grasping, clawed hands. By some miracle they didn't scratch her flesh, only clawing at her torn and stained school uniform.

Ellie kicked, sending the feral girl flying, before running.

[The Goddess Freya has heard your desperate plea.]
[You have been Chosen!]

"Huh?" Blue words hovered before Ellie's eyes, echoing in her mind. In that instant, Karlie's hand closed around her ankle.

Ellie spun, kicking her friend as a sudden burst of energy flooded her veins.

[SYSTEM ONLINE!]

"Get off! Let me go!" she cried, kicking desperately. Suddenly Karlie went flying. A blast of energy shot from Ellie's hands, hurling her friend through a window.

"KARLETA!" she cried. Instinctively, a System skill activated. Ellie rushed to the window, peering down to where her friend had fallen, but she needn't have worried. Already Karlie was scrambling back up the wall, joined by several more nekodrow.

Name: Elerra Hali
Level: 1
Class: Necromancer Aspirant

HP: 12/20
MP: 10/30
STR: 7
CON: 5
DEX: 6
ARC: 3
SEN: 4
EGO: 10
FAITH: 6
RESISTANCES: Cold (10%)
    BUFFS: Heart of the Explorer (SSR), Blessing of Freya (SSR)
    DEBUFFS: Starving
    SKILLS: Animate Bones, Force Push Lvl 1, Force Pull Lvl 1, Summon Minor Skeleton Lvl 1, Sense Dead Lvl 1.

The display hovering in front of her caused the girl to stumble back in shock, but there was no time to process any of it. Already, Karlie and her pack were nearly at the second floor.

Racing out of the bedroom, Ellie beelined it to a window on the opposite side of the building, clutching her gold bar. She opened the window and leapt, landing on a nearby roof.

A familiar, ear-piercing scream sounded out, one that Ellie now knew too well. The cry of the nekofolk, the cry of the pack.

As she ran, Ellie could hear them, *feel* them as they came from their hunting grounds. The nekofolk scratched and scurried from the shadows hellbent on mauling the last uninfected in the city.

Ellie.

Powered by pure adrenaline, Ellie leapt from black building to black building. Her purple eyes darted left and right, tracking the swarms of nekofolk closing in.

It's hopeless.

A quiet voice, *her* voice whispered inside her mind. It repeated the phrase every time her ragged lungs gasped for breath, every time her muscles cried out for rest, every time she heard another scream.

She climbed a steeple, clambering up the side of the spire. Something slipped from a hole in her pocket, plummeting to the streets below—the gold bar.

"NO!" she cried, watching her last assurance hit a Drowthraki on the head. The rest of the nekodrow backed off, avoiding the gold. It granted Ellie just enough time to haul herself under the belfry of a shrine, hand over hand. As she rested her aching body, she noticed something odd on the back of her hand: a pattern, and quite a familiar one at that—the emblem of her Lady in Silk. But she didn't have time to ponder what this meant or examine the annoying words flooding her vision. Her life was in danger!

Sometime later, she finally reached the top. With nowhere else to go, she looked down. Already, the infected were starting to climb after her. Hordes of them, from every direction.

"What do I do?! What do I do?!" Tremors seized her limbs, and her heart pounded away in her chest. It was all too much. The blue screen in her face, the constant screams of the horde, of her *friend,* her own heartbeat pounding in her ears—it was just all too much. That quiet voice had never seemed louder than now.

At the front of the pack, her best friend led the charge to infect her. Finally, Ellie's legs gave out. Her chest jerked erratically as she sobbed, all her complaints about wanting an adventure flashing through her mind now. She regretted each one.

Give up, why bother? Like a gangrenous sickness, hopelessness began to infect Ellie. She had tried her best, yet her best... wasn't enough. It seemed it was never enough. She was a disappointment to her mother. Her teachers said she'd never amount to anything. And even her talent was... subpar at best.

She wanted to explore the world, yet she could barely get out of her own hometown.

Now she would succumb to the horde like so many before her. Just another feral catsified Drowthraki.

Crapbins.

It began to rain. Golden droplets of water that fell from the heavens, filling the air with an acrid odor.

She reached out, touching the rain, perhaps the last sensation she'd ever—

"OW!"

Ellie recoiled, clutching her hand as she was shaken from her stupor.

Suddenly deafening cries of pain sounded out, shrill screams so loud Ellie was forced to cover her ears and shut her eyes to protect herself from the ungodly decibels.

But the noises simply would not cease. The girl fell to her knees, clutching at her head as her entire body seemed to vibrate.

"BURNS! BURNS! AAAAAAGHHH!"

At the sound of voices, *coherent words,* Ellie's eyes peeled open.

The nekofolk, they were being reverted back!

At the spectacle, her jaw fell open. But what was she to do as people screamed in pain?

Her eyes fell to Karlie. The drow girl's skin was burning, peeling... regenerating. Each time the golden water melted it away, it came back.

Ellie reached out, desperate to help, but the burning water forced her back.

"What do I do?" she wondered, gritting her teeth.

Suddenly the golden shower turned purple.

The acrid smell melted away, replaced instead by a scent of sun blossoms, a flower native to the Portr regions.

The screaming began to fade. Cries of relief took its place as the burning smells faded.

"E-Ellie?" Karlie exclaimed, looking up.

"Karlie!" she cried. The young necromancer aspirant wasted no time climbing down, embracing her friend in the purple rain.

* * *

"Go. Get out there," Adam commanded, lifting his goggles as he stared out of a window.

At his command, the cured Drowthraki kitted out in full plate armor and armed with various flasks took off, moving to hunt down the remaining nekodrow and cleanse the town of the infection once and for all.

"I must commend you, Chosen of Freya," a tall Drowthraki with greying hair and deep violet eyes said. The woman stroked her sharp chin. "Your plan saved my people and may have even saved the world. On behalf of all Drowthraki, I thank you."

"Nonsense, Grandmaster. I merely presented the cure; you made a way to mitigate its side effects. These people will live because of you," Adam said, using his best girl imitation as he stood beside the Grandmaster of the Academy.

"My, aren't you humble, Priestess."

"What I do, I do in the name of our Lady in Silk. I apologize that I could not arrive sooner," he replied, a devious smile on his face as the woman in charge of the city showered him with yet more praise, as surely as his cure showered down upon the city.

Catpurr 45

Heroine of the Drowthraki

"As requested, two plates of duckysaur. No citrus, no garlic, chamomile, or cloves," intoned a male Drowthraki butler wearing a shackle around his neck as he wheeled in the silver cart, decorated with golden trays of food. "Will there be anything else, Voice of Our Lady in Silk?"

"No. That will be all. Thank you. And remember not to disturb us while we decipher these texts," Adam said, waving off the man. He bowed and took his leave, closing the velvet-red door behind him.

"I can't believe that worked..." Junith said, peering out of the blue tinted window of the deluxe bedroom that she and Adam shared. From the top of a grand spire, their view overlooked the entire city.

"And yet you doubted me," Adam said, sitting on a king-sized bed, fitted with soft, blue sheets and royal-purple pillows. As was typical, he was deeply engrossed in a book.

"No. Seriously. HOW?!" Junith yelled, completely flabbergasted. One moment they were sleeping on piles of books, and now they were staying in an all-expenses paid suite exclusively reserved for heroes.

Adam sighed.

"None of this was supposed to work. And yet! *Yet*! Somehow, you tricked everyone into thinking you're some hero sent by the goddess!"

"Heroine."

"What?"

"Heroine. Female version of hero," he corrected. In his lap, his book's pages depicted a medical diagram of the duckysaur's anatomy. One of his skelecats approached him, bearing a plate of steaming duck. "This ruse only works so long as we don't make any mistakes. Especially with the amount of eyes on us now."

Junith took a breath, pinching her nose. Her claws had been hidden with a new set of fancy leather gloves, all in black. "So what's the plan now, *Voice of the Lady in Silk*?"

Adam narrowed his eyes but recalled the events that had led up to this point.

The Ouroborus.

During his cleanup of the academy, he had come across a feral elderly woman in a lavish dress hanging around a spacious office. However, it wasn't the dress, the lavish decor, or the books torn to shreds that gave the nekomancer pause, but rather the necklace she still wore.

It was a pendant bearing the symbol of Eli, his own supposed patron.

After spritzing the Drowthraki with the cure, Adam of course questioned her, asking where she got the symbol and her relationship to Eli.

To his dismay, the woman became ecstatic, calling him the savior of Drowthraki-kind. A messenger from Freya herself, as only the true followers of the Lady in Silk recognized the symbol. It was ordained that in their darkest hour, her Chosen would come

This answer of course just raised even more questions.

Who was Eli really? What was his relation to Freya? How was it they shared domains? Why did she think the symbol belonged to Freya, when it belonged to Eli?

Amongst the many gifts the Director had given him in gratitude, one of the ones he cared for most was a massive old tome. Presently it lay on the luxurious bed, beside him.

According to her, it was an indecipherable holy tome, an artifact of the gods that was waiting for a Chosen of Freya. A relic that belonged in the hands of the Chosen.

As he inspected the item, Adam was careful to avoid touching it, ever since the Head Mistress had left it on the bed. A dire warning was embossed across its cover in gold calligraphy.

[Freya's Secret Diary! Don't touch or I'll turn your organs into vineweed!]

This of course left the nekoboy with a dilemma.

While curiosity dictated that he read it, self-preservation told him not to touch it for fear of being... *restructured.*

Still, perhaps insight could be garnered into the lives of the gods. After all, the Mistress had handled the book, even flipped through its pages to reminisce before she handed it off to Adam.

So it had to be safe...

Right?

He shook his head and sighed. "We need to get our bearings." For now, he would table his research and instead focus on a different task. "Restock, experiment, and see about clearing the trial."

"Oh?" Junith raised her brow, poking at the fried bits of duckysaur. "You want to clear the trial now? What brought about that change?"

The words caused his ears to press flat, and his hackles to rise.

"A debt," Adam spat. Like the haunting drums of war, an unseen duck quacked relentlessly in his ear. From his eye fell a single, silent tear, tracing a path across his cheek. For all the books lost, the ducks must pay.

"Wait, what do you mean by experiment?" Junith hissed, visibly worried.

"Well…" Adam said, pulling up his System and accessing his evolution tree.

[Cat Tail Module]
[Enhanced Muscular Ligature]
[Reflex Sensitivity Tuning V2]
[Ocular Sharpening]
[Lightweight Body Optimization]
[Bone Density Upgrade]
[Healing Factor Boost]
[Sound Perception Tuning]
[Smell Refinement]
[SEALED until 4/5 improvements are selected!]

He still had a point available, and now that he was in a safe space, he could finally put it to use.

"I have a theory on how to cure us of this disease," Adam said. Junith seemed to perk up, interest glinting in her eyes.

"A theory? Well, let's hear it, necromancer!" she demanded, dropping the piece of meat in her hands and turning to the nekomancer, eager to be done with her catsified state.

"What if in order for gold to revert us, we need to be more cat-like," he surmised, thinking out loud.

"Like crap on the floor and scratch up things? Because I'm not doing that."

"No, you've already done both of those things," he said, causing Junith to go red. "What I'm saying is, maybe if I became more catlike, I may be more susceptible to the cure."

"What *are* you saying?"

Adam sighed. He didn't want to use this evolution point on it, but if it'd give him a shot at the cure to return to his old self, he'd take it.

Of course, it was a shot in the dark, but at this point he'd do anything to get out of this form.

Even if it meant...

"I'm getting a tail," Adam sighed as Junith looked at him with confusion. "Make sure no one bothers me while I sleep."

"Uh?"

His finger pushed against the System screen, making his selection. No turning back now. Tremors began, first in his hand, then gradually spreading to the rest of his body. The nekoboy sprawled across the luxurious bed, passing out.

Catpurr 46

Problematic Adam

Moments after waking, Adam frantically looked around as he realized he couldn't move. He was being held down, buried, by something that obstructed his vision.

Had he been the victim of a cave-in? But he was intimately familiar with the weight and feel of dirt, and this was completely different. Instead, it felt oddly soft, rough in some areas, but comfortable and warm.

Light was visible in the distance. With haste, he struggled until he escaped the pile of haggard, naked bodies... lying in the middle of a forest?

What?!

Adam nearly yelped, his eyes going wide as he realized he had been buried underneath a pile of sleeping Drowthraki women. Not only that, he was also naked!

He freed himself, backing away slowly as a woman let out a moan. From behind, there was an unnatural sensation. A cushion of wind seemed to caress his—tail? Tail!

It was a foot-long, fluffy, red and crowned by a white tip.

But there was no time to process this new appendage. He had to get away from the pile of women that was now slowly waking up.

What the Nyx happened?! he hissed to himself, taking off through the woods and pulling up his System menu. Where the Nyx was Junith?

One task! I gave you one task!

Companion sense informed him that she was quite near, in fact, she was closing in on his location!

As they each turned a tree, they came into each other's view. Like a perfect reflection each neko froze, pointing at the other as they simultaneously cried out, "You!"

"YOU'RE NAKED!" Junith screamed, turning away.

"I KNOW!" Adam yelled, spotting his cloak on the paladin's shoulders. "WHERE'S MY STUFF?! MY ITEMS?!"

"Put some clothes on, moron!" she cried, covering her eyes.

"Newsflash, idiot, I don't have anything to wear! What the Nyx happened?!" Adam said, grabbing a hold of the nekogirl.

"That's what I want to ask you! And I'm not an idiot!" Junith cried before punching Adam. She reached onto her back, grabbing his cloak of invisibility and throwing it at him. "Cover your unmentionables!"

"Tell me what you know," Adam demanded. They didn't have much time; growing louder, he could hear voices.

"Soon," Junith said, as her mark illuminated. "We need to get to safety first. There are search teams looking for you."

"What?"

"No time!" she yelled, grabbing Adam's wrist.

* * *

After walking for roughly thirty minutes, Adam and Junith came to a massive hole in the ground, surrounded by numerous massive duck tracks.

Adam peered down, eyeing the grappling hooks on the edge of the hole that led into the Drowthraki city below.

"Here, put this on," Junith said, handing Adam his wig. She looked to either side and grabbed the rope.

The pair rappelled down, making their way into the city where a patrol of golden-plated guards, armed with gilded weapons and flasks of golden shower, were guarding the road to the surface.

"Lady Junith! Grand Priestess Adama! You've returned!" a guard yelled. In no time a crowd of Drowthraki was gathering, all eager to meet their savior.

Adam's eyes darted nervously as the crowd pushed towards him, blissfully unaware that he wore nothing but a wig, a storage ring, and a cloak. One wrong move and he would be exposed—quite literally.

"Uh, Grand Priestess, what's that under your cloak?" a guard asked, noticing some strange movement.

Adam spun, realizing his tail was moving on its own.

"BACK! OFF!" Junith suddenly barked, standing in front of Adam and releasing a shout laced with mana. The skill sent the Drowthraki immediately to their knees.

"Our apologies, Lady Junith!" the crowd chorused in unison, each Drowthraki looking directly at the ground.

"Let's go!" Junith hissed, taking Adam through the crowd and back to the Grand Spire where their quarters lay.

After bypassing multiple guards, adoring fans, and eager servants wishing to be used, the nekopair finally made it back to the lavish suite, where Adam breathed a sigh of relief upon seeing his gear.

"What the Nyx happened? Why was I in the middle of the woods buried under women and naked?!" he demanded.

"You don't remember?" Junith said, her brow furrowed.

"Of course not! If I did, why would I be asking you?!" he yelled, grabbing his gear and re-equipping his pants and armor.

"You transformed!" That caused Adam to pause.

"Transform? Elaborate," he said, summoning his notebook with his interest piqued. "What happened when I lost consciousness?"

The look she gave him truly spoke volumes of what she thought of him, but documenting the phenomena came first. Junith described how Adam had begun yelling and screaming about his items before stripping and growing.

"You mean... I turned back into my adult form?" Adam asked, looking up from his notes.

"With cat ears and a tail. Then you leapt out of the window, causing pandemonium." She gestured quite helpfully at a nearby shattered window.

Adam frowned. A transformation...

This was unexpected, but interesting.

He hesitated before asking his next question. "What did I do?"

Junith seemed just as reticent to answer. "We don't know."

"What do you mean, you don't know?"

"We don't know! You ran around butt naked kidnapping women and—"

"HOLD UP! I did *what*?!"

"The constables are still investigating the crime scenes and are—"

Junith's lips were moving but words weren't coming out.

Or rather, Adam's ears had stopped working. A loud whine dominated his sense of hearing, as his brows furrowed deeper and deeper in thought. Certainly this explained some things, like why he'd been buried under the body of a naked woman or five. But did that mean he had...?

No...

Adam shuddered, disgust roiling through his innards.

A sudden knock at the door drew their joint attention.

"Lady Junith!" the Headmistress yelled, banging on the door with urgency. "Are you in there?"

And Adam still wasn't completely dressed. His tail fluffed up with alarm.

"Stall!"

Adam swan dived to the floor, clutching his cloak close in the instant the door opened.

"What do you mean they're out of pizza?" he hissed, activating his cloak.

"Lady Junith, I heard the Grand Priestess was found and came post-haste!" the woman yelled, entering with various guards. "Where is she? We must protect her!"

"She's currently—"

"Oh! Priestess!" the Headmistress yelled, walking around the bed, where Adam was clearly visible. "What are you doing down there?"

Huh? He could still be seen? But how was that even—

MY TAIL!

Adam quickly shot up, sitting down on the bed. As he sat on his tail, his entire body jolted with pain and he struggled to hide his wince.

"A-Are you okay?" the Headmistress asked, reaching out.

"I'm fine!" he squeaked.

"We were so worried when we found out you were taken by the feraling," the Mistress said. "Do you remember anything that happened?"

"Uuh. No, sorry," Adam said, shifting his body as a numbing sensation creeped through his tail. "I was knocked out. I woke up in the middle of the woods with Junith rescuing me. Sorry, I don't have any information."

The Mistress frowned, her shoulders sagging. "That's the same thing most of the survivors said."

"Survivors?" Adam asked.

"Yes, we've recovered a few of the women that were taken. We've been interrogating one of the groups left in a pile."

"P-Pile? Groups?" Adam said, confusion on his face.

"Yes, Grand Priestess, several groups of women left alone in groupings of three or four. The largest was twelve, that we just found. According to most, they were coerced by a smooth talking, red-haired nekoman that compelled them to follow him."

"I-Is that so?" Adam stuttered, visibly sweating. "And, uh... What else do they remember?"

The Headmistress narrowed her eyes. She peered towards a guard, cheeks flushing purple.

Oh no.

"They... cuddled."

"Cuddled? Is that a euphemism... for coitus?" Adam asked, his worst fears—

"No. Oddly, the women weren't ravished, but rather made to cuddle before the being got bored and left, knocking out the women using some form of hypnosis," the Headmistress said. "We believe he's the culprit of the infection, and we're are doubling and tripling our guard rotations. More gold armor is being crafted, and when next he shows we'll be ready."

"Ah... Is that right?" He was still in danger, it seemed.

"We'll triple security around your quarters for your protection and have guards escort you everywhere—"

"I don't think that will be necessary, Headmistress," the nekoboy cut in with a nervous laugh.

"But—"

"We must protect the citizenry!" he reasoned, slamming his fist into his palm." The guards will be more useful in tracking down any infected holdouts and giving people peace of mind."

The Headmistress and the guards shared a look.

"So noble. Truly, you are worthy of being our Lady in Silk's Chosen," she acknowledged with a bow. "If there's anything you need, I'll leave a couple of guards posted. In the meantime, I've procured the maps you requested and the data from the duckysaurs' lair."

"Thank you," Adam said.

The woman left and a scribe brought in a bundle of papers. The child froze, eyeing Adam—they recognized each other immediately.

Ellie stood as still as a statue in the doorway, staring at the nekopair with obvious shock.

Catpurr 47

Wereneko

"What are you doing, scribe? Drop off the documents and get going," commanded a guard.

Ellie jolted from her stupor, shaking her head. Why had she just been standing around? The last thing she recalled was being asked to drop the documents off with the Grand Priestess who was actually this boy pretending to be a girl!

[Item located!]

A large tome sitting on the bed caught Ellie's eye as she set the papers down on a desk. Myriad questions burned in her mind as she took her leave.

But she said nothing, Adam's narrowed eyes lingering on her as she quickly made herself scarce, watching the potential loose end depart.

When the dark clicked shut, he breathed a sigh of relief, now he and Junith could focus on the issue of his transformation.

* * *

"Werewolf," said Redfield, from where he stood in a corner.

"Werewolf?" Adam asked, looking curiously. He had summoned the Death Knight to watch over him, in case he had another... transformation.

"In my world, there are myths about werewolves and vampires. What you've described is a werewolf, or, well... in your case, a werecat?

They're beings that possess high regeneration, strength, and transform during a full moon. They can infect others and turn them into werewolves, too."

"Interesting." Redfield's insight truly was invaluable, as was the man himself. "Your world has vampyres? I suspected it was a form of vampirism, but there's no craving for sexual fluids. Hmmm."

Redfield shifted his head. "Don't you mean blood, sir?"

"No, vampyres sap the strength of their victims via sexual fluids," Adam recalled. "They have red eyes, sharp fangs and—"

"You're talking about succubi, not vampires, sir," Redfield stated.

"No, I'm talking about vampyres. I'm a necromancer, I know my undead."

"Is it possible you're both talking about two different, but similar things?" Junith butted in, the paladin's eyes studying the maps of a location called Candy Mountain.

Adam and Redfield shared a look.

"Anyway, I think you're just like a werewolf, but a cat, sir. A werecat. I think there's a term for it, but I'm not sure," Redfield continued.

"What are a werewolf's weaknesses?" Adam asked, drawing an image of a wolf with a human head.

"Silver, if I'm remembering correctly, Liza would probably know more. She'd probably call it a wereneko or something, though."

"Liza? Why would that oaf know?" Junith asked.

"Well, as much as I hate to admit. I only know all this because she wouldn't shut up when I had her in custody. In fact, all she would do is yap about movies while we were running for our lives," Redfield replied. Adam's ears flicked up as he peered at the Death Knight.

That's right, they knew each other prior to trial three.

"Great," Adam muttered, opening his companion tab. Liza was still far away, doing gods knew what, but judging from the faint feeling of happiness, it couldn't possibly be anything good.

* * *

LIZA POV

"THIS IS AWESOME!" a sopping wet Liza screamed, riding atop a massive, four-legged lizard as it leapt out of the ocean and snatched a flying duckysaur from the air.

* * *

Adam POV

Adam took a breath. "So... transformation during a full moon..." he prompted, opening his notes. Earlier he had observed this world had two suns and one moon. According to texts, the day and night cycle of this world was vastly different than any he'd been to. Here, daylight lasted for thirty-six hours, while night itself only lasted for roughly six. From the position of the moon in its relation to the twin suns, a full moon was...

"Crapbaskets."

"What?" Upon catching sight of Adam's intense, almost obsessive expression, a cold shudder arced down her spine. That couldn't possibly be anything good.

"So here's an interesting fact. There's a full moon every day of the week, save for two," the nekomancer said.

His two companions stared at him as a fragile silence descended upon the room.

"How is that a good thing?!" Junith shouted.

"I didn't say it was good! I said it was interesting!" Adam yelled back.

"How is you turning into a pervert interesting?!" The nekogirl leapt beside Adam, screaming in his face.

"BECAUSE IT—huhlk!"

Redfield grabbed each by the scruffs of their necks, yanking them apart.

Burning eyes flared, gazing at the two nekofolk with disappointment. Each neko curled up in a ball, paralyzed in his hands.

Without missing a beat, the Death Knight deposited first one, then the other at a nearby table. When they threatened to protest, he quickly hushed them.

"Alright, kids—"

"I'm not a kid—" Junith began, but a gauntleted hand slammed down on the tabletop, cutting her off.

"If you're gonna behave like kids, I'll treat you like kids," Redfield growled, drawing a smug look from Adam.

"That's—!"

"No."

"He—!"

"No."

"This isn't fair!" Junith shrieked, rising as mana twisted off her form. "You're being biased!"

"Ha," Adam snickered.

"AND YOU!" Redfield barked, causing Adam to jolt.

"Me? What did I do?"

"You're not innocent either, sir. Both of you spend so much time arguing we seldom, if ever, make any progress. In fact, this entire ordeal has come about because you two won't stop fighting!"

"But—"

"You two are adults. Act like it! You have powers and abilities that not only affect you, but everyone else and can cause disastrous consequences. Grow up," Redfield said, the glowing dots behind his helmet flaring red for a moment before they calmed down. He took a deep breath, then finished, "Respectfully speaking, sir."

The undead had a point. Junith and Adam had been fighting nonstop. The entire outbreak had been due to their fighting and even the last trial's... unfortunate death count was because of their immature actions.

Granted, they hadn't then known about their abilities, but Adam couldn't help but think the death count wouldn't have been so high if they hadn't been fighting.

"Right," Adam sighed, his shoulders drooping. "You make a fine case. I admit I have been a bit childish. We should make plans to contain my transformed self. I'll see about asking the Drowthraki to assist. Discreetly, of course."

"Good," Redfield said. The nekoboy and Death Knight turned as one to Junith, as she sat with her arms crossed.

"What? I've done nothing wrong," she retorted, causing Redfield's helmet to flare with red flames. His ghostly blue eyes, too, became a deep red as he placed an arm on the nekogirl's shoulder, staring at her, his skull-like helm only inches away from her face.

"Ri—Right. I might have been a bit argumentative..." she finally admitted, turning from the Death Knight.

"Good. Now shake hands," Redfield ordered, like a father reprimanding his children.

Reluctantly, Junith and Adam complied. However, as they did so Adam could feel Junith's grip tightening, prompting him to do the same. Neither let go, each instead narrowing their eyes until they were both glaring at one another in a contest of strength.

Redfield's armored shoulders sagged. The Death Knight slowly turned to the ornate, shattered window. Forlornly, he gazed across the recovering city, barely illuminated by distant light.

"We're doomed." The undead knight sighed, wondering what other shenanigans were about to unfold.

Catpurr 48

Planning the Trip to Candy Island

"Are you sure this is our best course of action, sir?" Redfield asked. Ghostly blue eyes stared as Junith finished securing Adam within the upright golden coffin with golden chains, graciously provided by their Drowthraki hosts.

"I, for one, think it's a good look on him," the paladin in question said as she backed away and eyed her handy work. "One could say it's fitting."

"Ha... Ha..." Adam retorted sarcastically, wiggling around to make himself more comfortable. "You are... so amusing. Have you considered being a jester as your next career? I think that would be pretty fitting."

She stuck out her tongue, which caused him to return the gesture.

"Respectfully, can we focus, kids," Redfield said, creating a *clack!* as he smacked his gauntlets together. "Are you sure this is our best course of action, sir? I feel a bit uneasy putting you in a coffin."

"Not much of a choice," Adam replied. "If I transform again and go running about, there's no telling what might happen or what I might do. This is just a necessary precaution. Besides, when your duration runs out it'll just be Junith here, and I don't trust her not to get in trouble if she has to leave this room to find me."

"Hey! What's that supposed to mean?" Junith spat.

"It means that you're a—"

Redfield shut the coffin lid. Adam's muffled cries could still be heard from within.

Junith quickly secured the coffin with yet more chains, a giddy smile plain on her face.

"You're extremely enthusiastic," Redfield commented as he stashed Adam's belongings underneath the bed.

"Of course I am! I love chaining up heretics!" she boldly declared before running in a circle around the coffin, making sure it was wrapped firmly. Next, she propped her foot on the coffin and began tugging. "Now all you need to do is pick up the coffin and drop it into the ocean! Or better yet, let's plug up all the breathing holes and listen to him suffocate!"

"I CAN HEAR YOU!" came the muffled cry from within.

"I know!" Junith replied, beaming.

"Yeah, I'm not doing any of that. I think you forget I serve him," Redfield said, slowly levering the coffin from its upright position until it lay horizontal.

Inside the coffin, Adam grimaced, wiggling around to get comfortable. His fluffy red tail was pressing up against his back, digging into his body. But it at least provided some padding against the chains digging into his skin.

Although initially puzzled, his Drowthraki hosts were more than willing to fulfill the so-called Priestess' request. In fact, they were so willing that they had stripped off their own jewelry and clothes in front of their savior to craft him a coffin made of solid gold. The whole endeavor surprisingly only took a few hours.

If only everyone else was as accommodating to my requests. The boy sighed as he listened to Junith and Redfield discuss the land's topography.

With resources provided by the Drowthraki, they were crafting a scheme to end the trial and go home. Well, their temporary home within the waypoint world. Research had allowed them to narrow Bullert's nest down to an isolated landmass known as Candy Island, thus named for the pink, edible plants growing on its mountains, loaded with high quantities of sucrose.

This unfortunately made it a breeding ground for duckysaurs who, Adam learned, were addicted to sugary sweets, often making them hyperactive and aggressive.

Finally, a break.

For now, he shut his eyes. In the morning he'd wake up rested and refreshed, ready to review their plans.

[TRIAL ACHIEVEMENT EARNED!]
[Exterminate 50 Duckysaurs! +50 to End of Trial Points]

Huh?

A blinking notification jarred him from his rest, alerting him to a new notification he'd apparently just earned.

"What is that idiot doing?" he muttered aloud, pulling up his companion menu and expanding it.

Bonded Followers: 03
    Junith Oatheart: T2 Lvl 20
    Class: Priestess of Eli
    HP: 1200/1200
    MP: 300/300

    Eh'liza Oktober: T1 Lvl 39 (Excited!)

BUFFED: Sugar High!

DEBUFFED: Poisoned! Wet! Nutritionally starved! Burning! Blinded! Mind-addled! Body fatigued! Crushed bones!

Class: Penitent of Adam

HP: 169/320

MP: 50/180

Kathrine Dominica: T1 Lvl 9 (Scared)

HP: 26/35

MP: 0/10

Class: Class selection available!

"Poisoned, wet, starving, burning, blinded, addled, fa— WHAT WERE YOU EVEN DOING?!" he shrieked as the many debuffs afflicting Liza scrolled past his vision. Between her achievements and her status, it seemed she was currently fighting for her life.

He thrashed about, opening his fanged mouth to yell out for Junith and Redfield, but a sudden wave of dizziness overtook him, his eyes rolling up into his skull as his body began to grow and warp, thrashing all the harder.

Outside, Junith and Redfield stared at the coffin, watching the golden box shake wildly.

"Do... you think that will contain him?" Junith asked, eying the box's straining chains.

"I'm unsure," Redfield said, stepping in front of the nekogirl. "Speaking of containment, he grows when he transforms, right?"

"Yeah, he turns into a feral adul— Oh..." As she trailed off she began to chuckle, imagining the heretic ballooning until he was strangled by his chains.

"Ma'am, you do realize that if you hurt him I will hurt you, right?" His ghastly voice echoed as his helmet swiveled to face her.

"Bring it, ghost," Junith snorted, her brow furrowed. "I can take you."

"You seem pretty confident, ma'am."

The two sat locked in a silent staring contest as the coffin jerked and wobbled in the background.

"You do realize that I don't have eyelids, right?" the Death Knight said.

"Yeah? So what?!" Junith spat. Despite how her eyes were growing red and twitchy, burning with unshed tears, she refused to blink.

"So, I don't blink.... ever. Like... *ever*." At that, Junith snarled and turned away, only to freeze. Hanging on for dear life from the bedroom windowsill was a familiar Drowthraki girl, legs kicking as she dangled thousands of feet above the ground.

"Huh?" Junith rubbed her sore eyes and looked towards the window again.

Upon realizing that the nekogirl and Death Knight had noticed her, Ellie cried out, "A LITTLE ASSISTANCE, PLEASE!" mere moments before slipping and falling off the window's ledge.

Catpurr 49

Ellie the Necromancer

"Please don't drop me! Please don't drop me! Pull me up, please!" Ellie cried, as she dangled by her wrist from Adam's Death Knight. His iron grip was the only thing between her and a thousand-foot plummet to her untimely death.

Redfield began to pull the Drowthraki girl up.

"Hold up, undead! Don't pull her up just yet!" Junith hollered. Ellie heard some commotion, before abruptly finding a broom handle being pointed into her face, Junith's sneer on the other end. "Why are you breaking into our apartment suite?!"

"Whoa! Whoa! It's me! Ellie! Don't drop me! Please!"

"I know who you are! I'm asking, why are you breaking into our room?! Why are you spying on us?!" she demanded. The broom handle bopped against Ellie's nose, causing the girl to sway in the open air.

"Uhm..."

"That's not good enough," Junith hissed.

"Uh! Uhm! UH! WAIT! I NEED YOUR HELP!" she screamed as the handle jabbed into her forehead.

Juntih paused. Behind her she heard Adam's muffled clawing and banging against the golden metal of the sarcophagus.

"Sorry. We're busy, if you couldn't tell. Go away."

"I can tell! I can tell! Don't drop me, please!" Ellie screamed. Suddenly she was yanked up and into the apartment.

"Hey!" Junith yelled. "I was interrogating her!"

"Oh, thank the Lady in Silk! Thank you, thank you, thank you!" Ellie exclaimed, kissing Redfield's plated helmet repeatedly.

"You were trying to push her off," Redfield scolded, his ghostly eyes flaring a bit as the girl's jaw dropped.

"No, I wasn't! See! It's so convincing, even you fell for it!" Junith exclaimed. From within the coffin came a single, sharp *thud,* causing all three to collectively turn their heads. Redfield was the first to speak.

"Is he—"

"Don't worry about that! Now speak!" Junith spat, pushing Ellie to the floor and drawing her blade. "Why were you spying on us, and what do you need our help for?!"

"Th-This!" Ellie exclaimed. She thrust her hand in the paladin's face, the symbol of Freya plainly displayed.

Junith stared for a long moment, before batting the offending appendage away. "Okay? A tattoo?"

"What? No! I mean, yes! But I'm a Chosen! Just like you guys are!" Ellie exclaimed, pointing towards a tapestry that hung on a nearby wall. "See! See!"

For a moment Junith looked between the banner and Ellie's hand.

"Huh."

"See! I need your help!"

"Sorry, we'll have to decline, on account of us being busy." The paladin gestured towards the gold coffin.

"B-B-But-but I'll die!" Ellie screamed, as a blue screen appeared in Junith's field of vision.

[Quest: Retrieve Journal of Freya.]

[**Description:** *An artifact containing dark secrets unfit for the world has fallen into unworthy hands. Retrieve the item without allowing it to be opened.*]
[**Reward: Experience x500, + S Rank Compensation**]
[**Failure: Death.**]

"Please! You've got to help me! I just need to retrieve that book!" She jabbed her finger towards the tome the Headmistress had left behind, still lying atop the bed.

"This?" Junith got up off Ellie, and the girl brushed herself down. The paladin approached, picking up the book as words on its cover caught her eye

[Freya's Secret Diary! Don't touch or I'll turn your organs into vineweed!]

Cautiously she sniffed it, and was about to flip it open, when a cry from Ellie stopped her.

"Please! Please don't!" she said, scurrying over on her all fours and begging on her knees. "I need it."

"Even though Adam—ma will be scuffed, we should give it to her," Redfield chimed in. "If it's required for her to survive, it's not only the moral thing to do, it's just."

Junith blinked.

"I don't need a morality lesson from an abomination, undead," the paladin growled. But then her eyes went wide, an almost unnerving smile breaking out across her face.

"You're right, this would make Adama angry, wouldn't it," Junith said, holding the book out to Ellie. "Here you go!"

"Oh, thank you! Thank you! I know you two are boys, but you guys aren't—"

"HOLD UP!" Junith barked, snatching the book back. "Did... Do... Do you think I'm a boy?"

Ellie and Junith stared long and hard at one another.

Gears seemed to turn in Ellie's head, keeping her mouth shut as she scrutinized the paladin's pout.

"A-A-Are you not?"

"YES!"

"Yes you aren't, or ye—"

"I'M A GIRL! A GIRL!" Junith yelled, spinning to throw the book out the window. But now the book was snatched from her by Redfield, who dropped the tome in Ellie's outstretched hands. "HEY!"

"Ah! Thank you, thank you, thank you! You're the best!" Ellie exclaimed as the item suddenly disintegrated, replaced by a pair of black gloves studded with green gems.

The girl's eyes widened, her pointy ears twitching as her mouth shaped into a smile.

"I leveled up!" she exclaimed before another blue screen appeared in front of her, displaying her stats to the nekogirl and Death Knight as well.

Name: Elerra Hali

Level: 2

Class: Necromancer Aspirant

HP: 20/20

MP: 30/30

Free Points: 2

STR: 7

CON: 5

DEX: 6

ARC: 3
SEN: 4
EGO: 10
FAITH: 6
RESISTANCES: Cold (10%)
BUFFS: Heart of the Explorer (SSR), Blessing of Freya (SSR)
DEBUFFS: None
SKILLS: Animate Bones, Force Push Lvl 1, Force Pull Lvl 1, Summon Minor Skeleton Lvl 1, Sense Dead Lvl 1

"I got points!" Ellie exclaimed as she did a little hop, completely oblivious to the dumbfounded Junith.

"Y-You! You're a necromancer?!" the fallen paladin spat, her eyes twitching. Behind her, her tail lashed viciously.

"Yeah! Isn't it great!" Ellie yelled. There was a *whoosh* as Junith's blade tasted the air, whizzing beside Ellie's head, the teenager was only saved as Redfield yoinked Junith back, tossing her to the other side of the room. A blossom of black shadows devoured her, keeping her tied down. Through it all, Ellie stood frozen.

"MHHHM! MARH! ARRRRRRRGH!" Junith screamed, frothing at the mouth. The girl's body shook as she viciously fought the shadows, but soon they consumed her entirely. This was a skill Redfield had been careful to keep hidden—he was certain Adam would abuse it when dealing with his companions otherwise.

"My apologies for her," the Death Knight said. Ellie's ears twitched as he bowed.

"I—I can understand you!" she said.

"Could you not before?" Redfield asked, cocking his black helmet. He thought back on their time running through the hallways together, seeing their previous interactions in a new light.

"Nope. I think it's because of this System thing."

"Yeah, it's pretty neat isn't it." Redfield smiled, his eyes flashing red for a moment.

"Wait, you have one too?!" Ellie exclaimed, clutching her pair of gloves tightly to her academy robe. "That's so cool!"

"Uh, not anymore. But I did," Redfield replied, walking over to a bundle of leftover chains as his body rattled. It was a sign that it wouldn't be long before he was sent back to Eli's realm, and *that* meant that in very little time, Junith would be set free.

"What happened to it?" Ellie asked, her head cocked to the side as she followed the Death Knight.

His ghostly orbs shifted to peer at the curious girl.

"Gone when I died," Redfield said before staring down at his armored gauntlet.

Catpurr 50

A New Necromancer

"Did you really use a slot just to protect your diary?"

"It's not a diary! It's a journal, okay! And yes! Of course! The stuff I wrote in here is too revealing for the minds of mortalkind!"

"I... Whatever you say, sis. But did you have to choose someone so weak? There are plenty of other candidates in that world to choose from."

"It'll be fine! It'll be fine! She's with Eli's Chosen, he'll take care of her."

"If you say so. You know Voltrain won't be happy. And neither will the admins. All they do is complain, even though they do nothing at all."

"IT'LL BE FIIIIINE! FINE, I TELL YOU!"

—**Freya & Unidine**
discussing Ellie's ascension to "Chosen"

* * *

Adam's body shifted, a groan rattling from his lungs as he slowly roused. Gradually he moved and stretched in the stale air of the coffin. Well, as much as he could—which was quite a lot. The coffin was oddly spacious. Too spacious, in fact. With a chill, Adam realized that the golden chains binding him, *lovingly* tightened to limb-numbing perfection by Junith, now lay shattered around him.

"Great," Adam muttered before knocking on the lid, giving the special signal that he was cognizant and able-bodied.

Eh'liza Oktober: T1 Lvl 39 (Sugar Crash!)
      DEBUFF: Sugar crash! Nutritionally starved! Body fatigued!
      Crushed bones!
Class: Penitent of Adam
HP: 89/320
MP: 82/180

Well, Liza's tab showed she was still alive when he opened his System to check on her.

From outside the golden coffin, a small voice broke the silence. But it wasn't one Adam had expected to hear.

"Are you okay or are you going to eat me?" whispered the young Drowthraki girl, Ellie, into one of the breathing holes.

Adam took a long sigh.

"I want to ask why you're here speaking on behalf of Junith. But somehow, I know I won't like the answer," he finally responded, as dread soaked his muscles.

"I'm going to undo the clamps now," Ellie said. Adam's ears twitched, faintly detecting the distant sound of Junith's familiar, muffled rage.

Please don't be like the Cinnabar Morgue incident, he repeatedly whispered. Light flooded in, temporarily blinding him as the coffin opened. As he blinked away the spots in his vision, he came face-to-face with a familiar, pointy-eared girl.

"Please tell me there aren't twenty guards about to stab me with spears," he moaned as he sat up. As he turned his head, he noticed Junith lying on the bed, bound up in gold chains and clutching a ball gag in her mouth. He raised a finger, inhaling as though about to ask a question, only to change his mind and shut his mouth. "I'm not even going to ask."

Suddenly he paused, realizing his wig wasn't on. With one rigid motion he turned to Ellie.

"Hello," the Drowthraki said innocently.

"Hi..." Adam replied.

The two stared at each other for a moment before Ellie jolted up. She dived underneath the bed and began handing him a series of items, his wig amongst them.

"Here ya go! Your Death Knight said you might want these immediately," Ellie said, pointedly ignoring Adam's sheer lack of disguise.

He took the wig, eyeing the black gloves studded with gems on the girl's hands as he donned his disguise, along with the rest of his armor and enchanted gear.

"Red said that, huh?" he mused. He tried not to, he really did, but he looked again at Junith and sighed. "Is there a reason for that, too?"

"Uh, she..." Ellie pursed her lips, her brow furrowing as she tapped her fingers together. "She tried to kill me after I showed her my System screen. So, your Death Knight gagged and tied her up for my safety. He said you could get her to stop once you awoke."

Adam raised his brow before cocking her head toward the paladin. She met his gaze with an intense glare—then rolled her eyes.

Adam was about to roll his own in return before he paused, snapping back to the girl. "Wait, you have a screen?"

"Yeah!" Ellie replied before the familiar blue box appeared.

Name: Elerra Hali

Level: 2

Class: Necromancer Aspirant

HP: 20/20

MP: 50/50

Free Points: 0

STR: 7

CON: 5

DEX: 6

ARC: 5

SEN: 4

EGO: 10

FAITH: 6

RESISTANCES: Cold (10%)

BUFFS: Heart of the Explorer (SSR), Blessing of Freya (SSR)

DEBUFFS: None

SKILLS: Animate Bones, Force Push Lvl 1, Force Pull Lvl 1, Summon Minor Skeleton Lvl 1, Sense Dead Lvl 1

"I hope you don't mind that I helped myself to the grilled duckysaur you had sent up. I haven't been able to really eat in days, so I really really appreciate the food!" Ellie exclaimed as Adam's face contorted into a smile.

Another necromancer.

"Summon your skeleton," he demanded. Ellie staggered back at the intensity of his tone.

"Wha—"

"Do it now," he said, leaning forwards.

"Uhm, o-okay." Her shaking hands extended. The green gems on the backs of her gloves lip up with purple glyphs as a pile of bleached white bones clattered to the floor. After only a moment they began to rattle and shake, assembling themselves before Adam's very eyes. In just a few moments a short, humanoid skeleton with ghostly blue pupils was standing before the nekoboy.

Adam's jaw dropped as he was suddenly hit with a wave of emotion. His eyes teared up as he clasped a hand to his mouth, softly choking.

"A-Are you okay?!" Ellie exclaimed. She tensed as the nekoboy suddenly lunged for her, and she was unexpectedly...

Hugged.

"Uhm... Okay. There there?" she tried. The girl was at a complete loss for words, and this had been the last reaction she expected. Stiffly she patted Adam on the back before she froze, as she spotted a long, bushy red tail flicking back and forth.

"I never knew I needed to see something until I saw it," Adam cried, much to the anger of Junith behind him. "You have no idea how good it is to see someone wielding the mighty power of the bones!"

It was now clear to Adam why Junith had tried to murder the child, she was a necromancer! A *necromancer!* Besides his master, Adam had always been alone, the only one who could truly understand the importance of the undead, the gospel of death that had no voice but was heard by everyone, eventually.

He stepped away, composing himself before he started bombarding Ellie with questions while the teen did her best to answer them.

"Who is your patron?" he started.

"Freya."

That gave him pause, and he cocked his head as his ears twitched. "Freya is a goddess of death?"

"Y-Yeah?"

"How did you get your powers?"

Ellie explained how she had only suddenly been Chosen, to her own surprise, only receiving her class after it happened. That piqued the nekoboy's interest. "Does this world not have a system for everyone?" he asked.

"No?" The confused expression on her face made that clear enough.

The conversation moved on from there, as Adam's inner scientist, never far away, now reared its head. He found she could only keep her summon active for about an hour tops, and that her **Heart of the Explorer** boon granted her bonuses to speed, climbing, and avoiding unpleasant things. Finally, he found he had exhausted his questions for now, and began to think about what he could do with a Chosen of Freya, now that he had one.

Aloud, he mused, "Where was the journal that was on the..."

He froze as he looked on the bed and realized that a certain item was missing.

Immediately he began searching for it, asking Ellie where it was. Suddenly the girl, who had seemed so forthcoming previously, became more withdrawn and shy.

"Uhm. I sorta needed it," she said before explaining to Adam her lethal quest for the item and how she had received it from Redfield

Adam's eye involuntary twitched, as the aura of the room suddenly grew heavy.

He sucked his teeth, visibly unhappy. But all Redfield's actions before now had always been reasonable and level-headed. He hadn't known the knight very long, but he resolved to trust his actions.

Still, a quest for the journal? There was obviously something inside that the gods didn't want Adam to see. Perhaps something damaging?

He stroked his chin. Perhaps this was a lead.

Regardless, it was out of his reach for right now. He sighed, moving over to the restrained Junith. "Great, there goes my reading material for the journey," he said, before undoing the gag ball stuffed into Junith's mouth. "Alright, please tell me you guys managed to get some work done before this."

"Filthy necromancers!"

"UGGGH. Are we still on this? Seriously, give it a rest already," he scoffed, looking down at the paladin.

"It's bad enough I have to deal with you, but now you're multiplying!" Junith screamed in horror.

"Yes, and soon there will be an army of the damned that will march upon your world and pillage all the temples of Voltrain."

At that, the paladin made a face. "You're mocking me."

"I am."

"When I'm freed, I'm going to punch you!" she yelled, snapping at the nekoboy's hand.

"Quick question, perhaps you might answer this for me, but how long have you been tied up?" he asked.

"What? Five hours, why?"

"I'd imagine it's about that time that your body will wish to relieve itself. To perform bodily functions," he stated. The paladin's visage of rage suddenly flushed. "Do you have to go pee?"

"N-No!"

"Oh, okay." He returned to his maps, beckoning for the young necromancer to accompany him as he planned for the end of the trial.

Catpurr 51
Oops, an Inquisition

The spacious room lined with bookshelves carved from black crystals and heavy with tomes was quite cool, and yet Adam sweated as he stood. Scrutinizing him from behind her obsidian desk was the Headmistress, as she pinned him with her gaze like an insect. Behind her was a portrait in a frame, apparently a pink-haired Drowthraki.

Apparently, because its face had been ripped to shreds.

"So... You're cursed? And the gold cure can't dispel it?"

Adam counted the ornaments and stacks of paper on the Headmistress' opulent desk. Though he was frozen by the sheer force of her gaze, his tail was held by no such bonds as it twitched and flicked, and indeed, it was his tail that held the Headmistress' attention now.

"Yes," Adam said. His voice had reached glass-shattering range, it felt, but the crystalline furniture surrounding him remained unshattered. His spine was ramrod straight as he played the part of the priestess. "Sadly, when I was kidnapped, I was infected. Thankfully, the power of... our Lady in Silk has managed to stave off its madness, but I'm afraid during the full moon I undergo certain... undesirable effects."

"Is that so?" the Mistress said. "This is certainly troubling news. So that is what the coffin is for."

"Yes. With the state the city is in, I didn't wish to alarm you and the others until I was confident that I could contain it," he explained.

"I understand your concerns. But for your safety, we'll have to triple our guard presence to prevent this sorry fate from befalling another. I can have our techens examine your body, to see if we might be able to engineer a cure?"

"Thank you, but no. I'm afraid that this... is a test from our Lady in Silk," Adam lied. "It is sadly my burden to bear."

"So admirable..." the Headmistress whispered, a glint in her eye as she took a seat at her desk, her long fingers interlocking with one another. "If there is a way for we of the academy to be of any use in curing this threat, the materials of the city and the full arsenal of our constables stand ready to assist in any way you need."

Great, Adam thought to himself. His ruse had yet to be discovered, and some pressure in his chest relaxed.

"Thank you, Headmistress. I may have to take you up on that offer sooner rather than later," he said. The woman raised one bushy brow.

"Oh? Anything for the Voice of our Lady in Silk," the Mistress said. "It is an honor to host you and your party. I only hope that our matriarch will consider our assistance to you in this time of peril when she sees our report."

"Riiiight," Adam said. The Headmistress still believed he had been sent from the capital. While he was wary of the contents of this report and his identity as a faker being revealed, as soon as he got what he needed, none of it would matter, he would be long gone by the time any of it was his problem.

"Please, state your demands of us."

The nekomancer schooled his expression into his very best poker face.

"My party and I are burdened with glorious purpose. We have been brought here by our patron to not only end the scourge of the catsification disease, but also the threat of Bullert."

"The king of the duckysaurs?" she asked, her mouth falling slightly open.

"Yes. A few others ordained by their own gods have also been sent, but I aim to win the race to end the threat and secure glory for our Lady in Silk before they do." The truth always made a lie slightly more believable, after all.

The Mistress's eyes widened.

"Gods? There are *other* gods?" the Mistress said. Adam's heart stopped, as his grin shattered into a grimace.

Oh, crapbaskets. Uhhhh, quick think!

"Indeed, there are. However they are inferior, annoying parasites that pale in comparison to our Lady, the one who spins the web of life and death," he said, channeling his inner Junith as he let his expression become one of self-righteous smugness. "They are interlopers in our world's affairs, hoping to seek dominion in a land that doesn't belong to them! Heretics that deserve no quarter and must be burned and flogged at the stake!"

Unbeknownst to Adam, every Chosen within the trial paused what they were doing. A great wave of unease settled over them from a source unknown. None could say why or how, but even those in the midst of fighting one another paused as their anxiety abruptly spiked.

The Headmistress stared at Adam, mouth fully falling open. Her expression twitched with horror—and then became one of jubilation.

"My word! This is news to me! Wonderful news! I will give you everything you need for the great journey!" she proclaimed. Ringing a bell on the desk, she summoned a pair of women into the office, clad in golden armor and wielding flasks of aqua regia.

"Great Priestess, Headmistress," they chorused, stamping their feet and bowing to the two. "How may we serve?"

"Tell Commander Erishta that her services are required by the Great Priestess. Anything she requires, the city shall provide."

"Yes, Headmistress."

"Thank you," Adam said. The elderly drow nodded.

"It is the least we can do. In the meantime, I must alert the other provinces of the existence of the heretics and launch a full inquisition!"

"Yes, of course, I'll—" Her words caught up with his thoughts. "An, uh... An inquisition?"

"Yes! Those who would profane our Lady's words obviously must be hunted down like the insolent curs they are," she remarked, as though discussing slugs in her garden.

Oh, crapbaskets.

"I— I don't think that's really necessary, considering the resources—" he tried, only to be cut off.

"Nonsense! You said so yourself, Great Priestess! They must be burned and flogged at the stake! No quarter given!" she declared, taking out ink and a fresh sheet of parchment. "It is my great honor to relay your orders! My, we haven't had a good inquisition since ninety-oh-five!"

"Ri—Right," he said, keeping a straight face. Inwardly he was screaming all the way to the office of the commander who would help him end this trial.

* * *

"You... You did what?" Junith asked. She pulled up her tunic, covering the serpentine symbol on her chest. "WHY WOULD YOU ORDER AN INQUISITION?!"

"How was I supposed to know I was ordering one?! I was just pretending to be you!" Adam threw his hands up in the air from where he lay collapsed on his bed. In the corner, Ellie was becoming one with the shadows. Since unleashing the volatile paladin, Adam had forced her to promise she wouldn't hurt, kill, or be mean to the young necromancer but still, Ellie was making an effort to avoid the pint-sized paladin.

'Me? ME?! I would NEVE—" Junith froze mid-word. A deep furrow appeared in her brow before she turned away, her lashing tail betraying her thought process. "Hmm... Actually a good inquisition is always fun. Do you think we could join in?"

"See! I was just being you! In a way, this is mostly your fault."

"My fault?! You're the idiot who can't learn to watch what you say!" she shot back.

As if the spirit of Redfield had warped reality to interrupt them, a knock sounded at the door.

Both nekos composed themselves, ensuring they were presentable before turning to the door, but neither made a move to answer it.

"Well?" Adam asked, expectantly eying Junith.

"Well, what?"

"Are you going to get the door?"

Her eye twitched.

"Why should I get the door?"

"Because I'm the priestess, and you're the servant."

"FAKE-priestess," she hissed. "I'm the one with the priestess class."

"Yeah, and don't you act like it, huh," Adam said, rolling his eyes as Ellie cleared her throat and yelled "Come in!" before the two could start fighting again.

The door opened, revealing a scarred, albino Drowthraki. Her pale white skin and sunset-orange eyes caused Adam to do a double take.

At second glance, she wasn't a Drowthraki at all, but a regular surface elf. Scars laced across her entire body like intricate embroidery, especially the side of her face.

"I am Commander Erishta of the Corydrun Civil Defense Force," she said in a haughty tone. Unlike the Drowthraki she made no effort to bow down to Adam, instead glaring down at the false priestess. "How may I be of service to the Priestess of the Spider?"

Catpurr 52

Embarking for Candy Island

"Is... this it?"

The wooden ships moored in the underground harbor bobbed gently in the water. Each about a hundred feet long, they were also alike in that all were equipped with two paddle wheels, a metal cabin, and a large, wooden mast bearing purple sails and lines. Adam stood on the dock with his entourage, marveling at the assemblage.

Commander Erishta stood behind them, frowning as she stared down at the boy clad in leathers and robes.

"Problem?"

"N-No?" Adam replied, turning, only to flinch as the full force of the commander's scowl bore down on him.

"Really?" She leaned closer, nearly touching him with her pointed nose. "Because it sounds like you have an issue with my vessels."

"It's... just interesting... I've yet to see a ship of its design before," he squeaked, shrinking away from the scarred woman's gaze.

Truthfully, Adam hadn't seen many a ship at all. His original world was mostly a single massive landmass that stretched nearly to the horizon in every direction. Boats and other water-faring vessels were largely restricted to lakes or rivers.

Rigellia had ships too, similar to those found in his original world, but this was the first he'd seen a ship with so much metal on it—and with such a unique design!

"Really?" Commander Erishta asked, raising a brow. Suddenly Ellie stumbled into her, laden down with an armful of stacked wooden containers. "Watch where you're going, scribe!"

"Oops! Sorry! It's just hard to see!" the girl cried, stuck behind the crates in her arms.

Ellie walked on by. Ever since catching wind of Adam's expedition, she had stuck close by, and she wasn't the only one—Karlie, or Carly, or whatever her name was hadn't been far behind. Adam frankly had no interest in remembering her name or even keeping track of her. As he recalled Ellie's pestering for an adventure, a headache began taking root in his skull.

The Girl-Whose-Name-Started-With-a-C? walked behind Ellie, helping to pick up dropped books and other knick knacks that spilled from her arms as she climbed the gangplank into the boat. The two friends seemed to want to spend as much time together as they could, before Ellie departed.

"You smell weird," Commander Erishta said, staring down at Adam.

"Ah, is that so? Haha. My scent has to do with my curse, sadly. It seems to produce a type of pheromone," he quickly explained.

"Is that so? And how is that curse? Is it contained?" Commander Erishta asked. To the side was a clanking commotion as a group of chained men were guided onto the boat by several armed guards. "I would hate for an outbreak to occur while we are in transit."

"It's contained, as long as the proper procedures are kept. My companions and I shall be no different than any other passenger," Adam assured her. Strapped to his Death Knight's back was a familiar golden coffin, which was constantly in the corner of his vision.

The procession of the armored undead, escorted by a parade of skelecats, had caused all dockworkers and soldiers to stop what they were doing and watch, with a confused mix of emotions.

"And all this luggage?" Commander Erishta asked. She reached out and grabbed one of the skelecats to take a closer look at the book in its mouth, raising an eye at its cover. "What use is the... *Fundamentals of Steampower* for an expedition to hunt Bullert? All this is doing is taking up valuable storage space."

Adam sighed.

"Have you heard the idiom 'knowledge is power,' Commander?" he asked. The pale elf only gave him a look. "I plan to create a weapon. And for that purpose, I must research."

"A weapon?"

"Yup," he lied. If he had judged Erishta correctly, this was the only thing that would save his books. He had no true interest in creating such a weapon. His plan for dealing with the duckysaur was just to have Redfield wail on him, re-summoning the Death Knight until they found victory. It was a simple plan, but it might take days, or even weeks to see it come to fruition.

He'd need reading material for those weeks.

Approximately seven months, three weeks, five days, and twenty-two hours remained until Junith's people came for her. Plenty more time for Adam to grind and accumulate assets.

"Is that what the lab equipment is for?" Erishta asked, as Junith berated several soldiers loading gear, wielding a checklist against the much taller warriors.

"Yup," Adam replied again. In reality, he was just taking everything not nailed down, as the Drowthraki had equipment foreign to all worlds he had visited so far, and he'd be a fool not to take everything with him.

The plan was for the expedition fleet to travel to Candy Island. The extra ships were just ferries for Adam's luggage.

Much to the Headmistress's dismay, Adam was adamant that only essential personnel be brought along. After all, the city needed to conserve its resources in case of a duckysaur attack or the red haired nekoman returned.

Though Erishta concurred, she was dismayed that rather than mounting an attack, her forces would only be used as a mule to establish a beachhead.

"I just need your ships to get us to where we need to go," Adam said, sketching the boat design. "Once we're there, we'll make sure to take care of everything."

* * *

As he boarded the boat and struggled to keep his balance amidst the rocking motion, Adam took note of the rows of slaves, chained to the boat deck. Oars were laid out at their feet.

Looks like they are our main mode of propulsion. Soon, however, he was distracted by the giant paddle wheels to either side of the boat.

"Commander, what are these wheels for?" he asked, indicating them.

"Thrust."

"Thrust? Really?" Fascination gleamed in his eyes.

"Have you ever been on a boat before?" Erishta asked, tone intense.

"Sadly, I've never had the pleasure," Adam replied, his stomach suddenly churning as a light wave made the boat shift.

"Is that so..." Erishta said. Adam couldn't help but feel he'd made some misstep. "You said you were from the capital, right?"

"Yes," he lied, eyes unblinking. A wave caused the boat to bob again, and he struggled with his nausea.

"Interesting," she muttered. Perhaps the nausea wasn't from the ship's rocking motion. It could have just as easily been the way she was looking at him now. "How old are you again?"

"I'm—" A familiar sensation seized him, causing his insides to cramp and his expression to twist. "I'm—I—"

"What? What's wrong?!" Erishta demanded. She laid a hand on the hilt of her sword, following him with heavy steps as the nekoboy dashed to the edge of the boat.

"BLEKH!" Rainbow goo disappeared into the dark water below as the boy spilled his guts. "Hhuuumg."

"Impressive... We haven't even left port yet," Erishta said. The seasick priestess slouched against the side of the boat and slid down off the guard rail. "Is your vomit color also part of your curse?"

"Y-Yes," Adam groaned, wiping his spittle-covered chin. As she stepped aboard the boat, Junith was quick to not only notice the spectacle, but point and laugh.

Catpurr 53

RE-LEASE! THE QUACKEN! PART 1

Ellie stood at the edge of the deck literally, and additionally at the edge of a precipice metaphorically. After taking a deep breath, she opened her quest log.

[Warning. You have reached a point of no return!]
[Once you depart from Corydrun, you may never return, and you may never see anyone you know ever again. If you seek risk and reward, board the ship. If you wish for a peaceful life, return to your home…]
[Quest 1: Board the Ship]
[Reward: A Memento, System Access]
[Failure: Loss of System Access, Demotion from Chosen status, Riches, Blessing of Freya EX1]

Her palms felt oddly sweaty as she took another breath. This was it. This was exactly what she had always claimed to long for. Adventure, exploration, risks and rewards. All her wildest dreams. And all she had to do was board the ship.

Board the ship, and…

Say goodbye to Karlie. Despite how she had begged Adam and Commander Erishta to allow Karlie to come along, neither would approve.

And Adam made it clear that this would be a one-way trip, so for now...

Not far off, Karlie was currently organizing what remained of Adam's luggage, the books and equipment that had yet to be loaded. Ellie watched from only feet away, committing every detail she could of her friend to memory.

She bit her inner lip, again feeling the weight of choice. This really, truly had been her dream—to explore, to see the world. But she couldn't just abandon her one and only friend, not at the end of the world.

But... Adam was planning to end the threat. And she really liked the System, as it allowed her to summon a skeleton and gave her powers.

She could help save everyone, with the power given to her by the goddess.

Karlie noticed Ellie staring at her and approached.

"What's wrong?" she asked, hands on her hips as she narrowed her eyes.

"Karlie, I... I don't know what to do."

"Are you getting cold feet? You better not back down after going on and on about adventurers all these years," Karlie said. "You'll finally get to see the ocean, go to the surface."

"Yeah..."

"Hey."

"Yeah..."

"Hey!"

Suddenly Karlie grabbed Ellie by the face, locking her lips with the shocked Drowthraki girl.

HUH?!

Karlie pulled back, a mixed expression coloring her face. While her mouth was quirked up into a smile, it didn't hide the downward tilt of her eyebrows. "There, one thing off your list."

Ellie's cheeks were left flushed with red, as her mouth bobbed like a gasping fish's. "W-W-Wha—"

"Y-Y-You complained b-before that you never got a kiss," Karlie said, the tips of her ears going red. If it was possible, Ellie felt her face blushing deeper, from her ears to her neck.

"You..."

"I..."

"You kissed me!"

Ellie buried her face in her hands, as Karlie freaked out, gesturing with her hands in a storm of movement.

"Sorry! I thought it was gonna be a cool thing!" she exclaimed, grabbing Ellie by the shoulders and shaking the girl. "Motivational! I did it for motivation! Motivation!"

"Does this mean you love me?!"

"Motivation! *Motivation!*"

"You stole my first kiss! You've unvirgined my lips!" Ellie cried as Karlie kept shaking her, crying, "Motivation!" over and over again. Then in an impulsive motion, Ellie grabbed her friend in an embrace.

"Thank you," she whispered. Karlie's hand raised, wrapping around Ellie's waist as she returned the gesture.

* * *

Two days later.

The spartan cabin's innards were dimly lit only by a faint, flickering bulb, the light catching on the fold. Adam's face twisted as he leaned against his coffin, trying to keep his balance.

"I don't... I don't want to be here anymore," he moaned, before grabbing at the bucket beside him. Another mouthful of rainbow spit joined the collection staining the bottom.

"Stop being such a wimp," Junith called from across the cabin. The paladin was busy swinging her sword around, tail swishing as a counterbalance while, Ellie dabbed at Adam's mouth with a cloth, preparing to take the bucket.

"Hhhughhhahaja," the nekoboy groaned, falling all fours and crawling underneath his desk where he curled up in a ball. "We are not... fish. This is awful. We were never meant for the sea."

He opened his System, dull eyes taking in its data points. It shared with him nothing of interest, except that Liza was still wet and on another sugar high.

"What is that idiot up to...?"

He lay there, his stomach continuing to churn. Despite not eating anything for days, Adam continued to vomit, painting bits of his wooden cabin in rainbow colors. A new feature of his curse, apparently.

"I just... wanted to read..." he moaned, cursing Eli under his breath. "I swear... I'll infect you and turn you into a cat..."

Ellie helped Adam up, grabbing him by the armpits and dragging him from under the desk. Their destination was a cot, bolted to the floor, which served as the nekomancer's bed.

"I'll go get another bucket," she said.

"Hhrnnn. Bleh," Adam groaned before throwing up on himself. Then with a piteous sound he gazed at Ellie with teary eyes that begged to end his suffering.

She quickly made her way out of the room, taking with her the full bucket.

* * *

Donning a poncho and exiting the room with the bucket filled with rainbow sludge, Ellie made her way through the hallway lined with cabins. Prying the door open with her foot, she ventured into the cold, stormy rain.

"How is she?"

"Heh?!" Ellie let out, jumping as Commander Erishta appeared beside her, nearly making the girl spill the vomit on herself.

"My apologies, scribe, I did not mean to startle you," Commander Erishta said, from where she leaned on the door with her arms folded, indifferent to the rain bouncing off her armor.

"Scared? Who was scared? Haha." The Drowthraki girl scurried to the side of the boat and dumped yet another bucket of vomit into the churning gray waves below, where fish visibly leaped and writhed within the waves.

But as she tried to return to the relative dryness of the indoors, she found her path blocked.

"You haven't answered my question, scribe," Commander Erishta said in a tone that brooked no argument.

"Uhm. She's fine."

"Really? Because every night we've been hearing scratching and screaming coming from the room. And every time I ask, the bodyguard says everything is fine." The commander loomed above Ellie. "So now I'm asking you."

"W-Why me? I'm just a simple scribe," Ellie replied, as from the corner of her eye she noted the Commander's hand had moved to the hilt of her blade.

"Because I've gone over the logs. And I've found it suspicious that on the day of their arrival, the outbreak just happened to occur. They claim to be from the capital, yet they have never set foot on a boat," Erishta said, scowling. "I don't understand the circumstances that have bound you to these two, but as a citizen of Corydrun, it is your duty to notify your betters of a potential threat."

"I..." Ellie began, suddenly aware of just how much taller than her the pale, scarred elf was. "I don't—"

There was a noise of perfect incoherence as Adam pushed past the Commander and stumbled out into the rain. The white-haired priestess staggered a few steps before screaming "WHY?!" Then she fell to her knees, as another bout of vomiting capped off her outburst.

"Sorry, I don't know anything," Ellie replied quickly before dragging the incoherent Adam back into the boat.

"Hateboats," Adam moaned as Ellie ushered the wet nekoboy inside. Hs wig was beginning to break, revealing strands of his natural red hair. "I hate boats... I hate boats..."

"What are you doing outside when you're sick?!" Ellie asked. She received a loathsome noise of torment most wretched in response.

"I haft to... I hafta move around. Learn about boat. Only way to beat this dungeon," he slurred as tears fell from his eyes. The now drenched nekoboy had entered a state of delirium. "I have to fight the boat boss! IT'S THE ONLY WAY TO BE FREED!"

"It's okay, it's okay," Ellie repeated to him, unable to do anything else as she led him back to their room. Commander Erishta was following them closely behind. "Let's get you in bed."

"Scribe, if you would allow me," Commander Erishta said, moving to grab Adam by the shoulder.

Ellie hesitated, but as Commander and leader of their vessel, it would be too suspicious if she refused.

"Hrrrn?" Adam mumbled as Commander Erishta laid him on his cot on his side. Then the woman laid down too beside him, pressing her hand against his stomach as she guided him into the fetal position. Soon her bulk was curled around his smaller form.

"I've found that during my special time of the month, laying in a fetal position with pressure on my stomach helps to alleviate bloating and the pain on my ovaries," Commander Erishta said matter-of-factly, laying with Adam. In the corner of the room Junith facepalmed, muttering to herself.

"Mmm. Cozy," Adam hummed, cuddling into the woman. His bushy red tail curled around his body, and he grabbed onto it in a hug.

For a moment, Ellie was worried that the large elf might discover the boy's secret, that he was wearing a wig. But she needn't have worried—within just a few moments Adam was out like a light, no more groaning or throwing up, only peaceful, angelic slumber. The commander rose, wrinkling her nose.

As Erishta passed by Ellie she stopped, addressing the girl in a serious, but hushed, tone.

"If you know anything, tell me, scribe," the Commander said. Then she shot a look towards Junith, whose face was presently buried in her palms.

"Okay, I will," Ellie replied, seeing the woman out. When the door shut behind her, Ellie released an exasperated sigh.

"I can't... I can't believe that worked..." Junith said. She approached Adam, her arm raised into a fist to punch him, only to stop. Her hand dropped to her side as she walked off with a sigh.

Ellie slid to the floor, trying to categorize her messy feelings. *This is turning out to be a* great *start to an adventure...*

Catpurr 54
RE-LEASE! THE QUACKEN! PART 2

Three days later.

At last, Adam awoke from his long slumber. Rubbing away the crust encasing his eyes, he found himself lying in his coffin in a pool of drool, snot, and rainbow vomit. The disgusting mixture had stained his cheek.

Is it because I'm not a worshiper? he lamented in his mind. *Is it because I don't have Faith?*

* * *

Elsewhere.

"Good question."

Sitting in a throne of graphite and bone, the skeleton clad in a pink bathrobe and bunny slippers lifted the TV remote held in his skeletal hand.

He aimed it, the remote's sensor connecting with the sixty-foot-wide television screen and pausing his show, freezing on the image of a blonde boy in a blue shirt and white hat, accompanied by a laughing, stretchy yellow dog.

Eli turned, waving his fingers and summoning a two-way mirror. Within appeared the image of an orange-haired adult woman with feline features, sitting in a solid gold bathtub as she shaved her furry legs, nude.

"ELI?!" Bastet exclaimed, dropping her razor and covering her exposed chest.

"Why did you give my Chosen rainbow vomit?"

"What?!" Bastet screamed. Frantically she tried to power down the portal, but the godly power fizzled and died. Such was the way of things when a weaker goddess opposed a Primordial God.

"Why did you give my Chosen rainbow vomit?" Eli repeated as a Dullahan entered his chambers for his master's scheduled foot massage.

"Because I needed to offset the perks of lycanthropy and gradually convert him! CLOSE THE DAMN MIRROR!" Bastet screamed. Finally the mirror closed, and Eli resumed his TV show.

"Hmm... Maybe I'll give him something to alleviate these issues," Eli mused.

* * *

"Are you ready to be let out?" Ellie asked, tapping on the coffin.

"Yes," Adam moaned.

"You have to say the password."

"Schrödinger," Adam muttered. At last the coffin opened, and light filled it. Surrounded by the beams was Ellie's face, shielded by a face mask, rubber gloves, and wielding cleaning supplies like she was about to go to war. Adam ventured the question, "Are we there yet?"

"Nope."

Of course...

After a vicious and thorough cleaning, it was time for Ellie to reapply his makeup, then he was dressed again in his gear, just in time to help clean the rainbow vomit from the coffin's insides. Sluggishly, Adam made it to his desk of scattered books and maps. A bucket had been secured to his chest, looking much like a baby Björn.

He looked down, eyeing the maps. By his estimation, they should have reached landfall yesterday. Yet here they were, the boat still rocking and Adam on the verge of throwing up. Again.

"Ellie, can you call Commblehar Erishta here." His words were muffled somewhat, as they were interrupted by yet more vomit. He did not even blink. "I need to have a word with her about our progress."

* * *

"This storm is unnatural," Commander Erishta said, eyeing the map. "My navigator and crew have attempted to enter the bay, but every time we near, the waves push us further off course, or the fish begin to swarm our boat, acting as a natural barrier. We've tried having all our slaves run faster and generate more thrust, but they tire too quickly. Additionally, the local marine life seems attracted to us for some reason. The same issue applies to the rest of the fleet."

Adam frowned.

"Ah, that is something I've been—one moment." The dulcet sounds of fresh vomit caressed Commander Erishta's ears. "—wondering about. How is the thrust generated? I assumed oars and sails, but you've told me the slaves have been running?"

"Yes, of course," the porcelain-skinned elf said, narrowing her eyes before beckoning Adam to follow her into the ship's guts.

* * *

"Huh," Adam said. His entourage was now within the deepest bowels of the ship, in the so-called propulsion room.

He and Junith stood, watching as dozens of collared, half-naked men of various species ran on a moving sheet attached to a moving platform that connected to machines embedded in the ship's hull.

"So you have a problem with speed?" Adam asked, observing the prisoners running themselves ragged on the wheels. Their collars were chained to metal bars above preventing them from stopping or fleeing.

"Yes, usually we would have them running to operate the paddles when we need to achieve great speed for ramming or fleeing, but right now they are the only things keeping us near the island," Commander Erishta explained as a gold armor Drowthraki whipped a familiar looking man who had a ball-gag in his mouth.

Huh... Small world, Adam mused. The bandit was Grig, and now that he looked, Adam could spot the rest of his band of bandits here as well. All were running with tears in their eyes.

Grig turned, spying Adam. Recognition lit in his dull eyes. The man unintentionally slowed down, nearly bumping into the runner behind him before he was whipped by the enforcer.

"What... crimes did these men do, again?" Adam asked, wondering what the Gangpunchers had been up to since last he'd seen them.

"Unsure. But they're men, so they're guilty of something. I believe that one in particular tried to enter into the city wearing a wig to pretend to be a girl, and thought we wouldn't notice such an ugly man," Commander Erishta said, pointing at Grig. "Look at him. Disgusting."

The man's expression wilted, tears visibly falling from his eyes. Behind them Junith snickered, imagining Adam running on the wheel. Visibly she seemed quite delighted.

"Ah—" Adam began, before holding up his fingers and summoning Ellie to his side. The girl seamlessly held out a bucket as the nekoboy threw up again. "So the issue is speed."

"Exhaustion mainly, and running speed. The problem is the fuel, not the gear," Erishta said, indicating the men were the fuel she meant. "Although we do keep getting fish stuck in our paddle mechanism."

"I see," Adam said, stroking his chin. A ringing bell echoed in the room, and another group of men were led in to change running shifts. "What if I were to give you guys a boost?"

"A boost?" Commander Erishta said, raising her sharp eyebrow.

"Yea, with all the parts and equipment you brought onboard—one moment," Ellie held out the bucket just in time "—I can assemble a lab and concoct a potion."

"A potion?" Erishta repeated as Ellie scurried off with Adam's bucket, tossing the vomit out the window. As she did so, she glimpsed a massive shadow following the boat, formed by a truly immense school of fish.

"Yup," Adam replied.

* * *

Two days later.

"Adam..." Redfield said. The Death Knight stood stock still, hands filled with vials. Fumes wafted out from them, drifting towards the ship's open windows.

He'd been summoned to be Adam's assistant, helping to move equipment and hold various things in place for his master, including a bubbling pot.

After a day of helping to set up air vents and hoses to better the lab room's ventilation, it finally dawned on Redfield what Adam was making with all the equipment and jugs of various liquids.

"Adam... This is meth."

"No, it's mirsomone, a stimulant," Adam said, looking up at the former police officer.

"This is meth. You cooked meth."

"You're repeating yourself, but I still don't understand the problem," he said before pausing. "Ah, is this another miscommunication thing? Is meth what your people call mirsomone?"

"I..." The Death Knight's eyes vanished for a moment as Adam poured the contents of his *special* blend into a jug of water to be served. "Adam, you can't feed people meth!"

"Why not?!" he asked, slushing the green jug around. "I worked hard on this!"

"This is not okay. You can't drug them, Adam."

"It's not drugging, it's boosting. No different than a magic potion to boost mana power or strength."

"It's addictive, there's a difference."

"So what you're saying is I need to take the addictive properties—*blehk*—out."

"No, Adam... I— I... I, uh... hm." The Death Knight's eyes vanished again as Ellie replaced Adam's bucket.

"What's da problem?" Junith asked from across the room. The nekogirl was gazing at herself in a mirror as she tried on a pair of blue faulds. "We just need to boost them enough to generate force necessary to get across the barrier, right? Once we do that, they stop being our problem. Plus, they're criminals. They deserve everything they get."

"It's cruel and inhumane," the Death Knight replied, his red eyes boring holes into Junith as she picked up a pair of red faulds.

"Love to burst the bubble, but none of us are human," Junith replied. She turned to Ellie as the girl dragged a vat of ether across the floor. "Red or blue?"

"I like red," Ellie replied, wiping her brow.

"Blue it is."

"Still, the sentiment remains," Redfield argued.

"Fine, I guess I could work on a version that's less addictive," Adam replied, eyeing his cocktail. "Though I'm unsure if I have the materials. I may need to try and contact a different boat and have them use their catapult to launch another slave over with supplies..."

* * *

"Well, I'll be," Erishta said. Before her, the bandit Grig was running at top speed on the wheel set up in Adam's lab. She gazed in something like her equivalent of awe at the nekomancer's experiment. "You're actually useful."

"I... take offense to that, Commander," Adam replied, notebook in hand. "Did you doubt my words or capability?"

"Hm." Her eyes moved pointedly to the jugs of water held by Adam's Death Knight. "How much can you make?"

"Enough for all three ships to have a go at breaking through the barrier," Adam said, recording Grig's results. "I've managed to remove most of the addictive qualities for the most part by replacing the reactants that give positive reinforcement for negative."

"Is that why he's so angry?"

"Yes. In order to reduce the addictive quality of the concoction, there are a few downsides. Namely, increased agitation, higher sweating, body temperature, loss of more advanced cognition, fatigue crash, decreased appetite, increased thirst, hair loss, acne, constipation, hyperthermia, blurred vision, loss of bladder control, skin wrinkling. Most of these are just conjecture, but we won't truly understand the side effects without further testing. There also may be muscle growth with continued use, as I tried to tinker a bit," he rattled off.

"I believe I understand," Commander Erishta replied. "If we can get enough of the chattel to run at this speed, we should be able to generate enough thrust to bypass the currents and make our way through. How soon can you produce the necessary potions?"

"Mmh. It is a delicate process. Really, I just need more hands to help stir and move materials around. Can be done in a day or two, I just need to check the manifest to make sure I brought enough of the materials," Adam said, stroking his chin.

"If hands are what you need, then hands you shall have," Erishta said, signaling to an armed guard nearby.

"Excellent, let's get to cooking."

Catpurr 55
RE-LEASE! THE QUACKEN! THE QUACKENING!

Standing on the bridge of her ship, Commander Erishta peered through the periscope she held up as the crew of her second ship, *The Strider*, pierced the murky weather with the light of a gas lamp to signal.

"Okay! That's it! The last ship has finished administering their sets of potions," Erishta called down. Immediately one of her knights rushed off, leaving Adam and his entourage where they stood in the rain. Their ponchos only did so much to keep the inescapable wet at bay.

Adam made a noise of discontent as, like the true talent he was, he managed to combine a sneeze with throwing up again. Like the true professional she had become, Ellie replaced his bucket. "Are all the preparations complete?"

"Yes. Any moment now, the operation will begin. The *Strider* and *Merrigell* are awaiting my signal. I recommend you brace yourself against something," Erishta said, checking a compass as Ellie walked off with Adam's sludge.

"Aye aye, captain." Adam sniffled, grabbing the railing as Erishta gave the signal. From her upturned palm a glowing ball of light shot into the air, and soon exploded into a blinding flare.

Adam turned his head, eyeing Junith who stood with her arms crossed. "You should brace yourself."

"Hmp. Unlike you, a warrior of my calibur possesses impeccable balance and I have mastered the use of my tail to further enhance my—"

Suddenly the ship lurched, the paddle wheels on both sides of the ship beginning to turn. Abruptly the boat jolted forwards and nearly caused Junith to fall over.

"—see? Impeccable balance."

"Right. I'm not going to jump into the water to save you if you go overboard."

"Save me? Please. The day I need your saving is the day I renounce Lord Voltrain."

"Uhm, but I've literally saved your life multiple times."

"Uh huh! And whose fault was it that I was in danger IN THE FIRST PLACE?"

Adam stared at her incredulously as she smirked back, oblivious to his thoughts

"Y... Yours?" Adam said, to which the paladin only rolled her eyes as the boat hit another wave.

"Ah, here we go," he muttered, gripping the guard rail of the bridge as the ship visibly began to move against the current of the waves.

"We're gaining speed! Shift axles! Half sail! Keep us straight as he goes!" Erishta ordered. A group of knights, each lashed to the railings so as not to be swept overboard, set to work, throwing levers that controlled the central mast.

From on the deck, Adam watched a distant wave. The more the ship advanced, the more intense the storm grew.

"BRACE! BRACE FOR WAVES!" Erishta barked. Adam's stomach chose this moment to invent skydiving. He opened his mouth, splattering Junith as the ship dipped sharply.

"AH, GROSS!" she screamed, looking down at her now rainbow armor. Fortunately, an opportunity would soon come to wash it right off as a massive wave crashed over the ship's deck, knocking several knights over as Adam lost his grip on the rail. Had Erishta not caught the nekoboy by the tail, he would have been swept out to sea.

"Ow! Hey!" he screamed. Overwhelming his cry was Junith, shrieking her lungs out as she was dragged away by the might of the wave.

"THIS IS WHY I SAID HOLD ONTO SOMETHING!" Adam screamed. He wasted no time in summoning Redfield, who dove into the sea after the nekogirl.

"Woman overboard! Woman overboard!" Erishta yelled, ringing a bell. For one single moment the ship stabilized, just as another wave appeared. A group of knights swarmed the side, searching for any sign of Junith in the crashing grey waves. But she had vanished without a trace. All signs of life were consumed by the endless slate-grey sprawl.

"Ah, this is so stupid! I haven't even gotten to go on an adventure and now I'm going to die!" Adam heard Ellie cry out. The teenaged Drowthraki was clutching at the railing like a child would a teddy bear. "I should have stayed home and had babies with Karlie!"

"Commander!" Adam barked, yelling over the torrent of rain.

"What?!" Erishta yelled back. Her hands were firm on the ship's steering wheel, both arms shaking violently as she tried to keep the vessel straight.

"We have to go back!"

"WHAT?!"

"We have to go back! My friend fell into the water!"

"I know, but we can't!" Erishta yelled over the sound of wind and water.

Adam clenched his teeth. "COMMANDER! AS PRIESTESS OF THE LADY IN SILK! SENT FROM THE CAPITAL! I AM ORDERING YOU TO TURN. THIS. BOAT. AROUALSKHCA—!" His epic speech was interrupted by untimely vomit.

Commander Erishta suddenly did something unexpected—she laughed.

Her eyes were touched with mania as the foreign sounds left her lungs. Finally, she raised her head and met the nekomancer's eyes. "GIVE IT A REST! I KNOW YOU AREN'T FROM THE CAPITAL!"

"WHAT?"

"I KNOW YOU AREN'T FROM THE CAPITAL!"

"YEAH, I HEARD YOU THE FIRST TIME! I WAS ASKING—NO, NEVERMIND! TURN THIS BOAT AROUND!" Adam screamed. It didn't matter what the Commander's suspicions were or what she thought. Right now, Adam still needed Junith, and he needed her alive.

"EVEN IF I WANTED TO! I CAN'T! WE'RE TOO FAR IN AND IF WE ATTEMPTED TO TURN, THE WATER WILL BROADSIDE AND CAPSIZE US!" Erishta yelled back. "WE'LL HAVE TO MAKE LANDFALL AND TURN THE SHIP TO COME BACK FOR THEM!"

Adam clicked his teeth and ran to the stern of the ship, scanning the water below. His teeth ground and clenched.

"Nyx below! You stupid idiot! Why don't you ever listen to me?!" he yelled out into the distance, only to be greeted with a faint voice that yelled back, "I'M NOT AN IDIOOOOOT!"

Well, at least she's still alive!

Slowly he let his forehead bonk against the railing. It was nothing compared to the migraine pounding away within. Then he jerked forwards, letting more rainbow spews join the colorless waves below.

"Ahhh! This sucks! This really, really— Huh?" Adam paused, wiping his mouth. Below the railing, dozens of fish were throwing themself out of the waves and towards the boat, but they weren't what gave Adam pause. Rather, that would be the twin, beady red orbs glowing from below the water's surface. The truly *massive* red orbs.

What the Nyx?

Not only were they already massive. Gradually, they grew larger and larger, getting closer—and the already-immense shadow grew with it. A wretched sound echoed in Adam's ears, one that would haunt his nightmares forevermore: a faint *quack, quack, quack,* in time with the bubbles reaching the ocean's surface and popping below. Adam's blood froze with an unthinkable realization.

Then he spun, boots slipping against the drenched deck as he sprinted towards the Commander.

"COMMANDER! COMMANDER!" Adam hollered, waving his arms. The scarred elf turned with a characteristic scowl.

"WHAT?!" Erishta barked, her face twisted in anger. Then it went slack, her eyes growing larger and larger as her head tilted gradually up. Adam's pace slowed to a stop as he felt a dark shadow swallow him. He did not want to turn around—but he *had* to see it with his own eyes.

An obscene figure towered above them. Feathers the color of putrid, yellow bile were wet and clumped with seawater, and beady red eyes fixed the ship with a baleful glare. The macabre being from deep beneath the surface had been awakened, resembling a capricious and vengeful god.

Quack, it boomed, and its voice seemed to shake the very heavens.

"DUCKYSAUR!" Adam screamed, flailing as the deck of the ship gave way beneath his feet. The ship was the fowl, two-hundred-foot-tall sea monster's toy now, to do with it as it pleased, and none would deny it.

The boat was thrown into the air, flipping end over end. As Adam's stomach emptied itself of its contents for the last time, the great wheels of time seemed to grind to a halt, the nekomancer's life flashing before his eyes as he questioned how, exactly, his path had led him here.

Is it my luck?

Did I not eat enough vegetables?

Is it my fault for being a bad pet owner and losing Schrödinger?

I really wish I had my cat right now.

A scream filled his ears, one he soon realized was his own. Uncontrollably his body flailed about until finally, he managed to fling his hand and activate the gauntlet of the magic hand, the ephemeral hand tethered to his glove clamping onto a railing and the boat flipped in mid-air. But all too soon, it fell with a mighty *crunch.*

-40 HP!

Barely seconds had passed since the beast revealed himself, and already a large chunk of Adam's HP was *gone,* but one supposed it was enough of a miracle that the boat had landed upright at all.

[CATSIFICATION! YOU ARE WET!]
-20% to ALL STATS!
STR: 25 -> 20
CON: 46 ->37
DEX: 25 ->20
ARC: 162 -> 130
SEN: 23 -> 19
EGO: 43 -> 38

Another thunderous roar caused Adam to wince, clutching at his ears as he doubled over.

Deep within, a low groan was building. Finally, he vocalized it, and followed it up by spitting out, "I'M SO SICK OF DUCKS!"

"BATTLE STATIONS! BATTLE STATIONS!" Commander Erishta yelled. Somehow, the woman had remained on board throughout the entire dilemma, still positioned at the ship's steering wheel. Clinging to her back like an anxious koala was a trembling Ellie.

What knights remained onboard immediately ran to the sides of the ship, grabbing bows and various other gear from under the floorboards of the ship's deck.

Scanning the scene, Adam saw a group of Drowthraki pulling at a rope leading off to the side. A chant of "Woman overboard!" had gone up amongst them. Seeing their distress, Adam took off, racing to the edge of the ship where he saw a golden armored knight dangling at the side of the ship and barely above water.

"Hang on!" he yelled before grabbing the rope, much to the dismayed looks of several knights. "What? What are you all looking at?! PULL!"

At Adam's words, the trio of soldiers pulled and with his help, managed to retrieve the woman who fell overboard. However, as she came up, she went wide-eyed, staring at Adam.

"You—You're a—"

A pale blur distracted the nekoboy. As he turned to see if Erishta was beckoning him, he realized the blur wasn't a person at all—his wig, utterly bedraggled and nearly grey with grime, had come off in the mayhem, now snagged on the massive duckysaur as the beast rose higher and higher into the heavens, revealing more of its body armored with white feathers and red scales.

"Ah, so... Funny story." The knights stared him down, their expressions unreadable. But before he could make up an excuse, the gods seemed to take mercy upon him—or perhaps just had a particularly cruel sense of humor. The fowl monster unfurled its wings, and the water billowed like fabric. A massive tsunami, easily thousands of meters tall, cast a deep shadow over the ship's deck.

Adam's ears folded as his jaw dropped, his eyes seemingly trying to escape his skull as the wave that blotted out the skies. Truly, only one word could describe this sight.

"Ah... Crapbaskets..."

Catpurr 56

Candy Island and the Magical Liopleurodon

On a golden-sand beach lay a cat-eared corpse, seaweed half-strangling its body. As a wild crab scuttled up to investigate its find, it pinched at the fluffy red tail, utterly sodden and drenched, attached to the corpse.

The body, better known as Adam Glow, squeaked, and the crab scuttled away, as the nekoboy then rolled onto his back, letting out a low and torturous groan in the summer heat.

At last, the boy shakily pushed himself to his feet, coughing up sand and ripping off seaweed shackles as he did. Sprawled around him was a tropical locale flush with vibrant, pink bushes.

"Well... As far as happy landings go..." the fatigued Adam moaned, grabbing at his neck that was sore, stiff, and slightly sunburnt. "I'm alive."

Begrudgingly he opened his followers list.

Bonded Followers: 03

    Junith Oatheart: T2 Lvl 20 (Wet, Annoyed)
    Class: [Subdued] Priestess of Eli
    HP: 960/960 (1200)
    MP: 300/300

Eh'liza Oktober: T1 Lvl 39 (Sugar High!)
Class: Penitent of Adam
HP: 278/320
MP: 120/180

Kathrine Dominica: T1 Lvl 10 (Wet, Confused, Scared)
Class: Class selection available!

"Well, that idiot is still alive at least," he muttered before violently sneezing. As he rubbed his nose, he took in his surroundings more closely. It was midday and he still had clothes, torn and tattered as they may be, so he hadn't undergone his transformation yet, meaning he had a few hours to get his bearings before he lost control of his body again.

On the horizon was the stationary storm, serving as a natural barrier against travel, while surrounding him were various other items that had washed ashore—planks, crates, pillows, and random junk. No other survivors in sight

With a sigh, Adam summoned his most faithful undead, but an odd message was displayed instead.

[The Death Knight Redfield has refused your call.]

Huh?

It was the first time he'd ever received such a message. He tried again.

[The Death Knight Redfield has refused your call.]

"He can do that?! Why are you refusing me? Did I make you angry? Is it the meth thing?" he wondered aloud, more bewildered than annoyed.

"Nyx below." No, standing had become too much effort. He flopped down onto the golden sands to continue taking stock of the situation.

Fortunately, he had had the foresight to stow his most important items in his storage ring, keeping his staff and Junith's armor of Smo, and all their other most important and expensive treasures, safe.

"Well... At least I'm no longer on that accursed boat."

* * *

Slow progress was made as Adam charted his surroundings, creeping through the jungle laden with pink flora. Everywhere sugarweed grew, stiff petals in all shades of rose, flamingo, and fuschia, containing truly ludicrous quantities of sucrose just as the name suggested.

Even though it was a much-loved commodity, the plant native to this island was highly invasive everywhere else. This led to most of the world burning the fields of pink wherever they were found and restricting the plant to this singular archipelago.

Sadly, this meant the island was also a nesting ground for the duckysaurs. The massive fowls were almost addicted to the taste of the sugarweed and had collectively flocked to this island, forming an army of enraged ducks ruled by Bullert. On top of possessing high quantities of sucrose, sugarweed also possessed an addictive quality, one that, when consumed in high concentrations, made the ingestor enraged, among other effects. And a troop of highly aggressive, addicted duckysaurs on a sugar rush had quickly spiraled into the current state of things.

White-hued seedlings adhered to a stiff sugarweed leaf briefly halted Adam's progression as he took samples. Then he sighed heavily, wiping the dripping sweat from his forehead.

"So much for just setting up a research lair..." he lamented, opening his storage device and taking out a vial. He had reserved a slot in his storage ring for just such an occasion.

Since the sugarweed wasn't a liquid concoction, his polite belt of potions wouldn't accept the vial, something Adam had learned when he tried to take plant cultures he'd seen during his run of the Drowthraki academy.

Sadly, with this last item, every slot in his ring was taken: one for his journal, the stielhandgranate which he kept inside for fear of exploding himself, his staff, Junith's armor, and now finally the sugarweed seeds.

Adam's stomach growled. A wave of fatigue was settling deep into the nekoboy's bones as several days of being too sick to eat finally caught up with him.

"Uhk. This sucks," he complained, his stomach gurgling as it demanded sustenance. The neko doubled over, his insides twisting into knots. "Ah, but at least I'm no longer vomiting."

His forehead pressed into the jungle dirt. And there he laid for a period of time, as life in the jungle continued on around him, indifferent to the nekomancer's presence—until a pair of bare toes entered his field of vision.

Golden eyes slowly panned up. Before Adam stood a woman, or rather a teenager. She was half-nude, with wild pink hair, the local flora having been repurposed into makeshift clothes for her, and a shining, gleaming tiara sat perched upon her head, clashing with her disheveled state.

"Oh, there you are. I was wondering how long until you got here," Liza said, biting a chunk out of a fruit.

"Y-Y-Y-You—" Adam began, his eyes twitching. Was this an illusion? A symptom of starvation? Or had he simply finally gone mad?

"Jeez, what took you so long?" Liza said. She plucked a pink leaf from her makeshift tank top and popped it in her mouth.

"You?! Where have you been this entire time?!" he barked as Liza lifted the weakened Adam up by the scruff of his cloak.

"Oh, ya know, here, there," she said nonchalantly as Adam's ears twitched. Sounds of rustling leaves filled the nekoboy's twitching ears. Unconsciously his eyes flicked towards the source, which Liza seemed to notice. "Oh, don't worry! That's just my friends!"

"Friends?" Adam muttered before his eyes bulged as he hung limp, his jaw falling open. From the neon foliage emerged a massive gray creature with large flippers for arms. The long jaws set in its smooth, moist head parted, revealing a set of serrated teeth. "FRIENDS?! THAT'S A MONSTER!"

"NO! IT'S A LIOPLEURODON! AND HE'S A CUTIE!" Liza exclaimed excitedly, accidentally strangling Adam as he began to weakly flail, attempting to get away from the beast's expanding maw.

"Adam, meet Tiffany. Tiffany, Adam!" Liza said, preventing the bedraggled nekoboy from escaping as he was manhandled and forced to greet the twenty-foot-tall creature.

"Ah! Its breath smells like cakes and sugar!"

"I know! Isn't it great?!"

"NO!" he exclaimed as the monster stuck out its long, slimy, pink-coated tongue. Lining the appendage were thick bristles that were akin to a hairbrush as it licked Adam's face.

"Uhwjwkan!" He shuddered, his whole body cringing but unable to fight back as fatigue took hold.

"Aw, he likes you!" Liza laughed, taking another bite out of a crunchy pink leaf.

"Stop! Stop this thing from licking me or I'll blow it up!" Adam yelled, summoning his staff. Already the crystal was shining.

However, much to his dismay, Liza only laughed at his threat. Below them the ground trembled. Then a multitude of massive Liopleurodons appeared, surrounding the nekopair.

"What? No! No! NOOOOOOOOOO!" Adam screamed in horror before dozens of slimy tongues descended upon him in a singular licking frenzy.

* * *

Covered in slime with a particularly deep and exasperated frown on his face, Adam examined Liza's camp with a critical eye. It had been situated in a lagoon shaped like a skull—something the average person may find somewhat unnerving, but which made Adam feel right at home.

"How the Nyx did you get here before I did?" he asked, walking around the spacious, slick black cavern festooned with various trinkets and items.

Mostly knickknacks and loot in the form of crates and other scavenged items. No doubt taken from wrecks like his.

"Well, when the space pupper flung me out, I landed out in the water. That's when Tiffany here caught me!" Liza said. Her companion's head poked out of the water as the nekogirl cuddled it. "Isn't that right, Tiffany! Isn't that right! You tried to eat me, you little goober you! Yes, you did! Yes, you did!"

The creature let out a yawn then licked Liza with its long, bristled tongue.

This is why cats are better, Adam wisely considered. Then he cringed as the monster left a trail of sticky drool across Liza's smiling face.

As the tongue approached him again his ears twitched, and he staggered backwards.

"No! Bad monster of the depths! No licking!" Adam yelped, barely evading another overenthusiastic Liopleurodon as it rose from the waters. "Bad!"

The creature hissed as Adam summoned his staff and booped it on the head, the twenty-foot-tall monster sticking out its tongue once more.

"Just let Charlie lick you," Liza called out. The nekogirl leapt from the cavern floor and onto the back of the beast called Tiffany. "They like the salt on our skin."

"I refuse," Adam said flatly, making the mistake of turning his head away from the four-flippered monster. Immediately it seized the opportunity to violate his personal space.

"UHK?!" he squeaked before spinning, ready to smack the creature but it fled, denying the nekomancer as it leapt back into the water with a loud splash.

"Hey! Don't scare Charlie! He's very sensitive!" Liza yelled, pulling her mount up beside Adam, whose knees gave way, plopping him to the ground.

"Please don't tell me you named every one of these creatures?" he asked, his stomach letting out a rumble that echoed throughout the cavern.

"Of course I did!" Liza said, matter-of-factly. "They're my friends and they deserve names after all they've been through!"

"Oh? And what exactly have your friends been through?" Adam scowled, narrowing his eyes at Charlie whose snoot poked out of the water.

"Well! Good thing you asked!" Liza exclaimed, reaching over and patting the boy on the head before she yanked him onto her mount.

Aboard the gray monster, the pair began to delve deeper into the cave.

"Ya seeee," Liza began. The nekogirl grabbed a torch, getting into an odd position. Then she opened her mouth and began to... sing? *"This island was their home, and deep down below, the temple was a place of freedom only they could go! Aeon after aeon, a haven only they know—"*

"What... What is this?" Adam said. From seemingly nowhere a melody seemed to emanate and fill the cavern, as the water began to glow.

"—but tragedy struck, the temple fell low! The ancient shrine and customs, all ending with the show!"

"What is even going on?! Why are you singing?! Where is this music coming from?!" Adam yelled, looking around the cavern as light arced along the walls in familiar patterns, which he swiftly recognized as runes.

Adam blinked, turning away from the singing Liza. The familiar etchings and symbols demanded his full attention as several in particular caught his eye.

Eli, Freya, Nyx, and Voltrain.

The symbols of the gods were here, and they were everywhere!

Catpurr 57
Team One

Adam hopped off the Liopleurodon, leaping on the outcrop of land to more closely examine the symbols as Liza sang.

He made a noise of interest, taking out his notebook to get a rubbing of the runes as dozens of questions burned in his mind.

Who were the gods really? Why were these walls carved with their symbols?

"Blah blah blah blah blah!" Liza continued, singing to the melody.

What did these other symbols mean?

"Blah blah blah! Blaaaaaah!"

What was this cave?

"Blaaaaaah! Blah blah blah."

Why was Liza insisting on singing in his ear?

"BLAH! BLAH BLAH!"

Seriously...

The caterwauling of the nekogirl's song abruptly fell silent, and just as suddenly the faint glow faded, the runes vanishing back into ordinary cave walls.

"Seriously?! Hey! I'm talking to you! I worked hard on this song!" Liza complained. Adam slowly turned on her, narrowing his eyes. Was this really so important?

Instead, he turned back to the wall, and the more important question. "Where'd the light go?" he muttered, rubbing along the walls. But they were completely smooth, not giving the slightest indication that runes had been inscribed within them.

"Well, the cave only works if someone is singing," Liza explained.

"What?"

"You heard me. If you want your scribbles, you'll have to SIIIIIING!" Liza shrieked, her voice like nails on wood to Adam's ears.

"What? Why?! Who ever heard of—" A sudden splash of water cut him off. The nekoboy turned to meet the gaze of a familiar bald, bronze-skinned man riding a Liopleurodon.

"Yo! What's up, sexual chocolate!" Liza exclaimed, waving to Abdullah.

"Ah! Kytah! It is by the will of God we should meet again!" Abdullah laughed, hopping off the creature. Disembarking with him, Adam recognized another familiar face.

The blonde dual wielder in a floral robe.

He eyed Adam yet said nothing, walking with a bundle over his shoulders.

"Okay, did everyone arrive here before me?" Adam said as the shirtless Abdullah approached and hugged him. The man's bronze skin was rough and bumpy from the scars coating his body. "Okay, you're hugging me. Why are you hugging me?"

"Ah, it is good to see you alive and well, huntah! Yashwah be praised! Another ally in our fight for survival!" Abdullah exclaimed, raising the boy aloft by his armpits before placing him down.

"Okay, pause. Everyone pause. I need an explanation how and why you all managed to get here before me?!" Adam asked. There—There was a barrier! One that had required his intellect to get past! There was a *duckysaur!*

"Ah! That's easy, kytah! After we sniffed out the information as to our objective, we quickly... Ah. What is the word, pink one, that word you used—"

"Procured!" Liza offered as Abdullah clapped his hands.

Ah, so stole, Adam mentally translated.

"Yes! Procured a ship from some locals and made haste in our journey to end this trial," Abdullah said, patting Adam on the back with a laugh.

"How long have you all been here?" Adam asked, raising his brow.

"Uh? Three?" Liza said, turning her head to Abdullah and the blonde man. The pair had begun feeding the monsters.

"Days?" Adam said, eyeing the camp. As Liza and the blonde man fed the monsters, Abdullah was dragging a net filled with fish to feed the gathering Liopleurodons.

"No, weeks. I think. Although I've been here since the beginning," Liza said as Adam went back to staring at the cavern walls where he last saw the inscriptions.

"Weeks? Give me all the information you have," he demanded, wanting to get appraised of the situation.

"Information?" The blonde warrior looked up, a scowl on his face as he shooed away a Liopleurodon attempting to get into Abdullah's net. "Look left, look right. Duckysaurs everywhere. The king lies on the mountaintop, surrounded by his guard and preventing us from getting close."

"What my frustrated friend here means," Abdullah said, stepping in and guiding Adam towards a crude map on a table, "is that there is much prey in these parts. The hunt is good, but their numbers know no bounds."

"So, you know where Bullert roosts? That's good, now we just need to figure out how to fight a two-hundred-foot tall duckysaur," Adam said, standing on a chair to study the dimensions of the island and various markers.

"Two hundred?" Liza said before giggling. "Oh, that's not Bullert."

"It's not?" Adam frowned, his face going pale.

"No, that's *Roger*. Bullert is about twenty feet tall."

"Wait. What?"

"Yeah, Bullert is about twenty feet tall, wears a top hat, quacks. He's a bit adorable, minus the death ray and all."

Adam blinked. "I'm sorry, did you say death ray?"

"Oh yeah, the top hat has a crystal that vaporizes things with a *pew pew!* Immediately into chunks," Liza said, making sound effects. Then she took out a severed arm from her bag.

"Just the other day, Tom got too close and was spotted then, *BOOM!* Gone. All he left behind was this arm. Poor Tom," she said sadly, using the severed forearm as a back scratcher.

"And... Who's Tom?" Adam asked, eyeing the appendage.

"Oh, some dill weed from the other team," Liza added. She hopped beside the nekoboy and pointed at a crude drawing of a boat. "The mangy mutts and their army are also on the island. Well, mostly on the beach with their boats."

Adam's frown somehow deepened.

"An army?"

This was just getting worse and worse!

"Yerrrrp. World Coalition Forces or something. They've attacked us a few times but we're better than those losers." Liza giggled, twirling a dagger as Abdullah laughed.

Adam pinched the bridge of his nose.

Oh, Nyx below, I can sense a headache forming...

"What's their numbers?"

"About a hundred?"

"I see," Adam said, looking at the crude drawing of a behatted duckysaur. "So we're here, and the duckysaur is here. Any battle strategies?"

"Nope, we've pretty much given up at this point and just sit around hunting ducks," Liza said, walking off to lay on her Liopleurodon that was resting on a pile of bones. "The mutts have screwed off after the last attack and have pretty much promised to leave us alone if we don't interfere."

"Oh..." Adam said. Internally he debated if he should continue his plan to end the trial, or just let the mutts do it.

Trial reversion would mean doing another trial and earning more rewards, but at the same time, he wasn't very keen on doing more and more trials.

But.

At the same time, the duckysaurs still needed to pay, and Adam was still feeling pretty vengeful...

"So? Where's the idiot at?" Liza asked, feeding the severed arm to her monster like a snack. "Ooh, who's a good prehistoric dino! You are! You are!"

The monster shuddered, its tongue flopping out of its mouth to lick Liza and leave another long, sticky tendril of drool behind.

"Somewhere. We got separated during our trip here. She's alive, so knowing her, she'll turn up somewhere," Adam replied, staring at the map before he summoned several skelecats and sent them off.

"What are you thinking, kytah?" Abdullah asked, standing at the opposite side of the table.

Adam narrowed his eyes, stroking his chin before his pupils settled on Abdullahh's dark-skinned hand.

"I'm unsure," he said finally before turning his attention towards the walls. Finally, his gaze settled on Liza, who raised a brow. "I'll think about it, but in the meantime. Liza, sing."

"Nope."

Adam blinked. "What do you mean nope?"

"You've lost your song privileges," she said, turning her head and crossing her arms as her Liopleurodon yawned. "If you want a song, you'll have to sing yourself. I had this whole thing planned out and even had a dance number."

"Yes, it has been very annoying," the blonde man said, laying down in a hammock set up on a wall.

"Hey! I don't complain about your farting, don't complain about my singing!" Liza yelled, throwing a bone from the ground at him. The man lifted an arm and sliced the projectile in half.

"And I told you, sugar makes me gassy. Yet you insist on only cooking with it, you addict," the blonde man spat, turning over to face Adam and Liza.

"Don't like it, don't eat it!" Liza exclaimed. "Anyway, if you want your song, you'll have to sing yourself."

Adam frowned, taking a breath, an air of annoyance surrounding him.

"Fine," he said, preparing to sing.

Catpurr 58

Clues

From somewhere beneath the waves, a particular Death Knight sighed, and spoke in a voice no one would hear, "Man... It's a good thing I don't need oxygen..."

* * *

Adam closed his eyes for a moment and inhaled, composing himself before opening his mouth.

Liza raised her brow, her eyes going wide as the soft vocals coming out of her master's mouth began echoing through the cave.

Abdullah turned his head, watching the boy as the water in the lagoon began to glow and the runes blazed to life.

"In the moonlight, where shadows play, a kind necromancer lights the way," Adam sang, recalling a nursery rhyme from his master as he touched the sigils. *"With a gentle touch, restoring peace, attending in silence to every resting place."*

Around the cavern, the Liopleurodons began to poke their heads out of the water, the crowd of monsters gathering around Adam, listening to the nekoboy sing his melody.

"Through the veil of night, a friendly gaze," he continued, jotting down the runes and glyphs. *"Children need not be afraid. Bringing solace to the gone, the necromancer's work is never done."*

[Title Obtained!]

[Melodic Voice]
[Your voice has attracted the fascination of a small crowd.]
[+20% favorability from all sentient beings.]

Adam ignored the blue screen, working furiously to copy down the runes before they faded again.

He walked along the wall, sketching as fast as his pen would let him, singing absentmindedly as a crowd of monsters followed him.

"Hmm." He paused, as he reached the end of the cavern where the runes vanished into the water, the source of the light.

As the light faded, Adam frowned. He gazed down at his pages of notes, the images he'd drawn being that of a sequence of events when read backwards.

The initial glyph showed a grand shrine of some kind, people offering a sacrifice to a circle made of runes that represented gods Adam was familiar with.

But, unlike the six symbols joined by Eli's symbol that Adam knew about, the wall displayed twelve symbols.

"Huh..." he hummed. The images depicted a person, one being sacrificed, before said person seemed to ascend, melding with the symbols.

From the context clues, one could surmise several things.

One. These worlds weren't artificial areas created for the trials, as he'd been told.

Two. These trials seemed to be gateways to obtaining or ascending to some form of godhood.

And three. They were being *used.*

There wasn't enough here to confirm the actual specifics, but from the fact that there were so many Chosen and trials, the participants were being used to accomplish a task of some sort.

Junith and others like her would believe themselves to be champions of their gods, heroes chosen to act as their hands upon the worlds. But Adam felt something more... sinister afoot.

Without a doubt, the last image of a man stabbing a person on an altar didn't bode well. Neither did the ascension part.

The purpose of the trials seemed to be to cultivate the champions, grow them and reward the participants... But for what purpose?

Adam frowned as Liza grabbed him, while Abdullah and the blonde man applauded.

"Wow! You have the voice of an angel! We should take your voice on the road! Become famous pop stars! Oh! Have you tried screamos?! Let me hear your scream! WE COULD START A HEAVY METAL BAND CALLED THE KITTY CATS!" Liza exclaimed, shaking the nekoboy violently and nearly causing him to drop his notebook.

"Easy, you idiot!" Adam spat, closing his book and smacking the excited nekogirl on her head.

"Ehk!" she squeaked, biting her tongue as Adam's eyes were drawn to the shadows coating the entrance of the cave.

Immediately his eyes widened. So caught up in the runes and taking notes had he been, he forgot one crucial fact about his condition.

Ah, crapbaskets.

He transformed during the night.

Adam took off in a panic, pushing the sobbing Liza to the side and leaping above the gathering of Liopleurodons to find something, *anything*, he could use to bind himself!

"Huh? What's wrong?! Why are you so frantic?" Liza asked, tracking the speeding blur of a nekomancer tearing the camp apart.

"Chains! Ropes! Coffin! I need something to contain me!" he yelled, searching through everything he could until he found a pair of chains and began spinning in circles, wrapping himself in a frenzy.

"What? What?" Liza asked in confusion as Abdullah narrowed his eyes.

"I TRANSFORM DURING THE FULL MOON!" Adam yelled, unwrapping himself and stripping naked. "Find something to bind me!"

"Transform? During—" With a great gasp, Liza's jaw dropped, her ears twitching rapidly as her eyes went round and she quickly put two and two together. "YOU'RE A WERENEKO! WAIT! DOES THAT MEAN I'M A WERENEKO?! OMG! EVERYTHING MAKES SO MUCH SENSE NOW!"

Liza began staring at her claws, sheathing and unsheathing them over and over again as her excitement grew.

"Kytah, what is this?" Abdullah asked, watching Adam roll around on the ground.

"Gah!" the boy replied in frustration, opening several portals in the process and depositing various skelecats. "Abdullah, you've got to find something to chain me down!"

The cat skeletons clattered on the slick cavern floor, shaking themselves before moving to join the effort to pin their master down.

Sensing the urgency in the nekoboy's voice, Abdullah and the blonde man hurried off, grabbing rope, chains, netting, and other objects as the sunlight in the cave began to dwindle.

Liza ran off, grabbing stakes that the blonde man used to pin the netting and chains into the earth, using a construct of green light that was shaped into a hammer to nail the spikes into the floor.

Abdullah stood to the side, chanting for a moment before clapping his hands and shifting the slick soil, the ground forming a layer of dirt that rose out of the ground to entrap Adam with his head sticking out.

"Will you speak to me of the matter, my friend?" Abdullah said, crouching low to bring himself to eye level with the immured, squirming nekoboy.

Adam let out a sigh before explaining the specifics to the members of his team while the Liopleurodons kept attempting to lick his head. Thankfully, the massive monsters were wary of his skelecats, allowing him some reprieve from the would-be onslaught of sticky tongues wanting a taste of furry feline skin.

"Interesting," the blonde man said, stroking his chin as Abdullah raised a brow. Not far off, Liza was busy singing a song about werenekos swimming in the ocean and causing a commotion.

"So, whatever you do! You must make sure I don't scratch you or get free!" Adam yelled, his anxious gaze locked on the sun setting in the distance. Before long, he was out like a light, a wave of fatigue washing over him and knocking him out cold, when a wicked sound filled the cavern.

Catpurr 59

OH GOD! HE'S HOT!

As malevolent laughter echoed through the cavern, a blinding light shone out, forcing Liza, Abdullah, and the blond man, whose name was Jack, to close their eyes and turn away from the nekoboy.

When the light settled, the much younger-looking boy was now gone. In his place now was a muscular, half naked, red-haired man sitting upright in the dirt. The chains and ground did nothing to stop the nekoman as he began to rise.

"Oh..." Liza let out, her face completely red as her jaw dropped at the sight of the nearly seven-foot-tall man with muscular arms, long, silky red hair, and face that was eye-catching to say the least.

"Well, this is new," the transformed Adam said in a gruff and deeply masculine voice, rolling his broad shoulders. The man's sharp, golden gaze fell upon Liza as she let out a high-pitched scream of excitement.

"OMG, omg, omg," Liza said, doing little hops in place as she clapped. "YOU'RE SO HOT!"

"I'm sorry? Who are you?" Adam said, sauntering over until he towered over Liza. The woman suddenly found herself backed up against the nearby slick wall.

"Oh—I'm—Uh—Huuuurrr," she hummed, staring at Adam's abs. "Holy twin towers you could grind meat on those things!"

"Oh, you're one of mine, aren't you?" the nekoman said, his hand placed beneath Liza's chin, lifting her head to meet his hypnotic gaze.

"I will be whatever you want me to be," she replied, drool coming out of her mouth as her ears folded.

"Huh... It doesn't work on you," Adam replied, a tinge of boredom in his tone as he shifted away from the fawning nekogirl.

"Kytah? Is this... Is this your true form?" Abdullah asked, the bald warrior astonished by the sudden transformation of the nekoboy into a man.

Adam blinked, eyeing Abdullah up and down and cocking his head to the side.

"Why are you black?"

"Pardon?" Abdullah replied, confused at the question.

"You're human, right?"

Suddenly Adam was standing in front of Abdullah. The bronzed-skin warrior flinched and summoned a large, round shield, as sand rose from the ground and shaped into several sharp spears.

Abdullah's eyes narrowed. He hadn't even seen Adam move!

"Hmm, you certainly smell human. Huh, you don't smell like chocolate," the nekoman replied before licking the warrior, much to his surprise. Then he shrugged, walking past the stunned Abdullah. "Don't taste like it either. Salty."

"W-Where are you going?!" Liza called out.

"On a walk. To stretch my legs. You're more than welcome to join, luv," Adam replied, flashing a wolfish grin at Liza who hopped and scrambled, quickly latching on to the nekomancer's large bicep.

"Hehehe, *muscles*," she giggled as the adult sized Adam took a step forwards, only to pause and raise his brow at the warrior barring his way.

"Not so fast, kytah," Abdullah said, standing resolutely at the entrance of the cavern. "Mine own eyes can see you are not yourself.

You charged me earlier to protect you, to make sure you were bound. I shall fulfill the request honorably. Return to your prison."

At the man's words, Adam cocked his head from side to side, his large, bushy tail moving back and forth before laughter erupted from deep in his chest.

"Ah, you're funny," he said, patting the warrior on his shoulder with a wicked grin. "If you think you can stop me, you're more than welcome to try."

At the provocation, Abdullah's spears disintegrated into sand.

"Nyah?" Liza squeaked, as Adam suddenly lifted her into the air. A tidal wave of sand swamped her form, and the nekogirl sputtered.

"BLEHBLEH BLEHG BLASAJWK!" she spat, flailing. The tiny grains soon parted to form a sphere around her and Adam.

Adam looked around boredly, not a care in the world as he allowed himself to be surrounded by the attack.

"Entomb!" Abdullah cried, clenching his fist. The sand sphere rapidly closed like a rubber band let loose, releasing a snap that echoed throughout the cave as a large sand ball formed.

[Target Entombed! 1/3]

A blip displayed in front of Abdullah. The bald hunter narrowed his eyes as the blonde man named Jack laid in the back on a sack, eating a snack and observing the unfolding chaos.

As his notification showed only one had been snared, it was a good assumption that Adam had managed to avoid his attack. Now the question remained, where was he?

"You'll have to do much better than that, my chocolate covered friend."

Abdullah spun, eyes wide at the man who stood behind him, half naked, with his hands clasped behind his back and bearing a wide smile.

"Kytah, do not shame me under the gaze of Yashwa," Abdullah growled, releasing Liza from his sand prison who made a "Blehp" sound as she hit the floor. Suddenly, her Liopleurodon leapt out of the water, snatching the girl up whole in its maw before leaping back into the river.

"I wish not to harm a friend," Abdullah said as sand began to snake across the cave, quickly coating the floor and cavern walls while the Liopleurodons fled.

"Harm me? Wouldn't you need to be able to first touch me?" Adam replied smugly. From the entrance of the cave came a sudden wall of golden light, and the nekoman turned. "So that's how this is..."

At the entrance, the blonde man had finally gotten up, golden energy wafting from his raised palms to form the prison.

"Kytah, lie back down," Abdullah said, a pit opening in the earth as nearly every inch of the cavern was coated in sand.

"No. No, I don't think I will," Adam said, his hands shaping into claws as the nearby Liopleurodons scattered.

"Fine," Abdullah said, the bald warrior's face darkening before becoming a wicked smile. Two copies made of sand formed, standing at his sides. "Then by Yashwa's grace, I thank thee for a worthy foe."

* * *

It wasn't long before a bloodied Adam was walking alone in the trees under the moonlight, chewing on a large pink leaf as he made his way to the only source of light in miles.

Under the moonlight, his vision was perfect, completely unobstructed by the darkness as he approached the wooden wall where voices could be heard.

"All I'm saying is, why are we even listening to those dog folk? Everything so far has sucked so hard. If we're gonna do nothing and stand around, we should have stayed in Cadia."

"I'm sure the higher-ups are doing their best."

Adam grinned, spotting a man and woman in the darkness above the wall, the two armored soldiers unaware of his presence.

"Ugh, what kind of man are you?!" the brunette in steel armor and purple livery yelled, throwing her hands in the air. "All you do is praise Command, I'm sure you have problems!"

"Well, sure I have problems, Private. But I'm your superior. I don't gripe to you. Gripes go upward," the man said, unrattled.

"What?" the soldier said in confusion.

"You complain to me, I complain to Lieutenant Lambert, Lieutenant Lambert complains to Knight Eskel, Knight Eskel complains to Knight Captain Geralt, Knight Captain Geralt complains to Commissar Vessimer. Up, you gotta go *up* with the gripes, not down."

There was a rustling of armor as the woman crossed her arms. "Okay, but let's say I was Lieutenant Lambert. What would you say to me then?"

"Then I'd say this is an excellent mission. We're fighting on behalf of the world, and I would be honored to stand guard on this tower in the middle of the night, surrounded by predators and an annoying private who never stops talking."

"Aw, come on, Sarge! You don't mean that. You love meee, Sarg— HUH?!" Suddenly the two soldiers spun, turning to face the looming, shirtless man who towered over the both of them. Somehow, he had managed to sneak up on their pair in their bickering.

"Who are—?!" the sergeant yelled, attempting to draw his sword only to be sent flying by Adam's hand as it knocked the man out instantly.

"SERGEANT BARIN—!" the private attempted to yell, but stopped as Adam grabbed her by the head and held the woman aloft, her muffled screams hitting his hands as he brought her to meet his eyes.

"Stop struggling," he ordered. The woman's eyes went wide as she stared into the pair of shining golden orbs that probed at her mind, overwriting her desires to break free.

The soldier's hands immediately fell to her sides as her muffled screams stopped, her eyes taking on a golden hue under Adam's trance.

"Ah, it still works," he said to himself, licking his lips as he released the woman who now stood at attention.

"What... What do you need from me... sir?" she asked, her flushed face unable to make direct eye contact with the nude, buff nekoman.

"You're a soldier, right?" he asked, his finger running up the woman's neck to caress her chin and turn her head to look at him.

"Y-Y-Yes, sir," the soldier's voice broke as she let out a moan.

"Are there others like you?" the nekoman asked, the woman now sucking on his thumb.

"Dozens, sir," the enthralled woman whispered, her body shaking.

"Interesting," he said, smiling to himself as he gazed out at the encampment of tents and boats that lay not too far away. "Time to have some fun."

* * *

Elsewhere.

"Hrrrn," Junith groaned, frowning as she sat in an iron prison cell with her arms folded while a battle-scarred Commander Erishta paced back and forth. The woman was stripped of nearly all of her clothes and armor. "Can you quit your pacing! you're making me nervous."

"It helps me to think," Erishta said, before banging her handcuffs against their cell's iron bars.

"Hmm," Junith grunted, flicking her gaze at Ellie sleeping nearby, then towards the cage filled with Adam's *test subjects,* like Grig, who were strung out. Their pulsing muscular legs kept them upright even in their sleep. "We aren't going to get out of here sooner with you pacing about."

"Oh? You sound like you have a plan."

"I don't," the nekogirl grumbled, looking at the mana siphoning cuffs that had been slapped onto her while she was unconscious. "But I'm pretty sure we won't be here much longer."

"Oh? And why's that?" the elf replied, banging her cuffs against the iron again.

"Because a great calamity is approaching," Junith said ominously, as the light of the full moon empowered her sense of where Adam was. She could feel the annoying necromancer rapidly approaching, no doubt drawn in by the light of the camp. "I can only hope that we survive the chaos."

Catpurr 60
I am Darkness. I am Night. I am... Catman?

Up on the wooden watchtower that overlooked the Coalition Army encampment, Adam crouched low, his golden eyes sweeping across the beach where dozens of soldiers milled about between the blue tents.

He stroked his chin, brooding, a wicked smile creeping across his face as he eyed his future subjects.

Between the boats brought on land and the giant machines of war in the form of catapults, only one area in particular caught his attention. It was the bonfire, swarming with men and women of various species eating and drinking around large tables. Some had scales, others wings, a few even fur—something that made Adam curious

His hind legs shook back and forth before he leapt, soaring through the air until he landed twenty feet below on all fours.

Not a sound was made.

Satisfied that no one was any wiser to his presence, Adam stood up, the half-naked wereneko shrouded in the shadows that the nearby torches failed to dispel.

Swiftly, silently, Adam stalked through the camp, surveying the soldiers like a predator hunting prey. At times, he would stand beside soldiers milling about, the armored humanoids completely unaware of his presence, despite how uncomfortable it was for him to move in pants that were several sizes too small.

How unskilled. Hmm, purrhaps a new pair of pants is needed, he mused, tapping a bipedal lizard soldier on the shoulder.

"Huh?" The lizardman spun, his eyes going wide and he opened his maw to scream—but a large, furry hand clasped over the scalie snoot, silencing it.

"Be still and obey," Adam hissed, his hypnotic gaze boring into the man's psyche and compelling obedience.

"How may I serve, sir?" the lizard said in a guttural voice as he stood to attention.

"Strip and give me your uniform," Adam commanded. The lizard immediately complied, undressing and handing the nekoman his clothes.

"Excellent, it even has a hole for my tail," the man mused, before looking at the now-naked lizard standing at attention. "Go play in mud, or whatever it is lizards do for fun."

"SIR!"

The lizardman took off, eager to obey Adam's command as the latter began dressing.

Now fully decked out in the purple livery of the soldiers, Adam stepped out of the darkness, a smile on his face as he made his way to the large gathering of humanoids singing and eating.

As he walked, the man noticed that those who spotted him immediately tensed up, many scrambling to get out of his way so as not to impede his path, saluting him.

Whispers abounded, men and women alike commenting on his appearance, some wondering who he was and where'd he come from, and others questioning how it was that none had noticed someone so handsome in their midst.

Adam heard it all, each word boosting his ego and improving his stride.

Upon reaching his destination, the music around the bonfire stopped, dozens of eyes looking at him before each person present stood to attention and saluted the nekoman.

Picking his ear, Adam raised a brow before shrugging and calmly making his way through the silent camp to sit at a table, where various plates of food were available. He reached over, swiping a plate of cooked meat a horned woman had been eating to begin stuffing in his mouth.

He ate in silence, not a word or sound made as all eyes focused on him.

Adam paused in chewing.

"What? Is there something on my face?" he asked. The crowd surrounding him said nothing, simply continuing to salute.

Adam shrugged, and went back to eating, causing multiple people to look at one another before they resumed their dinner.

"Hey, are you going to eat that?" he said, pointing at the half-eaten fish a pig-faced person had on a skewer in their hand, mouth wide open as they froze amid taking a bite.

"Errh. No, sir," the pigman said, handing Adam his food.

"Thank you, you're so kind. How would you like to be my commander-in-chief when I conquer the world?" Adam said. The pigman's eyes boggled, and he looked at his comrades only to be met by equally confused stares. "Actually…"

Adam turned his head, eyeing the woman beside him, little horns gracing her head.

"Hey, you're pretty cute. How would an exquisite gem such as yourself like to conquer the world with me?" he offered, smiling at the woman. Her skin color darkened as her horns changed color.

"Wha?!" she let out high pitched shriek, unable to formulate a sentence as Adam wrapped his arm around her waist and brought the soldier close.

Before long, the nekoman was surrounded by people laughing, serving him food, and offering him drinks. Dozens of soldiers simply wrapped around his finger.

"Wow, sir, it's not every day we get an officer that can outdrink an orahac!" a man laughed, gesturing at the pigman that lay face down on the table.

"What can I say, I'm not your everyday guy," Adam replied. "Now, pour me another one!"

Cheers sounded out.

"Sir, siiiiiir." A soldier drunkenly stumbled over, falling into Adam's lap. "You're one of da good ones."

"Yeah! Most of the officers 'ere dink theya betta than us, and ogg all da good git!" a drunk woman yelled, before falling out of her chair to the sound of applause.

Other soldiers joined in the complaining and groaning, their echoes of discontent spurred on by a smiling Adam, a woman beneath both his arms.

The soldier laying on Adam's lap suddenly began to weep as the nekoman found himself stroking the man's head like a pet, soft hiccups coming out from a drunk soldier. They came to a stop as Adam lifted the human's head, locking eyes with him.

"Tell me, soldier, what does your heart desire?" he asked, his gaze transfixing the human.

"I want to see my home... one last time before I die," the man replied in the most lucid manner, all hints of drunkenness gone as his pupils dilated.

Adam smiled.

"Then be at peace, and sleep well," he replied, snapping his fingers. Only a moment later, the man passed out.

"Aw, somebody get Henry and drag that lightweight to bed!" a soldier called out, as two of the man's friends apologized to Adam before dragging the man away.

"WHAT IN ISLANDR'S NAME IS GOING ON HERE?!" a voice roared, as everyone present but Adam flinched and snapped to attention, as a six-foot tall human woman with blue hair donning heavy, purple armor bedecked with red livery stepped into the light.

"Ma'am!" a soldier croaked, dropping his beer mug.

"IS THAT ALCOHOL, SOLDIER?! Who authorized *booze?!*"

"Oh, that would be me." Adam waved, still reclining at the table and munching on a stick of skewered fish meat.

The woman narrowed her slanty eyes, blue irises looking the nekoman up and down as he prompted the woman with horns on her head to resume drinking. But now she was rebuffing his efforts, frantically.

"And who... are you?" the armored woman scowled, her face contorting with barely contained rage.

"Who am I? Who are *you?*" Adam replied. Every jaw in the area dropped at his flippant remark, some soldiers even sneakily trying to flee.

"I! Am! General Motoya Veldora! Leader of the Coalition Liberation Forces!" the officer spat, her body glowing as a majestic double-headed silver axe adorned with red velvet ribbons manifested in her armored hand. "And I don't know you. Where did you get that uniform?"

"Well," Adam said, crossing his legs and yawning before his eyes locked with the woman's. "I'm Adam, and might I say you have a lovely set of aqua eyes."

"Answer my question," General Veldora demanded, towering over the still sitting Adam.

"But first, answer mine. What does your heart desire?" he asked, smiling at the woman whose scowl deepened as her eyes twitched.

The officer blinked; her brow furrowed as her face twisted. Something was wrong, *weird*. A completely alien feeling stirred up her insides as her mind compelled her to answer the man.

"Last chance. Answer me," Veldora reiterated, the smug smile from Adam's face fading as his compulsion unexpectedly failed.

"Huh... interesting," he said, smiling, prompting the woman to swing her mighty weapon, pulverizing the table and cracking the earth—missing her target entirely.

"Rude," Adam said, walking behind the general and grabbing a plate of food from another table.

"INTRUDER! SEIZE HIM!" Veldora roared, spurring her soldiers on. Immediately they shook themselves from their stupor and took action.

Or, tried to.

In an instant, the first group of six that attempted to rush Adam were out cold, the trained veterans incapacitated so quickly the other soldiers were forced to pause, still processing what happened.

Even Veldora's eyes had trouble keeping up with the man's speed, but somehow, she had managed and was now forced to reevaluate the man before her.

Six of her veterans, survivors of Bullert's desecration of Cadia, seasoned warriors. All knocked out in a flash—and to add insult to injury, the man used only one hand to punch them, as his other held his plate of food.

"Fall back! Alert Commander Dorn and summon the Outworlders!" Veldora ordered. Her soldiers immediately fled to fulfill their General's orders. "You..."

"Me," Adam agreed, walking slowly and stacking various bits of food onto his tray.

"You're an Outworlder. Are you here to break the truce?"

"Lady, I have no idea what that is," he said, reaching down and picking through the pockets of an unconscious soldier, examining some gleaming coins. "But let's say I am, what then?"

"First, I'd ask you to stop robbing my men. Then I would ask if you are here to help or to hinder our efforts."

"Robbing? I simply have no idea what you're talking about," he replied, stuffing his pockets with his ill-gotten gains. "Say, how would you like to be one of my commanders?"

"Hinder it is."

In a flash of purple lightning that echoed with a boom, the woman vanished, reappearing a half-moment later. Every fiber of Adam's being stood on end.

HUH?!

Adam went wide eyed, dodging as the axehead moved at impossible speeds and bit through his skin, slashing his chest and finally forcing him to drop his platter.

He backpedaled, stabilizing his footing with his swishing tail as Veldora seemed to balloon in size. With her axe head held aloft, the silver weapon radiated purple lighting as she chained her attack into an overhead swing.

The world erupted into brilliant light, the ground shattering as the purple lightning descended from the heavens to strike Adam where he stood.

Or, where he *once* stood.

As the smoke cleared, the red-haired man could be seen at a distance, standing amidst debris as he clutched his chest. Sizzling sounds and smoke seeped from his wound.

"Rude," he stated, all traces of mirth gone as the contestants from the opposing Chosen team rushed over, alongside dozens of soldiers.

Catpurr 61
Wereneko vs Werewolf

The moonlight illuminated the bleeding gash on Adam's chest as it rapidly began to close. The wereneko frowned as he inspected the ranks of armored beings surrounding him.

"Surrender," General Veldora ordered, pointing her axe.

Adam smirked, eyeing the wolfman armed with a spear, the green man pointing axes, and the lizard woman, three Chosen that were familiar, but still strangers to the adult nekoman.

"Make me."

Veldora turned, eyeing her newly arrived comrades and soldiers. Armored knights, bowmen, spear users. The reinforcements brought to bear prepared to overwhelm Adam with their numbers.

"Take him."

At the command, the now-armed soldiers rushed forwards, brandishing swords and spears at Adam as the Chosen stayed back, observing the situation. The canine faces scowled, while Sethis and the green-skinned man readied their weapons.

Adam eyed the charging crowd, his expression indifferent as he bathed under the moonlight. His fanged mouth opened.

"Defend your king," he commanded, his golden pupils shining. The dozens of soldiers who met his gaze suddenly dropped to one knee.

"WHAT?!" Veldora barked, her expression one of confusion. Many of the still standing soldiers in the crowd who had resisted Adam's hypnotic gaze shared her bewildered look.

Suddenly, the men and women who had knelt rose, turning as one and swinging their blades at their own comrades.

"What is this?! Have you all lost your minds?!" Veldora roared, her voice falling on deaf ears as the soldiers, who now sported golden irises, attacked. It took the commander a moment to process just what had happened—her own troops had been enthralled. "All forces, fall back! Disengage! Do NOT LOOK INTO HIS EYES!"

Adam laughed, now surrounded by several knights, their shields raised as the coalition forces fell back.

Huh, why does this all feel familiar?

An annoying feeling crept up on the nekoman, a sensation of annoyance and longing. A deep sadness that distracted him for a moment as he stared at his clawed hands.

"Schrödinger" he muttered, reaching up and catching an arrow that inches away from his crying face.

Adam's expression twitched, his fangs baring as an overwhelming sense of loss flooded him.

Then his golden gaze narrowed slightly. "Kill them all," he ordered, sending his converted soldiers at Veldora. Feeling his bloodlust, the men and women around Adam began to glow, responding to their master's will and raging, screaming. Their voices combined into a fury unbridled that whipped the thralls into a frenzy.

"What... What is this?!" Veldora yelled in confusion as the gathered Chosen all flinched, each of them receiving a debuff and a quest.

[Emergency Quest!]
[Kill Adam Glow!]
[This is your chance to earn the attention of the Gods!]

[REWARD: 10 Stat Points, Class Evolution, Legendary Loot Drop, Blessing of Voltrain!]

* * *

Elsewhere.

"WHAT ARE YOU DOING?!" Freya demanded, spinning the angry God of Light around to face her.

"What you lot are afraid to do! I'm putting an end to Eli's project, once and for all!" Voltrain barked. After sitting and observing Adam nearly unleash a neko plague with the potential to wipe out the world, the angry god had had enough.

The nekomancer was too volatile. Too unpredictable. Voltrain shuddered to think what would happen if the man's existence was allowed to persist. Already, there were distortions popping up in every realm he left—even the strengthened Rest World designated to gather and collect Chosen was undergoing a massive change thanks to Adam's dungeon running amok.

All around Voltrain, moving images appeared—hundreds of crabs firing laser beams, a world overrun by nekofolk, a white cat breathing fire and burning down one of his temples.

Every scene was something related to Adam, infuriating the God-King and Lord of Light.

Enough was enough.

While he was prevented from directly disintegrating Adam thanks to Eli's protections, that didn't mean he couldn't interfere in the trials.

* * *

Adam frowned as Sethis and the green-skinned humanoid approached through the bloodbath of fighting soldiers. He could see it in their eyes—avarice, a greed that propelled their legs forwards to greet their nemesis despite the chaos.

"Oh? Instead of running, you're approaching me?" Adam said, pushing his way through his honor guard before raising his hand and beckoning to his would-be assailants. "Well, come on then."

Sethis and the green-skinned man took off at supernatural speeds, the lizard hissing as the other roared, unleashing a skill called **War Cry**.

[You have resisted the effects of Warchief Joe's cry.]

Adam raised a brow at the blue box in front of him, the wereneko's expression twisting with confusion as he parried the snake woman's spearhead with his hand.

"Oh? What's this thing?" he said aloud, leaping over Sethis's sweeping tail before kicking off the green man's chest, performing a somersault over Sethis.

The snake woman spun, stabbing at Adam with her pike. His head moved to the left to narrowly avoid the sharp spearhead as his ears twitched.

Reacting on instinct, Adam kicked, planting his foot squarely in the snake woman's chest. That made her eyes bulge and sent the bipedal snake woman flying as a large glob of acid and blood flew from her mouth.

He sidestepped the green acid ball as it flew, and it instead impacted a nearby soldier with an audible sizzling sound, making the man scream as he was quickly dissolved into a bubbling pool of acidic goo.

"Ehhk." Adam winced with a frown, kicking a pauldron left behind as it hissed, slowly being dissolved like the rest of its set.

Seeing the handsome, red-haired man distracted, a nearby unarmored soldier huffed, taking a deep breath, psyching himself up before screaming "CAAAAAAAAADIIIIIIIIIA FOREVER!" and charging Adam.

Immediately dozens of eyes turned, loyalist and thralled alike, each person enraptured by the lone footman brandishing his sword aloft and screaming.

The crowd parted ways for the man, forming a line of honor guards that bolstered the soldier's spirited charge.

"WITNESS ME!" the man yelled, leaping into the air with his sword aimed at Adam's neck.

Adam ducked under the sword, and with one fluid motion his fist came up, striking the soldier squarely in his unarmored crotch.

From Adam's point of view, everything moved slowly as his fist connected with the man's gonads.

The soldier's face contorted, twisting as pain signals shot through his spasming body and his eyes bulged. Tears were already in his eyes as would-be future generations flashed through the man's mind's eye, only to turn to dust a moment later.

The soldier let out a high-pitched wail, his voice melodic and akin to an angel's hymn as he dropped his weapon and fell to ground, clutching at his manly pearls.

"W-Why?!" he lamented, before slipping into blissful unconsciousness.

"Huh, now I feel bad," Adam said. And then something knocked him off his feet.

The nekoman rolled, sticking a hand out to flip when he was hit midair with an attack that severed his arm.

Veldora pressed her advantage, giving the laughing Adam no reprieve.

Adam snatched up his wayward limb as he backpedaled, the woman's supercharged speed keeping up with his.

Up, up, down, down, left, right, left, right. Purple lightning-infused attacks came from all directions, as Adam deftly dodged them all.

He spun, avoiding an overhead axe swing while using his arm like a cudgel and smacking Veldora in the face.

The general blinked, pausing her assault.

"Did... Did you just slap me with your severed arm?!" she spat.

"Here, need a hand?" the man said, holding his limb out with the palm facing the general.

Veldora's face scrunched as if she'd eaten an entire lemon, her mouth opening to say something but stopping as Adam withdrew his arm.

"Ah, but you'll have to get your own, this one is mine," he said, dodging the green-skinned man and kicking the Chosen so hard he flew through a nearby tree. "And then there were two."

Scanning the area, the only remaining people that possessed power were the woman in purple armor and the canine-faced man with his posse of wolf people.

Adam reattached his severed arm, the flesh sizzling and releasing steam as the appendage rejoined its master.

He clenched his fist, testing his grip strength before staring indifferently at the general's wrathful glare.

"Return my soldiers to me, Outworlder, and I promise I won't take your head," Veldora growled as Adam smirked.

"Swear fealty to me and you'll get your soldiers back, as my commander," Adam laughed, drawing the woman's ire even further.

"Stand back," the wolfman said in an oddly noble tone, pushing past the woman to stand face to face with Adam. "You are no match for this foul creature of the night. I will take you on."

"Oh? Do you think you can?" Adam replied, brow raised.

"I do," the wolfman said, before howling, releasing a burst of energy that sent a multitude of nearby soldiers flying.

"Interesting," Adam said, eyeing the Chosen wolf as it began to grow taller, his appendages elongating as his body ballooned in size.

Power. The wolfman radiated it, the creature's slanted pupils turning silver as its gray mane grew further. White hairs sprouted from its bulging body.

Adam smiled, unfazed by the silver energy radiating off the wolfman. "Now that's what I'm talking about."

"Creature of the moon! I know what you are!" the werewolf roared, his body still transforming. "For generations, the Belmorrs have made it our life's mission to hunt abominations such as yourself! And I honor that tradition! Even at the cost of my own humanity! You, who prey on the weak! You, who—UHK?!"

It happened in an instant. One moment the werewolf was beginning to monologue, and the next he was choking, thanks mainly to Adam's fist punching against his throat.

"UHK! Ueeehlgh?! Ugk!" the wolfman squawked, stumbling around and grabbing its throat. Then Adam sent his shin into the creature's manhood with enough force a crushing sound was heard.

"Why do people insist on monologuing?" The wereneko wasted no time, his fists flying and punching the canine in the face repeatedly before he could recover.

"C-C-Coward!" one of the wolf people cried, charging Adam, who picked up the crawling werewolf by his tail and spun him around in a circle before throwing him at his comrades.

"And then there was one," Adam said, his hand grabbing the handle of the electrified axe that was held an inch away from his face, its electrical discharge singeing his skin and burning him. "As my commander, you'll have to try a bit harder than that."

Catpurr 62

Chaos and Disorder

"DAMN IT, ELI! NERF YOUR CHOSEN! HE'S TOO DAMN OP!"

"Nah."

"I MEAN IT! HE'S DISRUPTING THE BALANCE OF OUR TRIALS!"

"Nah."

The measured discussion between almighty deities quickly devolved into an equally measured screaming-and-hair-pulling session. Regrettably, Voltrain was at a disadvantage in this new contest, because skeletons were infamously lacking hair.

—Elli & Voltra
in having a civilized discussion

* * *

Adam punched Veldora in the nose, causing the woman to wince and loosen her grip on her axe. The nekoman wasted little time wrenching it from her grasp.

"Ooh, shiny," he remarked, just as the lightning crackling around it dimmed and disappeared. "Huh... Why did it turn off?"

Adam began shaking the weapon, moving it up and down and attempting to find some kind of button or switch.

"Y-You can lift it?!" Veldora gasped, her eyes wide with disbelief as Adam began twirling the ornate weapon around. "That is a sacred treasure! HOW?!"

He only shrugged. "I'm just awesome like that. Hey, how do you turn this o—"

Suddenly the axe shifted, moving towards Veldora's open palm. Or, at least tried to. Adam maintained a firm grip, brow raised and smirking as the weapon struggled to return to its owner.

"Give me back Sinestra!" Veldora roared, the axe suddenly arcing with purple lightning. It zapped Adam, who smiled as his frazzled hair and bushy tail stood on end.

"Shiny!" he giggled, laughing like a child with a new toy as he swung the electrified weapon around, even as it kept burning his regenerating flesh.

"*UNHAND THIS ONE, YE UNWORTHY HEATHEN!*" a posh, feminine voice suddenly boomed, causing Adam to pause and look down at the axe. On its head it had sprouted a solitary eyeball, currently glaring at the nekoman.

"You can talk?!" he exclaimed, his eyes wide. He drew the axe near his face, and it shocked him with another bolt.

"*YES, YOU CUR! NOW REMOVE THINE FILTHY PAWS!*"

Suddenly Veldora screamed and charged the nekoman, attempting to take her sacred treasure back. Adam dodged to the left and kicked the woman's leg, the General releasing a scream as her appendage bent at an inhuman and awkward angle.

"*VEL!*" the axe shrieked, screaming its master's name as the general hit the floor. Undeterred, she began immediately crawling towards Adam, demanding her weapon back.

"How do you work?" the man in question asked, inspecting the weapon as it violently vibrated. "In fact, how do you talk? Where is your voice coming from?"

He ran his hands along the axe's shaft, moving them up and down, caressing the weapon as he explored every nook and cranny.

"S-S-STOP TOUCHING ME YOU OAF!" it screamed.

He lifted the weapon up, eyeing the silver pommel, his innate curiosity propelling his hands back and forth, rubbing the end bit of the shaft. Sparks began to fly from the handle.

"STOP IT!"

"Oh? Is this how I get you to work?" Adam said, his hand picking up speed as he rubbed over the shiny pommel of the weapon. That made the axe begin to scream and holler.

"LEAVE SINESTRA ALONE!" Veldora screamed, grabbing Adam's ankle and trying to pull herself up to take the werecat down. Adam ignored her, rubbing even faster as the purple discharge escalated.

"Ah! AH! STOP! STOP! STOP, YOU PETULANT MAN-THING! Y-YOU'RE GONNA—!"

Suddenly the weapon exploded into a massive ball of light, releasing lightning that fried Adam as bolts of purple electricity rained down from the sky and struck him in rapid succession. The ground seemed to quake, and the night sky turned to day, the electrical storm chaining through the metal armor worn by the scores of coalition soldiers and electrocuting them as well.

Adam blinked as the light died down, lowering his hands. His attention focused on the naked, silver haired woman with pointy ears and purple horns glaring up at him through purple irises, trembling with unspeakable rage.

"I can't! I can't believe thee!" the weapon-turned-humanoid yelled, the woman flushed with embarrassment as the scent of cooked meat flooded the air from all the fried soldiers. "T-Thou—! Thou shalt have to take responsibility!"

"Errrr. What now?" Adam raised a brow, suddenly taking a step back, shaking off Veldora, who clung to his foot.

"Where?! Where art thou fleeing off too?!" the weapon screamed as Adam continued his retreat. "COME BACK HERE!"

"I'm just... I'm just gonna go get some milk! I'll be back!" Adam assured it, before taking off at a full sprint. The lady shrieked obscenities at the nekoman's retreating backside.

* * *

"What is going on out there?!" Erishta exclaimed before a blinding burst of light momentarily evaporated the night and hundreds of pained screams sounded out.

"What? What's happening?! What do you see?" Ellie asked from her prison cell, as it was devoid of a window.

"Calamity," Junith sighed, sensing that a certain wayward nekoman was getting closer and closer. She could feel his presence, each step he took towards her intensifying the bond between them until finally, the door at the end of the hallway suddenly went flying as a foot collided with it.

The prison immediately came alive, as the noise of the door being kicked off its hinges woke up all of Adam's test subjects, who began to scream and holler, their muscular legs stomping at the bars.

Erishta did a double take as her eyes went wide, the Drowthraki commander staring at the smolderingly handsome, red-haired man, who bore a strong resemblance to the short boy who had pretended to be a girl.

"Well, well, well. What do we have here?" Adam said, squatting down to bring himself to eye level with the scowling, black-haired nekogirl.

"Voltrain above, I hate it when you're like this. Somehow, you're even more insufferable," Junith spat. "Why do you smell like you've been cooked?"

"What a weird way of thanking someone for coming to save you," the smoking hot, and literally smoking, nekoman replied. "I could just leave you in here, ya know."

"Please do."

"Please don't!" Ellie screamed as the banging from the bandits began to escalate and the iron bars of the prison started to shift, the test subjects whipped into a violent frenzy upon spotting Adam. "Pretty pretty pretty please, don't! That purple lady talked about making us into rations!"

"See, now *that's* how you ask for help. Sure, I'll rescue you, little lady," Adam said, walking over to Ellie's cage and bending the metal bars until a big enough hole was made for the Drowthraki to step through. "What's their problem? And why are their legs so swole?"

He gestured to the mouth-foaming bandits.

"As with every ill-conceived thing, *you* happened," Junith spat, folding her arms.

"Interesting, sounds like other me is keeping things not dull." Adam shrugged, walking over and removing Junith and Erishta's cell door. "So, you guys wanna get out of here?"

Erishta hesitated, before cautiously exiting the cell while Junith sat still. The nekogirl frowned, until her eyes went wide as Adam picked her up by the scuff of her neck.

"GAH! LET ME GO! I DON'T WANT TO GO WITH YOU!" she screamed, flailing about before Adam adjusted his grip and the woman scrunched up.

"Come on, no subordinate of mine is gonna be locked in a prison cell," he said, carrying Junith in a way that was reminiscent of a mother cat moving their young. "Oh, I guess you two can come along as well."

Suddenly a massive quack sounded out in the distance, causing the group to stand stock still. More and more quacks joined it, rending the night air

"Duckysaurs!" Erishta spun to Adam, her eyes narrowed and hyper focused as she offered up her handcuffed wrists to him. "We cannot fight with our mana inhibited! Can you break our cuffs?"

"Sure thing, anything for a pretty lady." Adam laughed, grabbed the cuffs, and crumpled them.

"We need to procure our weapons and armor, I believe they kept it in a trunk somewhere," Erishta said, rubbing her wrists.

"Sure, I'm always willing to loot from the rich and give to myself." Adam shrugged. "Lead the way, pretty lady."

"Commander Erishta," the elf suddenly spat.

"Huh?"

"My name is Erishta, *not* pretty lady."

"Sure, whatever you say, Commander." Adam smirked, before breaking out into a wide grin as his eyes flared with golden light and his claws came out. "Say, you wouldn't purrhaps be interested in a job, would you?"

* * *

Elsewhere.

Emerging from the moonlit ocean, a black armored knight with red eyes finally set foot upon the dry, sandy beach. The undead Redfield scowled beneath his helmet as he pulled the chains that connected to a golden coffin layered with seaweed, fishes, and barnacles that had tagged along from the ocean depths.

He sighed, removing a starfish-like creature that resided on his helmet and tossing it back into the churning waves as he spit out water from his undead mouth.

He scanned the pink treeline, his glowing eyes flaring red before fixating on the bursts of energy in the distance.

"I don't get paid enough for this," he muttered, eyeing the lightning in the sky. Every sense he possessed, most especially his common sense, told him that his foolish master was responsible.

"Well, time to get to it," Redfield grumbled, his entire being sighing as he dragged the golden sarcophagus into the pink laden jungle.

Catpurr 63
Multiplying Nekofolk Problem

Waking up with a groan, a now miniature and naked Adam coughed, white fur flying from his mouth as he groggily took in his surroundings.

"What. The. Nyx?" he said aloud, as he noticed he was having trouble moving. The nekoboy blinked, allowing his pupils to adjust to the sunlight, before it was blocked out by the silhouette of a nekogirl and an armored knight. "Junith?"

"Nope," Ellie responded, as the now catsified Drowthraki stood over Adam with folded ears, clutching his enchanted gear in her hands.

"WAIT—" Adam let out, before pulling up his System menu with disbelief.

Bonded Followers: 04
    Junith Oatheart: T2 Lvl 20
    Eh'liza Oktober: T1 Lvl 39
    Kathrine Dominica: T1 Lvl 11
    Class: Class selection available!
    Elerra Hali: T1 Lvl 1

"No!"

"Yup," she replied. Yet another nekofolk was added to Adam's growing group of felinoids.

"HOW?!"

"Well...." Ellie said, trailing off as she helped him up. "It happened because—"

* * *

Four hours ago...

"Say, you wouldn't purrhaps be looking for a job, would you?" adult Adam said, smirking at the pointy-eared commander as she peered out through a window at the chaos going on outside.

"What?" Erishta replied, turning her head towards the pair of golden orbs boring into her soul. She could feel the nekoman's will, his hypnotic gaze attempting to overwrite her mind into obeying his whims. "W-What?!"

"I'm in need of a commander to lead my armies. What say we ditch this place and go conquer the world?" he offered, his hand outstretched.

Erishta's face scrunched, as the woman shook her head at the odd touch on her mind. She blinked, scowling at Adam as her eye color stubbornly remained unchanged.

"Huh. Interesting, it didn't work again," Adam mused, before turning to Ellie. "You."

"Me?" Ellie blinked.

"Serve me."

The Drowthraki girl blinked again, frowning as her crest lit up, the symbol on her hand warding off Adam's mind manipulation.

"Maybe I'm losing my touch," he muttered, toying with the ring on his finger.

"What did you do to me?" Erishta complained, grabbing her head. The commander leaned against the nearby wall.

"Eh, nothing," Adam said, before Junith leapt up and smacked him on the back of the head. "Ow! Hey! Watch it, you idiot!"

"You're the idiot here! Don't go around hypnotizing people! This is exactly how you ended up in the last mess!" she hissed as the ground suddenly rumbled, more quacks echoing out.

"We need to get out of here. If the duckysaurs begin a stampede, there will be nothing of us left!" Erishta yelled, recovering and taking off.

Shrugging, Adam walked at a brisk pace as everyone followed the elven commander's retreat.

* * *

"Sildera! To me!" Veldora screamed. The purple-haired woman transformed back into the sacred weapon as her master ordered her to her hand. Upon closing her hand around the axe's handle, a surge of energy coursed through the general's body, her broken leg suddenly creaking and cracking as the shattered cartilage and bone began to repair itself.

"Soldiers! On your feet!" the general barked, shakily rising to her feet to muster her troops. "Man the machines of war! Archers, form a line and prepare to fire! Squad leaders, break into kill formations and isolate your targets accordingly!"

Despite being fried and steaming, the men and women under her command were still alive. Mostly.

They were the best of the best, survivors all, each armored person of the coalition wearing enchanted gear that had protected them from the lightning involuntarily let out by her weapon.

The soldiers rallied to Veldora and their officers, even those who had previously been under Adam's spell.

Thanks to the sudden electrocution, which had broken the nekoman's control and freed the soldiers, they had returned to their commanders as if nothing happened.

Veldora didn't have a chance to question it, only to process two things: that her men were now free, and the coming threat.

A chorus of quacks echoed in the distance, massive torrents of flames shooting out into the darkness and illuminating the night.

"FIRE!" Veldora screamed, a torrent of black arrows flying into the air and striking at the horde on the horizon that was nearing their walls.

The ducks had come.

Attracted, no doubt, to the sounds of clashing and warfare emanating from her camp, thanks to the redheaded nekoman.

They had managed to keep them away thanks to the Chosen and routine guards keeping an eye out for members of the never-ending swarm, hunting down the duckysaurs and establishing their presence on the island with an endless tide of violence during the day and peace at night.

Veldora gritted her teeth.

Now that peace was broken. The duckysaurs were whipped into a frenzy, no doubt due to their sleep being disturbed. Now they were about to bear down on them after they'd already taken a beating.

The general turned her head, frowning at the so-called-champions of the gods.

The green man was half-dead, stuck in the trunk of a tree, three soldiers attempting to pull him out.

The snake woman was being treated by several medics, her rib cage fractured with multiple broken ribs with blood pooling out of her mouth.

And lastly, the wolfman... he was dead.

Well, unconscious, with his wolf people companions crying over his crumpled body as if he were dead.

These were the greatest bastions of her fighting force. And now they were all incapacitated, with her own injuries and mana also reducing her own fighting capabilities.

"Great," Veldora let out before her eyes tracked the redheaded culprit of this mess trailing behind her prisoners.

"KILL HIM! BRING THEE HIS SKULL!" her weapon demanded, rage fueling the axe's electric lightshow as the usually calm and collected relic now boiled with emotions.

Screams sounded out, officers and NCOs trying to make a defense. Yet she could see her soldiers were tired.

"No, we need him." Veldora gritted her teeth, attempting to temper her weapon's anger as it shook violently. "HEY! RED!"

"ME?!" Adam yelled back, his voice traveling across the camp.

"YES, YOU!" Veldora barked back.

"WHAT DO YOU WANT?!"

"HELP US OR WE ALL DIE!" Veldora screamed at the nekoman as multiple explosions detonated from the catapults delivering their payloads.

"WHAT'S IN IT FOR ME?!" Adam replied, walking backwards as a Drowthraki girl beckoned him.

"WHAT DO YOU WANT?!"

"BE MY COMMANDER?" he asked back, hands held up in a shrugging manner.

Veldora paused, the woman frowning.

"Oh, thou canst not be serious in considering this preposterous notion!" the sacred weapon in Veldora's hands screamed as the duckysaurs broke through the outer perimeter.

"WHAT DO YOU NEED A COMMANDER FOR?!" Veldora asked for clarification, before directing her soldiers to engage the quacking duckysaurs. They needed to buy her time to recover as her mana regenerated and her leg mended.

"FOR WORLD DOMINATION, OF COURSE!" Adam boldly declared, bellowing a laugh through the erupting chaos.

"Huh?" Veldora's face twisted with confusion as sounds of battle raged on. She didn't have long to process the madman's words as a scream of a soldier being swallowed whole by a duck disrupted her thoughts. "What? Fine, whatever! Just save my soldiers!"

"Ha! That's all I needed to hear!" the redheaded wereneko said, breaking out into a wide grin before cracking off the ground with explosive speed.

The wereneko dashed into the conflict, much to the dismay of his companions, who were more interested in fleeing.

Adam leapt, wrapping his arms around the neck of the largest duckysaur and taking it with him as he crashed into the ground.

There was a lull in the battle. The duckysaurs shifted their beaks, turning to the blood-coated wereneko ripping and tearing at their fallen brethren with wild savagery.

Adam looked up from his feast, his mouth holding feathers and dragon scales alike that were being chewed as if they were fresh venison.

"QUACK!"

"QUACK!"

"QUACK!"

At the sight, the horde became incensed, every duck opening their maw and spewing flames that created a towering inferno.

"FALL BACK! FALL BACK! RETREAT!" Veldora commanded, as insane laughter echoed from within the flames.

"AND JUST WHEN I WAS FEELING A BIT CHILLY!" Adam roared, the flames peeling away to reveal a gruesome sight.

The naked wereneko stood in the burnt field, his flesh melting off his body like heated cheese with his charred body standing upright with golden eyes staring at the moon.

Veldora and the many witnesses recoiled, horrified at the sight of a moving corpse that was visibly stitching itself back together and regrowing skin, returning back to life with the wereneko regaining his muscular form, albeit without clothes.

"My turn." Adam smirked, baring his fangs at the ducks stomping on the ground, preparing a stampede. "COME ON!"

What followed next was a bath of blood and feathers. The massive fowls were utterly ripped to shreds by a monster that made monsters afraid.

* * *

Present time.

"So... At what point did you get turned into a nekogirl?" Adam asked, still picking tufts of white fur out of his mouth and raising a brow at the gold coffin covered in sea life nearby.

"I'm getting to that! I'm getting to that!" Ellie said quickly, her face a little flush.

* * *

Three hours ago.

Ellie stood with her jaw dropped, her eyes wide at the scene before her.

"What is your obsession with finding a commander when you have no army?!" Junith yelled, kicking Adam in his shins, as he sat on the neck of a duckysaur while the army mopped up the surviving ducks.

"Every great king has three things. An intelligent queen, a competent commander, and a strong army," the nekoman said with a smirk.

"Gah! You're insufferable! What if you had died?! What would I do?! Your life is mine to claim, necromancer! MINE!"

"Aw, it's cute to see how much you care about me." He smirked. "Admit it, you love me."

"L-Love?! LOVE?!"

"Yuhp."

"Ha! As if you'd ever get anyone to ever love you!" the black-haired nekogirl spat.

"Says the girl in love with me."

"NEVER!" Junith hissed.

"Oh, don't play coy. I might not have all of day-Adam's memories, but if there's one thing I know for certain, it's that you love me," the man laughed, resulting in the nekogirl fuming.

"I'D RATHER HURL MYSELF INTO THE MAW OF A DUCKYSAUR THAN EVER BE ROMANTICALLY INVOLVED WITH A BLASPHEMOUS HEATHEN SUCH AS YOURSELF!"

"Says the girl who hounded me for years! That kind of obsession is called love. Just admit it. *You looove me! You looove me!* And who wouldn't? I'm a roguishly handsome man," he said smugly, completely apathetic to the chaos of quacks and death around him.

"I DON'T LOVE YOU!"

"Prove it, then."

"FINE! YOU WANT PROOF?! THAT'S IT! I'M THROWING MYSELF INTO THE MOUTH OF A DUCKYSAUR!"

Adam clapped. "Do it!"

"RAAAAAAHG!" the nekogirl screamed in frustration before Ellie noticed movement in the night.

The wolfman.

He was up and moving, creeping low, weapon in hand with a scowl and white vapor coming off his body, as he avoided the soldiers running back and forth.

"Uhm. Adam!" Ellie called out, attempting to get the attention of the nekoman who was busy arguing with Junith.

"You are absolutely insufferable!" Junith screamed.

"I prefer the term handsome and endearing," the insufferable neko in question replied.

"Do you even hear yourself?!"

"Yes. No. Yes. No. Odd, every time I stop talking my voice stops."

"UUUUUUGH!"

"Uhm! Adam!" Ellie exclaimed as the wolfman moved. But Adam was too engrossed in making Junith mad, too distracted to see the werewolf summoning a spear and moving.

The wolf moved, but so did Ellie.

She wasn't sure why she did what she did, but her legs propelled her forwards, the forty-year-old Drowthraki youth intercepting the weapon that pierced through her body and diverted the blade meant for Adam.

Pain shot through Ellie's body, her eyes wide at the canine man who snarled before he flung her body away.

What happened next was a blur. Ellie remembered only being cold, and a sense of lightness touching her body as her eyes stared at the spinning stars above.

She could hear roaring, explosions, every second that passed seeming to make the world sound dull and the view less vivid.

And then she saw Adam, the blood-covered man standing over her with hyper-focused eyes as her breathing produced only gargles.

* * *

"Aaaaand that's when you bit me to save my life. Junith didn't have mana to heal cuz of all the cuffs, and you didn't have much of a choice," Ellie explained as Adam finished getting dressed and stood up, frowning as rows upon rows of soldiers entered his field of view along with contestants from his team.

"How did you know about the parts you weren't there for?" Liza asked, popping out from a nearby bush and spooking Ellie as a woman in purple armor walked from the gathering of soldiers and knelt.

"Sir, the army is ready to move at your command," the officer said as her weapon, which appeared to be an axe, shook violently under tight wrappings.

"I'm sorry, did you say army? And who are you?" Adam blinked, scratching his head, still trying to wrap his head around Ellie's story.

"I am Commander Motoya Veldora, leader of the coalition forces which are now under your command, General."

"G-Gen—" Adam stuttered.

WHAT THE NYX DID I DO LAST NIGHT?!

"This is what *you* wanted," Junith said, placing an armored hand on Adam's shoulder as Abdullah limped out and waved.

"Maybe the other guy, but not me!" the nekoboy pleaded as he clutched his head and fell on all fours. "I JUST WANT TO READ AND RESEARCH!"

Catpurr 64

Planning Phase for the Ducky Raid

[CONGRATULATIONS! You've won 5 Cicero Coins!]
[Daily attempts left: 00!]
Gacha coins: 170

"Ugh! UGGGGH! ARRRRRRRGH!"

Adam frowned as he sat in a green tent flush with various amenities, pulling out tufts of red hair as he did his daily gacha pulls.

"WHY DO I EVEN BOTHER IF I NEVER GET ANY GOOD PULLS!" he called out in frustration, his tail smacking against the hard chair he sat on. "This is rigged! Rigged! Is this made to purposely make me angry?!"

* * *

Elsewhere in a casino, there was a sudden sound of manic laughter.

* * *

"Sir," Veldora said, as the purple-haired woman entered the tent. "Are you ready for the meeting?"

"Yes, yes, give me a moment," Adam grumbled, closing his gacha menu before hopping off of the table and following the Commander.

Outside, he frowned at the sight. Everywhere he looked, men and women of various species walked, slithered, or crawled. It was a fascinating view for Adam, one that made him want for nothing more (besides petting Schrödinger) than to interview and document all these sentient folk. However, there was a time and place, and right now there were more important, time-sensitive matters to be discussed.

Namely, Bullert the magical duckysaur, and the victory his *other* self had promised, both of which were giving Adam a headache.

Walking through the encampment, Adam drew odd looks, every set of eyes fixed fearfully on the nekoboy walking through their camp, littered with duckysaur bodies.

Not that he was too bothered. He understood the why, however a slight feeling of uneasiness grew as their gazes reminded him that he wasn't in control of his own actions. At least he now had an army and could complete the trial successfully, while every member of team two was mending their broken bones and injuries.

"General!" Two guards, a pig-faced humanoid and a goat-like person, saluted as Veldora and Adam neared the entrance of a large, expansive red tent that served as the command apparatus for the raid.

"At ease," Veldora said, before directing the nekomancer inside where Junith, Abdullah, and the rest of his companions of team one stood around a large table. "Now that we are all here, let's get down to business to—"

"DEFEAT! THE HUNS!" Liza screamed, suddenly standing on a chair and singing. *"DID THEY SEND ME DAUGHTERS! WHEN I ASKED! FOR—BLEHP!"*

Liza's singing was cut short as Junith kicked the chair out from under the nekogirl, resulting in her hitting her head on the planning table, before sprawling unconscious on the floor in a pool of her own blood.

"Ehp?!"

Junith stepped on the girl, causing her to exhale as she gazed at the others from atop her new step-stool.

"—anyway, as I was saying before," Veldora said, continuing where she left off. "Now that we're gathered, let's discuss the plan of attack for this raid."

Various nods went out, with each person listening intently to the plan to cut a swath towards the monastery atop the mountain, where Bullert roosted.

They would use catapults, crossbows, cannons, and bows. Seeing how Bullert seldom left his temple, all they had to do was push their catapults within range of the mountain and let loose, the combined might of twenty machines of war more than enough to collapse and kill the duckysaur.

At least, that was the plan, one that team two had devised.

"So, we're relying on an ambush?" Adam said aloud with skepticism, also standing on Liza. "Using force and a bunch of rocks?"

"Not a bunch of rocks," Veldora replied. "Alchemifire."

To which the nekoboy raised a brow. "Alchemifire? On a fire breathing duckysaur *resistant* to fire?"

"Resistant, not immune. And alchemifire is magically enhanced flames that stick to anything it touches when in the presence of air," Veldora explained, opening a nearby chest that contained dozens of flasks, each filled with green liquid. "They don't spread, and instead latch to whatever they touch until it burns to ash."

"Fascinating," he said, eyeing the flasks with greedy eyes. "So, the plan is to coat him in magical fire, then watch him burn?"

"Precisely. However, we need to bring the catapults in range and secure the area which will involve thinning out the horde that protects Bullert. Thanks to you sending all of our previous champions into the infirmary and killing the canine and his companions—"

"I'm sorry, I did what now?" Adam blinked. This was the first he heard about him killing someone.

"Oh, uhm," Ellie let out, the newest addition to Adam's collective looking away sheepishly. "I may have left that part out..."

"*May have?* I took a person's life."

"To save mine?" Ellie offered sheepishly as assurance.

A sudden ***bang!*** turned everyone's heads as Veldora slammed her armored gauntlet on the table.

"*So,* you can see that our fighting force has been diminished. So we'll be relying on you," she stated, as all eyes turned next to Adam.

"Errr. You mean, *other* me," he said.

"Whichever one is most powerful," Veldora stated, before moving several blocks on the table as Adam frowned. "Here is our position in relation to Bullert's nest."

"One question, emirtah," Abdullah said, raising his arm that wasn't broken. Veldora nodded to the warrior. "What will our next course of action be, should our efforts prove futile?"

"Even if it fails, it should still weaken our quarry enough that we can try the old-fashioned way," the commander replied, eyeing her axe, trembling where it lay wrapped in velvet.

At the proclamation, Abdullah beamed a wide, happy smile. The warrior, even injured, silently prayed that the main attack would fail so he could get a glorious fight.

"A full-frontal confrontation with a duckysaur doesn't sound like one where we walk away unscathed," Adam remarked, voicing his concerns. "Especially against targets thrice our size."

"No plan survives contact with the enemy," Veldora replied, causing the nekomancer to frown.

"This is still a tactical disadvantage. I don't think this is a good idea," Junith added, agreeing with Adam for once and causing him to raise a brow at her. "What? It's obvious."

"Nothing, I guess the bar for your intelligence isn't as low as I thought. I'm honestly impressed."

"Can you shut up, Adam?! This is why you're gonna die alone!" Junith spat.

"Rather die alone than be an idiot," he countered.

"Uuuugh! I'm not an idiot!"

"PEOPLE!" Veldora shouted, interrupting the pair as smiles settled on several officers' faces. "Focus."

The two nekofolk frowned at each other before turning back to the table.

"It would be, if they had the height advantage," Veldora continued. Adam's brow raised as she signaled a nearby soldier, a woman with one bulbous eyeball on her purple-haired head who nodded and left. "But fortunately, we've got a new toy to fight these titans."

The one-eyed woman returned, this time with a crate that she placed on the floor beside Veldora before saluting and leaving.

Adam hopped off of Liza, walking around with the others to crowd the now opened crate displaying metal contraptions.

"Boxes? Are these a trap of some kind?" the blonde dual wielder named Jack asked.

"No," Veldora explained, before a soldier reached down into the box and grabbed what appeared to be a harness and began strapping it on. "Omni-propulsion gear. Developed shortly before Cadia fell, these hooks and wires allow us to maneuver in trees or cities. With this, we can turn their size to our advantage."

Junith and Adam eyed the contraption made of metal and wires, their heads shifting in unison to stare at the items being attached to the soldier's harness that extended from the shoulders down to the feet, wrapping around the boot.

Adam inspected it out of curiosity.

Junith, out of interest in a new weapon.

"How does it work?" Adam asked, getting closer to the twin boxes connected to both the wires and a harness resembling a belt of some kind. There were triggers and a tube, gears visible from the opening where a hook lay.

Veldora smiled, her eyes wide with a threatening gaze that made him uncomfortable.

"I'm so glad you asked," she said as an ozone smell filled the space from the weapon all across the room.

Oh no.

Catpurr 65

Death Knight and the Assistant

"UGH! ARRRRRRGH!" Adam let out, throwing up before going limp as he hung, suspended upside down in a tree by the harness connected to the omni-propulsion gear.

"Okay, right. This is obviously not for you. And here I thought cats had good balance," Veldora said as she stood beneath the tree with folded arms, eyeing his rainbow-colored vomit as the nekoboy groaned and began slowly spinning, the wires tangling him up.

"I... have... BLEH! Great balance... too much movement..." he groaned, swaying back and forth as Liza zipped by with a "WHEEEEEEE!"

Suddenly, two hooks embedded on the tree beside Adam, as Junith landed beside them but a moment later.

"Man up. This is child's play," she said, pressing a button on her control stick and retracting her hooks.

"Junith... Sit," Adam ordered. The woman frowned. Her geas activated, and she was sent flying from the tree and into the ground. "Ha... ahahaha... BLEEalcnkancw!"

Veldora inhaled and closed her eyes, taking a moment as the nekogirl, now covered in dirt, began screaming at the boy hanging upside down and vomiting.

"Hold on! Imma get you!" Ellie yelled, landing on a nearby tree with a *crunch* as her propulsion gear hooks retracted.

"I've... been thinking," Adam said as he spun round and round while Ellie tried to free him. "Why aren't we conducting this operation at night?"

"Because visibility is poor and there are untold numbers of monsters that lurk in the shadows, which could threaten our work," Veldora replied as Liza zipped around, doing fancy tricks in the air before landing on the tree near Adam. "My spotters need to be able to see the fortress if we are to adjust our attacks accordingly."

"Okay... but I can't fight in this condition," Adam said, still spinning as Ellie shimmied across the tree branch and reached out to grab the wires to stop his perpetual motion.

"Well, tough luck. You took out my other champions and they all knew how to do this," Veldora replied as Ellie hit the release on Adam's OP Gear, sending him to the ground—but not before he froze midway.

[CATSIFICATION CURSE ACTIVATED!]

Adam paused mid-air, making a ninety-degree spin before landing on his feet.

"More and more, you amaze me, kytah," Abdullah said, as the bronze-skinned warrior landed next to Veldora, the woman scratching her chin.

"How about everyone does the fighting, and I just hang back? Offer moral support in the way of skeletons. We also have the Liopleurodons that can help," Adam offered, summoning a pack of skelecats that came out and formed a bed for him to lay on.

"That's the third time you've done that. Do you always land on your feet?" Veldora asked, ignoring the nekoboy's plea.

"Yeah, I think so," he groaned, clutching his temple as a sense of lightheadedness began to take root.

"Interesting," she replied with the same fascination that Adam used when he inspected ruins.

Oh no.

"So you always, *always*, land on your feet, do you?"

"Y-Yeah?"

"So, you aren't in any real danger if you're in the air and falling."

"I... suppose... not?" he replied, wondering where the veteran was going with this.

"So," Veldora said, casting a long shadow over Adam as she loomed above him. "That means you can train all day and not get seriously injured."

"I— No? I—" Adam stuttered, his mouth ajar. Veldora's body crackled with energy.

NOnononononononNOnonoNNonono!

"Get up, soldier!" Veldora barked. "NOW! NOW! NOW! NOW! NOW! NOW!"

Adam jumped off his mound of skelecats, standing upright with his cats scurrying in a panic as Veldora began screaming at him.

"I don't—"

"I DON'T CARE WHAT YOU THINK, SOLDIER! STAND AT THE POSITION OF ATTENTION WHEN I'M TALKING TO YOU!"

He blinked, making a face as confusion took hold.

"ARE YOU DEAF? AT ATTENTION!" Veldora yelled before physically moving Adam, correcting his posture as she gave orders. "Left heel against right heel, turned at a forty-five-degree angle. Legs straight! Not stiff! Hips and shoulders leveled, chest up, soldier!"

Junith smirked from the side, watching the wide-eyed Adam frozen in place like a statue as he maintained the position Veldora had put him in.

"At ease!" the commander barked; Adam was still stuck until she moved him.

The next twelve hours were hell, with Adam constantly being yelled at, screamed at, and ordered around by Veldora, who stuck to him like bone on marrow. The woman even went so far as to don omni-propulsion gear to follow the nekoboy and scream at him mid-air.

"Are you a quitter?! ARE YOU A COWARD?!" she screamed at Adam, crawling on all fours. Smeared behind the nekoboy was a trail of rainbow-colored vomit, akin to a slug slithering.

Adam hiccuped, crying. "N-No! I'm not a quitter!"

"What?! I CAN'T HEAR YOU!"

"I-I'm! *Blejacnk, uugh!* NOT! A! QUIIITTER!" he shouted through tears, all covered in rainbow filth.

"THEN GET BACK ON YOUR FEET AND GET! SOME! ALTITUDE!" Veldora screamed as Adam raised the mechanisms that would fire his hooks and stood on wobbly legs. He shifted his waist, aiming at a nearby tree. "That's it! Go! Go!"

All around him, people watched, his companions and Veldora's soldiers, the crowd cheering him on to rise.

[Tenacity trait acquired!]
[Thanks to your constant unyielding spirit and hard work, you've proven yourself a tenacious being!]
[+5 Ego]

Spurred on by the blue box, Adam hit the mechanism, the boxes on his waist propelling him forwards—only for the wereneko to anticlimactically smack into a tree.

"HEK?!"

-20 HP

"Ow..." he groaned, before doing the thing he should have done when it was available. He summoned Redfield.

"Sir?" the Death Knight said, drawing audible gasps from the crowd as a sudden influx of ozone flooded the air.

"Reeeed," the neko whined, splooting out of exhaustion, his eyes closed and unaware of Veldora gripping her axe in preparation to do battle. "Take me away, I don wan be here anymoah."

"Yes, sir," Redfield said, the armored knight picking up Adam off the ground and princess carrying him through the crowd as it parted for the Death Knight.

There were murmurs and whispers, people pushing over one another to eye the spectacle of an undead knight carrying its master through the camp.

"Hey... You aren't mad with me, are you?" Adam inquired, limp in Redfield's arms, every muscle in his body sore and swollen as it ached for rest.

"Hm? And why would I be angry, sir?" the knight replied, taking Adam back to his tent as a multitude of eyes tracked them.

"Ah, you refused my summons. Didn't know you could do that."

"Well, sir, after I dove in after Junith upon your command, I realized too late that I can't actually swim. So instead of meandering and letting the sealife nibble at me, I decided to be useful and bring the coffin to shore," Redfield said, entering the nekomancer's tent and dropping him into his golden coffin. "I figured you'd need it, sir."

"You're so reliable... Why is it so hard to find good help," the nekomancer in question mumbled, his eyes half asleep as he began whispering about exploring ruins and how this just proves that undead were superior.

Redfield looked down, eyeing his sleeping master as Ellie suddenly rushed in carrying bundles of wrapped somethings and a jug of water.

"I got food!" she said, the droopy-eared nekogirl quickly hushing up as she realized Adam was asleep. "Oops."

"Did you get non-citric foods?" Redfield asked. Ellie quickly nodded her head.

"Yup."

"Non-herbs?"

"I think so," she said, unwrapping the ration bundle to reveal bits of dried jerky. "No garlic or chives, leeks, onions, oregano or anything citric. Since the chef didn't know what any of that is, I just asked for dried, unseasoned meat."

"Good, it's exceptionally important that you understand that these ingredients are fatal to you now," Redfield said, patting the folded-ear nekogirl on the head with his armored gauntlet. "Unlike the idiot and the... other idiot, you're the only one who seems to have Adam's best interests in mind."

"Well, of course! He saved my life and helped open my eyes to the world! I even have a cool System thing!" Ellie replied excitedly before checking her tone.

"Good." Redfield's ghostly eyes flared beneath his helm. "Look after him when I'm away. Unlike the other two. They would most likely throw him under a bus the first chance they get. The only thing stopping them is the geas on their bodies and their self-preservation."

"I see..." Ellie nodded. "What's a bus?"

"Uh, it's like a really long car."

Ellie's head turned, exhibiting the same trait Adam did when he found something curious.

Do all nekofolk become like this? Redfield thought to himself before answering the girl. "It's a can of metal with wheels that is powered by... magic. People from my world use it to get around."

"Oooooooh," Ellie said, fishing out her own notebook, inkwell, and duck feather from her child-sized clothes. "Can you tell me more about your world?"

Redfield smiled beneath his helm.

"Sure. Let me tell you about Earth, kid."

Catpurr 66

One Thing Not to Do...

"Okay, whatever happens, whatever anyone says. Do *not* open this coffin. Do. Not! No! Nada! Do you understand me?!" a naked Adam yelled, addressing his reluctant companions as his hands wrapped around Liza's head, tugging at her pink-furred ears. "Do you all understand me?!"

"Nyah!" Liza let out, making a face at Adam, who reached eye level with the help of a convenient stool. "Why are you singling me out?! It's unfair!"

"Because out of all the idiots that follow me, you're the one most likely to let me out!" he snarled, his dark-spot-covered eyes wide with anger. "Say it! Say you won't let me out!"

"Nyaaaaah," she complained, as Junith rolled her eyes and Ellie giggled. "You're always bullying meh!"

"Say it, you nitwit!"

"Fine! I won't let you out!" she cried. Adam finally let her go and sighed as the sun began to set.

"Okay, it's getting late. Junith, do the honors," the wereneko said before walking over to his gold sarcophagus and laying down.

Junith stood above Adam, a wicked smile on her face.

"I can't wait to do this for real," she said, shutting the coffin as Adam made a face and mimicked the palacat's tone in a childish manner.

"And remember! No OPENING MY COFFIN!" he quickly yelled as the coffin slammed shut and Junith locked the mechanisms in place.

* * *

Thirty minutes later.

"So, who wants to crack this bad boy open?" Liza said, balancing on Adam's coffin as it shook violently.

"No! Bad fluffy-pink ear!" Ellie yelled, taking a spray flask from her waist and spraying the girl with water, causing her to hiss.

"Ow?! What the frick! What was that for?!" Liza yelled, rubbing at her face as she suddenly became sluggish.

"Redfield said to spray you if you did something bad," Ellie said, aiming the spray bottle and spraying the neko again until she began hissing and backed off into a corner. "Adam's instructions were very clear! Don't let him out!"

"Unfortunately, I need big Adam," Veldora interjected, entering the tent. Ellie quickly brandished her spray bottle at the general, who raised a brow at the cat displacer.

"Well, I'm sorry! But Adam said no," Ellie reaffirmed, spraying Liza again when she tried to sneakily open Adam's coffin.

"Let me handle this," Junith said, stepping around Veldora and approaching Ellie. "Look, I've known Adam for a very long time. And because I've known him for so long, I know his strengths and weaknesses. We've been talking, you've seen how he was out there. If things—"

Ellie narrowed her eyes.

"Didn't you say we should throw Adam overboard while he was in his coffin?"

"I mean, I did but— HEEESSHH!" the paladin spat, recoiling from the water being spritzed on her face.

"Look, we can either do this the easy way, or we can do this the hard way," Veldora said, as a faint scent of ozone wafted from her weapon.

Ellie frowned, suddenly finding herself in a three versus one stand-off as the space around her began to get crowded.

"I said back! Back off! I'm not afraid to use this!" she yelled, spraying the leader of the coalition forces in her face with the spray flask.

"Right... Hard way it is," Veldora sighed, wiping her face as the trio began to close on the folded-ear nekogirl.

"No! No! NOOOOO!" Ellie screamed, spraying her water flask everywhere before she was apprehended and pinned down by Veldora and Junith. "Redfield! Red! Help!"

"Relax, what's the worst that can happen?" Liza said, her symbol of Eli glowing as she unlocked Adam's coffin.

* * *

The next day.

Adam woke, blinking under the sky that had become familiar to him as the sound of quacking echoed nearby.

"Of course... I tell her not to do the one thing..." He sighed, realizing he was pinned under something.

He looked down, eyeing the miniature duckysaur sitting on his naked chest.

"Hello? Can I help you?" the nekoboy said, eyeing the creature that was the size of a regular housecat.

"Quack!" the creature let out, glaring down at its captive.

Adam moved, and the duck fell upon the floor, where it began to quack frantically and nip at his bare feet.

"Ow! Ow! What the Nyx?! Gah!" Adam yelped, kicking the tiny duckysaur, sending the monster cartwheeling into the air before it hit a nearby tree.

"Just my luck," he groaned, feeling the top of his head that was apparently covered by a large black top hat. "Huh?"

The tiny duckysaur returned, smacking at Adam's ankles repeatedly and nipping at him as he inspected the black hat, bedazzled with a large purple gem.

"Quack! Quack! Quack!" the duckysaur squeaked, hopping around until it snagged the brim of the hat and began pulling.

"Fine! Fine! Is this what you want?! Take the stupid hat!" Adam yelled, letting go as he spun. He took in his nearby surroundings to try and figure out where he was.

"Ah. Why is it so cold?" he grumbled, rubbing his sides before he spotted a large black robe on the floor, and put it on.

"Ugh. I'm definitely putting Liza in naptime when I get back," he determined, fastening the robe around him when a shadow fell upon him, and soon began to descend.

Adam's ears bristled, the ground beneath his feet seeming to shift as he recalled Liza's mentioning of a top hat and a disintegration beam.

The wereneko spun, eyeing the once miniature duckysaur that was now mushrooming in size, pushing away the trees and soil as it grew and grew until it was nearly twenty feet tall.

"Ah... Crapbaskets." He sighed as the now transformed duckysaur let out a mighty "QUACK!"

Catpurr 67
Battle of the Kaijus

"Aaaaaaagh! WHY?! WHY?! WHY?! WHAT DID I EVER DO TO YOU?!" Adam screamed, barely ducking beneath a blast of searing red duckysaur flames.

"QUACK!"

In retaliation, Adam summoned Redfield. The armored Death Knight rose out of the fragmented depths of the earth to defend his master—only to be trampled by the rampaging duck.

"AHK?!" Redfield squawked, crushed beneath the duckysaur's weight and left in a flipper-shaped crater in the ground as Adam screamed.

"IS IT BECAUSE I KICKED YOU?! I SAID I WAS SORRY! WHAT MORE DO YOU WANT?!" the nekoboy yelled, opening various cat-shaped portals, a plethora of skelecats leaping out to latch onto the mighty, feathered fowl.

"DAMN YOU, LIZA! I TOLD YOU ONE THING! ONE THING!" he screamed, searching his body for anything he could use as a weapon or tool.

"My staff!" Finally, he called forth the magical item into his tiny hands and pivoted. The regal scepter radiated icy blue hues as the wereneko activated **Regal Smash** and smacked the charging beast with the glowing staff, resulting in an explosion that unexpectedly launched Adam seventy feet into the air.

Doing cartwheels through the open sky, the bloodied Adam could do nothing but scream as his limbs flailed about mid-air.

"CRAPCRAPCRAPCRAPCARPAACAELKCMALKA!" he shrieked, rapidly plummeting to his death with his eyes wide on his soot covered face. "HuLP?!"

Suddenly his free fall to the ground turned into an aerial diagonal climb, his body caught by a certain pink-haired nekogirl wearing omni-propulsion gear and laughing out loud.

"YOU!" Adam snarled from where he was tucked under Liza's arm. Immediately he began to struggle. "YOU NUMBSKULL! IDIOT! YOU ABSOLUTE MORON!"

"Stahp! Stop! You're gonna make me drop you!" Liza yelled as she recalled her OP gear hooks and re-adjusted her aim to hook onto a large tree.

"WHY DID YOU LET ME OUT?!" Adam demanded, smacking Liza.

"How are you sure it was me?!" she exclaimed as a loud, wrathful, titanic quack echoed through the woods, shaking leaves loose from the trees.

"Because you're you! I know it was you! I'm so sure it was you that I'd cut off my own tail!" Adam shouted, before realizing he'd lost his scepter. "GAAAAH!"

"You found him!" a voice called out, turning his attention to Junith, Ellie, and Veldora heading in their direction, with a dozen soldiers outfitted in OP gear.

"Oh, what happened to plan A?!" The nekoboy sagged, wondering why everyone was out in force. "I thought we were gonna do this all from the safety of distance!"

Several soldiers landed beside Adam, with one carrying a box that contained gear for him to put on.

"Come on! Get dressed, we got a world to save!" Veldora barked, causing the boy to tense up. "GET TO IT NOW! We don't— UHGK?!"

Suddenly a blast of swift, purple energy struck the commander, smacking against the axe. She barely managed to reposition in time to catch the attack that sent her flying out of the tree.

"GENERAL!" a soldier screamed before "QUACK! QUACK! QUACK!" could be heard, the very ground shaking and causing Adam to drop his OP gear as he tried to maintain his balance.

"Ah, crapbaskets," he muttered.

"BULLERT IS BEHIND US AND CATCHING UP!" a soldier screamed as several leapt to ground level to assist Veldora.

"Alright, let's get out of here. We need to gain distance and figure out a plan of attack," Adam said, turning to Liza, who raised a brow and brandished a smile. "What?"

"Do you want uppies?" Liza replied, smirking at him as the shaking got louder and the soldiers scattered.

"What?" Adam reiterated. "This is no time for games! Get me up and let's go!"

"Awww the nekoboy wants uppies," Liza replied, booping him on the nose and causing his face to involuntarily twitch. "Say you want uppies! Say you—"

"QUACK!" Bullert was now visible, the massive duck spotting Adam and lifting its giant yellow bill skywards, where it released flames into the air.

"Uppies?" Liza repeated.

"YES! YES, YOU MORON! I WANT UPPIES! NOW LET'S GO, YOU IDIOT! BEFORE WE DIE!" Adam screamed, grabbing the woman as the duck barreled through the forest towards its target, smashing trees and leaving enormous flipper prints in its wake.

"Up, up, and awaaaaaay!" the pink-haired neko exclaimed, shooting off into the distance with Adam in tow.

"Hurry up! It's getting closer!" he cried, wiggling about as he summoned a sabercat skeleton out of a portal. The oversized feline slammed into the duckysaur.

Adam winced, watching as his sabercat bravely attacked Bullert, only for the duckysaur to ram through his skeleton and scatter its large bones in every direction.

Ugh! I don't have much mana left! I should have spec'd into different kinds of summons!

Suddenly Adam's eyes moved, involuntarily tracking the movements of the coalition forces that flew from out of the nearby trees.

"NOW!" Veldora barked, and the aerial soldiers unleashed attacks from handheld tubes in their hands that shot out devastating explosions.

A deep, pained quack sounded, signs that their attacks were working. Yet, despite their efforts, it wasn't enough. Bullert screeched, releasing a baritone quack that radiated with rage.

"It's still alive! Scatter!" Veldora ordered, the soldiers immediately fleeing as flames and purple beams of energy began to bisect and mince the nearby shrubbery, even consuming several soldiers.

As the attacks rained down on everything, the feathered fowl began to balloon in size, growing even larger until it cast a massive shadow that eclipsed the suns.

Adam's eyes wide at the now two-hundred-foot-tall duckysaur. "Seriously?!"

"Wow!" Liza let out against the flurry of panicked voices. Enraptured by the massive duckysaur, she became distracted, smacking into a tree that sent Adam careening into the air.

Fortunately, he was caught just before he hit the ground by Ellie zipping by, grabbing the nekomancer by the robe and exposing his bare butt cheeks to the mercy of the bushes and leaves, scraping his skin.

"PULL ME UP! PULL ME UP!" Adam exclaimed, grabbing his nethers as Ellie attempted to, but failed. The pair went tumbling to the ground with Adam rolling feet first.

"Fall back! Fall back!" Veldora cried as explosions detonated against Bullert. Seeing the feathered fowl, the catapults from the encampment had joined the attack, unleashing their payloads at a target that was nearly impossible to miss.

However, this did nothing but anger Bullert, the massive kaiju duck letting out another ear-shattering quack that reverberated through the air and forced Adam to cover his ears.

"HOW ARE WE SUPPOSED TO DEAL WITH THIS?!" he groaned, balking at the massive ducky. Then it dawned on Adam—the hat.

The nekomancer narrowed his eyes, turning his attention to the top of Bullert's massive head which fired blasts of purple energy randomly in every direction as small tufts of green alchemifire burned its feathers.

"Ellie!"

"Y-Yes?" Ellie said, shaking her head that was full of leaves and dirt as Liza and Junith landed beside Adam.

"I need you to bring me to its head," the boy said, walking up to the only one in his party that didn't have ulterior motives.

"W-What?! I'm sorry, did you say bring—"

"Yes. The size of that duckysaur is unnatural! If we can remove the hat, we can even the playing field. There's no way this trial is meant to be *this* impossible," he asserted, narrowing his eyes at the duckysaur stomping its way towards the source of the catapults.

"It's too big! And the hat itself shoots too many beams! I don't think I can get close to it," Ellie replied as the ground beneath their feet rumbled from Bullert releasing a titanic beam of energy from its top hat.

"Then we need a distraction." He turned to Liza, whose eyes went wide.

"Oh no, nope! Nada! Zero!" she said, waving her arms and shaking her head. "Not gonna do it! I don't want to die!"

"Yes! You will do it!" Adam spat, the geas on Liza shining as her hackles rose and her tail fluffed up.

"Why me, though?! Why not the idiot?!" Liza exclaimed, pointing at Junith.

"Because out of everyone here, you're the least valuable. If you die, it's fine," Adam said deadpan, causing Liza to wilt with a sad expression. "I need Junith alive to get back to my world, and Ellie is at least helpful. You, on the other hand, are just a constant irritant that isn't even useful."

Liza blinked, looking at the ground with downcast eyes as her geas compelled her to obey.

"Oh... Okay," she murmured, turning around. Her shoulders slumped as she made an odd hiccuping sound. "I'm useful... I can be useful. I CAN BE USEFUL! FINE! GARFUNKEL! GARFUNKEL! *GARFUNKEL!*"

In an odd twist, Liza began to yell, scream, and shout, hollering the name 'Garfunkel' over and over again with tears in her eyes.

"I think you finally broke her," Junith said, raising a brow as Adam pinched the bridge of his nose in exasperation.

Suddenly, the ground began to rumble. The crust of the earth itself shook in a way that was unnatural and made the hairs on Adam's body stand on end.

Something was wrong. The quivers from the soil beneath his feet weren't from Bullert, no. These were from something else. Something big, something that made Adam clench his teeth.

"GARFUNKEL! GARFUNKEL!" Liza continued to scream, much to the dismay of the gathered party until a sound that dwarfed even the mighty Bullert's rampage echoed out.

Answering Liza's call, an ancient beast slumbering within the depths of the Skull Lagoon awoke, the titanic Liopleurodon hidden beneath the temple that had yet to be accessed by Adam, rising out of the sea to honor its pact with Liza.

The island itself seemed to part, massive waves striking into the archipelago and consuming various islands from the creature's awakening. Adam and his gang were forced to take to the trees to avoid the surge waves that threatened to topple the high-rise flora.

"Oh, what the Nyx is this?!" Adam exclaimed as a gigantic Liopleurodon rivaling Bullert's size appeared in the distance, billowing flames as it roared its challenge against the massive duckysaur.

"Me! Being! Useful!" Liza exclaimed as the battle of the giants began.

Catpurr 68

Climatic End of Arc

"WHEN WERE YOU GONNA TELL ME YOU COULD SUMMON A KAIJU?!" Adam hissed, yelling at Liza over the gushing storm.

"I was! But then you interrupted my song!" Liza spat as the wind around them picked up.

"Why can't you just be normal?! IT WOULD HAVE TAKEN FIVE SECONDS TO JUST TELL ME YOU COULD SUMMON A MONSTER! BUT NOOOO, you just had to be difficult!"

"IT'S NOT A MONSTER! IT'S MY FRIEND, AND SHE'S A SWEETHEART!" Liza screamed as the world quaked from the two titans clashing.

Adam winced as the two-hundred-foot-tall Bullert and the even taller Liopleurodon clashed, both unleashing blasts of flames at each other that collided, creating a massive cloud of heat and gas. It hovered between the two before exploding and sending a shockwave that shook the world.

"WHAAAAA?!" Ellie let out, as the folded-eared nekogirl went flying. She was caught by Junith, who reached out and grabbed her, only to slip and fly into the air herself. Next Adam reached out, grabbing the nekogirl by her boot before the tree he was holding onto was toppled by the waves, causing him to lose his grip.

Fortunately, Liza was quick, leaping into the air and grabbing Adam by his tail, resulting in a chain of nekofolk, all holding onto one another as the pink-haired one shot her OP hooks into a nearby tree that was still standing.

"DON'T LET GO! HOLD ON!" Adam screamed, voice drowned out by the deafening winds and cries of the two clashing titans.

"SAY I'M USEFUL!" Liza yelled, causing Adam to do a double take.

"WHAT?!"

"SAY! I'M! USEFUL!" she screamed, looking Adam directly in the eye with a madness in her gaze that gave the nekomancer pause for concern.

"BUT YOU AREN'T USEFUL!" he spat, his brow furrowed as the duckysaur screeched and delivered an uppercut to the Liopleurodon. "YOU'RE LIKE THE OPPOSITE OF USEFUL! USELESS!"

"THAT'S IT! I'M LETTING GO!" Liza screamed, her hand reaching down to the release mechanism on her omni-propulsion gear.

"JUST LIE TO HER, ADAM!" Junith exclaimed as Ellie began to cry, "We're gonna *die!*" over and over again.

"NO!" he snarled. "Why would I lie and say she's useful when she isn't!"

"SAY IT OR I LET US GO!" Liza screamed, tears in her eyes.

"JUST SAY IT! PLEASSSSE!" Ellie cried, her little arms dangling uncontrollably in the wind.

"NEVER!" Adam roared, staring madly into Liza's glaring eyes.

"ADAM! IF YOU SAY IT, I'LL HELP REUNITE YOU WITH SCHRÖDINGER!" Junith yelled as Bullert sent a beam of energy at Garfunkel from his massive tophat.

At those words, Adam's eyes went wide, and his face morphed from panic-stricken to the most stern expression he could muster as he told Liza what she wanted to hear.

"Liza, you are the most useful person in the history of usefulness. Never in the world has there been a more useful person. If anyone were to ask who was most useful, I would interject and tell them you were the most useful person. In fact, I know ten useful people and you are nine of them," he said, looking Liza directly in the eye as he lied to her face.

Liza's face scrunched, her hand still reaching for the release on her propulsion gear.

"WAITWAITWAIT! I TOLD YOU YOU'RE USEFUL!" Adam cried.

"I DON'T BELIEVE YOU! PLUS, YOU HURT MY FEELIES!"

"WHAT?!" he screamed, flabbergasted.

"SAY IT LIKE YOU MEAN IT!"

"I DID, THOUGH!"

"NO, YOU DIDN'T!" the nekogirl scowled over Ellie's crying and Junith's yelling.

"YOU'RE USEFUL! YOU'RE USEFUL! YOU'RE USEFUL! YOU'RE USEFUL! YOU'RE USEFUL! YOU'RE USEFUL! NOW HOLD ON, YOU IDIOT!" Adam hollered.

"Nah," Liza said, hitting the release on her harness.

"NOOOOOOOOOOOOOOOOO!" Adam screamed, as the four-person ladder of nekofolk went careening into the wind.

Round and round they spun, Adam releasing a load of rainbow-colored vomit as each nekofolk held on to one another as they flew, until suddenly, their uncontrolled spin was halted by Veldora who rammed into the group, sending them crashing into a tree.

Immediately Adam was up, his head covered with leaves and twigs as he climbed over tree limbs and grabbed Liza by the neck. Then he began to strangle her.

"WHY, YOU LITTLE! DIE, YOU IDIOT! DIE, IDIOT! DIE, DIE, DIIIIIE!" he spat, choking the pink-haired nuisance.

"What are you lot doing?! Get to work!" the leader of the armed forces barked, pulling the two apart.

"We're gonna die! We're gonna die! We're gonna die! I SHOULDA JUST STAYED HOME!" Ellie exclaimed as she rocked back and forth in the tree.

"SNAP OUT OF IT, SOLDIER!" Veldora spat, smacking the sense back into the nekogirl.

As Veldora attempted to restore order to the chaotic party, the world tremored as Garfunkel smacked Bullert with its tail, sending the massive duckysaur careening backwards where it crashed into the island.

Releasing massive quacks, Bullert flapped about, rolling on its side before it climbed back to its feet and charged the prehistoric monster, drop-kicking the dinosaur with its giant flippers.

The two kaijus were locked in, both monsters giving it their all as they pulverized the archipelago and shook the world with their battle.

Suddenly, another quack sounded, one that didn't belong to Bullert—but rather another duckysaur, the one Liza had named Roger. The titanic yellow beast emerged from the ocean depths, joining the fight as it slammed into Garfunkel.

"NOOOOO!" Liza screamed, her eyes wide as she witnessed her companion suddenly being smacked around and blasted with flames from both duckysaurs.

"That thing isn't going to last long against Bullert and Roger, we need to get in there and assist," Velodra yelled, adjusting her gear.

Calming his raging emotions, Adam spun, turning to the Commander of the Coalition Forces.

"Commander!" he yelled, catching the woman's attention. "I need you to get me to Bullert's head! The source of his power is the hat! Can you do that?!"

Veldora looked down, eyeing a gauge on her OP gear.

"I can, but I only have enough fuel to get to the top. After that, that's it. We only get one shot at this!" Veldora replied, holding her arms out for Adam, who quickly ran up and embraced her.

"Ellie! Stay here and protect Junith! And make sure Liza doesn't do anything stupid!" he said as he was suddenly hit with the Wet debuff, the wind pouring enough water on him to activate his curse.

Fatigue cursed through Adam's body, but despite that, he held onto Veldora as she aimed her OP gear and took off towards the rampaging kaijus.

Up and down the trees the pair went, dodging debris and large waves, and maneuvering at absurd speeds through thick foliage and harsh winds. Adam's stomach bubbled, causing rainbow bile to leak from his mouth, but he held it in, attempting not to distract Veldora as the Cadian veteran used all of her experience to get the outworlder to where he needed.

Dodging left and right, the pair finally managed to get close enough to Bullert to where the shiny scales on his body became visible beneath his feathers. Attempting to use Bullert as a latching-on point for her OP gear, Veldora shot her hook at the creature, only for the metal to bounce off with her forward momentum, sending her and Adam slamming into the side of the two-hundred-foot-tall monster.

"UKH!" Veldora let out as she bounced, beginning her descent downwards into the raging waves with Adam in her arms.

"HOLD ON TO THIS!" she roared, grabbing her silver axe and placing it into Adam's hands before she threw it, nekoboy attached, at Bullert as the sea claimed her.

Round and round Adam spun, a cartwheel of vomit leaving his mouth before the sacred treasure bit into Bullert and found purchase.

He dangled from the axe, his body flapping in the wind as he tried his best to hang on but was quickly losing his grip.

"Crapcrapcrapcrapcrap!" Adam let out, slipping and flying but not before he was suddenly caught by the wrist, the sacred treasure transforming in a flash of light into a woman with purple hair that was now screaming at him.

"CLIMB YOU FOOL!" the woman yelled before throwing Adam onto the back of the duckysaur, where his claws dug into space between Bullert's scales.

Adam wasted no time. He began moving, climbing, scaling the as rain, wind, and heat from the clash of the titans threatened to cast him into the sea.

You do this for Schrödinger! You do this for Schrödinger! You do this for Schrödinger! You do this for Schrödinger! The sentence repeated in Adam's mind, spurring him on as the mysterious woman helped him climb.

"JUST YOU WAIT, SCHRÖDINGER! I'M GOING TO SAVE YOU!" Adam hollered. He held on for dear life, while Bullert's body abruptly trembled. The duckysaur was now aware of the little nekoboy climbing it and attempted to shake him.

Unbeknownst to Adam, each scrape of his claws were poisoning the massive duck, his catsification curse slowly infecting Bullert to a degree that his presence became noticeable.

"I can do this! Because I must! For Schrödinger!" Adam screamed, climbing until he finally reached the top of Bullert's head, where the tophat firing a laser beam became visible. Now came the next issue, how was he supposed to remove the massive hat? He didn't know, but he'd find a way as the nekomancer pushed on and climbed the brim of the hat.

"Ah, crapbaskets!" he hissed, grabbing ahold of the large patch of silk wrapped around the tophat to maintain his balance. "How the Nyx do I remove the hat?!"

"Use this one! Strike the gem!" the axe screamed, taking Adam's hand and transforming back into its weapon form, which was surprisingly lightweight. The boy grimaced, eyeing the sacred treasure in his hand as it sparked with lightning, invigorating his body and giving him strength.

With a mighty roar, Adam charged, the tiny nekoboy braving the storm with lightning dancing off his body as he ran around the brim of the top hat towards the purple gem, preparing to fire another beam to finish off Garfunkel while he was still pinned by Roger.

"RAAAAAH!" the nekomancer screamed, eyes wide with madness and slamming the sacred treasure into the gem where it shattered, causing a massive explosion that immediately darkened his world.

Catpurr 69

Do Gods Dream?

First, came Darkness.

Out of the void of nothingness awoke a consciousness shaped in darkness.

Alone, Darkness was left to ponder the things he could feel and touch but couldn't see. Eons alone in… nothingness.

Then, came Light. Blinding light that illuminated Darkness with stars and galaxies, giving sight to darkness, who didn't shy from the light but instead embraced it as colors exploded around the universe.

Upon the two meeting,

A question was asked.

An answer was given.

Without cause, and without purpose, the two beings unexpectedly coexisted. Companions, forever aimlessly wandering through the cosmic expanse that seemed to expand as they searched for purpose in the void.

After a supereon of aimlessness, a phenomenon occurred.

"Hey! Hey! Come quick!" a hyper-voice beckoned, one that caused the being obscured in shadows only visible when Light was near to turn in surprise.

The two bright orbs of blue that adorned Darkness's head settled on the humanoid body formed of gentle starlight as she crouched over a two-way portal, excitedly clapping her glowing hands with glee.

"Look! Look! Things!" Light exclaimed, pointing down at what appeared to be beings shaped like themselves—but these were pale, less colorful, and huddled together, staring back at Light with fear from inside what appeared to be a cave.

"Hmm. It's just dust," Darkness replied, uninterested in the collection of dust motes.

"Oooh, they look scared and confused!" Light exclaimed, pulling Darkness in, who could only go wide-eyed. "Hello, life forms!"

The beings shrunk back, terrified, with several even bowing.

"What are they doing?" Light asked. "Do you think they understand us?"

"Doubtful," Darkness replied as Light suddenly began to glow brighter.

"Whoa! Whoa! I feel stronger?" Light said. Darkness's curiosity was piqued as he too felt what Light felt.

"Fascinating," he said, poking his head through the portal, whereupon several of the beings immediately fainted from the ice-cold grip of oblivion before Darkness was yanked back.

"Stop! Stop! You're scaring them!" Light exclaimed.

Darkness turned, gazing over the beings that were immobile, with several amorphous globs of energy floating above each now vacant husk.

Both primordial beings went wide-eyed, staring at the motes of power that were so similar to their own cores but so different, so... *weak.*

As if a gentle solar wind could disperse the cores.

Darkness reached out, grabbing the cores and pulling them through the portal, allowing the energy that made up the beings to dance in his palm.

Fascinated, Light watched with wide multicolored eyes as the cores changed shape and form into doppelgangers of the husks left behind.

"I think... I think we've found it," Light whispered, barely containing her jubilation.

"These things?" Darkness asked with cold indifference as he cocked his head to the side. "Is this our purpose?"

Light suddenly shrunk down, condensing herself to bring her body to the same stature and size as the beings on Darkness's palms, her body morphing to resemble theirs.

She looked up, smiling at Darkness in the form of a pale-skinned woman with colorful, bright hair that rose up like flames emitting from her head.

"Hi! I'm..." Light said, only to pause, as she was still a being with no name. "Sol! And this is my friend Eli."

Darkness raised a brow, wondering what the primordial being of light was up to as she grabbed the hands of the spectral beings and danced in his palm.

* * *

Eli woke. The skeleton was sitting slumped on his throne as he stared out into the darkness that was his domain.

Moments passed by in darkness as he sat, the only sound in the damp cave being the odd clacking of bones as his servants scurried around outside his champers.

The skeleton sighed with non-existent lungs before he turned his skull over to a portal he had opened, casting light directly into his chambers.

Then Eli rose from his stone throne, walking over to the moving images of humans fighting against a massive dragon spewing flames in a manmade jungle of concrete.

The primordial being shifted his skeletal finger, zooming out the image until a blue marble came into view. Eli paused for a moment, looking at the cradle of humanity that they had nurtured before zooming out once more to the star that dwelled in the center of the Earth's star system.

Feeling oddly, nostalgic, Eli stepped through the portal, appearing beside the blistering yellow star that did nothing to the elder god.

"Sol..." Eli murmured, suddenly growing flesh and muscles, pink and red globs of meat adorning his bones that were soon covered by unnaturally cold, pale skin.

He stood there, floating in front of the star named "Sol," allowing the heat of the gaseous giant to warm his skin.

Now with blue eyes tinged with gold, Eli hung his head low as he stood in front of the last legacy left behind by his first friend.

"I am all that remains..." Eli said. The primordial god drifted into the star, allowing the flames to consume him, allowing the heat and warmth to caress his skin... yet it wasn't the same.

Nothing was.

Before long, a blue portal opened next to Eli as he lay in the center of the heated cosmic fire.

"There you are, Eli!" Freya exclaimed, shirking back from the heat coming out of the portal.

"Can I help you, Freya?" he asked, gazing out at the flames indifferently.

"*Yes!* Voltrain is up my ass about your Chosen! It's been three months! Where have you been?!"

Eli sighed. As he finally turned his head over to the goddess, the little gremlin, Islandr, climbing on her shoulders.

"Is that Eli? I can't see! Let me up! I wanna say hello!" the war goddess exclaimed.

"Yes, yes, I'm on my way back," Eli said, forcefully closing the portal before Freya could hound him for a task.

Three months, that's how much time had passed since Eli had come to visit the grave of his friend.

To Eli, the time that passed was less than the blink of an eye. For everyone else, even the so-called gods, time was a constant plague that weighed heavily on everyone's mind.

But to Eli... what was time to a being that had witnessed the inception of the universe? Who played a hand in its creation?

"It will only be some time now, Sol. This time I've got it right," Eli said as he closed his eyes and the flesh on his skeletal frame melted away.

Catpurr 70

My Ultra-Grade Dungeon is Now a City for Looters

Screaming, Adam and his gang of nekofolk fell from the sky, culminating in a heap with Adam buried under his nekompanions. The cattyduck then landed atop them with a mighty "Meowk."

"Uuugh," Adam let out, squirming as he tried to pull himself out from under the pile of nekofolk.

"Yay! We're back!" Liza exclaimed, leaping up with excitement as Ellie looked around, confused.

"Alright, everyone knows the drill. Scarves, hoods, anything to cover your ears," Adam said as he tried to get his bearings.

"Huh?" Ellie let out, watching as everyone else around the nekomancer began to pull up hoods and cloth to cover and conceal their identity. "What? What's going on?"

"Oh, nothing, just we have to hide our ears. Otherwise, we'll be hunted and skinned alive for our soft skin and tails," Liza said with a smile on her face.

"Huh? Huh?! You're kidding right?" Ellie exclaimed.

When no one said otherwise, the girl began to panic.

"Someone tell me this is a joke?"

"This world is a bit backwards in its thinking. They hate necromancers as much as they do demi-humans," Adam grumbled, summoning multiple skelecats and sending them off to find the nearest road.

"So... We're fugitives?" Ellie asked with worry as Dominica ripped off the bottom half of her raggedy shirt and used it to cover her cat ears, causing Junith to scoff.

This isn't going to work.

Adam took off his cloak, drooping it over Dominica, who immediately became flustered as the nekomancer put the hood over her head.

"I cannot accept this!" Dominica exclaimed as Adam fished out the trickster's persona from one of his leather pouches.

"You can and you will. It would be odd with you walking around in rags," he explained before realizing something.

Huh... I could have totally used this during my visit in the Drowthraki city...

"Of course, I bow to your great wisdom, Emissary of the *One Who Waits*," Dominica said, bowing as Adam rolled his eyes beneath the mask on his face.

He turned his attention to one of his skelecats ambling out of the bush, the creature having found a road.

"Alright," Adam stated, looking at his entourage of nekofolk that had expanded with his latest trial and realizing, with a frown, that the amount of people he needed to take care of had increased. "Nyx below..."

"What?" Junith asked.

"Nothing," he grumbled.

The cluster of nekofolk followed the skeletal cats through the woods. This culminated in the gang standing on a large road paved with stones.

"Well, at least we're next to a major city," Adam said aloud, looking both ways at all the wooden signs that had various advertisements offering goods.

"How do you figure that?" Junith asked.

"Well, I suppose I'll explain it to you since you're obviously lacking in brain power. Paved roads don't typically lead to small settlements and nowhere places, Junith," he said. Junith wasted little time leaping up, attempting to take a swing at him, but she was intercepted and held back by Ellie and Dominica.

Feeling around his leather armor for the map of the Vilenciel region, Adam pulled out the rolled-up parchment, now wrinkled and blurred by constant water damage. Not far away, Junith ranted, swiping with her claws, just a few inches from reaching the back of his head.

"Ah... Great."

The nekoboy frowned. While he could make out the largest stretch of highway on the map, it left him puzzled, as the highway that was visible wasn't located by any large swaths of trees.

Great... Did we seriously get teleported out of Vilenciel? That was a reason for worry

"Are we lost?" Liza asked, peeking over Adam's head.

"Seems like it," he said, spotting a carriage moving towards them.

"Oh! There's people!" Ellie exclaimed. Adam realized that he'd have to get a language crystal for both her and Dominica, if they were going to be of any use.

I need to find Tim, he thought to himself before shushing everyone as the carriage drew near.

"Hello!" Adam called out, waving down the wooden carriage laden with goods, only to pause as the black-haired driver with sleep deprived features and a green-haired woman with matching eyes gawked at him.

"ADAM?!" the duo said aloud, shocked by his re-emergence after three months.

Okay, so I am near Vilenciel? But then where did this highway come from? Adam frowned before putting on a smile. "Hi. Surprised seeing you all around here."

Before long, Adam's crew were riding in the back of Sehn and Titania's cart. The duo was on a mission to deliver supplies to a new guild hall that had been set up in the region.

"New guild hall, huh?" Adam inquired, sitting in front between the two adventurers. "Are we not near Vilenciel?"

"Oh, we are, it's just the increased traffic to the Selkuin area has made it economically beneficial for the guild if we set up near the dungeon," Titania explained. "Because of its danger—"

Immediately alarm bells rang in Adam's head as Titania's voice faded to the background.

"I'm sorry, did you say dungeon?" he asked, realizing that they were near his hideout.

"Oh, you were in a trial, weren't you? So you wouldn't know, huh?" Titania said, fiddling with the iron cuff on her wrist. "Well, a few months ago, we started getting reports there of increased monster activity in the region. After the first few rounds of successful exterminations, adventurers began to disappear, and more and more monsters began to show up."

Sehn scowled, the coffin-wielding berserker's face scrunching.

"So, naturally they sent us disposable minions to investigate—"

"And then we found the cause. Which so happened to be an ultra-grade dungeon with so many monsters, everyone began gathering hoping to uncover treasure," Titania finished, sounding every alarm Adam possessed as he tried to discreetly pull up his System and view the dungeon tab. He hadn't bothered looking at it since he'd last been in this realm.

[UR Dungeon Name: Dungeon]
[Level: 32]
[MODE: Defense in Depth]
[Status: *Constructing floor, recycling human remains, gestating monsters, constructing additional pylons, cleaning floors...*]
[Mana Reserves: 78900/500000]
[Floors: 45]
[Minions: 3201]

Huh? HUUUUH?! R-R-Recycling human remains?!

"Oh, we're nearly there," Titania said, oblivious to the boy's internal panicking.

It took all of Adam's cool not to flip out as he scrolled through the information. The edge of a massive town came into view on the horizon.

I GAVE YOU ONE TASK! BE DISCREET! STAY HIDDEN! HOW IS THIS HIDDEN?! He wanted to scream. The hideout that he was counting on to stay hidden was now surrounded by a *massive* trade town filled with adventurers, traders, and officials looking to collect taxes.

"So, who are your new friends?" Titania asked, pushing the thin sheet that separated the front seating crew of the wagon to the bed, crammed supplies and nekofolk. "Seems like every time we see you,

you're multiplying. Hey! Get out of that! Close that! If any of those metal pipes get damaged, it's my butt!"

Liza stopped what she was doing and waved happily at Titania, as if she hadn't just been caught cat-handed looting their goods.

"Cousins of mine," Adam grumbled as the wagon pulled up beside the gate that was manned by two Vilenciel guards. For a moment, Adam was worried, wondering how they were going to explain the extra passengers, but his concern was for naught as the next interaction alleviated his growing anxiety.

"Dave."

"Sehn."

Sehn and the guard addressed each other, and Sehn tossed a bag of coins to the man, who caught it before waving the wagon through.

"That's it?" Adam asked. "No searches? No identification?"

"Nope," Sehn replied as he yawned. "As long as the crown gets their coin, they don't really care what happens here. This place is pretty much borderline lawless, unless you piss off the Black Hand or any of their affiliates."

"Oh," the boy let out, scanning the crowd of heavily armed men and women going about their business, as peddlers attempted to sell their wares.

"GABBAGES! GETCHA GABBAGES!" a familiar man pushing a cart called out. "Please, won't somebody buy my gabbages?!"

"Screw his gabbages! Buy my kakarots! Guaranteed to give you super strength!"

"Lies!" the gabbage merchant exclaimed, the two vegetable peddlers soon getting into a brawl.

"Say," Adam began. "You wouldn't happen to know a merchant by the name of Tim, would you? He works with the Black Hand?"

"Huh? How do you know about the Black Hand?" Titania asked. Adam pointed to the mask on his face. "Right, that makes sense. Especially with how you were able to avoid everything for so long."

"Tim is around. Although he's kind of banned from being anywhere on the surface... or... anywhere next to people," Sehn explained. "You can find him on floor thirty. Good luck reaching him, almost no one has gotten past floor twenty."

"Huh... you don't say," Adam said. "And where is the entrance?"

"In the center of town," Sehn answered. "There's a large, pink house. Not sure why, but the entrance is shaped like a home."

"I keep telling everyone that the dungeon is really just an old wizard's home who doesn't want to be disturbed," Titania said, as Sehn rolled his eyes.

"Here we go again. If it was someone's home, why would it be flooded with monsters?"

"I don't know! What kind of dungeon has hand-crafted furniture and pink fluffy pillows dotted all around?!"

"The kind that has an entire floor that's just lava. Has skeletons roaming around and ten-foot-tall crabs that shoot lasers!" Sehn barked back. "I still have crab bite marks on my back from all those things falling out of the ceiling on top of me!"

"And whose fault is that?! I told you that we should just leave the dungeon alone. I keep telling everyone that!"

Adam kept his mouth shut, hoping that the pair wouldn't connect the skeletons, crabs, and other shenanigans to him.

"King?"

Suddenly a voice touched against the nekomancer's mind, a fanatical voice that called out with excitement.

Uhhhh.

"KING! KING! KING! KING!"

Suddenly and without warning, the ground began to tremble, the very road beneath their carriage moving. Every pedestrian nearby scrambled for shelter as the vibrations violently increased.

"What? What's going on?!" Junith exclaimed from the back of the carriage. Then the ground erupted, spewing a geyser of hundreds of tiny crabs, each firing laser beams from their eyes and setting the nearby shops and stalls on fire.

"MY GABBAGES!" a voice despaired as a massive shadow descended on Adam.

"KING! KING! KING! KING! KING! KING!" Krabby chanted, as the now *enormous* Morian crab, wearing oversized cat ears and a monocle on its shell, broke forth from the earth like a long dormant monster answering its master's call.

Titania and Sehn both leapt off the cart, the seasoned adventurers ready to do battle as shouts and screams resounded from everywhere.

"K-Krabby?!" Adam stammered before the geyser of crabs turned, the swarm falling towards the nekoboy, who could only gawk at the shadow about to consume him.

"KING!" a thousand voices cried out, slamming atop Adam and covering every inch of the cart that was pulled into the ground, despite Titania and Sehn's desperate attempts to stop them.

Catpurr 71

Lord Adam

"HUAAAHWHAA!" Adam cried, tumbling out a hole and landing on a surprisingly soft surface.

"Welcome home, Master Adam," came the soft voice from a tall, lithe woman with white cat ears as she purred.

Shaking his head, Adam quickly got his bearings, and his face scrunched in anger.

"YOU!" he snarled, reaching out in a fit of rage to pounce at the woman, only to wilt as the spitting image of his former teacher beamed a soft smile at him.

"Yes, me, Master Adam, how may I be of assistance?" Dungeon asked, causing the boy to short-circuit.

"I... Uh... Err," he stammered, his jaw agape as the avatar of his Dungeon stood before him in a scantily white dress and a large, wide brim hat. Her bushy white tail swept back and forth behind her.

"Y-Y-You..." Adam quickly began to grow red, his face flustered as the avatar leaned close.

"How may I be of assistance, Master?"

"Uhhhh," Adam let out before he quickly got his wits about himself and realized the others weren't around. "Where... Uh, where are the others?"

"In their accommodations, Master," Dungeon said, summoning several mirrors that revealed Adam's companions.

"Don't!" Adam's face twisted before his voice dropped to a whisper. "Don't call me master, please."

"Yes, Lord Adam," Dungeon replied, causing him to sigh as he eyed the mirrors.

Junith had a simple, wooden room filled with weapons, training dummies, and armor.

Liza had a room painted with eye-hurting pink walls, pink furniture, and giant, pink stuffed toys that littered the room as she bounced around.

As for Ellie and Dominica, they had barren rooms with only a singular bed each and shelves filled with random books, some stained with odd splotches of brownish red.

Adam looked around the room he himself sat in, eyeing all the amenities that furnished it. A simple desk, shelves of books, a large circular bed, and a cat tree large enough for a house cat that immediately made Adam nostalgic for Schrödinger.

Soon.

With a sigh, Adam looked up at his avatar and asked a simple question.

"Why?"

"Why what, Lord Adam?"

"Don't call me Lord."

"Of course, Mi'lord."

He shook his head, red ears going flat. "Nope, not that either."

Dungeon was undeterred. "Of course, your Excellence."

"No, stop!"

"Of course, Superior One."

Adam hung his head low and groaned. Seeing the visage of his old master address him in such a manner disturbed him to his core.

"How do you set their rooms up?" he instead asked with curiosity as he spied his companions roaming about through the portals.

"The data I have of their preferences comes from your memories, Superior One," Dungeon replied.

"And the materials to make these rooms? To make all this?" Adam asked, looking around the chamber he sat in and the plush soft bed beneath his body. "Where did you get them?"

"From intruders, Superior One," Dungeon answered flatly.

"Elaborate."

"Of course, Superior One," Dungeon said. The woman in white bowed before describing in detail how it all began when Krabby had come, searching for any trace of his master.

It had led Krabby to the dungeon, where he and what remained of the crab army were fleeing from the humans intent on exterminating them.

Dungeon immediately recognized a loyal servant, and quickly directed Krabby into the safety of her nest while unleashing minions to deal with the humans.

After repeated clashes and severe losses, eventually the humans gathered at Dungeon's doorstep. By then Dungeon had gathered enough data and materials from the dead to evolve new, stronger monsters.

It wasn't long before the humans were beaten back. Even with the Duchess's daughter spurring the humans on, they were incapable of standing up to the new tide of monsters.

This then led to calls for adventurers, with a small settlement being established near the premises before it began to expand and grow until, after enough bloodshed, it had come to encompass the entire entrance of the dungeon.

From there, expeditions quickly began to take place, with Dungeon rapidly scrambling to rebuff their advances and expand her floors.

Thus began a battle of man versus Dungeon, until a stalemate was called, and a reprieve was had, allowing for Dungeon to reorganize their defenses.

Before long, Dungeon had grown to forty floors, while the surface settlement had expanded, bringing in thousands of humans keen on exploring the ever-expanding labyrinth below their feet.

"This... was the opposite of what... I asked for..." Adam groaned.

"My apologies, Superior One. I have merely followed my directives in defending the domicile and burying the core while accumulating resources," Dungeon stated, prompting Adam's ears to twitch.

"Loot?" he said, before a long list of materials and supplies appeared before him.

Wood x2300

Stone x3901

Iron x31

Various Pelts x30

Copper x99

Obsidian x16

Mana Crystals x50

Sacred Jewel Spheres x1

Chaos Emerald x1

Zinc x12

Silver x45

Gold x19

Sulfur x200

Coal x34

Bones x1370

Sapphires x12

Emeralds x5

Amber x20

Rubies x3

Silk x6

Cotton x30

Enchanted Material x3

Wool x10

Satin x1

Galvanized Iron x3

Glass Shards x9

Steel Bars x20

Magical Item x30

Paper x5

Charcoal x57

Steel Bits x12

Human Weapons x300

Human Remains x20

Rotting Flesh x40

Chaos Cores x20

Plant Fibers x100

Plant Seeds x40

Fresh Meat x2000

Adam blinked, looking over the list.

"So little?" he muttered.

"Each number represents a unit, Superior One," Dungeon replied.

"A unit? What's a unit?"

"One pound or a rough equivalent, Superior One."

Adam's brow raised, eyeing the list of resources he now had at his disposal, which equated to metric tons of loot.

"Where are we keeping all this?" he asked. Dungeon then displayed multiple portals that revealed chambers full of materials and monsters of various species, all organizing loot.

"I have organized the acquired materials into antechambers buried deep within the dungeon, with minions facilitating the upkeep and management of the assorted goods for future expansions," Dungeon said, bowing. "I eagerly await your instructions for future development."

Adam raised a brow as a transparent screen was pushed upon him with no prompt from himself.

Pushy, much?

"Great..." he muttered with a sigh, wondering what new problems would come for him in the coming days. He had wanted to be discreet, to hide away, yet here he was, being presented a whole new workload and problems *literally* at his doorstep with a gaggle of companions he never asked for.

"This sucks," he spat, sitting down grumpily on a chair that manifested for him as he rubbed his temples, and his thoughts turned to his one and only true friend.

Just a few more months, and I'll have you home, Schrödinger. Just you wait, I'm coming, buddy, Adam said to himself, sighing once more before opening the dungeon panel management.

It was time to get to work.

Thank you for reading a MoonQuill original novel. More exciting stories can be found on our website, www.moonquill.com.

We would greatly appreciate it if you could take a moment to leave a review. Every review helps the author and supports their ability to continue writing fantastic books for everyone to enjoy!

Additionally, we're looking for dedicated ARC reviewers and experienced readers to join our beta reader team. To learn more, drop us an email at info@moonquill.com or stop by our Discord.